MW01697950

Patches of Grey

By Roy L. Pickering
Jr.

Published in 2009 by M.U.D. House Books

Published by M.U.D. House Books

ISBN-10: 0578005816

ISBN-13: 978-0578005812

CHAPTER ONE

A photograph captures one's image but is incapable of containing their essence. Before Tony lay a camera created impression of Janet Mitchell. In his mind were countless other pictures he had mentally processed. Visions of how she walked, and spoke, and smiled. The song her laughter played, the oasis of her eyes. The stuff of dreams.

Dreaming was something he did much of, not only with Janet as subject. Each day as he gazed out his bedroom window, Tony looked beyond what his eyes could see. To another place in a time yet to come. Far away from the ironclad grip of the projects.

As sweet as his dreams were, he would awaken to the sting that they were only fantasies. Pictures that in spite of their clarity, also held no essence.

Present day reality showed a greatly contrasting portrait. Long lines of brown bodies waiting impatiently at the welfare office. Equally long lines of teenage girls at abortion clinics. Food stamps serving as currency, except when it came to the purchase of narcotics, which was strictly a cash or sex business. To every side of him were faces that showed hunger and longing to be no longer filled with hunger and longing. Single mothers struggling to keep their babies fed, anonymous fathers in search of another bed. Sex, alcohol, drugs and church the most frequented routes by which one might find God and ask Him why. When a thunderous silence served as reply, it was translated as "why not". No use arguing with that logic.

Where Tony wished to be was more of an idea than a zip code, since it had not been experienced firsthand, merely glimpsed on television, in magazines, and books. Tomorrow appeared as a montage of popping champagne bottles; yachts setting sail for tropical locales; tuxedos and evening gowns twirling under chandeliers made of diamonds; luxury cars;

luxury suites; the luxury of laying down one's head on a bed soft as a cloud, content that the world had been conquered and would service all needs, satisfy every desire. These things were "seen" by Tony through a shimmering haze, in the center of which one vision shone bright and clear.

"Still jerking off to the picture of that white chick?"

Tony slammed the yearbook shut as if caught leafing through a pornographic magazine by his bible toting grandmother.

"I can't believe you spent good money on that bullshit when you aren't even a senior. Just so you could drool over Barbie."

Tony looked up from his bed towards his younger brother, C.J. The young men were three years apart in age, possessing near identical cheekbones and matching sets of midnight clear eyes, C.J. having slightly more melanin in his skin tone, Tony with deeper waves throughout his hair. Their physical resemblance to one another was not matched by their senses of fashion. Tony was dressed comfortably in a pair of Khaki pants and a ribbed tee shirt. C.J. was clad in a plaid flannel shirt and a pair of jeans sized well beyond what his waist required. This provided a clear view of the Loony tune characters adorning his boxer shorts. Atop his head was a black bandanna decorated with skull and crossbones. The foreboding image was replicated on his right forearm by an artlessly rendered tattoo. Around C.J.'s neck were three gold chains of varying widths and styles fighting to out-sparkle each other.

Rather than respond to his brother's prodding, Tony opened a textbook. He had a trig exam the following day. Without further studying he felt confident that he could probably get a grade in the low eighties. He intended to do considerably better than that.

On the opposite side of the cramped room, C.J. lay down and adjusted the fit of his faux diamond studded watch. It was the latest addition to a collection of timepieces that was nearly sizeable enough for him to wear a different one for each week of the year. He then began tapping on his bed's headboard to the beat of a song playing in his head.

"Do you mind?" Tony snapped after a minute. "I'm trying to study. You might try it yourself for a change."

"Nigga, please. I don't need that bullshit to get mine."

Tony tried returning to his schoolwork, but was forced to stop reading when a shadow blanketed the page he was focused on. C.J. stood directly in front of him, having approached without being detected, a neat trick that he frequently put to mischievous use. He yanked out the yearbook that Tony had tucked beneath his chest, then flipped it to the page it was accustomed to being opened to. On it was a close-up photo of Janet in her cheerleading outfit.

"Don't you get it up for sistas no more?"

"What?"

"Don't play dumb, you know exactly what I mean. I'm not saying it's bad to get with a white girl. Pussy is pussy. But you're drooling about more than just waxing that ass, I know you are. A white girl is all you need to completely cross over, and this one, fine though she may be, is as white as they come."

C.J.'s first word on a topic like this one was rarely his last, so Tony knew that attempting to ignore him would be futile. Instead, he addressed the accusations with the best comeback that came to mind.

"You might want to wipe away the shit before talking out your ass."

C.J. snickered. He was bored and his big brother made a convenient target. Irritating Tony was as good a way to spend some spare time as any.

"Just admit it. You want to sell out completely. You want to go to some white college. You want a white suit and tie job. You want a house in a white neighborhood with a white wife by your side. Tell me I'm wrong."

Tony shook his head. "I'll give you this much, C.J. It's true that I don't have anything against being educated. Nothing against getting paid well either. And I happen to look damn good in a suit."

"Why am I suddenly in the mood for an oreo cookie?"

The wisecrack slowed Tony's momentum no more than a mosquito ramming into a windshield. If C.J. wanted to wage a verbal battle, Tony was happy to oblige him. Trigonometry could take a temporary back seat.

"You're damn straight I won't be living in the projects my whole life. And when it comes to the girl I choose, I happen to be color blind."

"Blind like hell. Your little jimmy knows exactly what color it wants." C.J. tugged lightly on the crotch of his jeans. This was done out of habit rather than a gesture intended to accompany his statement. "Don't think for one second you're fooling anyone," he continued. "I know what the real deal is. You want to prove that you're as good as them, and what better way than by having one of them on your arm? But you can't prove what people refuse to believe."

C.J. drowned out any chance of a rebuttal by turning on his boom box. The volume as usual was at maximum. Their room became filled with a thumping bass line and a rapper bragging in rhyme about the women he had bedded and the men he had killed.

Taking another glance at his watch, C.J. noticed that it was no longer running and the glass casing was cracked. The kid he took it from had surprisingly put up a fight, even managing to get a shot in. C.J.'s retaliation destroyed the very thing he was trying to obtain. He tossed his prize into the waste paper basket.

Tony reached over and lowered the radio, which had been acquired by C.J. from someone who committed the cardinal sin of being smaller and less battle tested than him, not to mention the folly of being insufficiently observant in the wrong place at the wrong time. Tony sadly understood that what C.J. didn't forcibly take for himself, he purchased with money earned on the streets by preying on the weaknesses of crackheads and other assorted addicts. This left him with very little interest or time for matters such as trigonometry.

"You got a problem with white people?" Tony asked, determined to finish what had been started. "You think they look down on you? Then don't allow the insult to ring true. Don't trap yourself in a little box and then accuse them of stuffing you in there. The only one who can limit you, is you."

Tony was saying nothing that C.J. hadn't heard from him before, though he did manage to sound even more self-righteous than usual. This probably had something to do with the white girl in the yearbook photo. C.J. pulled a stack of bills from his back pocket and began sorting through it.

"Whatever," he said nonchalantly. "I've got better things to do than argue with you."

Tony shook his head. "So you got a few bucks on you."

"A few hundred is more like it. Better study your math a little harder."

"That supposed to impress me? Congratulations, you can rob people and sell them drugs. What's the next act in your minstrel show? Cotton picking, tap dancing, or watermelon eating?"

C.J. twirled a chain around his index finger, another subconscious habit, but this one seemed more symbolic than the others, emphasizing that he was satisfied being the person he was, regardless of approval. "It definitely ain't doing impressions, cause you'll never find me imitating Whitey like you. I'm not ashamed of who *I* am."

He put the money back into his pocket, then lay down and closed his eyes. C.J. had grown weary of the argument he'd initiated, for he believed words to be a futile method of persuasion. Two things made the world go round. Fear and money. The rest was just what people tried to be satisfied with. Some even managed to delude themselves that they were happy. That was their choice and their lives, but not his.

"Wanting to be successful doesn't make me any less black," Tony said. "No matter what garbage Dad would have you believe. And it doesn't make me ashamed of who I am."

"Don't bother trying to convince me. Tell your little fairy tale to that white girl."

Giving up on ending the argument on his word, Tony sighed and returned to his studies, refusing to acknowledge C.J.'s self-satisfied grin.

CHAPTER TWO

Tony and Charlie first met in second grade, having chosen the same girl to impress with their skills in distance spitting. They both promptly lost interest in her when the conversation turned to professional wrestling. The merits and character flaws of the various combatants were debated, and with a friendship thus forged, they had been inseparable ever since. In the ensuing ten years they had ridiculed and heaped abuse upon each other as only the best of friends can. They were also each other's greatest sources of support.

"Even if I get a scholarship, it will probably only cover tuition," Tony said. School had just let out for the day, turning loose a flood of adolescence onto the surrounding streets. "I'll still need to pay for books and a place to live."

"What part-time job do you know of that could pay for all that without putting your ass in jail?"

"I'll find one."

"Stay home and commute. Sponge off your folks as long as you can. It's the American way."

Charlie's advice was both practical and sound. This mattered little to Tony, for his strategy was based on far different guidelines.

"I can't deal with him anymore. I have to get out."

Charlie massaged his head, momentarily dulling the gleam of the sun off his dark chocolate dome. He had been caressing it virtually non-stop since shaving it bald a month earlier, as if the existence of his scalp was an unexpected surprise.

"You've dealt with him this long. A few years more can't hurt."

"He thinks he can turn me into him. I ain't going for it."

Tony reminisced about the childhood wars waged with his dad at the dinner table. They would stare at each other for what felt like days, neither of them willing to concede defeat. His mother would try to mediate, but to no avail. Finally Tony would force a piece of broccoli into his mouth, disgusted by the texture and taste, but mostly by the smirk that would creep upon his father's face in his moment of triumph.

Then Tony would vomit the green intruder back up, the grin would vanish, victory would be seemingly his. That is, until his father stated that he would either have to finish eating his vegetables or else go get his belt. Broccoli always won out over his father's aged leather belt, a fashion accessory that somehow managed to grip the skin of one's behind as if it possessed razor sharp teeth.

"So when are you planning to talk to Janet?" Charlie asked.

"As soon as the time is right."

"A fine girl like that won't stay available for long. If you don't make your move soon, someone else will."

"I've got it under control." Tony didn't need to be reminded of his cowardice, for it haunted him daily. Rather than allow his false claim to be disputed, he continued the game of musical chairs with conversation topics.

"How's it going with Sheila?"

Charlie's hand returned to his scalp and his persuasive grin went out like a light bulb that had just used up the last of its watts. Sheila was the one subject guaranteed to cast a cloud over his sunny outlook. "That's over with."

"Really? Yesterday you were willing to walk across the East River for her."

"Well today I wouldn't cross the street to spit on her if her hair was on fire."

"I thought she might be the one, after breaking the two month mark and all."

"I kind of thought so too," Charlie admitted. "But dem's the breaks. I'll get over it soon enough."

“What up homies?” said Larry Faulk in greeting as he caught up from behind and wrapped an arm around each of their shoulders.

“Not much,” Tony answered. “Did you ace our last Spanish test like you usually do?” Larry would never be mistaken for a scholar, unless the subject was either hip hop videos, NBA statistics, martial arts movies, or female celebrity posterior comparisons. But he always excelled in the tests given by Mrs. Sanchez, who happened to be Polish, but presumably Mr. Sanchez was not.

“Of course. You know I spend crazy hours studying that language. If I want to impress these fine ass Boriquas and Morenas, I need to be able to conversate with them real smooth in their native tongue. You know what I’m saying?”

“I hear you.”

“You guys hear about the prank Billy Frazier and his boy Shaqawn played on Mr. Flaggs in fourth period?

“Yeah,” answered Charlie. “Everybody was talking about it.”

“Them niggas are crazy. I guess that settles the debate about whether he wears a toupee or not. I heard they got mad detention, like three months. But Shaqawn practically gets his mail there anyway, and you know Billy is just going to sleep through it just like does most of his classes. I can’t stand how Mr. Flagg be trippin’ over every little thing. He was all on my case the other day just cause I blew a bubble with my gum. He would have made a great Nazi."

Larry had been affectionately dubbed the blackest white boy alive by his friends, and certainly not due to the constant ruddiness of his cheeks. He was so deeply immersed in African-American culture that they were waiting for the day when his hair would start to kink up. He never gave the impression that he was trying to be anything other than who he naturally was, pretending to a throne he did not rightfully inherit. Rather, it was clear that he felt sincere passion for a culture that was not his birthright, but he nonetheless fit into like an old pair of slippers.

"I'm out of here, fellas. Gotta join the huddled masses. I'll be getting my own ride soon. I picked out this phat Corvette. It needs a lot of work, but if definitely beats the alternative. The honeys are not overly impressed by my bus pass." He sprinted towards the bus that had pulled to a stop at the corner and was quickly filling to capacity.

Tony and Charlie resumed walking until they reached the intersection where they were to part company for the day.

"See you tomorrow, Charlie. Don't go breaking any hearts."

"I'm the one who always gets his heart broken. That's what happens when you're a sensitive guy like myself."

"No, that's what happens when you're an asshole."

Charlie laughed and stuck up his middle finger as a farewell salute. Tony headed towards the library, alone again with thoughts of Janet.

* * *

A few hours later Tony stood waiting outside of his home. In an institution of learning he felt in control of the actions that would help determine his fate. He knew what to prepare for and how to go about it. His efforts achieved tangible results, and each A grade was another stepping stone towards the future he envisioned.

The world behind the door he now stood before was of another sort entirely. No amount of preparation helped to appease the unquestioned king of this particular castle. From the commotion inside, it was obvious that his father was enraged over fate's latest helping of grief. 'Here we go again' was the thought that leapt to mind as Tony put his ear to the door in order to calculate how much of a mess he was about to walk into.

"There's no need to get worked up over this," he heard his mother say. "The strike will be over in no time."

"Caren, they can easily replace me with some kid for half the pay. You think they give a damn that I have a family to support?"

"Then you'll get another job."

"Oh yeah. A middle aged nigger with nothing more than a high school diploma. That puts me right at the top of the hiring list."

“There are no struggles too difficult for God’s love to guide us through.”

"We got nothing to sell, nothing to mortgage. Might as well lay down and die. They'd love that. Another black man broken by the system. Another nigger goes on welfare."

Lionel Johnson's bemoaning came to a halt when the front door opened. Tony had decided that a good time to enter would not be coming any time soon.

“If it isn’t my son the bookworm. Got all your college applications out the door, boy? Need a few dollars for tuition and dorm fees? Well you better wait in line, towards the back I might add, because you’re not the only one wanting to empty out my wallet.”

Lionel looked expectantly at Tony, though he was waiting for something other than answers to his questions. He seemed to want a confession. The accusatory look in his fiery eyes could not be mistaken. They issued condemnation of the smugness he perceived in his eldest son's demeanor. Tony was no doubt looking down on him, thinking that once he was out on his own he would never allow himself to be imprisoned by poverty. He would not accept limitations that others attempted to impose on his options. He had no intention of blaming racism for that which was brought about by submission. In other words, Tony had arrogantly concluded that he would never become his father.

Tony stepped quickly through the living room towards his bedroom as if afraid the laser-like gaze of his father could penetrate skin and bone. There was nothing to say that would be welcomed, no place to go that the disapproval of Lionel could not reach.

CHAPTER THREE

For Adam it had been easy. He was the only guy around, so of course Eve would go for him. It didn't matter if food was stuck in his teeth, he stumbled over his words, or had toilet paper dangling from the hem of his pants. No one else could be more charming, or clever, or handsome. Eve's only alternative was solitude.

"There she goes," Charlie said. "By her lonesome."

Nevertheless, Tony suspected that Adam's palms still sweated and his hours spent preparing for the moment seemed inconsequential. Regardless of the odds, women tended to have that effect.

"I see her."

"So go talk to her."

"About what?" Tony asked, quite reasonably in his opinion.

"Just ask her out. How hard can that be?"

That serpent in the Garden of Eden had probably used this same line of logic.

"Very hard, since I don't even know the girl."

"Then get to know her," Charlie almost shouted. He paused to control the volume of his voice. "Introduce yourself. See how it goes from there. And if you can't then shut up about her, cause words are cheap."

Charlie was right, of course. If he wanted to get to know Janet, there was nothing else to it but to step to the plate and take a healthy swing for the fences. Yet Tony felt his hesitation was warranted, for Janet Mitchell was not exactly the typical girl around the way. Among her many wondrous traits was the ability to grow a little more beautiful with each passing day. Even indoors, her hair seemed to reflect all light the sun had to offer. Her eyes were twin oceans inviting him to dive in, her lips the petals of a rose in bloom.

If only his desire was matched by his nerve. If only his confidence about so many other matters could be summoned when it came to being around Janet. Another girl took the seat next to her in study hall that Tony would have taken, if only.

"Well, she's not alone anymore," he said.

"No, but you are. Alone and pathetic. I don't see what the big deal is. Worst case scenario she'll blow you off and you'll become so depressed that you'll kill yourself. That's not so bad, is it?"

Charlie had a knack for putting matters into proper perspective. What would be the worst outcome? Janet would reject him and he'd feel bad for awhile. Damn bad, but he'd get over it. There were plenty of girls out there. Pretty soon he wouldn't even remember her name. Well maybe not pretty soon, but eventually.

Tony had inherited the khaki colored skin and inviting eyes of his mother, along with the strong jaw and wavy hair of his father. He had grown accustomed to a fair share of attention from female admirers, and was not usually the shy sort around girls. Except for some maddening reason when it came to the one he wanted most.

His previous girlfriends had all been either black or Hispanic. An opportunity to sample further had not presented itself. Little thought was given to this until the day he looked up from his seat in the cafeteria and beheld a vision. From that moment on, Janet was never far from his thoughts. Like the cough of a lifetime smoker, her image would fade only for as long as it took to build up strength again.

He went about discreetly finding out anything about her that there was to know, except for one crucial fact. Would she be interested in him? Tony suspected that had she not been white, he would have discovered the answer by now. This aspect of the situation took on more weight each day she remained a stranger. He knew that regardless of her skin tone, she would either give him a chance or not. Yet much to his chagrin he continued to regard it, and was thus frozen in inaction.

Was Janet destined to remain nothing more than a fantasy? Could the reality of mortal flesh live up to his fevered dreams? He would never know until he was able to lay his hands on her milky skin.

Then it happened. The event transpired in mere seconds, but worlds had been shaken to their foundation in less time. What Tony expected least while wanting most is precisely what took place. Janet turned back towards him and smiled. When her friend also snuck a peek, Tony concluded that he was the subject of their conversation. He glanced at Charlie, whose grin confirmed that he had witnessed the silent exchange.

"Go for yours, Casanova."

Tony did not respond, in fact showed not a trace of the euphoria swelling within him. He could not count how often he had vowed to overcome his phobia regarding Janet. Every missed opportunity gnawed at him with the persistence of a dog lunging at a pot roast left unguarded on a counter top. But this no longer mattered, for he knew with a certainty never before experienced that the next time would be the only one to matter. The bell went off signaling everyone to head to their next class.

"You going to the game today?" asked Charlie.

"Nah."

"Why not?"

"I have to look for a job."

"You're set on getting that apartment, ain't you?"

"My dad went on strike yesterday," Tony explained. "I'm just trying to help out."

"Well good luck. And don't worry, I'll keep an eye on Janet for you."

"Who's going to keep an eye on you?"

"I'm sure she will," Charlie answered, right before darting down the hall, narrowly avoiding Tony's playful kick.

* * *

It was already past eight o'clock, nothing left to do but go home. Tony's only reward for his day's travels was a pair of weary feet. Job openings were more scarce in this neighborhood than sushi bars, frustration more plentiful than fried chicken shacks. As he spoke to each shopkeeper, he could feel his father's expectant presence lurking in shadowy corners.

As Tony matured and began reaching his own conclusions about the world and the mechanisms that made it go round, the rift between he and his father grew steadily wider. The two of them were simply unable to look at the same thing without seeing it in different ways. But now an opportunity to reverse the momentum of their relationship had presented itself. His willingness to help the family out financially in troubled times would earn him respect at long last.

His father had previously been on strike seven years earlier. Every morning he ventured out to march on the picket line, and each evening returned drunk. Once home he would explode at the slightest provocation. Static on the television, lack of beer in the refrigerator, the Mets losing another ball game. No longer helpless to do anything but watch and cry, Tony would pitch in and lighten his father's burdens this time around.

Activity taking place about thirty yards ahead sidetracked his thoughts. The nearest streetlight was broken, so details were sketchy, but it appeared to be a fight.

Drawing closer he made out four guys, each around fourteen or fifteen years old, maniacally beating up on a single one of their peers.

Tony wondered if he was about to see his first live homicide, and briefly considered taking action on the victim's behalf. But that would just make two casualties. The thing to do was turn around and take the long way home. This was none of his business. Nevertheless he was drawn helplessly to the violence, common sense overwhelmed by natural instinct which caused the shedding of blood to be the basis of a variety of spectator sports.

A police siren wailed from a distance too close for comfort. "It's Five-O. Let's get the fuck out of here."

Even if the speaker's face had not been clearly made out in the lamp light, his voice was easily recognized.

After the assailants ran off, Tony walked over to the boy they left behind. Blood trickled from his nostrils and mouth. He initially appeared to be unconscious, but then opened his eyes and spoke.

"You see my glasses anywhere?" He sat up and let loose a spray of scarlet.

A pair of glasses lay on the ground nearby, twisted out of shape and one lens shattered. Tony handed it over, which produced a look of great irritation instead of gratitude that it was his eyewear rather than his skull to have been damaged beyond repair.

"Shit. My mom is going to flip out." He effortlessly rose to his feet despite the beating just taken, then spat another puddle of blood onto the pavement. "Thanks, man."

As he walked away, the letters RD shaved into the fade on the left side of his head were spotted. A downward glance at his Timberland construction boots confirmed Tony's assumption. He was a member of the Raw Dawgs, a neighborhood gang comprised of Puerto Rican kids. They were usually seen in Corollas without bumpers, the flag of their motherland on every antenna. Much of their time was spent working on these vehicles. The rest was spent looking for and finding trouble.

The Raw Dawgs were the chief rivals of the Kaos Krew, the gang his brother belonged to. The main source of friction between them was the right to be the sole supplier for the numerous junkies who inhabited their miniscule sector of the Bronx.

It was a group of Kaos Krew members who had just fled the scene, and C.J.'s voice that had been recognized. Tony feared that one of these days his brother was going to be on the flip side of the violence he could not resist.

Staring at the blood stains on the sidewalk for a minute, solemnly aware that the difference between life and death could be measured by the size of such a stain, Tony wondered as he often did what he could do to make C.J. see the inevitability of his downfall. Then the sirens cried louder and he decided to ponder this question on the go.

* * *

Tony arrived home to the sight of his father in the tattered recliner that he alone ever sat in, a can of beer in one hand and remote control in the other, eyes fixated on the television set. The sound of canned laughter reverberated throughout the apartment. Paper thin carpeting which matched the colorless hue of the walls and ceiling created a claustrophobic ambiance that lack of size could not quite bring about on its own. The mix and match utilitarian furnishings borrowed more heavily from the rainbow's spectrum.

With everything the world had to offer, Tony marveled at how the golden nectar of barley and a box filled with moving pictures managed to placate his father. Why didn't he need more, or at least comprehend why others might?

Tony was about to open the door to his room when a stern, commanding voice held him in place.

"I've been wanting to talk to you." Lionel held off on his lecture long enough to take a sip of beer.

"When I was your age I was helping support my family. I didn't have the luxury of daydreaming about nonsense, and despite what you might think, neither do you."

Tony forced himself not to grin as he informed his father than he had just been out looking for a job.

"Is that right? About time you got your head out of the clouds. You need to start bringing some money in here. Your years of leeching are over. You're grown now, at least in the eyes of employers, and they're the ones who matter. They're the ones who can keep you fed, not them books you're always buried in or those colleges you keep talking about."

It came as no surprise to Tony that a pat on the back would not be forthcoming, just another dose of cynicism and criticism.

"I'm looking for something temporary," he said. "My head is in the same place it's always been."

"I guess then you've figured out how to pay for college."

"Like I've said a hundred times, I should be eligible for financial aid, plus I might win a scholarship. If it isn't meant to be, I'll deal. But I'm not going to give up without even trying."

The chuckling that followed must have dried Lionel's throat, for as soon as the sound left, cold beer filled the void. This silenced him for but a moment.

"Just keep in mind where that money would be coming from. White people aren't in the habit of simply giving money away, especially to us. What they do is make investments. They take a few dollars from their back pocket, and then that's right where they have you."

"Is that right?" Tony could have finished each of his father's sentences. He could not recall the last opinion expressed by him that was surprising or new.

"Debt is a powerful thing. You better think long and hard about who you're willing to owe, cause the white man's pocket is mighty snug. Get tucked back there, you may never make your way out. And while you're daydreaming about tomorrow, don't forget that there are bills to be paid and bellies to be fed today. Any luck with your job search?"

"No, not yet. I filled out a few applications. We'll see what happens."

"Keep in mind that it's called work for a reason. Getting a free ride tends to spoil a person. Well that ride has stopped."

Tony took a seat on the sofa. His father was just getting warmed up, so he might as well make himself comfortable.

"I remember what I had to endure when I was your age to make a few bucks. Everything short of picking cotton. I even shined shoes for a little while. You didn't know that, did you? I shined their damn shoes."

Lionel closed his eyes, transporting himself back to a time and place he wished he could forget, but knew he never would.

"You'll do pretty much anything when you're young, and just got married, and have a kid on the way. You'll do whatever white folks will pay you for, even if they don't think you're worthy to eat where they eat or piss where they piss. If you're lucky, you won't have to go through half of what I did. But I don't hold much stock in luck."

Tony tuned out the personal history lesson by reflex, much like someone who lived near an elevated track would eventually cease to notice the periodic rumbling of passing trains.

"Times have changed, Dad. You can piss wherever you want to nowadays."

Tony was fed up with the lectures and berating. He had been told once too often that he did not talk right, or walk right, or breathe right. All because he was preparing to do what his father didn't have it in him to imagine, or to tolerate.

"You think a couple of new laws and some tokens in high places makes everything fine and dandy?" Lionel asked. "You don't actually believe that changes what they think of us, do you? Getting good grades in school don't mean you know shit about life, boy. I could have five PHD's, but that wouldn't change nothing. I could click my heels and think good thoughts all day long, but they'll still see me as a nigger. You're my son, so how do you think they see you?"

Lionel brought the can to his lips, found the taste of aluminum unaccompanied by beer, so went to get another. Tony got up and headed to his room. If his father refused to see a better way to live, that was his choice. But Tony was his own man, and saw the world with his own eyes.

* * *

In the shadows cast by Bronx public housing, a young couple gazed at each other with the passion only first love brings. Longing spread over the girl like rays of sunlight over a field of lilies, charged through the boy like a bull past a matador's teasing cape. The girl's smile overtook her entire face, her cheeks dimpling into little caverns, her wide eyes shimmering like fireflies over a lake. The boy's chest puffed out with pride at having landed the fairest maiden, though it also felt inevitable, for he knew himself to be the most charming prince in their particular kingdom. The two of them kissed, tenderly at first, growing stronger as lust assumed command. After a few minutes the girl reluctantly pulled back.

"I better go in," she said. "My dad's going to throw a fit."

"All right. But let me give you something first." The boy, who was a little closer to pretty than handsome, had a glint in his lightly colored almond shaped eyes that suggested an inflated sense of self. He was the only child of a single mom and the only grandson of her mother, and as soon as schoolgirls his age began noticing boys, he was usually first on their short list. His popularity only grew as he smoothly navigated adolescence and became expert at how best to wield it.

After reaching behind his neck to undo a gold chain with name pendant on it, he placed the jewelry on his girlfriend while simultaneously drawing her to him, his tongue and hands bolder now that he had placed his brand upon her, roaming with abandon. His purposeful momentum directed them to a poorly lit corner.

The sound of boisterous laughter from a group walking by startled the girl, bringing ardor to a halt. Her suitor tried to resume once they were alone again, but he was gently held away.

"I really do have to go."

"Okay. He knew it would take little effort on his part to convince her to stay out longer so he could reap a little more reward from his gesture of commitment. But there was no need to rush anything. He had this situation well in hand and knew that the opportunity to take full advantage of it would come soon enough. “I'll see you tomorrow, baby."

Only after he was out of sight did Tanya Johnson enter the building her family resided in. Hell would be caught for coming home so late, but this realization scarcely penetrated her euphoria.

Walking on tip-toe with breath held, Tanya inched the front door open and peered in. Her father was slumped in his easy chair, snoring away as a local newscaster chatted from the television that often acted as a sedative on him. She stepped in and closed the door gently, hopeful that she could get to her room undetected. But it was impossible to avoid the creaky floorboards that constituted a natural alarm system for the apartment.

"What time is it, young lady?" Lionel asked as he rubbed the sleep from his eyes and pulled himself back to consciousness.

"I know, I'm sorry. I lost track of the time."

"You've been doing that quite a bit lately. Sit down. I want to talk to you."

Tanya did as she was told. A punishment of some sort was inevitable. She could only hope that its severity would be reasonable.

"Were you out with this Eric fellow again?"

"Yes, Daddy," answered Tanya in her most innocent sounding voice.

"You've been seeing a lot of him."

"I guess so."

Tanya fidgeted uneasily. She had been staying out late with Eric practically every night, always mindful of her curfew, but repeatedly failing to meet it. She was fortunate that her father tended to be easier on her than her brothers, but this luck seemed about ready to run out.

"You're too young to be running around like you've been doing. You're going to earn a reputation you won't be able to erase. I don't want you going out in the evening for awhile until you've proven you can act responsibly."

Usually a definitive period of time was given whenever she or one of her brothers was grounded. The vague duration of her stated punishment was therefore troubling, and also indicative of the fact that her father's position would be inflexible from here on out.

"That isn't fair?"

"Maybe, maybe not. Either way, it's what I've decided and that's all there is to it."

"I promise I'll never break curfew again," Tanya said, knowing that her usual ploys were not likely to be of use. "Please give me one more chance."

"You've already used up that promise."

"I'm not doing anything wrong, Daddy." A change of tactics would be her only chance, although it was a bleak one at best. "I'm sixteen now. All my friends are dating. I'm not your baby girl anymore. Why can't you accept that?"

"You want reasons, I'll give you two. One is because you're still living under my roof. So when you come home one day with a bellyache which turns out to be a lot more than that, I'm the one who'll have to feed it. And there's enough hungry mouths around here as is."

Lionel stood up and walked behind Tanya. He rubbed her shoulders as he often did as a sign of affection, but his tone remained firm.

"Reason number two is that I'm the father and you're the daughter, so what I say goes."

Tanya realized that there was no point to arguing further. Her father's mind as usual, was unchangeable. But so was the fact that she was in love. She could be kept at home, but no one could keep her and Eric apart.

CHAPTER FOUR

Tony had been walking for hours, making dozens of unsolicited offers, rejection waiting at every stop. Now he knew what it was like for Jehovah's Witnesses after countless doors had been closed in their faces. Upon sighting the Help Wanted sign in the window of Jensen's Supermarket, he felt like a dying man in a desert who had just spotted a water fountain. He only hoped it wasn't a mirage.

The store manager, Mr. Jordan, was a stout balding man with the stub of a cigar protruding from the corner of his mouth like a natural extension of his two day's growth of beard. His facial expression could only be interpreted as a frown, but it appeared to be a permanent characteristic, such as a mole or dimple, rather than an indicator of his mood. He took the cigar from his mouth and blew out a puff of what smelled like vaporized sewage.

"You don't mind me smoking, do you?"

"No, sir," Tony replied, sensing that honesty would not be the best policy in this situation.

"Good answer. All you have to do is lift boxes, unpack 'em, and shelve what's inside. If you show up on time and do what I just said, things should work out fine."

Tony wasn't sure how much longer he could hold his breath, but would break the world record if that's what it took to get the job.

"The only people I got a problem with are jerk offs who go around complaining about other people smoking. The surgeon general can warn me all he wants, but if he ever came down here and tried to take away my stogie, he'd be the one needing a surgeon. What's your name, son?"

"Tony Johnson."

"Which school you go to?"

"Lincoln."

"Nice and close, that's good. The job pays seven dollars an hour. I need someone to work from four to eight on weekdays. That sound okay to you?"

"It sounds great, sir."

"In that case you got yourself a job. Can you start tomorrow?"

"Sure can. Thanks a lot, sir."

"You can thank me by being a good worker. Hey Howard, come here."

The guy headed towards him put Tony in mind of beautiful, tanned people downing soft drinks on a California beach, their gleaming white teeth like freshly painted picket fences. He was the embodiment of Madison Avenue's most enduring creation, the All-American boy. His demeanor exuded a brand of self-assurance possessed by those accustomed to having the world handed to them on a platter.

"Howard, this is Tony. He'll be working with you starting tomorrow."

"Good to meet you," Howard said.

"Same here."

"I better get back to work. I'll see you tomorrow."

"Yeah, see ya."

He would have to rearrange his schedule, studying at home rather than the library. A few all nighters would probably be necessary on the days before exams. Nevertheless, Tony did not doubt that he would be able to keep up his grades. And once his father started working again, he would have extra spending money. He would update his wardrobe, buy a used computer, put money away for college, and if he started dating Janet, *when* he started dating Janet, be able to take her out in style. His pace quickened. He couldn't wait to get home and share his good news.

The time-beaten easy chair was vacant, so he walked into the kitchen where his mother was almost a permanent fixture. She was a modestly pretty woman, but when in certain moods that caused her expression to change just so, a deeper form of beauty would sneak up on the eyes which beheld her. As many years as Lionel had been gazing upon her, this still happened when least expected. Signs of middle age were just beginning to appear on Caren's face. The faint lines around her eyes were ironically named, for life had given her too little to laugh about.

"Hi, Mom." Tony planted a kiss on her forehead before heading to the refrigerator in search of food with minimal prep time required. He found some cold cuts and decided on a sandwich.

"You have a good day at school today?" asked Caren, pleasantly surprised by the demonstration of affection. Her children would never know how much she cherished such moments. At least not until they had children of their own.

"It was okay, but I had a better day after school."

"Why is that? You have any luck job hunting?"

"If you call getting a job that I start tomorrow luck. Personally, I call it skill."

"You got a job? That's great. Doing what?"

"I'm a stockboy at Jensen's supermarket. With Dad on strike, I figure every penny is going to count."

Caren pinched his cheek, a habit she had acquired years ago when his cheeks were considerably fuller and never quite managed to shake.

"You're a good son, you know that? I'm very proud of you."

"Aw Mom, you're making me blush," said Tony with a laugh. He headed out of the kitchen with the bologna and American cheese sandwich he had assembled. His unwillingness to wait until dinner was due to the inedible quality of what his school's cafeteria presented as lunch earlier that day.

"Don't even think you're leaving without cleaning up this mess."

Tony made a mock groan of displeasure before doing as he was told.

On the way to his room, he decided to drop in on Tanya. Fortunate enough to be the only member of the family with a bedroom to herself, she treated it as a sanctuary. He knocked on her door and she called out for him to enter.

It was unnecessary to ask how she was feeling. Heartache resonated in the air. Tony knew about the punishment she had been put on and realized that Tanya was paying a dear price not so much for her tardiness, as for their father's fear of what her boyfriend might tempt her to do once the sun went down. Her crime was sullying the image of Daddy's little girl.

"Cheer up. The world hasn't ended just yet."

"You wouldn't say that if you were the one being held prisoner."

"No, I suppose not."

It was easy to sympathize. Tanya had held out the longest, but none of them was beyond their father's clutches. When he saw joy, he was determined to squelch it. If he couldn't take pleasure from life, why should anyone else?

Tony took in the sight of his sister's walls. Almost every square inch was covered by pictures of who she thought were beautiful, black men. They were taken from her massive magazine collection that she began acquiring nearly as early in life as her first literary encounters with seeing Spot run and Dick hanging out with Jane. Michael Jordan in his youthful Chicago days soared over Denzel Washington and Wesley Snipes in full vampire slaying mode, her tributes to the old school alpha male. They were sandwiched by Tyson Beckford and L.L. Cool J. A few other rapper/singer/actor/athlete hybrids held court at the head of her bed along with the host of a music video show whose name Tony could not recall, but if memory served he was the only one amongst them with a first *and* last name, plus he was the only one wearing a shirt. If Lionel ever ran into any of these guys they would be well advised to make a hasty exit, for they had stirred up the hormones of his virginal daughter.

"I better go do my homework," Tony said. "And you have to figure out how to see Eric without Dad knowing about it, right?"

"Yeah, I guess."

Tony left his sister alone to sulk. She was the latest victim of their father's refusal to accept the choices made by his children. But the time would soon arrive when they got to decide for themselves. At the age of sixteen, Tanya still had to accept his final say. Not so with Tony, who was on the verge of emancipating himself.

* * *

A congregation of twenty waited restlessly behind McKinley High School. Rusted and rimless backboards loomed above, pillars supporting their own private section of sky. Shards of glass from broken beer bottles shimmered to rival the stars that watched over them. The school C.J. attended was only a fifteen minute walk from where his brother and sister went, but the differences were striking. Both were public schools, but one had to do well on a test to get into Lincoln while anyone who cared to could attend McKinley. Whereas McKinley was firmly nestled in the projects, Lincoln stood at a border line between a lower class neighborhood and one proudly bearing the mantle of middle class. McKinley high school was no place for children at night, nor for law abiding adults.

The youngest of the group was thirteen, the oldest twenty. Despite their youth, or perhaps because of it, they were dangerous. They hungered for power. Not the kind gained through politics or from money. That was beyond their reach. So they strove to earn it in the streets. If they couldn't get out of the ghetto, they would rule it. People knew who they were, and to stay out of their way. As long as they stood unopposed, they got whatever they wanted.

But now they *were* being opposed. Not by the mayor putting more cops on the streets, judges handing out stiffer sentences, a community patrol, or anything of that nature. The only danger that mattered to a gang was another one who laid claim to the same territory.

The Kaos Krew did not like sharing power. They refused to accept that there were now people who couldn't be pushed around so easily, and certain things it was best not to take. They missed being untouchable.

"I think I hear them coming," said Tyrone, the baby of the group in age but no less savage than the others when occasions called for it.

"Yeah, that's them all right," said Louis. "I can smell the rice and beans from here."

Louis was the leader of the Krew and the rest of them looked up to him with awe. He had done things very few would dare try, for money, reputation, or just for kicks. Fear was a stranger to him and life of minimum value. So he risked his own with little regard, and for those in his way he held none.

He stepped forward and watched the Raw Dawgs approach. They stopped five feet away except for their leader, who walked right up to Louis, nearly close enough for the sweat on the tips of their noses to merge.

"Let's do this," Felix said.

Most didn't see the punch that followed, for its swiftness allowed Louis to draw first blood with the subtlety of a mosquito. But everyone saw Felix fall to his knees, and with that the battle officially began.

The fighting was fast and furious, and despite the unity they tried to embody, once the blows started coming it was every man for himself. The younger ones who were less experienced flailed wildly. The elders circled each other, looked for an opening, then struck with chilling ferociousness. The prize at stake was honor. They felt victory would mean supremacy. But all it really meant was something to gloat about until the next time. For losing only made them angrier, and anger made them stronger. Death alone could stop them.

They rarely thought about dying, though. Each of them felt surrounded by an aura of invincibility. And as long as they stuck to damage inflicted by hands, which the gangs had sworn to do tonight, they were relatively safe.

C.J.'s opponent was a heavyset kid who threw windmill punches intended to decapitate. After ducking safely under a flurry, C.J. blocked a right cross headed towards his temple and retaliated with a roundhouse right that connected flush on the jaw, dropping his adversary on his back. C.J. pounced on him and landed a few follow-up punches for good measure. He then looked around for someone new to take on.

Seeing that Louis had Felix up against the fence and was whaling on him with a passion, C.J. took a moment in the midst of the chaos to admire his gang's leader. Muscled arms pumped like pistons, pounding their target mercilessly, dredlocks dancing like the mane of an enraged lion. It surprised C.J. when Louis suddenly backed away, until he noticed the knife Felix bared. The fair fight agreed upon had grown decidedly unfair.

Louis reached towards his pocket, but was deterred by the knife's blade slicing across his forearm. As he clutched at the wound, Felix moved forward like a starving alley cat with a broken legged pigeon in its sights.

Without thought, C.J. withdrew his own knife and raced to Louis' aid. He moved swiftly, but someone else managed to arrive before him.

C.J. stopped and stared in horror as Felix thwarted his attacker by slashing at the blur caught in his peripheral vision. Tyrone lurched back and fell hard to the ground. A stream of blood sprayed past the blade now imbedded in his chest.

As one, the members of the Krew rushed at Felix, who wisely did not wait to greet them. The Raw Dawgs followed closely on their heels. Oncoming traffic was brought to a halt as they overtook the street.

Only two people remained in the schoolyard. One was C.J., who stood motionless while watching the unimaginable. The other was his best friend, Tyrone, who at the ripe old age of thirteen lay writhing in pain, his eyesight blurred by tears as he did the only thing he could think of, call out for his mother.

* * *

It was a quarter past eight and Lionel had still not come home. Caren was trying to keep busy. Her fingers nimbly interacted with knitting needles to create form from the ball of yarn beside her, a hobby she had abandoned years ago and recently taken up again. Her initial goal was to make a blanket, but she had scaled down her ambitions and settled for a scarf. Even so, she had been at it almost two weeks and was only halfway finished. Between her part-time job and full-time role of housewife, she was not a woman with a great deal of leisure time.

Tony could see she was worried. His father was usually home well before this time and could reliably be found before the television with a beer in hand. He favored old westerns, old game shows, sports and infomercials.

There was no way to reach him, so Caren did what she could to distract herself, a task she was failing at miserably.

Someone struggled to put a key in the lock of the front door, accompanied by the sound of frustrated cursing. After several seconds passed with no sign of success, Caren could no longer refrain from getting up and opening it herself. Lionel stumbled into the apartment.

"Are you crazy, woman? Never do that again."

Caren wasn't listening to him. She wasn't even concerned about his being drunker than usual. Drunk was drunk. Her attention had been grabbed by the fact that his clothing was drenched.

"What happened to you?"

Lionel walked unsteadily to his chair and sat down. "I had a slight difference of opinion with someone at McCann's."

"With who?"

"Phil."

"Phil?! He's your best friend."

"*Was* my best friend. Until he tried to be Mr. Big Shot and started offering handouts." Lionel yanked off his shirt and explained that Phil's teenager assistant had accepted another job. When offered the vacated position, Lionel expressed in a manner that left no room for doubt what he thought about being treated as a charity case. A brief and sloppy shoving match followed, and an unfortunately placed pitcher of beer ended up as the lone casualty.

"Like I'm gonna hand him paint brushes for minimum wage."

He reached for the TV remote control. When in his chair, Lionel routinely held a beer can and the remote - his throne and his scepters.

"What's for dinner?" he asked as Caren walked to the kitchen.

"Stew."

"Again?"

"I'm trying to conserve our money. The last time you went on strike it lasted over two months. If we hadn't borrowed..."

Lionel slammed his hand down on the coffee table. His flashes of temper, especially when drinking, were something Caren and the coffee table had long grown accustomed to. Both however, were worse for the wear.

"I don't owe Manny a damn thing. I paid him back every cent, with interest. So don't go making him out to be our savior. Just get me something to dry off with."

He took aim at the television and searched for a program that might soothe his nerves. Caren went into the kitchen, emerged seconds later with a dish towel which she tossed to him, then retreated like a turtle darting in and out of its shell.

Tony had been patiently waiting for an opening to speak. His good news would surely serve as antidote to his father's agitated state. Every father wanted to be proud of his son, and at long last, Tony was providing the perfect opportunity.

"Guess what, Dad. I got a job."

Lionel stared ahead as if completely engrossed in the commercial for women's deodorant on the television screen. Tony was confident that he had been heard, but the lack of response forced him to repeat himself.

"I said I got a job. At Jensen's Supermarket. I start tomorrow."

Lionel turned and looked at Tony curiously, seeming uncertain for a moment of what language had been spoken to him.

"Well ain't that something," he said finally. "Caren, bring us out a couple of beers. Our son is a working man."

His tone of voice was difficult to translate, perhaps because the alcohol in his system blurred the line between sarcasm and genuine satisfaction.

“What do they have you doing there?” Lionel asked. “Are you managing the place or what?"

"I'm just working in the stockroom a few hours after school. I figured we could use the extra money."

Tony wanted it understood that his motivation had been the best interest of the family. He wanted credit. Although unwilling to abide by many of his father's wishes, a part of him could not help but seek approval. He was of the same flesh and blood, not some objectionable outsider, and this deserved to be acknowledged. It was long overdue.

"With me out of work, right? Boy, I don't know how we ever got by before. But now everything's going to be all right. I figure between you and your mother, I might as well retire. Caren, hurry up with those beers."

The now obvious ridicule made no sense to Tony. But why should it? When it came to pleasing or at least appeasing his father, there was no right and wrong to choose between, only wrong and dead wrong.

"It's time to make room for the new generation," Lionel continued. "Women and children first. Shit, I never thought that would apply to getting paychecks."

He threw the soaked towel across the room. "Where the hell are those beers? I know she heard me." He stood up, took a moment to make sure of his balance, then started towards the kitchen. "Go on strike a couple of days and no one listens to a word you say."

Tony jumped up to prevent what his father's frustration was leading to. He gently put a hand on Lionel’s shoulder.

"Dad, relax. I'll get the beer."

Not gently enough.

"Look at this. You telling me what to do? You figure your new job gives you that right? Well, you figured wrong. Now get off me, boy."

Lionel shoved his son back as if Tony was an irritating fly on his rough hide. Then he entered the kitchen.

"Didn't you hear me? I asked for two beers."

"You've had enough to drink, Lionel."

"I don't remember asking for your opinion."

Caren realized she was positioning herself in a path that might soon be steamrolled. But she refused to play barmaid, would not provide her husband with fuel for his fire. Lionel had never needed much help getting drunk, and he wouldn't be receiving any assistance from her today.

"Neither your legs nor your hands look broken to me. You want more beer? Get it yourself."

Lionel raised his hand, but was unable to bring it forward. He turned back and looked into the eyes of his son. Tony had found the courage to go this far solely on instinct, but once his father faced him, he could will himself to do nothing but remain standing. Lionel, having forgotten about Caren, the beer never received, and the smack he had been set to deliver for her insolence, yanked his wrist free and backed Tony into the living room.

"Lionel, no!"

Caren's plea was ignored. "You want to take me on? Let's see what you got." Lionel clasped his hands behind his back in invitation.

"What are you waiting for? You want to show the world how much better you are than your old man, right? Well fuck the world. Show *me*."

It was as if Lionel had attained the power of Medusa. Tony was unable to take a breath or blink an eye.

"Come on, stockboy. Show me!"

Lionel would not get his wish. Tony's brain finally succeeded in transmitting its message to his legs. He stepped back and continued doing so until reaching his bedroom. Caren looked on in shocked silence. She had witnessed many of her husband's lows, but this one bottomed them all.

Tony slammed the door behind him and fell onto his bed. He wanted more than anything not to cry, but couldn't help it. Here he was eighteen years old, less than a year away from starting college and perhaps even moving out on his own. Yet when push came to shove was he really anything more than a little boy? His father was right. It didn't matter how well he did in school, what kind of job he ended up with, or how much money he may earn someday. One either stood up for who he was and what he believed in, or else he ran away, cowered beneath his pillow, and asked himself why tears fell.

Was it because he was angry? Was it because he was scared? Or were they shed because he hadn't been able to show his father that he was a man, and doubted he ever would be?

* * *

In the dream, *Tony ran as fast as he was able. Though his lungs were at the point of bursting, he didn't dare stop. Close behind was a vicious beast of monstrous proportions, each of whose plodding steps equaled ten of his own. The face of the creature was the grotesquely deformed but still recognizable visage of his father.*

The ground beneath Tony vanished and he found himself hurtling through an abyss, just beyond the outstretched claws of the beast. His mother, sister and brother came into view. If he could only get to them, he was certain he would be safe. Drawing nearer though, he saw that each of their throats were slit, and they were not standing on firm ground but sinking into quicksand.

He plunged in. Only his head remained above the surface. Looking around desperately for help, he spied

Janet. She was dressed in a white gown that danced about her in the wind, her hand extended. When he reached out, the movement caused him to sink deeper. Now only the upper half of his face was above the surface of the murderous slime. He stretched again, but Janet was just outside his reach. He went under and waited for death to overtake him.

Suddenly he was pulled to safe ground. He wiped the quicksand from his eyes and looked up at the most beautiful vision ever beheld.

Then he noticed the thin red line that marked where Janet's throat had been cut. Her body fell aside and in her place stood the monster. It raised its dagger-like claws and...

Tony jerked upright, his face bathed in a cold sweat, heart beating quicker than a drum solo on a jazz record. He looked at the clock beside his bed and saw that it was one o'clock in the morning. Having been wrenched from sleep's grasp, he would not fall back easily. He was contemplating a trip to the refrigerator when the door to his room opened and a familiar silhouette floated in.

"About time you dragged your ass home."

"I was at the hospital," C.J. said, tossing his jacket onto his bed.

"You all right?"

"I'm fine, but I can't say the same for Tyrone. We threw down with the Raw Dawgs and he got stuck."

"Is he hurt bad?"

"Well he ain't hurt good. He was bleeding like a mother fucker. Sounded like a little baby, rolling around on the ground crying for his mom. But he ain't no baby, he's as tough as they come. He's gonna make it, just wait and see."

Tony's concern disintegrated. He could not understand C.J.'s determination to court death on a daily basis. Or maybe he did understand, and this was what caused his frustration. So many found the same solution his brother had. Selling death to their own people. The money was a difficult lure to resist. Additionally, the fear elicited from their hard core posturing proved nearly as addictive. They demanded to be heard, even though it didn't seem they had much to say. Perhaps the futility and smallness that characterized their lives was too overwhelming to articulate in any manner other than a primitive, incoherent scream. Maybe it was inevitable that those who felt they had no stake in society would opt to destroy it.

Whether Tony understood or not, he had to do something. He couldn't change the world, or even this one ghetto neighborhood. But perhaps it was still possible to get through to his brother.

"You're better than this, can't you see that? Why throw your life away over meaningless bullshit?"

C.J. flashed an infuriating smile. The one that said "I know everything worth knowing, so don't bother trying to teach me".

"That was beautiful speech. Almost brought tears to my eyes."

Tony lay back down and closed his eyes in surrender. C.J. was like the pilot of a small plane taking off without regard for riotous weather, hell bent not so much on reaching a particular destination, as on riding the storm.

CHAPTER FIVE

Tony awoke the following morning with a vague recollection of his nightmare. He didn't dwell on it for long. Morning was intended by God to be the eraser of night. His thoughts were focused onward, to a day brimming with possibilities. He intended to do no less on this day of days than act out what destiny had pre-ordained. Janet would succeed in reality where she failed in fantasy. She would be his salvation.

While doing toe touches in gym class, he confided to Charlie what his plans were. The smirk of response could be translated as nothing but, "I'll believe it when I see it".

Tony had been rather inattentive to Mr. Mahoney's dictatorial instructions throughout the semester, for he was busy becoming an expert on Janet's behavioral patterns. For example, she always did a few extra stretches before starting to run. When minutes later she remained true to form, Tony did not hesitate. He walked towards her purposefully, the theme song to Rocky playing in his head just as it did before big exams and other critical tasks. His tranquility did not surprise him, for he was as prepared for this moment as any man had ever been.

Three steps away. That's how close he managed to get before the familiar demons of inaction came out from hiding. He stooped to re-lace his already adequately tied sneakers. When he was done he looked up, prepared to see that Janet and the moment were gone, ready to heap curses upon himself for allowing fear to again be his master. Instead he saw that she was still there, fiddling with her own sneakers. Fate had given him a reprieve. Or perhaps she too was stalling.

"Hi." His journey of a thousand syllables had begun.

"Hello."

"I'm ..."

"Tony Johnson."

He failed to hide his surprise. "How'd you know that?"

"We have some mutual friends. All I had to do was ask."

Tony was quite pleased with how this was going so far, but tried to remain composed. Girls were turned on by composure.

"Okay. Why did you ask?"

"I'm the curious type."

“Curious about me?”

“Curious about anything or anyone who seems kind of interesting.”

“So I intrigue you?” Tony asked, while suppressing a grin that threatened to pass by both ears and meet up at the ends behind his head.

“Maybe.”

"This isn't social hour, Johnson," Mr. Mahoney bellowed. "Hit the track!"

They began to jog, going at the same pace to continue their conversation. Tony's mind had gone blank. What was it that he was supposed to say next?

"I've been wanting to meet you for a while. Just couldn't work up the nerve."

That wasn't it, but was hopefully better than silence.

“What made you want to meet me?” asked Janet.

“I thought you seemed kind of maybe interesting too.”

“Is that so? Well I'm glad you worked up the nerve. What finally brought out your courage?"

"I had three boxes of Wheaties for breakfast this morning." Tony was pleased by his unrehearsed display of wit. He anxiously awaited a reaction.

Janet smiled. Tony remembered to breathe. Janet was being friendly, inviting even. Half as much interest from another girl would have adequately bolstered his confidence. Yet he was still unsure. If Janet's taste was judged by her previous boyfriend, Tony didn't see how he stood much of a chance. And yet he sensed she *was* interested, that she was in fact, waiting.

Their classmates had run into a black hole, the voice of Mr. Mahoney sucked into a vacuum of silence, the track and the school and the surrounding neighborhood dissolved like salt into water. All that remained was him and Janet.

"There's a rumor going around that you and Roger broke up."

"It's not a rumor, it's a fact. Roger has a lot of growing up to do. How about you and Sharice?"

“Sharice is a great girl. She’s attractive, and she’s smart, and the truth is, I can’t think of a single negative thing to say about her. But she wasn’t the one I’m looking for.”

“Who are you looking for?”

“I can’t really describe her”, Tony answered. “I only know that if a guy is lucky, he’ll see someone, and he’ll watch her from a distance for awhile, and he’ll ask around to find out what kind of person she is, and then he’ll finally work up the nerve to speak to her, to see if her smile will light him up and set his heart racing. And then suddenly, he’ll know that she’s the one.

Janet said nothing in return, but Tony could tell from the quality of her silence that she liked what she had heard and wanted more.

"Have you replaced Roger yet?"

"I'm trying to be more fickle the next time around," Janet answered.

It was now or never. Tony inhaled deeply and went with now.

"Do you only go out with quarterbacks, or does a courageous cereal eater have a chance too?"

"I don't know who I'll go out with until I'm asked."

"In that case, what are you doing after school today?"

The words were sprung from his mouth, and unless the laws of audiology had changed they had no doubt been transported through the air and into Janet's ears. His part was done. What happened next lay in greater hands. He said a brief prayer in his head. Please God.

"I had nothing special planned, but maybe you'll change that."

Tony exhaled an Amen. "We could go to Sanstone's and talk a little more over burgers."

"Okay. But I think I'll have a salad instead of a burger. Our cheerleading outfits don't hide much."

"I've noticed. That's why I never miss a game."

Janet gave him a playful tap on the arm as they finished up their laps.

"I'll meet you by your locker after last period."

"I'll be there," Janet said, before running to catch up with the rest of the girls heading towards their gym locker room. Tony stood and watched her for a moment, then joined the male half of the class. Charlie was waiting for a report, but Tony's grin had a mind of its own and broadcast his success in advance.

"I take it things went well."

"Smooth as butter."

Tony related his conversation with Janet as they changed out of gym attire. It was a much abridged version of the story, minus the overwhelming sense of anxiety, plus the sophisticated, charming confidence of James Bond. He didn't see how his plot revisions could do any harm. The final scene worked out the same. He had gotten the girl.

* * *

At Sanstone's Diner, Tony and Janet's first date was scheduled for the upcoming weekend as they shared a strawberry milkshake. Destiny was set in motion over a green Formica table, and it promised to be even sweeter than the frothy treat that had been blended for their enjoyment.

Shortly afterward Tony arrived at his new job, full of the vigor that only youth combined with good fortune can generate. In summers past he had been a day camp counselor, enjoying the feeling of semi-independence that earning his own keep brought with it. But mostly it had felt like babysitting unruly kids, keeping them under control mainly by distraction and steadily guiding them towards exhaustion. What he did at Jenson's Supermarket was definitely not a chore or task or way to simultaneously pass time and earn a few dollars, but bona fide work. Perspiration dripped from his brow as he and Roger strained under the weight of the cartons they carried, muscles taxed to near their limit.

As exhausting as the labor was, his coworker's steady stream of chatter made the time pass quickly. A large percentage of what he had to say was on the subject he was most interested in - himself. By the time they punched out for the day, Tony was an old hand at unpacking cartons. He had also become somewhat of an expert on the life of Howard Davis.

Superficial matters were disclosed at first. Howard was in his junior year of college, played the guitar a little, was considering getting a tattoo, and worshipped the ground walked upon by Pamela Anderson. This led to more personal revelations, such as the fact that his stepfather was an accountant who wanted his less than thrilling footsteps to be followed. Howard resisted at first, wanting to join the Peace Corps and see the world, or at least take a year off to travel across country by motorcycle like a latter day Che Guevara.

Discussion of his step-dad led to the topic of his biological father. He had died when Howard was only four, so was known through anecdotes more than memory. The tales told of an irresponsible, but irrepressibly charming man with an aversion to domesticity. Howard's stepfather on the other hand possessed a stellar track record for being home by dinner time.

For the past two years Howard had been dating a girl named Sandy. Since they went to different colleges, he didn't bother to resist the temptation of other girls. Tony concluded that if the fairer sex thought as much of Howard as he seemed to think of himself, though more in a confident than a cocky manner, this must have constituted a great deal of non-resistance. Shortly before quitting time, Howard disclosed one last nugget of information.

"Check this out. My dad hooked up a job for me with a friend of a friend of his. I'm supposed to be learning the family trade as we speak. He wants me ready to replace his partner when he retires."

"Is that right?"

"I couldn't stand it. Boring beyond belief. And on top of that, the guy was an asshole. I did everything I could to get fired, and it finally paid off. But I never told my dad. He thinks I still work there."

"When are you gonna tell him you don't want to be an accountant?"

"Probably after I've been doing it for twenty years or thirty years." Howard chuckled at his own sense of humor, but Tony found the situation less than amusing.

"Seriously."

"Just because it's funny doesn't mean I'm not serious. His heart is set. How am I supposed to tell him that I'm not interested in his plans?"

"You just do," answered Tony.

"Or I get a degree in accounting and eventually take over his business. There's good money in it, so what the hell. But I've still got a couple of years before I head down that road. I'll do this for awhile, build up my muscles some." Howard flexed his biceps to make sure they were still there and worthy of admiration. "Then when the summer comes I'll lifeguard, be paid to tan and get laid."

Tony knew more than he cared to about having a father who was intent on dictating his son's life. He was an expert at having to fight for his own principles rather than adopting those handed down to him like a set of used clothing. It wasn't easy, but that was no excuse for giving in.

Nevertheless, he kept these thoughts to himself in recognition that his new friend's situation was somewhat different than his own. Howard did not want to duplicate the recklessness of the man who had caused his mother much grief, nor disappoint the man who came to the rescue bearing the gift of stability.

So Tony opted for bringing up the subject of football. It turned out that he and Howard were both avid Jets fans, the seed to sprout a beautiful friendship if ever there was any. The Jets didn't look half bad this year; he was making some cash; and best of all, his first date with Janet was only a few days away. All in all, being Tony Johnson was a pretty sweet deal.

CHAPTER SIX

Tony was certain what would be most vivid in his memory from this night. Not the dog walked past that howled at the moon as if summoning an old friend. Not the sliver of lamplight caught for an instant by Janet's earring. Not the ticket stubs placed in his pocket as tangible evidence that heaven existed. Not the melody repeatedly surround sounded to convey the passion of onscreen lovers. Not the kernel of popcorn placed tenderly into his mouth by Janet, which he hadn't chewed right away, but delectably rolled around his tongue like the last savored morsel of a death row meal. Not the scent of Janet's shampoo intertwined with pheromones, luring him like a child to a batch of freshly baked cookies. Not even the rose purchased for three dollars which had sprung from the soil without knowledge of its destiny to be a token of his fervor.

The most memorable part of the evening took place in the darkness of the theater as his fingers slowly crept towards Janet's hand. The signs had been given, the time was undoubtedly right. She would welcome this first miniscule step upon the road leading eventually to a lover's embrace. So he sent his fingers onward until they were millimeters away from their female counterparts. There they set camp and refused to move further. His will had run smack up against a single, mortifying thought. What if he had misread the signs? There could be no standing still after this point. Everything would either go forward or head full speed in reverse. The world stopped. Then it started again, for Janet placed her hand into his own.

"I had a great time tonight."

"I did too," said Tony, frantic to discover something wonderful to say, coming up empty.

"I'm glad you finally asked me out."

Janet had been waiting for him to initiate things. She had been attracted to him all along, perhaps even fantasized about him as he did of her. It seemed absurd now, the wasted time.

And yet, even as she sat across from him in an intimate corner of Baskin Robbin's, even though she had made her desire clear, something still daunted Tony. How does one kiss an angel?

"I want to know everything about you," he said. "Your favorite movie, the music you listen to, what foods you like best, what color. Everything."

"Who are you, Barbara Walters?"

"I have been told that in the right light I kind of look like her."

Tony was then shown indisputable evidence that one of the most breathtaking sights for a man to behold was the laughter of a beautiful woman.

"That must be some light. Let's see. My most favorite movie is an old classic, *Murder by Death*. I love violet. I'm into Justin Timberlake, Green Day, Beck, Dave Matthews, Gwen Stefani, the Red Hot Chili Peppers, U2. I could go on. And my weakness is chocolate, particularly chocolate covered cherries. Your turn."

"The ultimate movie in my humble opinion is also an oldie but a goodie, *Weird Science*. Well, that and *Scarface*. I listen to Prince, Brian McKnight, Maxwell, Janet Jackson, Lenny Kravitz, Mary J. Blige, Black Eyed Peas, Jay Z. I could go on too. Nothing tops a barbeque steak, rice and peas after I've taken out all of the peas, and baked macaroni. You might want to write this down for when you make me dinner someday."

"How about you order it from the restaurant we go to on our next date?"

"Does that mean there will be a next date?"

"Most definitely. But you skipped your favorite color."

"That of your eyes." The source of the words was a mystery, so Tony assumed Cupid must have been kind enough to whisper them into his ear.

Janet blushed and he almost kissed her, but not quite. The perfect moment would come, and he would recognize when it arrived.

"Anything else you want to know, Mr. Walters?"

"Who was your biggest childhood crush on?"

"Oh, that's an easy one," answered Janet. "Big Bird."

"Excellent choice."

"Who did you like?"

"It was a toss up between Mary Ann and Ginger."

"Not Mrs. Howell?"

"Only on very special occasions."

They both laughed, and Tony thought how amazing life would be if the rest of it could be spent just like this. He had meant it when he said he wanted to know everything about her. The knowledge would make her real in a way that she wasn't yet. Up until now, Janet had been more of a symbol than a flesh and blood person. She represented everything he wished to possess, things he refused to believe were beyond reach despite all evidence to the contrary. But as he sat across from Janet now, she slowly transformed from fanciful idea into wonderful reality. It was like an old television set that takes a while to warm up, the blank screen becoming widely dispersed static drawing closer and closer until solid form appears. And now that she was revealed to be someone who was trying to find a place in the world just like him, he was more drawn to her than ever.

"So what do you want to be when you grow up?" he asked.

"When I was little I used to dream about being a ballerina. Now I go back and forth between the one where

I'm elected as our first woman President, and the one where I win an Oscar, an Emmy, a Tony, a Grammy award, and the Pulitzer Prize all in the same year."

"So I take it you're not very ambitious."

"Exactly. How about you?"

"I dream about a bunch of stuff. Winning the lottery, being heavyweight champion of the world, having a set of keys to the Playboy mansion. But mostly, I dream about you."

Janet lowered her gaze, causing Tony to worry that he had been overly honest, come on too strong. But then she looked directly at him and he knew he had nothing to fear.

"You must charm all the girls, Tony Johnson."

"I'd settle for just one."

This was no longer a fantasy. Tony leaned forward. Remarkably, Janet did not vanish when he briefly opened his eyes for verification. She continued to kiss back, and it was better than he had ever dared to imagine it could be.

* * *

Caren sat on the sofa watching soap operas and enjoying a pint of rum raisin ice cream, momentarily putting off her daily trip to the laundry room. There was a knock at the door. "Come on in", she said without taking her eyes from the television. It was unnecessary to confirm the presence of her best friend who lived down the hall.

"What's happening?"

"Susan is pregnant again," Ellen answered. "She doesn't know if the father is Roger, Brad or Victor. Dave and Felicia are back together. Whitney got into a car accident and now has amnesia. What's going on here?"

"Corey and Angela found out that they're actually brother and sister."

"You're kidding," Ellen exclaimed to no lesser extent than if they had been speaking of actual people rather than TV characters. "They made such a nice couple."

"Sometimes life throws you a nasty curve."

Ellen plopped down on the sofa. The women worked as nurses assistants at the same nursing home, Ellen full-time and Caren for twenty five hours per week. Today was an off day for both of them, so they were enjoying their favorite indulgences - soap operas and talk shows.

Caren, dressed frumpishly in loose jeans and a sweatshirt, was kept in constant motion by an endless list of household chores. Ellen's casual attire was considerably more on the voluptuous side, usually stretch pants and something showing cleavage, largely in case Mr. Right dropped by unexpectedly. Or expectedly. She received a remarkable number of packages from UPS. Her off-day itinerary consisted of dipping carrot sticks into a carton of yogurt, pedaling her exercise bike, and paying Caren sporadic visits to give and get soap updates.

"Speaking of life, how is yours going? Does Lionel think the strike will end anytime soon?"

"He has no idea." Caren muted the volume on the TV, a sure sign that the topic at hand was a serious one. "I think he's scared that things will get as bad as the last time, and he's not the only one."

The quaver in her voice hinted at a need to get her baggage out in the open, and that is what she proceeded to do, confiding in Ellen about the previous night, about the shred of self-respect that Lionel was clinging to by his fingernails.

"He's a good man," Caren concluded. "God knows he isn't perfect. But I've known quite a few women whose husbands *were* perfect, right up to the day they walked out on them."

Ellen shrugged at an attitude she found maddeningly typical. Caren could not curse Lionel without excusing him in the same breath. She could not cast unadulterated blame on her husband, for that would mean having to do something about it, perhaps even the unthinkable act of leaving. As Ellen saw it, some things could simply not be excused, regardless of circumstances. Excuses never solved anyone's problems. Dumb luck and taking action were the only two ways she knew of to get things done, and the latter was far more reliable. Whenever Ellen felt depressed because she had yet to find her life's mate, she consoled herself that at least she was avoiding the grief suffered by so many of her married friends.

"Now that he's out of work, he feels like he's failing us," said Caren. "He's angry at himself and some of it is spilling over."

"If it's only a matter of being out of work, he should cross the picket line."

"He wouldn't turn his back on his co-workers any sooner than he would on us."

"Then I guess you're going to have to wait for the strike to end."

"Suppose it lasts as long as the last one did," Caren said. "We might have to ask his brother for money again. No, it mustn't come to that." She put a spoonful of ice cream into her mouth, but the bitterness of the topic at hand spoiled the sweetness of her dessert.

"Being proud does not give him the right to be a bully."

"Don't say that, Ellen. I know you and Lionel don't get along, but there's no need to insult him."

"Who do you think you're talking to, girl? This is me, remember? The one you come to after he's smacked you around or drank up the rent money."

"That stuff happened a long time ago," Caren said softly. "He was out of work, he was drinking heavily. He wasn't himself."

Caren's description of the distant past bore far too strong a resemblance to recent days. If this was fair indication that history intended to repeat itself, she knew that things would become much worse before getting better again.

"Girl, please," Ellen said, exasperation etched both by her tone of voice and pained facial expression. "Is that your explanation for every time he screws up? That he's not himself? His is the only handprint that gets put on your face. I don't care how many moods he gets into. He's still responsible for every last one of them. And you're just as responsible if you stick around and take it."

"Don't you think I know that?" Caren tossed the blouse in her hand to the floor.

"I'm sorry. I didn't mean..."

"Maybe I do blind myself to his faults more that I should. But Lionel has never deserted me, and I will never desert him."

Ellen was well versed in the story behind the justifications her friend instinctively gave. Caren's father had abandoned her when she was a baby. Her mother proved unable to raise a child on her own, so Caren was sent to live with relatives. Her aunt asked her to leave when she became pregnant out of wedlock. Lionel did not miss a beat in proposing to Caren, and though she suffered a miscarriage, he stayed true to his vow of sticking around through the worst as well as the better.

In Ellen's opinion, Lionel fell far short of earning the devotion of such a good woman. But he had stayed in place, and in Caren's book this meant a lot. Perhaps one day she would find the strength to rewrite that book. Such fortitude would not be conceived from well-meaning words of encouragement, though. Caren would have to find it on her own.

"Guess I'll head back now," Ellen said. "If you need me for anything, come right on over."

Once alone again Caren turned the sound back up on the television, escaping into the realm of her soap opera companions. She envied these people in spite of the topsy-turvy lives written for them to endure. At least their trials and tribulations were suffered for no more than an hour a day.

CHAPTER SEVEN

Lionel pushed the button for his building's elevator, which had an annoying habit of breaking down at the most inopportune times. To his relief the doors opened right away. He stepped in, pressed the button for his floor, and leaned back to better appreciate the havoc being played on his senses by recently consumed whiskey. After spending the day walking through a frigid north wind on a picket line, he had been sorely in need of something to warm him up and mellow him out. Once again, McCann's bar came through in a pinch.

As the doors were closing, a hand reached in between them. They re-opened, and in walked his wife's friend. A single glance told Ellen everything there was to know about Lionel's condition, and told Lionel that Ellen would be giving him grief over it.

"Let me get some coffee into you," she said, no trace of hospitality in the offer. "Maybe we can make you semi-sober before you go home."

"It's my home and I'll walk in any way I damn well please."

"Well I want to talk to you first."

"About what?" asked Lionel.

"About your family."

"What business is that of yours?" The opening of the elevator momentarily silenced Lionel. Ellen wasn't the only nosy neighbor he had.

"Let's continue this in my place," she said, gently tugging on his arm until they were inside her apartment. "I'll make you that coffee."

"To hell with coffee. You got something to say, let's hear it."

Lionel surveyed the unfamiliar surroundings. What he found was himself, for much of the wall space was covered by mirrors. Some of them masqueraded as art, the rest pretended to be nothing more than the odes to vanity that they were. Her furniture came in a variety of neon colors, most of the pieces faux leather. Ellen's home perfectly reflected Lionel's opinion of her. Tacky, loud and cheap.

"I know the strike is tough on you," she said. "It's hard enough to make ends meet nowadays when you *are* working."

"I'm glad you know so much. Now if you don't mind..."

"None of that gives you the right to abuse your family."

Ellen took off her coat. As usual, the outfit she wore underneath revealed more than it concealed. She was dressed in the fashion of women fifteen years her junior. Her hair had recently been dyed an obscene blonde, as if anyone could possibly be fooled. She gestured for Lionel to have a seat, but he ignored her and waited to hear what else she had to say.

"I heard you tried to start a fight with Tony the other day. What kind of father are you? What kind of man are you, pushing around the people who are supposed to matter most to you, who you're supposed to be taking care of? Maybe Caren's willing to stand there and take it, but I'm not about to let that happen."

She took a step forward, getting right in Lionel's face. He had to give credit where it was due. The woman had balls.

"I'll call the police the next time. I'll get a gun and shoot you dead myself if necessary. But I will not let you mistreat them any longer."

"Thanks for the advice," Lionel said, his voice as serene as an ivory cloud concealing the tip of a brewing volcano. Before Ellen could say another condemning word,

Lionel walked out. Rather than feeling assured that she had done good, Ellen was left to wonder if her judgement would prove costly to those she had aimed to protect.

As Ellen worried, Lionel marched briskly home. A man's place was at the head of his household and it was essential that this be recognized. God was worshipped first and foremost because of the fear His power elicited. People might praise His infinite capacity for love, but it wasn't love that brought them to their knees in obedient prayer. When Lionel entered his kitchen he found Caren setting the table for dinner. A dinner the money *she* earned had paid for. What need did she have to be grateful to her husband, except for the merciful restraint he showed? But in order for the restraint to be acknowledged, a hint of power had to be displayed. Caren must be reminded of the fear.

"So I'm a real bastard, is that it?"

Lionel answered his own question by flipping over the dinner table, sending dishes and silverware clattering to the checkered linoleum floor. "How dare you tell Ellen I abuse you?"

Caren was momentarily distracted from the question by the mess her husband had created. A few plates and glasses had been broken. Fortunately, she had not yet placed any food on the table.

"I never said such a thing."

"I don't care how crazy she is. She didn't come up with that shit off the top of her head. She was quoting you."

"I told her you've been on edge because of the strike," Caren said. It would be no easy task to douse Lionel's anger. She would probably have to settle for stifling her agitation at Ellen for poking her nose where it didn't need to be. Caren knew that her friend had well meaning intentions, but stirred up trouble pays little heed to the purpose of its instigator.

"I break my back every day for this family. All I ask for in return is a hot meal and just maybe a little respect. You think I treat you bad? You don't know what bad is. But you seem to want to find out."

Caren was aware that the right choice of subservient words could placate Lionel. But thoughts had been placed in her head lately that she was unable to wish away, and these thoughts urged her to challenge rather than concede. Perhaps the self-respect fostered by her job of the past several months played a large part. Day by day, the woman who allowed herself to be intimidated by her husband was fading away. In her place, a woman who was just beginning to recognize her own value after four decades of living now stood. This woman was tired of such tirades, and even more tired of rationalizing her husband's occasional cruelty. Ellen was right. Lionel’s reign as tyrant had gone on long enough.

"I've got to run back and forth between work and keeping this place up,” Caren said. “You know what thanks I get? A drunken husband screaming at me like a baby who wants his bottle. You want a hot meal? Go eat it off the stove."

She tried to leave the room, but Lionel stuck out his arm to prevent her exit. It was then that Tony stepped into the kitchen, unheard over his parents’ argument and shielded from view behind his father’s tensed back.

"Don't you walk out on me," said Lionel.

He could not allow the matter to end on Caren’s terms. It was not supposed to have gone like this. Where was the remorse, the groveling for forgiveness? His wife needed to learn what life had taught him a long time ago. Pride would be knocked right out of a person who didn't have enough sense to hold it in check when necessary.

Caren read his eyes and found herself at peace in the retina of the tempest. Like the most experienced of sailors, she knew that nature’s wildness could not be fought, only waited out.

"What are you gonna do, hit me? Go ahead then. Get it over with if that's what it will take."

Caren staggered backward from the blow which followed, tripped over an outstretched table leg, and fell to the floor. Tony wrapped his arms around his father like a boa constrictor suffocating its prey.

"Who is this? Get off me. Get off me or else."

Tony ignored the commandment, holding on as if the fate of the universe depended on his grip.

"I'm not going to tell you again." Though his words were still acerbic, Lionel had ceased to physically struggle against the vise he was in. He was too drunk, and his son too strong with desperation. Nevertheless, Tony held on even tighter.

"You're going to regret this, boy."

Tony did not doubt that the truth had been stated, but refused to acknowledge it. No one would be allowed to harm his mother, not even the man he feared most.

"Let him go, Tony."

His mother’s soft spoken request accomplished what his father’s threats could not. Tony backed away from Lionel, hyper-alert to whatever might happen next. Lionel did not bother to look his son’s way, but simply walked out of the kitchen and left the apartment.

Caren knew exactly where he was headed and what he would do. Her husband would drink until his wallet was empty. Then he would come home, shamed and drunk enough to be willing to apologize in order to coax her into making love. She was used to the ritual and accepted it as she did the sun rising each morning.

"Are you okay?" Tony asked as he helped her up.

"I'm fine."

"I'll never let him hit you again."

Caren’s sudden burst of indignation had just as swiftly disappeared, replaced by a need to pacify and explain.

"Your father has a lot to deal with right now. He's angry about the strike and this is the only place he can let it out."

"He has no right to take it out on you."

"We're his family. If he can't count on us, who can he count on?"

Tony shook his head. Not only was his mother not distraught, but she seemed to have accepted what had happened and was asking him to do the same.

"You forgive him for everything."

"Of course I do. That's what love is."

Caren ran her hand through Tony's hair. She could see the hate in his eyes and wanted to remove it. No boy should hate his father. Life was tough enough as it was.

"I love you, Mom."

"I love you too, and so does your father. Promise me you'll try to understand him."

"I'll try," Tony said, not caring if he sounded sincere. He understood his father's brand of love well enough. It was based on orders being followed, his presence being trembled before. But the day hopefully was soon coming when it would no longer reduce Tony to a petrified child.

Mother and son stood in loving embrace. Caren reflected on what she had just said. That's what love is. Moments earlier she lay on the floor, her hand covering the handle of a fork. She had imagined shoving the tongs into her husband's eye. If Tony had not come into the room, if Lionel had advanced to finish teaching his lesson, would her fingers have let go before bad grew irreparably worse? She didn't know the answer so she silently made the same promise she had asked of her son. All was lost once people could no longer forgive.

CHAPTER EIGHT

Tony grabbed hold of the tickets he had just purchased, placing two dollars of change into his pocket. The twenty dollar bill in his wallet represented the remainder of cash on him. He did a quick mental calculation. The theater's concession stand would just about wipe him out. He and Janet were supposed to grab a bite afterwards, but unless soda and popcorn were passed on, he was certain to come up short on cash tonight.

This would make the second time in a row. Janet's help with the bill had been necessary on their last date, an experience Tony desperately wished not to repeat. Though she had certainly not made him feel bad about it, he required no assistance for his embarrassment. With his father's strike dragging on, increasingly larger portions of the money earned at Jenson's was being appropriated for the family's expenses. This left over precious little to spend on romance. Now that Tony was earning his own money, he truly understood the limitations on how far a dollar could be stretched.

Janet often spoke casually about places she had been and things she had done, unaware of how small the words made him feel because he could not afford to replicate these experiences with her. He cherished Janet as if she were the very air he breathed, and did his best to make her realize this. But words could only say so much. Tony feared that due to his scant resources, he would soon be diminishing in her eyes. He wanted to be Janet's hero, and heroes were usually able to pay for dinner.

From the perspective of youthful innocence, the most impoverished of upbringings seems ordinary and in no way ignominious. With love and attention in adequate supply, such a childhood is equally happy to those filled with prosperity. As he grew older, Tony began to notice the deficiencies in his family's lifestyle. He started to dream of things that would one day be his. But never did he feel shameful until all that he didn't possess was exposed in the light of what Janet was accustomed to. Like a man who finds a stain discreetly hidden in the pattern of his tie, although the garment was proudly donned prior to the discovery, the new found knowledge makes it a source of embarrassment. Tony had grown too aware of his circumstances to remain comfortable about them.

Circumstances by nature were usually temporary, and resourceful people found ways to work around them. He had vowed to do whatever it took to satisfy Janet's every need, for the strongest of causes motivated him. The love he felt made a heaven of his life in conjunction with the hell moments like this put him through.

He scanned the packed theater lobby. Three likely blockbusters had opened over the weekend and everyone wanted to see them before word of mouth lessened expectations. The smell of butter, or whatever that yellow liquid was that they poured into oversized bags of popcorn, was so strong that Tony could almost taste it simply by sticking his tongue out into the air. One of the features in the multiplex targeted family audiences. So in addition to the usual headcount of young lovers, there was also an abundance of people under four feet tall maniacally running circles around their impervious parents, wired from the caffeine content of tubs of soda, bedazzled by the wizardry of Hollywood.

An attractive, quarreling couple in their mid-twenties caught Tony's attention. The girl was giving her boyfriend a hard time because she had followed his wandering eyes to the seat of another girl's pants. The topic of their rather loud discussion did not seem to be a new one between them. The agitated girlfriend, who reminded Tony slightly of a meatier version of a popular anorexic looking actress more famous for the men she dated than the roles she played, was making some pretty valid points about how leering at others was disrespectful to her. After making a half hearted attempt at claiming that he had not even noticed the other girl, the flustered boyfriend was mostly reduced to nodding in embarrassment and acceptance of earned chastisement. Tony could emphasize. The object of desire who unknowingly managed to stir up such trouble was by no means easy to keep from staring at. To be ogled was obviously her intent for the evening. Her just about perfectly rounded ass threatened to burst from suffocatingly tight, low low rider jeans. To atone for his sin, the guy sheepishly stood with hands tucked in his pockets and held his girlfriend's accusing gaze, afraid to look elsewhere lest he inadvertently find something else to his liking and incur yet more wrath. Tony had taken his own lingering peek at the moveable feast, but either he was successfully discreet about it or else Janet was secure enough not to complain about inescapable human nature. One more reason to love her.

"Wait here a sec. I'll be right back."

Fortune had struck. While surveying his surroundings Tony noticed a friend from school. It took a bit of cajoling, but Larry came through with the loan that would secure his manhood for the evening. Hopefully his father would resume bringing home paychecks very soon. That would solve a host of problems. It was amazing how many of the world's ills were cured by money.

"I'm back," Tony said when he was again by Janet's side. "Did you miss me?"

"What do you think?" she asked in return, following her words with a deep kiss.

When able to speak, Tony said - "I think I'm the luckiest guy in the world." What he didn't say was that he hoped his luck wouldn't run out.

* * *

A short distance from the housing projects amongst where the Johnsons resided could be found a haven. Acres of grass made a welcome change from squared off pavement and streets of tar. Armies of trees rose majestically towards the sky. Long before the creation of cities separated the haves from the have nots, the ancestors of these trees had offered equal shade to all.

The wide open space invited Lionel's thoughts to wander where they might not otherwise venture. Surely he would not dwell on such matters in the overcrowded subway train that transported him to and from work. As he robotically went through the motions that up until recently had earned him an insultingly low wage, his mind did not take him back this far. When walking about the tenement buildings that sapped the strength from many an earnest dream, his memory usually showed mercy and let him be. In this park, however, a glimpse of the world as God intended it reminded him of his younger days.

Before being swallowed whole by the denseness of New York City, he had lived in a small southern town where cool grass was routinely trampled by his bare feet. The scent of jasmine floated perpetually in the air. His community was comprised of familiar faces rather than an indifferent mass of humanity. At night he would lay back and gaze upwards, intoxicated by the lullaby of crickets, blanketed by infinite stars. Due to the glare of streetlights, only a scattering of stars was visible from his current urban viewpoint. Perhaps this accounted for why he wished upon them far less frequently now.

Taking a break from the picket line, Lionel sat on a bench feeding pieces of bread to a gathering of pigeons. Although they were so commonplace as to be nearly invisible to pedestrians, and were considered by many to be little more than winged rats, he envied these birds. Theirs was a straightforward journey, no enigmas to solve other than where to flock for their next free meal. And if life on the ground ever did get stressful, they could flap their wings and escape into the wild blue yonder.

Lionel once believed that his own ascension was equally possible. But it was not to be. Instead of the eagle, the hawk, or even the less heralded pigeon, he elected to emulate the plight of the penguin. He was given the gift of wings, yet refused the magic of flight.

Rational thought was behind the refusal. More than that, there had been compassion and a sense of obligation. He hadn't thrown away his prospects on a foolish whim. But regardless of the reason, the end result was the same.

He had been given a choice. Be the good son, or think only of himself. His days since had largely been spent trying to figure out if the right decision was made.

At the time, Lionel was 18 years old and the recipient of a full college scholarship. A once in a lifetime opportunity, not to be passed up for any conceivable reason. Then his dad lost his job. No big deal. His father was a drunk, always in and out of work. It was what he did. He dreamt and he drank and grew mean and got fired and then sobered up, made his apologies, went back to work and began the cycle all over again. But this time he was staying drunk, and staying mean, and staying out of work. And he wasn't even sorry about it. He had given up on everything, including taking care of the family. Lionel's sister was only six years old. His mother's hands were full taking care of her. Someone had to make sure that the bills were paid and food was put on the table. That responsibility fell to Lionel and his brother, who had also received a full scholarship.

Lionel's dream of becoming a doctor was within reach. His shot at doing something of worth, the chance he had worked like a mule to obtain, cried out to him like a siren's song.

He begged his brother to cooperate, to make a small sacrifice until their father was back on his feet. At most they would start a semester late. Maybe a year. College wasn't going anywhere. They merely needed to take care of business at home, then go tend to the rest of their lives.

But Manny would have no part of it. He refused to let his plans be altered by their father. So he snuck out one night like a cowardly thief with his brother's future the loot, nothing left behind but a brief note of tepid explanation. For Lionel, the only remaining option was to stay and watch his dreams evaporate like ice cubes on a scorching Summer day.

Within two years their still unemployed father died of a heart attack on his way home from a bar. Caren had gotten pregnant, so Lionel did what a man is supposed to do and married her. His mother and little sister went to live with relatives. After the child was stillborn, Lionel and Caren decided a change of scenery was for the best. With a job in New York guaranteed by a friend, they left Georgia for good.

Twenty years later, Lionel sat on a park bench feeding pigeons. If it was possible, he would have preferred to share his sandwich with the flightless penguins. Stuck on snow covered terrain because they couldn't rise up and escape, not even for a ten minute cigarette break, having to make due with dips in the frigid ocean, they must have had a very good reason for turning down God's gift. Perhaps they made the right decision, everything considered. But Lionel knew that when they looked up and saw their brethren in the sky, it likely broke their hearts.

CHAPTER NINE

Death's aroma wafted throughout the corridors of the hospital. Its components as far as C.J. could tell were Lysol, blood, and freshly pressed linen. Tyrone had regained consciousness and his family was with him in his room. C.J. flipped through the pages of an old Sports Illustrated in the waiting area. The athletes gracing its pages and their stories of bravado and triumph over adversity failed to impress him, because his thoughts were otherwise occupied.

Earlier that week, he and several other members of his gang had crept up on a smaller number of Raw Dawgs. During the chase that followed, C.J. managed to run one of them down. He pinned the kid to the ground and held a knife over his throat. The continuance of his enemy's life lay entirely within C.J.'s trembling hand. The power of God was his for a very long and sobering moment.

A kaleidoscope of images raced through his mind. Tyrone writhing on the ground, as much from fear as pain. His friend being wheeled into an emergency room along with nameless faceless others, much like the endless row of meat he once witnessed his father handling at work. Tyrone frantically yet contentedly working the analog controller of a video game system, seated upon a cloud that presumably placed him in Heaven, all sins forgiven.

C.J. raised the knife above his head, prepared to strike. He tried to avoid it, but ended up looking into the terror stricken eyes that stared at him pleadingly.

Cries of agony could be heard, life blood was vividly seen draining, even though the boy remained untouched. C.J. was mesmerized by the look of realization that the end of everything was at hand. The face beneath him turned into Tyrone's, and then his own. C.J. set free his would be victim, who looked at him with an expression that was half bewilderment and half gratitude before fleeing.

A pretty nurse led Tyrone's parents and grandmother into the waiting room. C.J. stood up, unsure of what he should say. Tyrone's mother did not have the same problem. She moved towards him with finger pointed in accusation.

"Look at you, wearing that damn rag on your head as if it's something to be proud of. My baby nearly died because scum like you makes him think this fighting is fun and games."

She slapped him across the cheek and may have tried to inflict more damage had her husband not pulled her away. The grandmother did not follow them immediately, but stood staring at C.J. with not quite dead eyes. He stared back with equal intensity, mesmerized by the unrelenting final stage of the aging process. Her skin seemed to be dripping off her bones like wax from a burning candle.

"I'm a friend," C.J. said feebly. She answered him by using one her precious remaining breaths to spit at his feet.

Minutes later he entered the room that Tyrone was recuperating in. The various tubes and monitors made it appear as though Tyrone was no longer a kid who roamed the streets of the Bronx, but Frankenstein's latest creation. His doctor had said he was lucky. Half an inch more to the left would have meant certain death.

"What up, Tyrone?"

"I don't feel like much, but I guess I'm okay."

"We jumped a few of them on Saturday. Would have fucked them up real good, but they ran."

C.J. wondered if the shame was broadcast by his face. He had been given a chance to avenge the near killing of his best friend, only to throw it away.

A tightrope walker uncertain if he could make it to the other side probably would not. A racecar driver wondering if he was taking a turn too fast was likely to lose control. If a man feared death, whether his own or the taking of another's, death would surely come calling.

C.J. had once believed that he understood who he was, what he was about, what he was capable of. But when the moment came to act upon these convictions, he discovered that his knowledge of self was faulty. Had his lack of killer instinct been a momentary lapse, first time jitters? Or was there more to it than that? If not the fearless, remorseless man he supposed himself to be, then just who was he?

"They won't be able to run fast enough once I'm outta here," said Tyrone in a voice that had only recently begun changing from child to adult, yet declared such bold assertions.

"Louis said from now on it's war, no more fair fight bullshit. We're gonna be putting some fair bullets in their asses."

"I'm definitely down with that."

"So how's it feel to have your first battle scar?"

A scar was a source of pride, proof that death had been stared in the face and made to back down. The size and amount of them marking one's flesh were the most visible ways of judging a man's virility. Some have reasoned it is the brain that uniquely defines each of us. Those more romantic and less scientific in nature feel it is within the heart that our true selves dwell. A more mystical or religious conclusion is that an invisible, unattached organ known as the soul constitutes who we each are. But common sense declares we are no more than the raw materials that comprise us. This explains the metamorphosis that often results from minor cosmetic changes. Additional inches to hips and bosom convince a girl that she has become a woman. The sporadic emergence of hair follicles makes a boy believe manhood has arrived. There are many who feel redefined by the placement of a tattoo. A new hairstyle; contact lenses in place of glasses; the removal of braces; are just a few of the alterations which change someone's appearance, and in so doing, also transform a personality. What then to make of a permanent gash in one's skin? Can such a thing leave a body marked but the person unchanged?

"It's bigger than the one in the middle of Louis' back," Tyrone answered.

"No shit."

"Yeah, really."

"You're a hero, man."

Tyrone smiled, then closed his eyes. "I'll be back with you guys soon."

He was going to be all right. With this reassurance, C.J. realized that if his young friend could shrug off mortality and be anxious to challenge it once more, there was no legitimate reason for his own reservations.

In a moment of weakness, C.J. had forgotten that there was no room for mercy. For if and when the tables were turned, no mercy would be granted to him. Any hesitation, time taken to consider moral ambiguities or possible repercussions, could mean his downfall. Any vulnerability displayed would quickly be taken advantage of. One did not purposely cut himself while in a lake full of piranha. Like Tyrone he must be strong, for only the strong survived.

Had Mr. Darwin been able to communicate to him, he may have informed C.J. of the adjustments made to his views on this matter. He might have said that upon further reflection, he had concluded that the strong die much like the weak. At best, they took a little longer and went out in a somewhat more dignified manner. But death was death.

* * *

Tony was in the highest of spirits as he and Janet took their place on line. Cosmos was the hot new neighborhood nightclub that most Lincoln High School seniors could get into without particularly good fake I.D. He and Charlie had spent numerous Friday and Saturday nights on the prowl here. The irresistible ambiance of the place was composed of blaring music; lights flashing in a rainbow of hues; bodies dressed, perfumed and pampered to be especially alluring, writhing around each other to sensuous percussion; pulses racing against sampled tracks; sweat draining from all pores; the promise of romance or a suitable substitute as abundant as hairspray.

On this evening Tony was looking forward to showing off his beautiful lady to the public and reveling in the envy elicited. When other guys checked her out, he stared each of them down protectively while appreciating all the more that Janet was with him.

Eventually he began to realize that not every look expressed jealousy or admiration. When he and Janet were spotted by certain black couples, the girl would frown, then turn and voice a complaint to her date, who would cast a glance of equal displeasure before draping an arm around his girl, his brown skinned girl. On the first such occasion he figured it to be misinterpretation on his part. The second time around he reasoned that he had accidentally caught a dirty look aimed at someone else for reasons unknown and of no interest to him. By the third occurrence he could no longer ignore what was happening. The ostracism was reinforced when he spied a classmate and waved in greeting, only to be ignored. He was positive that Terrence had seen him. They were not the closest of friends, but were certainly on cordial terms. As usual, the colors of Africa were predominant in Terrence's wardrobe. His clothing advertised his social and political views. He was never shy about talking up the virtues of his people, nor did he hesitate to point out the vices of those fairer in complexion. It made sense that Terrence would not approve of his current choice of dance partner.

Had this complaint been verbalized, Tony may have pointed out that Terrence was scarcely a shade darker than the people he had such a problem with. It would take a very short climb up the family tree to find a relative of his no less white than Janet. Rather than increasing his tolerance, Terrence's mixed ancestry no doubt fueled his militancy.

Tony tried to convince himself that the opinion of a casual acquaintance with a significant chip on his shoulder mattered very little. He was moderately successful at doing so, decided this would have to do, and moved on to more pleasant thoughts that were soon interrupted.

Three couples headed towards the back of the line stopped before them. "Hi guys," said Janet cheerfully. "Isn't this line something?"

"It's like this every Friday night," said one of the girls. She was wearing a tight red mini skirt that provided the bare minimum of coverage. "Sometimes it takes almost an hour to finally get in."

"This is Tony."

He smiled in greeting. No one paid him the same courtesy, unless he counted a grunt as friendly salutation. He recognized the male half of the group as friends of Janet's ex-boyfriend, football players and hangers on.

"Can we talk with you privately for a minute," one of them asked.

"Sure, I guess so," answered Janet. "I'll be right back, Tony."

They had enough tact to take her out of hearing distance, and he was no expert at reading lips. Still, he was able to guess accurately enough at what they were saying. He fidgeted with anxiety and not a little anger, waiting for Janet's reaction to what was surely an attempt to take her away from him. Their conversation was turning into an argument. As voices rose he began to catch most of it.

"Look, you're not my keeper," Janet said. "I'll go out with whoever I want."

"What about Roger?" asked the short red head whose ample breasts earned her the attention that neither her personality or rather plain face were likely to manage, though one got the feeling that she had yet to figure this out.

"What about him?"

"He told me he wouldn't mind getting back together with you," said the least overtly sexual of the three girls. Even from such a distance her nasally voice wore on the eardrums like fingernails scraped down a chalkboard.

"I don't care what he told you."

The guy who had asked to speak to Janet whispered something for her hearing only. He was the only one of the group whose name Tony knew. Tim Braddock played wide receiver on the varsity football team, small forward on the basketball team, was involved with a volunteer group who brought food and company to shut-ins, and was in the top ten percent academically at their school. It was a minor miracle that he could be so accomplished and still find the time and energy to be as obnoxious as he was.

"You're an ass," was Janet's response, at which point she marched back to Tony's side. Rather than saying anything to him, she stared straight ahead, trying to act as if nothing had happened but not yet trusting that her voice wouldn't give away her distress.

Tony massaged her shoulders, completely aware of the six pairs of eyes on him. "You still want to go in?" he asked.

Janet nodded.

"Are you okay?"

She repeated the gesture.

If she had nothing to say on the matter, Tony was not inclined to pursue it. It was such a minor event. Nothing offensive had been said directly to him, or even overheard. But knowing this didn't settle the churning of his stomach. He had to say something.

"I don't think your friends like me too much."

"They're friends of Roger. They kind of want us to get back together. They don't like seeing me with another guy."

What she said was reasonable, yet the churning continued. Tony glanced at a lanky blonde guy standing in front of them and wondered if Janet's friends would have the same problem if she were out with him.

What did it matter? Why should he worry about the opinions of strangers? Why allow their narrow-mindedness to get under his skin? He wrapped his arms protectively around Janet's waist.

"They're just going to have to get used to seeing you with me," he said. "Cause I'm not going anywhere."

She turned around and gifted him with the smile he treasured. Tony let himself get lost in her eyes, where the rest of the world ceased to exist.

* * *

A pair of dust covered bulbs supplied most of the sparse light in McCann's bar. A neon sign advertising Budweiser beer was responsible for the rest. The sole window was tinted, so sunlight had little chance of penetrating the desolate air. An ancient jukebox sat neglected in a corner, mutely begging to be played, its request denied. The inhabitants of McCann's weren't there to be entertained. They came to drink their troubles away, and their elixir was in no short supply.

Among the patrons were Lionel and Phil, together for the first time since their disagreement. They had been friends for nearly twenty years, their paths first crossing not long after Lionel's arrival in New York. A difference of opinion augmented by circumstance and alcohol could not seriously jeopardize such a weathered relationship. So they uttered terse regrets about their previous encounter and it was disposed from memory. This done, Lionel began to speak freely of the matters most pressing on his mind.

"Used to be my word was law in that house, like it oughta be. Not any more."

As the result of many years of steady drinking on Lionel's part, inebriation no longer arrived swiftly. His body had grown accustomed to the onslaught of venom and now digested it like water. He would regularly down one drink after another, waiting for the kick he always expected to come, only to be perpetually disappointed that his state of awareness would change without notice. At some point during any given binge he would come to realize that sobriety was long gone, that once again, the invisible line had been uneventfully crossed.

"Even Caren is getting into the act. Now that she's got a little job and I'm out of work, it's changed her. And I guess I can't really blame her. Why should a woman respect her husband when he isn't supporting his family like he ought to?"

Lionel slowly poured the liquid fire down his throat. It should have helped him forget. Instead, he saw with greater clarity.

"Is this what I've earned for years of hard work and sacrifice?" He peered into his glass as if it was a crystal ball. If any answers were contained, the glass was keeping them to itself.

Phil wanted to console his friend with nuggets of wisdom, or at least an appropriate cliché, but at the moment he was as stumped as the glass.

"I did the right thing," Lionel said. "I should have been rewarded by now."

The two of them took simultaneous swigs. They usually drank at about the same pace to begin with, but as Phil began to wind down, Lionel would just be starting to pick up steam. Phil promised himself as he routinely did that he would cut down on the stuff. Besides being Phil's closest friend, Lionel also served as crash dummy, a three dimensional example of what must never be allowed to happen.

Lionel checked to see if any of the small but devoted group of regulars were listening in on the conversation. As usual, they were lost in their own little worlds, trapped in their own private hells. They gave as much of a damn about his life as he gave about theirs. It was Lionel's kind of place.

"The strike's going to end soon," said Phil, having settled on a line of hollow hope to dispense. "Everything will turn out for the best."

"You just don't get it, do you?"

Phil gestured for their empty glasses to be refilled. Lionel needed the liquor to keep talking, Phil to stomach listening.

"Any white man with my experience would be running that place by now. I know the operation like the back of my hand."

Phil nodded. Once Lionel got going like this, a minimum of encouragement was required to sustain his stream of consciousness. The slightest gestures and a bottomless glass were more than adequate support.

"I've got a mountain of bills waiting to be paid. You know what that means, don't you? I'll have to start kissing some white ass. And what thanks will I get?"

A man wearing a conspicuous blue pinstripe suit walked into the bar. He sat two stools away, ordered a vodka martini, and withdrew a cell phone from his breast pocket.

"Then you got these guys."

The newcomer was a cocoa colored man in his late forties with salt and pepper hair and mustache. He briefly glanced at Lionel, but found nothing of interest so turned back around to listen to his phone messages in peace.

"They get it all because of what guys like me gave up."

When no response to the goading came, Lionel stared at the mirror before him. It was not his present self reflected back, but his past. The next topic of conversation was one that frequently emerged when he was drinking himself back in time - his brother.

"At our mother's funeral, Manny stood before everybody and talked about how much he loved her. Never mind that he had deserted her. I kept waiting for someone to tell him off, but the only thing people said was how proud Mama had been of her college boy. All was forgiven because he was successful."

Phil knew the story as well as if it was his own. He could have done without hearing it again, but knew Lionel needed to heave the burdens from off his chest like a shot-put. Perhaps he believed if the tale was told often enough, its outcome could be revised. But neither the recapitulation of his existence nor the way Lionel felt about it would ever change.

"After the service he asked me how I was. He destroys my life, then has the nerve to ask how it's going." Lionel repeatedly flexed his fingers from open palms to clenched fists, as if unsure whether to slap or punch at his ghosts.

"I just walked away. I couldn't think of any words hateful enough."

Lionel and Manny had not gone out of their way to keep in touch after that day, but were unable to avoid each other altogether over the years. Their younger sister Angie had proven herself quite proficient at baby making. Each christening brought about another rejected opportunity for Lionel and Manny to make peace.

"Dwelling on stuff only makes it worse," Phil said.

Lionel did not heed the caution. He refused to forfeit his right to rail against an unjust world.

"Men like him get more and more while I get a whole lot of nothing." His eyes were focussed again, but not on Phil, or the mirror, or his drink.

"Now Tony wants to be one of them. He wants to go so far from who he is that he'll hardly ever be reminded. I know he's not thinking that way. He just wants to do better for himself than his old man did. I don't blame him for that. I want it for him too. But the things he wants have a way of changing a man. He'll start thinking that the money and the white man's learning are all that matter. He'll get himself a college degree and a paper pushing job, and he won't have to sweat and strain to make it from one paycheck to another. That's a blessing. But he'll take it for granted. He'll feel ashamed that no matter how different he acts and thinks and feels, he'll be seen the same as the rest of us. The same as me."

Lionel paused as if waiting for what he said to be refuted. Although he was met only by a sympathetic gaze, he went back on the defensive.

"Don't tell me I'm wrong. It happened to my brother. We came to the light of day one right behind the other, and for a long time we saw things as if with one pair of eyes. But once Manny got the so called good life in his sights, he couldn't see nothing else. He pushed me aside so he could take it all in for himself. He shoved his whole family out the way."

Lionel drained the whiskey far too rapidly for his taste buds to take notice. No matter, since it was not being consumed for their benefit.

"I know how it feels to aim for the stars only to end up in the gutter. I also know what happens when you do get what you want, because you didn't allow anything else to matter. If Tony is set on what will fill his pockets but empty his soul, I'd rather blind him now than let him look at me one day the way Manny does. I won't help make him into what I hate. I ain't sacrificing nothing for nobody no more."

Lionel smacked his hand on the bar to get the attention of the stranger he had been glaring at. "Tell me something, buddy. Did you ever so much as say thank you?"

The man looked at Lionel curiously, regarding him as someone who was possibly deranged, most likely harmless, but definitely too close for comfort. "I don't have the slightest idea what you're talking about. And I don't believe I want to." This said, he swiveled back to his drink.

Lionel stood up. "Don't turn your back on me. What the hell are you doing in here anyway? Shouldn't you be hanging out with your white friends in the Hamptons? You think cause you're some hot shot who's slumming for the day, that gives you the right to disrespect me?"

The man showed no fear, but also no inclination to carry things further, nor to explain that the Hamptons were not frequently visited this time of year. He took a casual sip of his drink. Phil was impressed by the show of self-restraint, but knew it would be ineffective. Lionel's mind was made up. The formally attired gentleman embodied those who had profited unfairly, while equally unfairly, Lionel had been held down and pistol-whipped by life.

"I take your silence as a request for an ass kicking."

"I wouldn't bet on it," the man said, not bothering to look in Lionel's direction. His statement issued a vague threat, but it was the lack of acknowledgement that was most insulting and challenging.

"Oh yeah." Lionel managed to say no more than these two syllable before doubling over. He grasped tightly onto the barstool with one hand while clutching his stomach with the other, groaning through gritted teeth. His antagonist looked on in disgust. Then Lionel began to vomit. Phil had never known him to throw up from drinking before.

"Couldn't you make it to the bathroom?" the bartender asked, summoning for the mess to be cleaned up. No one else in the bar noticed the disturbance, or if they did, they weren't disturbed very much.

The man in the suit was now finally in a state of agitation, because some vomit had landed on his shoes and the hem of his pants. He chided himself for not realizing that entering this shanty of a bar would be a regrettable choice.

"Teach your friend how to hold his liquor," he said to Phil. "And tell him he's lucky I'm not going to make him pay my cleaning bill."

He looked down at and on Lionel before walking out. "These are the fools who make certain we'll always be seen as niggers."

Moments later, the brunt of his pain having subsided, Lionel rose cautiously, reacquainting himself with gravity and the earth's rotation. Phil expressed concern and Lionel assured him that he was fine, though worse for the wear.

"Must have been something I ate for lunch. It felt like I got kicked in the gut by a mule. Damn. I was set to clock that guy."

"I know you were."

"Just one more break for him," said Lionel, shaking his head in wonderment at the utter lack of parity amongst God's creatures.

CHAPTER TEN

C.J. headed towards his girlfriend's house, mulling over recent events. When he believed Tyrone was going to die, his priorities had been thrown into disarray. The more he tried to make sense of things, the greater his confusion grew. Try as he might to drown it out, his brother's warning about dying for a meaningless cause kept echoing in his head.

Tyrone had reminded him that the cause wasn't foolish. Only fear was. It weakened resolve, made him his own worst enemy. So C.J. decided he would never fear death again. He would never fear anything again. He would never be weak.

When he turned the corner, Lisa came into view. They had been together for almost six months. This girl of emerald eyes and honey skin had captivated him from first sight. Love took him on and out like no rival on the streets ever had been able to.

He twisted the chains that adorned his neck. His allegiance belonged to his gang, what he obsessed about was gold. Lisa knew she was running third in the race for his affection. This only made her run harder.

She minded the jewelry considerably less than the Kaos Krew, and for good reason. Her older brother Mark had been in a gang, eventually trading in the colors of his set for prison garb. Her cousin Ron had been a gang member as well, and he too was cornered by the police while up to no good. Unlike Mark, Ron chose to shoot at them until they returned fire with greater accuracy.

C.J. wanted to calm Lisa's fears, but was not about to change his ways. She could accept him as he was or she could move on. He answered only to himself.

Lisa was leaning against a car, talking to somebody inside. As he drew closer, C.J. noticed the trademark flag of

Puerto Rico on the antenna flapping mockingly in the breeze. Operating on automatic rage, he set in motion.

He pulled open the car door and dragged its occupant out, who was no more difficult to manhandle than a rag doll. With considerable force he slammed the slender kid to the ground and pounced on him, throwing a wild, endless flurry of punches, not noticing or caring once he had beaten his victim unconscious.

"No!" Lisa shouted loud enough for the whole neighborhood to hear, but not the person closest to her. "You're going to kill him." She grabbed C.J.'s neck and tried frantically to pull him off. "Stop it, stop it!"

He finally did cease, his arms having grown weary. It was only then that he felt Lisa tugging on him. The two of them rolled onto the ground.

"What the hell's the matter with you? Victor's not in the Raw Dawgs. It's his friend's car."

It took a moment for the adrenaline to wear down enough for C.J. to realize what she was saying. His payback had been taken away. This fool wasn't a Dawg.

"How could you keep hitting him like that? What gives you the right to do this to someone? What the fuck do you think you're accomplishing?"

Lisa's profanity grabbed C.J.'s attention, for she rarely cursed.

"What happens if you kill someone? Is that something you'd be proud of?" She lay her head on Victor's chest. C.J. put his hand on her shoulder.

"I'm sorry, baby."

"Don't touch me," she said, jerking away from his touch as if he was a leper.

"It was a mistake."

"No, we're the mistake. I should have known better. My friends warned me, my family warned me, my own feelings warned me. I ignored everything because I thought you were different somehow."

C.J. took a good look at Victor, recognizing him now from school. He was a quiet guy who didn't mess with anybody. No serious damage had been done, but his face was a mess. This shouldn't have happened.

"But you aren't different," Lisa continued. "Your set always comes first. Before family, before friends, before girlfriends. You steal from people, hurt people, try to kill them, and it's all okay because it was done for that damn gang."

"I didn't mean..."

"No, you didn't mean to do this to him. You meant it to be someone else. Do you really believe that makes it okay?"

Lisa was blowing things way out of proportion. Why was she getting so upset? He was her man, not this fool on the ground who didn't have the sense not to be hanging out in a Raw Dawg car. The rules of the street were clear cut, and those who didn't obey risked the price to be paid. Victor may not have been in a gang, but by getting involved in the affairs of a member he had voluntarily put himself in danger. It struck C.J. that this also applied to Lisa. He put the realization aside.

"Nobody got killed all right, so there's no need to wig out on me. I fucked up, I'm sorry. Don't you understand that after what the Dawgs did to Tyrone, I have the right to want payback?"

"Your stupid payback isn't going to help Tyrone any."

"Listen to me." He grabbed Lisa by the shoulders and turned her towards him. "I said I'm sorry. What more do you want?"

"Let go of me." She squirmed to get out of his grasp. "How do I know you won't do this to me someday?"

"Don't be crazy. You know I love you."

"What do you know about love, C.J.? How can you do something like this one minute and talk about loving someone the next?"

Lisa was intimately acquainted with the sides of C.J. rarely displayed to others. He had confided to her his hopes, dreams, fears and insecurities. So she stood by him, waiting for the day he would give full expression to the better facets of his nature, hoping he would survive to see such a day.

Now she was acting as if he was a stranger, like she had reason to fear him. She had to know that he loved her, even if he didn't quite know how to show it. Even if he remained unwilling to prove it by doing what was begged of him. C.J. did not understand how Lisa could treat their relationship as if plucking petals from a daisy, moving quickly, callously and thoughtlessly from loving him to loving him not. He raised his hand to teach her about loyalty.

His hand lowered and the lesson remained untaught. He had seen his father hit his mother enough times to know one thing for sure. That was not the kind of man he would ever allow himself to become.

C.J. rose to his feet. He glanced down at Victor, whose eyes had opened, but he remained still as if the mere idea of movement was enough to intensify the throbbing in his head past the point of no return. The fact that he looked up without fear, merely a weary form of condemnation, was almost enough to re-light C.J.'s fuse and set a swift kick in motion. Instead he set his gaze on Lisa, taking one last stab at defending himself and earning her pardon.

"Nobody's perfect, you know."

"I never asked for perfection."

C.J. recognized the truth of her words, understood that they left him no choice but to walk away.

Lisa put her head back on Victor's chest, perhaps with hope that her tears could salve his wounds and pride. She cared deeply for C.J., wanted to be with him more than anything, but the violence was too much. In her fifteen years she had seen the lives of too many loved ones needlessly wasted. She was desperate for C.J. to quit his gang before it ruined or killed him. The former may already have happened. After that, the latter was only a matter of time.

* * *

Last night the people on the news spoke of terrible events. Men, women and children had been robbed, murdered and raped. Battles were raging on foreign soils. Starvation, tyranny and natural disasters eliminated souls by the thousands. If it could, Tony's heart would have gone out to these people. But it was already bursting at the seams, his mind consumed with a single thought.

"I'm really falling hard for her." He and Charlie were retrieving books from their adjacent lockers at school.

"You're always falling hard for some girl."

"Janet's different."

"Of course she is," said Charlie. "They're all different and they're all the same. Whether it's sugar coated or glazed, it's still a doughnut. I take it things are going well so far."

"Everything is great. Almost perfect." Tony shoved a copy of Moby Dick into his bookbag. He was enjoying the epic novel, but wished Melville's editor had made him trim more generously. The bulk was wearing on his shoulder.

"Almost?" Charlie folded the cliff notes for Moby Dick and shoved it into his back pocket. "Why not perfect? Don't tell me you've found a flaw. Let me guess. She doesn't floss."

Tony ignored the sarcasm.

"We ran into some friends of hers at Cosmos the other night. They're tight with her ex too, and I wasn't exactly made to feel welcome. I'm pretty sure they were badmouthing me."

"Fucking white boys."

Charlie's train of thought instantly jumped to another track when a cute but underdeveloped freshman walked by. He flashed a smile at her. Ordinarily Tony would have given his friend grief for setting his sights so young, but first he needed to clarify matters.

"Well, it's not as if they were wearing hoods and burning crosses. Like I said, they're friends of Roger. They probably feel like I broke up their little clique. Plus, me and him did come pretty close to throwing blows last year."

The girl passed by again and Tony paid closer attention on her second pass. There was certainly plenty of potential there.

"Maybe," Charlie said. "But I get the feeling there's more to it than you say. You think they'd be tripping if she was seeing a white guy?"

"Yeah, I do," Tony said, not wanting to admit that he had asked himself the same question and chosen not to answer it. "I don't have an us versus them mentality like my dad. I didn't think you did either."

"My mentality has nothing to do with it. I'm just calling things as I see them."

"You didn't see anything, and neither did I."

Charlie chose not to argue further. If he was wrong, he was wrong. If he was right, Tony would find out soon enough. In the meantime, while his mouth remained shut his eyes would stay open for what his friend might not see until it was too late.

When Charlie's attention drifted again, Tony followed his path of vision. He expected to find another girl at the end of it. Instead he saw several members of the varsity football team coming down the hallway. Among them was Tim Braddock, with a finger pointed in their direction. At center of the group was Roger Lane, Lincoln High School's starting quarterback and Janet's ex-boyfriend. His eyes met with Tony's like a car wreck.

"You guys want something?" asked Charlie in a tone suggesting he hoped that they did.

"Not from you."

"Well that's too bad, cause I'm who you got."

Roger smiled and perhaps was about to follow up with a less congenial act when a teacher walked past and stopped within viewing range. Getting suspended was not in anybody's interest, so physical aggression was put off for the time being.

"This ain't over with. We'll settle it some other time." His threat delivered with no wiggle room left for misinterpretation, Roger departed with his sidekicks.

"Assholes."

Tony did not debate the statement, but avoided eye contact when Charlie turned towards him. The stare-down had made him uncomfortable. It needlessly exacerbated the situation, and worse, flaunted what Tony wished to go unnoticed. When Charlie and Roger glared at each other, posed mano e mano, to onlookers it was no doubt seen as more than just two students trying to settle a disagreement by determining which one was tougher. The respective skin colors of the near combatants could not be ignored. The fact that one of them was black and the other white could not be removed from the equation, rendering the specifics of the altercation inconsequential. To anyone who happened to bear witness, it was nothing less that a mini race riot. If Charlie and Roger could not stand before each other without race taking center stage, Tony wondered if he and Janet would be able to love one another without the same thing happening?

Since the night at Cosmos he had been unable to resist searching the faces that took him and Janet in for displays of disapproval, and keeping his ears cocked for whatever disparaging word might be said. He hated thinking like this, wanted nothing more than to relax and enjoy his good fortune. Why seek what would probably not be found? What he did not want to find. But still he searched just to make certain.

Seeing that his effort on Tony's behalf was not supported or appreciated, Charlie shook his head in agitation and walked away. Tony thought to call out after him, but then remembered that he was supposed to meet Janet. Not wanting to keep her waiting, he chose to let Charlie cool off and headed to the other end of the building

"How was your day?" asked Janet upon his arrival.

"A little crazy."

"Well, I'm a little crazy about you."

Tony gratefully accepted his girlfriend's kiss. By the time their lips parted, the incident with Roger was gone from his mind.

* * *

Having finished cooking dinner and it being an off day for her at work, Caren was enjoying a few spare minutes of relaxation. With her on the couch was Ellen, who was describing her latest boyfriend. He was six foot four, twenty six years old, and according to her, as fine as they came. They had met in the parking lot of Pathmark on account of a fender bender. After coming out of their respective cars to confront each other, they decided to settle out of court and in a friendlier manner.

"I really hope this works out, cause the single scene has just about worn me ragged."

Caren didn't want to dampen her spirits by suggesting that the odds of an affair with some guy more than ten years her junior turning into marriage were pretty slim.

"Speaking of sex," she said instead, "I happened to overhear Tanya with one of her friends on the phone the other day. I couldn't believe the things coming from that child's mouth. Far too adult for my liking."

"Did you say anything to her?"

"No. I didn't want her to think I spy on her. My aunt used to listen in on me and I hated it. We've already had the big talk. Hopefully she uses good judgment."

Caren fidgeted with the rollers on her head. She was trying out a new hairstyle. Maybe it would please Lionel. Very little was doing that lately.

"Kids are growing up so fast nowadays. At least they're trying to. When I was her age, sex was the last thing on my mind."

"I seriously doubt that," Ellen said teasingly.

"Okay, maybe it wasn't last. But it wasn't at the top of the list either."

"Lionel was your first, right?"

"My one and only."

"That's incredible. It's almost scary."

"I've never wanted it any other way."

"Did you wait till you got married?" Ellen asked.

"No. I tried to. But one night we went to a party and got pretty drunk. I had never drunk hard liquor before. I was rebelling against whatever there was to rebel against at the time, and Lionel was more than willing to join me. One thing led to another and we ended up making love in a cotton field. I suppose you could call me a hypocrite, because the truth is, I wasn't much older than Tanya when it happened. And she probably feels she has just as strong a reason as I did back then."

"Caren, you slut you. How was it?"

"Quick." The two of them laughed. "He had been trying to get me into bed for months. I don't think either one of us fully believed it was happening, and fools that we were, we didn't take any precautions. I got pregnant from that first time."

"That was the baby who miscarried?"

"Uh huh."

Caren wondered on occasion if her life would have turned out much differently had she not become pregnant on that steamy Georgia night. She knew Lionel loved her and would have proposed eventually. But the baby accelerated matters. Control left their hands and was handed over to indifferent fate.

She picked up her half-finished scarf. Years ago she *had* completed a knitting project. A little yellow bonnet for the child who was never to be.

When he was young and naive enough to view the world with pure optimism, Lionel often boasted about how great their future would be. His eyes lit up when he spoke of becoming a doctor. To Caren there was still much to look forward to. She knew this without question, but Lionel no longer felt the same. Once his heart and spirit broke, they broke for good.

"How was your first time?" she asked, wanting to divert attention from her own bittersweet memories.

"Oh, it was great. His name was Darnell Pullman. He was the star running back for our school football team. All the girls wanted him." Ellen broke out in a smile of remembrance.

"We did it on the fifty yard line. He was back with his girlfriend a week later." Her smile faded. “The first of many good lays and many heartbreaks."

Over the years she had managed considerably longer relationships than the one with Darnell, but none much more substantial. From this Ellen had adopted the philosophy that all pleasure must be paid for somewhere down the line. No matter how promising a start she got off to, she would inevitably end up mourning the loss of another time in her life when the air was sweet and full of possibility. Whether in a cotton field with a lifetime lover or on a football field with one of a lifetime of lovers, the moments would undoubtedly be sublime, but sooner or later collection time would come around. The tender memories purchased would be paid for with unrelenting tears.

Ellen cut off her downcast thoughts before they managed to ruin her mood. She was a firm believer in having a positive outlook. Ignore the pain and eventually it would go away.

"A toast," said Caren, holding up a glass of diet Pepsi. "To sex, cotton fields, fifty yard lines, and of course, to love."

"Cheers," said Ellen as they clicked their glasses together. "And don't forget men. They're usually not worth the trouble they bring, but at least they give us something to do at night."

CHAPTER ELEVEN

C.J. peered out the car window at a massive stone building preceded by an impenetrable gate and mythical reputation. Numerous people had warned that this was his destination. Now that it loomed before him, he was thoroughly unimpressed. Taking away a man's liberty was supposed to be the ultimate punishment for wicked deeds. But if one already inhabited an environment of limited options, the risk of incarceration didn't seem too big of a deal. Steel bars were not the only, nor the worst way to keep someone imprisoned.

Jail could not be much worse than school. Teachers had the most pointless job in existence. They tried to make significant what would never matter. What was algebra going to do for him? The only math he needed was counting up the dollars he made. What good did it do to learn about sciences he would never bother to use, about places he would never travel to because where he was served him just fine, or about people long dead who had no impact whatsoever on how he would get paid today? He needed no instructions on preparing for tomorrow, because he had learned from those who had walked these streets before him, hustling, pimping, stealing, getting by through whatever means best suited their circumstances and talents. His present, past and future had been established before he was born, and algebra had nothing to do with it. He would not attempt to alter his fate, but would instead manipulate the rules that governed him to best advantage.

C.J. was not in search of a way out. He had seen too many others try and fail miserably. They thought if they worked enough hours, or learned enough of the white man's education, or got high on enough drugs, they would locate an escape hatch. C.J. knew better. He had no intention of trying to escape. He planned to be a man of consequence, someone to be reckoned with. But he would do so within parameters set around him as securely as penitentiary walls.

Those who lectured him made some reasonable points, and usually had his best interests at heart. What they failed to grasp was that he was not defined by what he did, although he did not blame others for getting this wrong, for he understood that most people had nothing but his actions to judge him by. He wasn't an animal who derived pleasure from hurting people, or taking from those not any better off than himself. But it was crucial that he be able to dictate the direction of his life's journey to some degree. C.J. would not become his father, controlled by bills, a measly paycheck, and his wife's fertility. Unlike his brother, he would not sell his soul to the devils in order to gain entry to their world. And he would not be like the pathetic addicts he supplied, searching forever for the perfect high, forever just an overdose away.

Along with C.J were Lisa, her little sister, and their mother. After the incident with Victor, Lisa refused to speak to him for several days. Each of his attempts to reclaim her was shunned. Flowers and candy and the stuffed animals she loved had not done the trick, nor even his grandest gesture, a slow paced romantic rap song that he'd custom written and performed for her. A rolling of the eyes was the most acknowledgment he earned. Just as he was preparing to accept that the situation was hopeless, she called. Not bothering to consider what had earned him redemption, he eagerly accepted the invitation to visit her brother in prison. Though he would have preferred a more intimate reunion, what mattered most was that Lisa had forgiven him.

Her brother had been locked up for the last five years on an armed robbery charge, a minimum of four years left to serve on his sentence. Lisa's mother, who had made it clear to C.J. that she wasn't especially fond of him, treated these visits sort of how a terminal, devout Catholic desperate for a miracle would view a trip to Lourdes. What miracle she was expecting to take place, C.J. could not figure out. He knew it must have taken a great deal of cajoling on Lisa's part to convince her mother to include him on the visit. So he kept a low profile, staying back and scanning the visiting room as Mark's family took turns greeting him. Mark was expressing the same sentiments replicated by various other convicts clad in blue wardrobes courtesy of the taxpayers. Everything was pretty much the same here; he was just counting the days till he was released; things would be different when he got out, for he was a changed man now; how are things with you?

C.J. knew quite a few guys who had come out of prison thinking this way. Melvin "Van Gough" Jacobs, so nicknamed for his skill in graffiti art and half of an ear he lost in a fight, had been sent up for three years. When he was released, he told anyone who would listen how much prison had changed him. The last C.J. heard of him, Melvin had earned a return trip upstate for robbing a 7-11.

Melvin was not an isolated case. Countless fools had come out of jail with a new attitude. Yet as changed as they were, or thought they were, the outside remained unforgiving. Those broken by the prison system had grown soft. They were gobbled up quickly, because softness didn't stand a chance beyond these walls.

C.J.'s thoughts drifted to another institution, the hospital where Tyrone was recuperating. Physically his friend's condition had greatly improved. The near fatal wound was healing ahead of schedule, and he was set to go home in a week. But Tyrone's mood was lagging far behind the state of his body. His parents had decided to move from the Bronx to the suburbs of Westchester. They were fearful that their thirteen-year old son had embarked on a path leading straight to premature death. The only way to win the tug of war for his soul was to drag him away. Better kicking and screaming than in a pine box.

Lisa whispered to her brother conspiratorially, then beckoned C.J. over.

"C.J., this is my brother Mark. I thought it would be nice if you got to meet each other."

The women of the family walked away to give them privacy. C.J. had nothing to say and wondered what Lisa thought they should talk about.

"My sister has told me a lot about you."

"She's told me a lot about you too."

"We used to be real tight before I got sent up. She's always been like older than her years, you know what I'm saying?"

C.J. nodded. He found his thoughts going back to a day long ago when his family visited a petting zoo. No older than five or six years old, he had been fascinated by the goats that ate from his hand. He.told his parents that he wanted one for a pet, and cried when they explained that the animals could not be taken home. C.J. cried because he did not get what he wanted, and also for the poor goats who had no choice about where they could be.

"I regret not being around to judge her first boyfriend, let her know what I thought of him," Mark bleated. "I was supposed to be the one who chased the guys away, you know what I'm saying? Instead, she had to fend for herself."

He bore a strong resemblance to Lisa, the strongest of the family. This didn't mean that his autobiography was of interest. C.J. already knew it. Mark had played the game, lost, so was here. End of story.

"When our father died, I became the man of the house. But I let everybody down. Instead of watching out for my family, I was running around getting in all kinds of trouble until I found myself here."

C.J. concluded that this lecture must be why Lisa had asked him to come. He tried to play along.

"Must be tough. I know some guys who got sent up, and they said it was real bad."

"You have to watch out for yourself," Mark said solemnly. "You need to figure out who to make friends with, who to stay away from, who to kiss up to."

This was proof enough that he had gone soft. If C.J. knew anything, it was that you don't kiss up to anyone.

"But I see myself as lucky, you know what I'm saying? If I hadn't got caught when I did, I'd probably be dead by now. I needed something to straighten me up quick. The worst part is being away from my family. I hope you're taking good care of Lisa."

"I'm trying my best"

"Bullshit."

"What?" asked C.J., surprised by this turn in a conversation that he had been rapidly losing interest in.

"You heard me. If you were really trying then she wouldn't be so worried about you."

"She don't have nothing to worry about. I'm doing fine."

"Sure you are," Mark said. "And you'll continue doing fine until your hands are in cuffs or you've got a bullet in your head. I told you how much my sister means to me. If you're who she chooses to love, there's nothing I can do about that. Not from in here. But I don't want her to get hurt."

C.J. didn't really give a damn what Mark wanted. Out of respect for Lisa, he kept this thought to himself.

"She's a strong girl, but I don't think she can handle losing another person she cares about."

"She's not going to lose me," C.J. asserted.

"Can you guarantee that? Can you guarantee that when you leave here, you won't run into somebody who intends to pop a cap in your ass?"

"No. But if I do, he's gonna be the one to go down. That I can guarantee."

"So you're invincible, is that it? You're trippin' big time, young blood. Thinking like that is the surest way to end up as a statistic."

A scare straight lecture. How comical. C.J. knew Lisa had his best interests in mind. Even her brother's heart was probably in the right place. But there was something these do-gooders needed to be educated about.

"You may have ended up a statistic, but I'm not you. I don't need to hear no sorry rap about where I'm headed. I know what the deal is. That's why I'm living large instead of making license plates or flipping burgers at McDonalds. You can't turn me into a sucker like you with some little jail bird speech."

Mark smiled and then spoke in a soothing tone, as if he was a dentist preparing a child for the pain of a tooth pull.

"I know exactly what you're going through. I did the same things. I know the sense of power you feel. But there are better ways to earn power. Getting an education, getting a good job, being respected rather than feared."

"You think you're gonna get that when they let you out of here?"

"Yes, I do. Because I'll make certain that it's so."

"Then you're the one who's trippin', man. You ain't getting nothing. You weren't given shit before you came here, and you'll get even less when you leave."

Any fragment of respect C.J. may have had for Lisa's brother was now gone. Mark had been converted by the system. He was the white man's latest poster boy for the rehabilitated nigger.

"You want to be my fucking role model? Let me tell you something number 948703, I ain't going for it. You want to know why? Cause I'm a man. I still own my balls, I haven't loaned them to the state."

C.J. leaned forward, getting right in Mark's face, and it wasn't to swap gang stories, share secrets, or recite a "be all you can be" speech. It was to irritate him, make him mad as hell, push him as far as he could be pushed. Because the fact was, there wasn't a damn thing Mark could do about it.

"I'd rather get smoked like your cousin than be a bitch like you. At least I'd go with my self-respect. You had too many dicks up your ass in here to remember nothing, nigga? No one's gonna give you shit. You got to take what you want."

On the streets these words would have demanded retaliation, nothing less than death. But Mark was no longer on the streets, so operated under a different set of guidelines.

"You're half right," he said, his composure unruffled and voice steady. "Nobody's going to give me anything. But I don't have to take nothing either. I can earn it."

C.J. stood up. "Okay, fine. We'll continue this four years from now. When you're out long enough to remember everything you've forgotten."

"I'll be there. I doubt you will though."

C.J. smirked. Lisa was actually worried that he would end up like this punk. Never happen.

* * *

"What did you say this is called again?"

"Mavi. It's spelled with a v which is pronounced like a b. A quirk of Spanish people that I'm kind enough to indulge them in, as long as they keep making the stuff."

"That's awful kind of you," Janet said, smiling at her boyfriend's silliness. "Mavi," she repeated. "It has an interesting flavor."

"It's an acquired taste."

"Kind of like you."

Tony smiled, then stopped walking in order to tickle Janet's sides until she squirmed into his arms in surrender.

"I used to play football and baseball in that lot over there," he said, pointing across the street. "I don't think kids use it much anymore. Too much broken glass and garbage lying about. It's a shame the city hasn't bothered to maintain it."

A group of boys aged eight to ten ran past, hollering at the top of their lungs for no better reason than it felt good. The sneakers on the smallest one were so threadbare that the soles flapped open and shut in the front like a hungry fish.

"This is where I get my hair cut. My barber is a real character. He's got something like eleven kids from eight or nine different women. He gets most of the customers in the place, partly because he's a great barber but mostly because he never runs out of wild stories. Sometimes bald guys plop in his chair just cause they need a good laugh. He sells everything under the sun on the side. Anything to make a buck. He may be irresponsible about birth control, but not about child support."

Janet walked along silently as Tony pointed out sites of significance and related anecdotes to accompany each one. He felt an unfamiliar fondness for the neighborhood as he nostalgically painted a portrait of his childhood spent here. Tony was as happy as he ever remembered being, and this cast a warm light on everything around him. His girl was by his side and nothing was on their hands but time to fill.

"On your right is the world's most poorly stocked candy store. I don't think you could find a stick of gum in the place less than three years old. It's really a front for a gambling operation. Montell will take you out for sure if you welsh on a bet, so hardly nobody ever does. But other than being a hard ass bookie, he's a pretty okay guy. Dresses up like Santa Claus every Christmas and gives away toys."

At the corner six young men were gathered in a semicircle staring at the base of a wall. One of them shook his arm like he was whipping a horse to greater speed.

"Come on," he said. "Shorty wants to be driven around in a brand new Benz."

A pair of die sprung from his hand, did their tantalizing dance on the pavement, then came to rest.

"I guess shorty will have to keep riding the bus", one of them said to the laughter of the others. Money exchanged hands and the ritual started over again. "Come on. Mama wants..."

Tony and Janet turned onto a residential street. When he was younger, Tony walked these streets alongside his parents and siblings on their way to church every Sunday. His father never failed to point out his favorite homes, pondering aloud how much they might go for. "This one has the biggest yard in the neighborhood," he would say. "This one is a little run down, but with some work it could be something." Or, "I know the guy who just bought this house. The bank foreclosed on it, so he got a pretty good deal. You got to be in the right place at the right time. That's what it's all about. In a few years we're gonna be living in one of these. An apartment is no place for a family. You kids need some space to run around. I'm gonna provide it for you, just wait and see."

Tony tried but failed to recall precisely when his father had stopped pointing out homes, stopped describing the dreams he held. What he did remember was that his father eventually stopped accompanying them to church altogether. The early morning walk and sermon that followed did not mesh well with his hangovers.

In the middle of the street several boys were gathered around a rectangular box that had been painted on the ground. Numbered squares were spread throughout, and the kids were flicking bottle caps around the board. When a car came down the street, each boy grabbed his cap protectively. Once the path was again clear, the tops were returned to their respective locations.

"I was the skelsies king back in the day," Tony boasted. "I used a plastic cap that had raised letters on it. I would scrape it against the sidewalk for about an hour until the letters were gone and the bottom was smooth as glass. Then I would fill it with melted crayon. That thing would glide forever."

Three high school age girls came walking towards them, talking loudly about a music video, dressed as if they were about to audition for one of the booty shaking variety. The trio smacked gum and sashayed their hips in perfect unison. Jewelry jangled and glittered from every conceivable body part, perhaps to reflect light off the girls' various tattoos.

Their festive mood changed when Tony and Janet were spotted. The conversation they were having paused, resuming with a different subject matter once the couple was behind view, but not quite beyond hearing.

"These niggas will forever be chasing after white girls."

"And sooner or later they find themselves one with a Mandingo complex."

Tony first hoped the nasty exchange had gone unheard by Janet. Then he changed his mind. He no longer wanted to be alone with his recognition of how they were sometimes perceived. Narrow-minded opinions were usually not stated directly to them. It was more common for displeasure to be silently expressed through less than subtle stares or behind the back sniping. Each occurrence would gnaw at Tony. It was time to share his uneasiness with his partner in crime. If he and Janet spoke about what had been unnamed till now, the attitude of unenlightened others could be laughed at. Faced alone, each episode made him a little angrier and frustrated that he had no outlet.

But he didn't want to be the one who broached the subject. Perhaps Janet's silence was best left untouched. If urged to speak, she might say that she was not strong enough to handle the slurs, that she was beginning to agree that the two of them should not be together.

So when several seconds passed without Janet speaking about what had transpired, Tony joined her in ignoring it and resumed his role as tour guide.

"You ever have a Jamaican pattie? I mean the real deal, not those you can buy in a pizzeria."

"I don't think so."

"You're in for a real treat then," he said, guiding Janet towards a West Indian bakery on the opposite side of a street in his neighborhood, giving her a glimpse at his world, opening and offering the better half of his heart.

CHAPTER TWELVE

Lionel's surroundings appeared hazy. To his right were the hoodlums who hung out front of his building everyday. He sensed that their carefree laughter was at his expense. The glitter of the gold they wore overwhelmed his eyes. They had sold their souls to the devil in order to obtain it, and he wasn't certain whether they deserved to be condemned for this. After all, the supermarket would accept their dirty money but he couldn't buy a can of soda with his clean soul.

He tripped over a step and one of the kids asked if he needed any help. He understood what type of assistance was being offered, so politely declined. The poison they peddled was not needed. His own eighty proof liquid variety did him just fine.

Lionel entered the building, stepped into the elevator, and squinted to determine which of the buttons was the one for his floor. Somebody called out for him to hold up. He managed to make contact with the "Door Open" button just in time.

Moments later, tauntingly curvaceous hips appeared before him, just the right amount of flesh for a man to get a good grip on. He raised his view and his pleasure ceased. It was Ellen. He braced himself for the requisite caustic remark. When none came he took a closer look at her. She was leaning against the opposite wall, apparently as drunk as himself.

"I hate men," she said. Her hand-eye coordination was in a slightly better state than Lionel's, so she was able to send the elevator on its way.

"I never took you for the lesbian type."

"Oh shut up," she said, but with less scorn in her tone than usual. She even managed a smile.

"Why can't guys be honest? If all you want is a one nighter or a casual fling, just come out and say so. Why do you have to promise us the moon and stars?"

Ellen adjusted the dress that was clinging to her hips. She wasn't hard to look at, Lionel had to admit. If she could only learn to keep her mouth shut, he might not mind her being around so much.

"If guys went around telling women that, they wouldn't get laid nearly as much."

"I guess that's true."

The elevator door opened and the neighbors squeezed together, trying to walk out at the same time. They started towards their respective apartments.

"Hey, I borrowed a blender from Caren the other day. Come in and I'll get it for you."

Moments later, Lionel seated himself on a lime green sofa while Ellen went into her kitchen. She returned with a blender in one hand and a glass of wine in the other. With a concentrated expression, she examined herself in the largest mirror hung on the wall.

"I'd offer you some, but this is the last of it."

"That's okay. I never had much taste for the stuff. Like they say, wine is fine but liquor is quicker"

Ellen turned to face him. "If I ask you something, would you give me an honest answer?"

"Maybe."

"Fair enough. "Do you find me attractive?" Once again she smoothed some wrinkles in her dress in case this would influence the answer to her question.

"What do you care what I think?"

"Just humor me," Ellen said. "Sometimes a woman likes to hear these things. Sometimes she needs to."

Offering commentary on Ellen's appearance was more pleasant than having her curse him out for being a louse, so Lionel chose to answer somewhat kindly.

"You don't need me to tell you anything with all the boyfriends you've had."

"None for very long, though. None for keeps."

She sat down beside him and practically inhaled the top half of her glass of wine.

"Let me tell you about this last guy I was dating so you can see what I'm talking about. He was beautiful, did some modeling even. Only twenty six. I know what you're thinking, robbing the cradle, right?"

Lionel shrugged.

"Maybe I was," Ellen continued. "But this thirty eight year old body was more than up to the challenge. I'm at my sexual peak, you know."

Lionel squirmed uneasily. He definitely did not need to be hearing this, did not care to hear about any of his neighbor's peaks. He shifted his line of vision to the carpet because he did not want to be accused of staring at Ellen's cleavage, although her pushed up breasts in her low cut apparel gave him little choice but to take notice. Doing some subtraction back to the year Ellen had thrown a 35th birthday for herself, even in his state of inebriation it was relatively easy to calculate by how many years she was currently lying about her age.

"I treated that man like he was a king. I cooked for him, redecorated his apartment, did his laundry. And I know I gave him the best sex he's ever had. So what does he do?"

Lionel felt confident that he could make an accurate guess, but did not bother to because Ellen obviously intended to do the answering as well as the asking.

"He does what all the others before him basically did. He gets a few good fucks, a couple free meals and clean laundry. Then he dumps me for some slut. Some twenty two year old slut."

Ellen drained the remainder of her wine like a seasoned drunk. She could certainly hold her own when it came to drinking. Lionel was forming a new found respect.

"Why can't I find the right man?" she asked.

Lionel recognized the same burnt out expression of exasperation mixed with alcohol that he often found in the mirror. Regardless of how different people seemed from one another, a single trait was held in common by all. Everybody had a sad story to tell based on something that had been long sought, but not yet found.

"I'm sure he'll come along soon."

"You're very sweet, Lionel. I've always been kind of tough on you. I'm sorry about that. I think we can be friends, don't you?"

"Sure, I guess." Lionel was still looking at the floor, so he was startled by the unexpected kiss on his cheek. Ellen then took hold of his hands.

"That's for being such a good neighbor."

Lionel didn't say anything. He was beginning to feel strange about how intently he was being looked at.

"You know, I used to go with a guy who you remind me of a little. We lived together for awhile. Then I got pregnant and gave him an ultimatum about getting married. He took off the next day."

"That why you give me so much grief? Cause I remind you of some old boyfriend who did you wrong?"

Ellen didn't answer the question. She was lost in the past. Lionel just wanted his hands back.

"He had such pretty eyes. Our child would have been beautiful. But I didn't give my baby a chance to be anything."

Lionel was starting to wax nostalgic for the days when Ellen couldn't stand him. He didn't need to hear her problems. He had more than enough of his own. Listening to Ellen's sob stories was supposed to be his wife's job.

"Want to hear something funny?" she asked.

Lionel didn't respond, but there was no need to. He would be hearing what she had to say regardless.

"After I got the heave ho tonight I went to a bar."

"No kidding," said Lionel, although he knew in advance that the sarcasm would be wasted.

"My only company was Captain Morgan's spiced rum, but I didn't figure on being alone for long. Since I'd lost one stud, I intended to go get me another. Not five seconds after my pick suggests we go to his place, his girlfriend walks in. Some nights you can't get laid to save your life. But you can always get drunk."

"This is true."

"It's not much of a replacement."

"I guess not."

"Besides, I'm out of wine," Ellen said. "So what do I do now?"

Neither of them spoke in the seconds that followed the question, but in Ellen's hungry stare, more than enough was said. Yet Lionel was still taken very much by surprise when she straddled his waist with her thighs. Without being conscious of willing his hands to any particular action, he found them wrapped around her back. A voice in the recesses of his mind yelled at him to stop, but primitive urges far stronger than conscience imposed a gag order. She was unbuttoning his shirt, clawing at his chest. Then she was kissing his neck, blowing in his ear. "Take me," she moaned. "Take me now." Her hand slid down his chest, down his stomach, lower, lower. The combination of alcohol and fast pumping blood had Lionel in a daze. How long had she wanted to do this? How long had *he*? "Oh God I want you," she purred. Her breasts had somehow sprung completely free. Lionel's face was guided towards the ripe, firm mounds of flesh before him.

His mind drifted to the one near infidelity of his married life. That had been seven years earlier. Maxine was a waitress at a coffee shop near his job at the time. Friendly idle chatter somehow led to a place where happily married men were not supposed to venture. He accepted the invitation to her home both in spite and because of his instincts. The intimate embrace of a woman with whom he had no history; no obligations; no hardships; only carefree laughter and the promise of much pleasure; was too exquisite to resist. But that is what he ended up doing, what he had to do, because life as in most every case left him no choice. Within five minutes of entering Maxine's apartment, he understood how his being there would change everything, even if forever kept a secret. So he issued hurried apologies and rushed home to Caren. The next day he found a new place to get his morning cup of coffee and accompanying bagel. The coffee wasn't nearly as good and many of the bagels were stale, but such are the sacrifices that life sometimes demands.

Temptation was now once again whispering in his ear, offering him just one little bite that would surely give birth to a ravenous appetite for sin. The woman had changed, the locale moved to frighteningly exciting proximity, but the enticement of passion without ties was the same.

Lionel looked across the room and saw the intertwined bodies of Ellen and himself infinitely reflected. Then the image of Caren appeared like a ghost in that house of mirrors. He loved his wife. More than he would ever be able to say. More than he could even think. The risk of losing her was not worth taking, no matter how sweet the short term reward. Temporary emancipation by a stranger's flesh could never make up for the trust he would be forsaking.

"This isn't right."

Ellen pressed her lips tightly against his. He tried to stand but she was holding him down. "She'll never know. Just this one time. I need someone tonight. She'll never know."

"I'll know." Lionel pushed her off a little rougher than intended, rose to his feet, hastily got his clothing back in order and wiped off the lipstick stains that he spotted in Ellen's mirrors. When he looked back in her direction, he found her sitting on the floor with her head between her hands.

"I'm so sorry. I'm so sorry. I'm so sorry."

Lionel couldn't spare the time to accept Ellen's apologies. He hurried home, blender in hand.

* * *

The motel room was far from luxurious, but was what Tony could afford and had more than served its purpose. It was softly illuminated by candles brought along for the occasion to create a romantic touch. Plus, Charlie had advised him that once the lights were turned off in this place it was best to leave the room dark, unless he did not mind the sight of a battalion of roaches camped around the bed.

Tony ran his fingers through the golden strands that crowned his princess, brushing them gently across his cheek. His finger traced the birthmark he had only discovered this evening, for its placement on Janet's thigh hid it from view under normal circumstances. But the circumstances of tonight were anything but normal. His life would now be catalogued under two distinct time periods, the one before this night, and the one after.

He marveled at Janet's beauty. Even after making love to her, and then again, and then again, he still had trouble believing she was really his. Never before had anything felt so right. This was what poet's wrote about, what songbird's whistled of.

"What did I do to deserve you?"

She smiled as response.

"When we're alone, it's like no one and nothing else exists. There's just us. I wish it could be like this all the time. Twenty four hours a day, seven days a week, always this simple and sweet and perfect."

"Mmmmm hmmmm."

Her purr of contentment was envied by Tony. Happy as he was at this moment, never before had he been so aware that the more one had, the more one had to lose.

An hour earlier he had arranged for accommodations with the desk clerk. The slightly built, disheveled and beleaguered looking man with the weakest chin ever seen by Tony held a blank expression. He seemed the type who rarely bothered to summon the energy required to form an opinion on anything, much less express it. Nevertheless, Tony issued a challenge with his stare, just in case he encountered disapproval or perhaps even opposition for trying to obtain a room for himself and a white girl. But he was confronted with nothing but indifference, the lone sentiment recognized being boredom. The only color of concern to the clerk was that of the money he was paid.

It was ridiculous to fabricate resentment and negativity where none existed. When given all you've ever wanted, allowed to experience life at its most sublime, the only fitting responses were to revel and give thanks.

"You know what else I wish. I wish I could figure out the perfect way to say how I feel about you."

But how could he possibly illustrate the palpitations of his heart? A new language would have to be invented. Not one any tongue could pronounce. A language only his heart could speak, and only Janet's could hear. Like most men, however, Tony didn't even know where to start. So he had to make due with that most plagiarized of oaths.

"I love you."

"I love you too."

He pulled Janet to him and held on until the rest of the world was gone. Once it was, he still didn't let go. They had time to spare and his passion had once again returned.

* * *

Tanya tried to make her mind blank, but this had not worked. Neither had attempting to think of something else, anything else. Her thoughts kept boomeranging to Eric, to how good he made her feel, and the fact that he was probably back with his ex-girlfriend by now.

The first obstacle to their happiness had been overcome. Eric did not warmly greet the news of her restrictive curfew. He thought it unfair that just as they were starting to get serious, he was now hardly able to see her. A lunch period here, a recess there, did not suffice. Tanya could not agree more, but there was little she could do other than wait the situation out. She knew better than to defy her father, who was on edge as it was. With difficulty, she was able to convince Eric to exercise patience.

Several weeks came and went until their next dilemma. Eric's parents were going away for the weekend to celebrate their wedding anniversary. This left him with an apartment to himself. Tanya was not allowed to stay out late, but her weekend days were still free.

Unlike herself, Eric was sexually experienced. She had expected the subject to come up sooner rather than later. From the night he placed his name around her neck, a request for a return on his investment had been a foreseen conclusion. They were a steady couple now, and sex was one of the things that often went along with such an arrangement.

Eric had not been pushy about it at first. He knew it would probably take a little while for her to warm up to the idea. And due to her punishment, opportunities were scarce to non-existent anyway. But this was no longer the case. The time to choose had arrived.

Without saying it in so many words, an ultimatum was declared by Eric. Tanya was to decide whether their relationship or her virginity would continue. She did not want to lose him, felt that perhaps she loved him, or was at least well under way.

Tanya had not known what she was going to tell Eric until the moment came to give him an answer. She learned at the same time he did that it was no.

So now, instead of being in Eric's loving arms, she was walking aimlessly and alone.

It wouldn't have been anything to be ashamed of. It was destined to happen eventually. There was no real reason to believe she would be better off holding out. If only she could go back in time. Just a week would do. But if she could, would her answer be any different?

She spotted her friend Cheryl walking with boyfriend of the month, Tariq Blackwell. He wore the same cheesy grin they all did before being sent away in favor of the next one.

Tanya had not told anyone about breaking up with Eric, because she was in denial and felt that saying it aloud would somehow make it official. Now she felt an overwhelming need to confess. She had Cheryl excuse Tariq for a minute and gave a quick recap.

"What do you think I should do?" she asked, although she already had a pretty good idea what Cheryl's opinion would be. She simply needed a second opinion that agreed with the amended one she was forming.

"You know what to do, you're just afraid to go through with it. Your problem is that you think too much. It's just a little bump and grind. You might even enjoy it. Speaking of which, I'm about to enjoy a little something-

something with Tariq. Is he cute or what? I'll call you tonight."

"Bye Cheryl. Thanks."

Sex had made Cheryl a bonafide woman while Tanya was still a child. This could change soon enough. The more Tanya thought about it, the less she understood why she had made such a big deal out of this. It would be beautiful. There was no point to stopping the natural progression of love and passion. Sex was okay if it was with someone you cared about. Everyone knew that.

Tanya had made herself miserable wrestling over whether she was ready or not. It was time to think in simple, concrete terms. She could make love with Eric and keep him, or hold out for reasons she barely understood and lose him. The matter was no more or less complicated than this.

She wasn't far from his home. It was with urgency that her steps were now taken. Within minutes Eric's two story apartment building was within sight. Her pace slowed as new questions began to surface. One in particular stood out. Only six days had passed, but it was still true that they were officially broken up. What if he wasn't alone?

Tanya moved onward until she was before his door. She turned to leave, then turned back. Having come this far, she might as well follow it through. What happened next would determine if this was meant to be.

She pressed the buzzer for the upstairs apartment. No one was answering. Maybe he was out. Maybe he wasn't. Maybe ... She pressed the buzzer again and kept her finger on it. If he wasn't alone, the incessant noise she created would certainly disturb what was going on. The door opened and there he stood.

"Hi," said Eric with the mischievous grin she could not resist, his cap of the day askew. Tanya immediately knew that she had made the right decision.

CHAPTER THIRTEEN

New York City was being treated to an unseasonably warm day for so late in the year. Everyone who could was taking advantage by basking in the sunshine. Late departing birds, those who wouldn't catch the worms, wondered if perhaps their procrastination had paid off and there would be no need to finish packing and fly south.

Tony and Charlie lounged on a park bench as people walked, ran, pedaled, skate boarded, rollerbladed and scootered past. No lovers quarreled, no parents were exasperated by screaming children, no person in sight was taking or getting taken. It was one of those rare days when nary a soul seemed to have a care in the world.

Due somewhat to his job and in greater part to his love life, Tony had been spending considerably less time of late with his best friend. Only because Janet had made plans for the day which excluded him had Charlie been given the opportunity to be consolation prize. Although it was at his insistence that she was off skiing with friends over the holiday weekend, and despite the fact that he had declined her offer to join them, he was still somewhat bothered that she went. It wasn't that he could even ski, or particularly wanted to learn. Two weeks earlier when she purchased tickets for a concert, he turned down her offer to claim one without regret. The main attraction was a boy band that performed pop songs of puppy love he could take or leave, and the opening act was a rock band with one minor hit to their credit that he could only leave. He had no problem accepting that Janet occasionally socialized without him, especially since their tastes in music and other forms of entertainment were far from identical. But even if he had wanted to go, the truth was that he could ill afford such luxuries. He worked hard for the few dollars he made, and most of his salary was allocated to pay his family's bills. Going skiing or attending concerts was not merely a matter of dipping into allowance money or asking his parents for it. That was not how it worked for him, but it did work this way for Janet. She always invited him along, but the invitations were frustrating rather than flattering because he usually had no choice but to decline.

Something else troubled him as well. Janet should have known that he would feel less than comfortable amongst the group she went on these excursions with. They seemed like cool enough people, but they had a private history of memories together. It was impossible for him not to feel like an outsider as they shared in-jokes and you-had-to-be-there stories.

He would conceal his disappointment in her lack of sensitivity, not wanting to come off as overly possessive. In truth, he wanted nothing more than to fully possess Janet. Especially the part of her that he suspected was shown freely to others while kept hidden from him. He ached to be let in on this secret side of the girl he loved. Yet he was equally afraid of what might be found.

"What are your thoughts about the military?" Charlie asked.

"Why?" The out of thin air question distracted Tony from his worries and brought him careening back to the moment at hand. "You thinking of signing up?"

"I'm thinking about the future in general. School is almost over. Got to do something with myself."

"Joining the Marines worked out pretty well for Jermaine," Tony said, speaking of a mutual friend. "It definitely straightened him up."

"Yeah, that's true. For someone who needs discipline and structure like he did, I can definitely see the benefits of putting on a uniform. Especially if no wars happen to be going on at the time."

"A bullet in the head from some Middle Eastern soldier would definitely cancel out the benefits."

"Jermaine landed a pretty good job when he came out" Charlie said. "But Franklin has nothing good to say about the Army. He says the military is no place for a black man to be."

"The way I figure, you get out of a situation whatever you put into it. No doubt Jermaine felt like telling a drill sergeant or two to fuck off. But he kept it to himself, did his job, made things work out for himself. Franklin probably reacted a lot differently. He's too hot headed."

"I see your point," Charlie said. "A brotha doesn't need to enlist to find a hard time. A white man neither, for that matter. You go around looking for a fight, you can always find one."

A group of girls walked by, their conversation temporarily ceasing as they crossed Tony and Charlie's path. This was because one of them was Charlie's ex-girlfriend. They exchanged not quite hostile, not quite friendly glances.

Charlie continued to stare off into empty space after she was gone from view. Or so Tony thought. But then Charlie pointed to an elderly man, stooped over from years of living, attempting with little success to light a cigarette that dangled precariously from his puckered lips.

"You see there? That was me and Sheila."

The old man lit another match, cupped his hand around the flame to protect it from an unpredictable wind, and drew it slowly to the cigarette's tip. Just as he began to inhale the sweet taste of nicotine that his body craved, the flame was extinguished.

"What in the world do you mean by that?"

"We were almost there," Charlie explained. "But just as we were getting started, poof."

They watched the old man's next attempt, having nothing better to do. There was something bizarrely heroic about his display of determination. His withered hand moved with the imperceptible momentum of a slug, extremely slow, remarkably steady, for the slightest quiver might betray his purpose. Once again, just as fire prepared to lick the tube of tobacco before it, a mischievous force of nature doused ignition.

Then he caught a lucky break when a fellow smoker approached and loaned his cigarette, allowing the old timer to light his own with relative ease. The first wisp of smoke escaped from his lips like the answer to a prayer.

The subject of Sheila was a touchy one with Charlie. He had yet to provide an adequate explanation for their break-up, but it was unnecessary to ask him who made the decision. Sheila was the one girl Charlie had not intended to love and leave. He strictly did the first part while she took care of the second.

"The day will come, just wait and see."

Tony figured that the day being referred to was when Sheila would come begging for another chance. The prediction seemed unlikely based on how nastily their relationship had ended, but he knew better than to share this opinion with Charlie.

"Well look who we have here. If it ain't America's most wanted, the junior version."

The remark was aimed at C.J., who was headed towards them. He bluffed throwing a punch in response to Charlie's teasing.

"Keep dissin' me and next time it might be for real."

"Just don't forget to put away your pacifier first."

"I don't know which one of you is cornier," C.J. said. "No wonder you two fags hang out together."

Tony smiled at what was the usual exchange of pleasantries between his brother and best friend. The mostly pretend friction was caused by Charlie's memory. He didn't need to delve particularly far into it to recall when C.J. was a wide eyed innocent trailing behind his big brother, the most violent aspect of his life being the cartoons he watched. C.J.'s itinerary had changed dramatically in the past two years. Very few of his current activities could be viewed as childlike. Nevertheless, Charlie delighted in reminding him that despite the hard core exterior he now presented, he had yet to fully outgrow the little boy he once was.

"Have mercy." Charlie exclaimed.

The remainder of the vote was wordlessly unanimous on the girl headed their way. Her hips swayed like a small boat on rough water, her short skirt left the bare minimum to imagination, her taut, exposed belly a golden shade of tan, her blouse parted to reveal twin globes that were still strangers to the laws of gravity. Heads of men young and old swiveled so quickly to catch her going as well as coming that a case of whiplash was a genuine possibility. Other girls also checked her out discreetly and otherwise. Most of their faces showed envy and disapproval, particularly those who had just lost the attention of their boyfriends. She stopped at a water fountain to refill her bottle, bending over to a tempting degree.

"This is a situation ripe for the picking, and I'm the right field hand for the job" Charlie said. "Unless one of you guys wants to claim first dibs."

"Nah, you go for it," C.J. said. "I could use a good laugh."

"Since I'm off the market now, I'll defer to you," said Tony. "Not that you have a chance in hell."

"Thanks for the support, guys. Just sit back and observe a true master.

"A true masturbater is more like it," Tony quipped.

"You better hurry up," advised C.J. "She's breaking out."

Charlie jumped up and headed quickly towards the girl. To his credit, he immediately engaged her in conversation. The two of them were beyond the hearing of Tony and C.J., but it appeared that Charlie was making progress.

"This isn't happening," C.J. said when he saw that the girl was looking into her purse. "He's getting her digits. I don't believe it."

Suddenly she withdrew a small can and held it to Charlie's face, who responded by backing away swiftly. Despite his retreat, the femme fatale still felt impelled to say - "Get your fucking black ass the fuck out my face, before I have to blind you and shit."

"Mace!" shouted Tony uproariously as Charlie made the long, lonely walk back to the bench.

"So how'd it go?" C.J. asked, failing miserably to keep a straight face.

"We decided to take things slow."

"A lot slower than that moonwalk you just did, I bet."

"She has some hostility issues," Charlie said. "Tony, I think I'm beginning to understand why you went and got yourself a white girl."

Charlie took his place on the bench, from which the young men continued to admire fair maidens and razz each other until the disappearing sun told them it was time to turn the park over to its night dwellers.

* * *

"What are we going to do?"

The question lay heavily in the air between Caren and her husband. Spread out before them was a collection of unpaid bills.

"I don't know" was the best answer Lionel could come up with.

"Most of these are final notice."

Lionel sighed in exasperation. "Do you think whining and complaining will get them paid?"

"No. But neither will ignoring them from the comfort of a barstool."

Lionel brought his fist down on their coffee table, sending some of the bills in flight as the table wobbled frenetically. The paperback book kept under one of the legs to maintain stability was a few pages short.

"I've been busting my hump trying to find work. You don't know what that's like, filling out dozens of applications, knowing nobody's going to call. You've never had to sit before people who make you feel like a bum begging for a quarter."

He took a final gulp from the can he held, as if the taste of beer could wash out his disgust.

"Their smiles don't fool me. I know exactly what they're thinking. They want to get rid of the nigger as quick as they can. They're too important, too white to have to deal with me."

Caren began picking envelopes up from the floor. Lionel grasped her arm. He wanted her full attention. Unlike the wall of condescension that he butted everyday, she *did* have to listen to him.

"I put up with enough shit out there. I'll be damned if I'm gonna put up with more when I get home. I need your support, but all you do is criticize."

He looked expectantly at his wife, waiting for a sign of contrition. Nearly a minute passed without a change of expression on Caren's face. If she felt at all sympathetic to his plight, she was keeping it to herself. He would have to generate pity on his own behalf. Lionel tried to be angered, but this required energy beyond his storage capacity. Caren had stood by him through times that would have shaken the resolve of a nun. From the day he first laid eyes upon her in the store she worked in at the time, asking her to help him pick out a gift for his mother's birthday, she had done everything in her power to please him, to show him that her love was true and enduring. But even true love only went so far. Her eyes did not cast blame, but neither did they request forgiveness. They simply said that enough was enough, and it was to this unspoken statement that Lionel responded.

"You ought to forgive a man for having a few drinks if they help him momentarily forget how much of a failure he is."

"You're not a failure, honey."

"Then what am I? The rent is way overdue, our fridge is empty. I'm supposed to take care of those things. I promised you the world. I never thought we'd end up like this."

"I know it's tough, but when has it ever been easy? We just need some money to tide us over till things get back to normal."

"Yeah, I guess. But our credit is shit. There's no way the bank will give us a loan."

"We do have one option," Caren said

"Don't say it. Don't even think it."

"What choice do we have?"

"I'll get a job soon."

"You've been saying that for awhile."

"The strike should end any day."

"You've been saying that too. But we need money now."

"Don't worry," said Lionel, taking one last stab at sounding as if he was in control of the situation, that the break he needed was only a good night's sleep away. "We'll get by, just like we always do."

"And if we don't?"

Lionel was through trying to pin down answers to questions that refused to stay put for a three count.

"I don't want to talk about this anymore."

"What else is there to talk about? What else do broke people talk about besides the fact that they're broke?"

"Don't test me, Caren. I've had a rough day. I've taken about all I can take."

"Fine, I'm going to bed. You can stay out here and think up the miracle that will make these bills go away." She stood up and walked to their bedroom.

Lionel sat and stared at the wall for what may have been ten minutes or may have been an hour. No miracles were to be found there. Money grew out of plaster as often as it did from trees. There was only one place he was certain to find what he needed. But he would die before turning to his brother again. There had to be some other way. At this point he would accept a deal from the devil as quickly as he would from God, but he wasn't asking for a damn thing from Manny.

Eventually he looked back down at the numerous requests for payment which were not making a sound, but nonetheless refused to be ignored. With a sweep of his hand he shoved what remained on the coffee table to the floor. But brute force, though occasionally effective on people, could not budge his debts an inch. So for the time being, he reached the decision usually found at the end of his dilemmas. He walked to the kitchen to get another beer.

CHAPTER FOURTEEN

Howard and Tony were hard at work unloading a truck in the back of Jenson's Supermarket. Tony appreciated the opportunity to earn an honest wage. He was glad he could help his family out and have a few dollars left over for himself. But he had also concluded that for the amount of work he did, he was being vastly underpaid.

When they decided to take a break in the storeroom, Howard began to recount his latest adventure. It seemed his stepfather had run into the man he was supposed to be working for, exposing Howard's clandestine work status.

"Is he going to let you keep working here?"

"For the rest of the semester. But in the Summer I have to work full time for him. So much for lifeguarding. He has no idea how much pussy he has cost me. This place is not exactly the type of meat market I'm most interested in, not that I haven't managed to parlay it into a couple hook-ups."

"You shouldn't let him run your life." Tony still felt impelled to help construct a backbone in his friend. The sons of the world had to support one another in the war against the fathers. "You've got to take a stand sometime."

"What's the point? Like it or not, I'm going to graduate with a degree in accounting. I might as well start preparing for it. I can't hide out here forever."

"Then I guess your crisis is over."

"Yeah, I guess so. Hey, check out who I hooked up with the other night." Howard reached for his wallet and withdrew a photograph that was obviously a professionally taken headshot. "Is she hot or what?"

The girl was indeed stunning, possessing a butter pecan complexion, sparkling almond shaped eyes, and hair like auburn strands of silk. She was probably a multi-blend of races. There was definitely some African-American and either Hispanic or Native American in her features. Whatever parts comprised her, the sum total was conclusively pleasing to the eyes. He and Howard had similar tastes in women. Then again, whose criteria could she possibly fail to meet? Even Charlie, who occasionally chided him for succumbing to the media's elevation of features associated with Caucasian beauty, would allow that this girl was exquisitely fine.

"Not bad," Tony enviously understated.

"You better believe not bad. My first model, or so she claimed to be. My first sista too. Fucked my brains out. This white boy didn't know what he was missing. I wish I could get her to give Sandy lessons."

Tony wasn't sure whether to be amused or offended by the racial profiling. It occurred to him that he had never mentioned Janet was white. He considered bringing it up now, but decided against it. The timing would only make Howard feel bad about his lack of political correctness and create unnecessary tension between them. Tony's least favorite people were those who couldn't take a joke. He would accept his co-worker's commentary as benign, take it with the lightness of spirit that was obviously intended.

Howard kissed the photograph before putting it away, probably joining several others. He had a carefree manner about him that indicated a high degree of comfort in his own skin. This along with his teen idol good looks was an effective combination. He sometimes surprisingly spoke of getting married to his girlfriend in a few years, but for now monogamy didn't stand a chance of making his top ten list of priorities. Not so long as he and his girl were in separate schools. One of these days Sandy might decide to take a peek through that wallet of his. He would have quite a bit of explaining to do then. But Tony would not bother to caution him. Some lessons could only be learned the hard way.

"Hey, did you get a chance to listen to those CD's I loaned you?" Howard asked.

"Yep."

"What did you think?"

"Not bad. Not bad at all. It took me a little while to get into. At first it just sounded like a lot of racket with all that heavy guitar and drumming. But eventually my ears got used to the groove and I started to see why people might dig it."

"I knew you'd like it," Howard said. "If you can appreciate Led Zeppelin, there's hope for you yet. I listen to them whenever I work out. I feed off their energy."

He stood before the cracked mirror hung to a wall and flexed his biceps. Satisfied with the reflection, he turned back to Tony.

"I'm gonna loan you some Springsteen next. You can't go wrong with the Boss."

"Unless you want something you can dance to."

"Man, I'm not talking about dancing. I'm talking about art. Real music moves your soul, not just your feet."

"All right, whatever you say, Professor."

"You're going to be grateful to me one day for opening your mind, Johnson. You'll forget at least half of what they teach you in school, but what you learn from me will stick in your brain. Mark my words."

Tony's attention was grabbed by a report on the radio, which he turned up. Outside of sports he usually wasn't much of a news junkie, but the words of the commentator today hit closer to home than usual. A schoolmate of his had been attacked two nights earlier and was now in a coma.

"Do you know him?"

"Sort of. He's in my history class."

The awful incident was the major topic of conversation spreading throughout Lincoln high school. Teddy Wilkins had been jumped by a group of men wielding baseball bats while walking through a predominantly white neighborhood. It turned out that he had been dating the cousin of one of the guys, an ex-convict who didn't approve of the interracial relationship.

"It's a damn shame," said Howard. "You think stuff like this is ancient history, and then wham, there it is again. I better watch my back when I go home."

"Why would anyone mess with you?"

"An eye for an eye. I'm white, ain't I?"

"First off, the attack on Teddy was personal. It wasn't as if they picked out the first black guy who passed by. But even they had, what's that got to do with you? You weren't one of them."

"It doesn't matter," Howard responded. "I hear black people talking. They see Teddy as an example of how they're all treated. If he can stand for a whole race of people, so can I."

There was some truth to the statement. Tony had also heard threats of beating on random whites as retaliation for Teddy's death from black people who probably had nothing better to do anyway. Most likely they wouldn't amount to anything. But there was no denying that a generic hatred had been stirred up. Wide spreading ripples can reach calm waters far removed from where a stone has been tossed.

"What happened to Teddy was fucked up. But he wasn't standing for anyone but himself. Too many people believe there's a race war going on because the anchorman says there is. It's just for ratings."

Tony was starting to become as angry over people's reactions to the attack as he was about the attack itself. If one in five or even just one in ten whites was a bigot, many blacks assumed this of the balance as well. The actions of one obliterated contrary evidence displayed by the others. Statistically, the behavior of one fourth of his own people deemed them a blemish on the good name of society. Could the other three ever be judged fairly? When it came to race relations, why was the exception so often taken to be the rule?

"You're probably right to be a little nervous," he conceded. "I'm sure there are people who are eating this up. They have an excuse to be idiots now. There's something specific they can point to."

Tired of the news, he tried to find something a bit more rhythmic to listen to but came up empty. So many stations and not a single decent song to be heard. Nothing but commercials and DJ's babbling.

"I've had it up to here with this black versus white bullshit. Look at us. Do you see any war going on here?"

A familiar scent invaded the storeroom. Before Tony and Howard had time to react to it by looking busy, the smoker of the cigar spoke.

"No, I see two kids I'm paying to sit around and talk when I could be paying two other kids to actually do some work."

"Won't happen again, Mr. Jordan," said Howard, as he and Tony hastily got back to emptying cartons.

* * *

"Come on, cut it out. We have to study."

"Absolutely," said Tony, momentarily ceasing the baby kisses he had been planting on Janet's collar bone. Seconds later though, his lips returned to the nape of her neck.

"We're going to fail out of school if we don't learn this stuff," Janet said, but she didn't pull away as her ear was nibbled on.

"We'll do fine. I'm naturally brilliant and you'll become brilliant by osmosis."

Janet grabbed a pillow off the bed and hit Tony over the head with it. This was a significant day in their relationship, an event that fell into the category of firsts. Previously he had escorted her around the outskirts of his neighborhood, but never directly into the housing development that cast ominous shadows of despair over the enclosure of poverty, never home sweet home.

He had been apprehensive about inviting her, imagining that Janet would see the projects as a hail of soot coming down upon her unblemished coat of snow white fur. But he decided that if his fears turned out to be warranted, it was best to find out sooner rather than later.

Tony had watched her face carefully when she walked into the apartment. Shame briefly crept over him as he saw his home through her eyes. But she did not seem bothered by her surroundings at all. He was not in love with a snob.

This did not remove his other concern. If sober, his father might be tolerable. But all bets were off if he was drunk. Janet would then surely be given a rather unpleasant exhibition of her boyfriend's origins. He did not know what he would do if the beast of his nightmares emerged, but he was pretty sure how she would react. She would flee for her life, and from his.

As it turned out, the meeting was uneventful. Janet and his mother hit it off right away, as expected. His father mumbled hello and went into the kitchen. It was the best that could have been hoped for.

Tony and Janet engaged in a brief pillow fight. The battle soon gave way to a truce of kisses.

"I like your mom," she said when they came up for air. "She's really sweet."

"She likes you too. I can tell."

"Your father seems like the strong silent type."

"Strong definitely, but I wouldn't call him silent. Maybe his not talking today was an early birthday present. It's the best thing he's ever gotten me."

"You two don't get along?"

"That's putting it mildly."

He had never spoken in detail to her on this subject, neglecting to divulge his father's contempt for white people. This was the last thing he wanted to think of when with Janet. He preferred to save his confessions for sweet nothings whispered in her ear.

"Why not?" she asked.

"Let's just say we have different ways of looking at things."

"How so?"

"Exactly like I said. Now can't we think of something more interesting to talk about?" He returned to the lobe of her ear, for he knew it to be her most sensitive easy access spot. "Or do." They fell back onto the bed, thoughts of studying, fathers, or anything else gone from their heads.

"Cut that out!"

Tony and Janet sat up quickly, the latter making sure that her clothing had been left in order by caressing hands. Tony expected to find his father enraged at the sight before him. Instead he saw C.J. standing in the doorway with an amused grin on his face.

"Don't you ever knock?"

"It's my room too, remember?" C.J. took appraisal of Janet, whose face had turned red with embarrassment. His brother may have sold out, but at least he had gone to the highest bidder. Janet's picture had not done her justice. She was a beautiful girl.

"Hello," she said, trying to regain her composure.

"Janet, this is my brother C.J."

"Nice to meet you. I thought Tony had made you up, like he did with his other so called girlfriends. But you seem real enough, and you're not even inflatable."

Janet laughed. "Oh really. Is there anything else I should know about him?

“Well he is my brother, so I try not to dis him to his face. Tony, would you mind turning around?”

“Chris Rock you’re not”, Tony said, but he failed to suppress a smile.

“You two probably want to be alone. Janet, once you get tired of this guy, you know where I live.” C.J. grabbed a few items from his dresser drawer and then headed out, pausing to deliver a message before closing the door behind him. "Carry on."

"Your brother is not without charm. And he’s adorable."

"Oh, is he really?"

"Mmmm hmmm. Not as cute as his big brother though."

"You got that right." Tony leaned forward to thank her for the compliment, but she kept him at arm’s length.

"I better get going now."

"Do you have to?"

"Yeah. I promised my parents I wouldn't be home too late. Besides, once we're apart maybe we'll actually do some studying."

"I'd rather study anatomy, specifically yours."

"Tell me something I don't know."

After he had walked Janet out and a gypsy cab whisked her away, Tony began thinking about what was soon to take place upstairs. He had brought a white girl home. He had fallen in love with the enemy. He now officially stood for everything his father was against.

The inevitable confrontation was not feared. It was almost welcomed. Nothing had ever felt as right to him as Janet did, and he was willing to defend her at any cost. Defiance radiated from his pores as he crossed the threshold of his home.

"So that's your girlfriend," said Lionel right on cue from the comfort of his easy chair. He had no doubt been salivating over Tony's return, holding still like a Venus Flytrap in expectation of insect footsteps.

"Yep, that's her."

"I wish I could say it surprises me, but it doesn't."

"You didn't think I was gay, did you?" Some fun might as well be had before things got ugly.

"You know what I'm talking about. Couldn't you find yourself a black girl?"

"Sure I could have. But what difference does it make?"

"Cause then I'd have proof that you're not ashamed of who you are. That you aren't trying to be something other than a black man, like this one here who gave life to you."

Though it had been seen coming, in the end this didn't matter. His father attacked from right out in the open, yet still managed to hit every vulnerable area he thought he had covered. No amount of indignation could fully cover his Achilles heel.

"I'm not ashamed of who I am, Dad. I'm not ashamed of being black."

"How else do you explain Goldilocks?"

Something turned either on or off inside of Tony. Whatever it was, it caused his fear of repercussions to vanish. It abolished his already faded instinct to be respectful, annihilated his habit of proceeding with caution. The time had come to speak his mind. His father would not be spared a single syllable of what he had to say.

"You're the one I'm ashamed of. Want to know why? Because you're so resentful of other people that you have to hate them to feel better about yourself."

There would be no more trembling son before omnipotent father. Their stand off would be man to man.

"You're right, I *don't* want to be like that. I don't want to consider everyone who earns more money, or has more education, or whose skin is a different color than mine, an enemy."

Tony was used to being on the receiving end as his father pointed out one supposed fault after another. Now the scene was reversed and the emotional release bordered on exhilarating.

"I'll tell you who I *can* hate though. Someone who tries to fill me with anger, because that's all he's made of. Someone who tries to hold me back, to limit me, just so he doesn't have to feel inferior."

Lionel was rendered speechless. He seemed to be wondering if his senses were playing tricks, causing him to hear things that could not possibly have been said. But the unblinking eyes of his son were ample confirmation.

Tony had stood his ground and discovered that it would not crumble beneath him. He and his father were now on equal footing. The bully had been stood up to, and as bullies usually do, he had backed down.

Lionel rose from his chair and walked to the kitchen. There was an expression on his face never seen before. A wounded look. Then it struck Tony what had just happened. A corner had been turned, and there could be no going back. The relationship between he and his father, for better or for worse, was irreparably altered. It was as if he had given birth to a new life, not the one bequeathed to him by his mother and father, but one that was uniquely, completely, irrevocably his own.

CHAPTER FIFTEEN

Caren put the finishing touches on dinner, which once again consisted of leftovers amalgamated into a stew. Her and Tony's part time jobs were just enough to put low budget meals on the table and pacify the various utilities companies, but their rent was yet to be paid. She and Lionel feared that the next time their superintendent, Mr. Weldon, came to visit, it would be with an eviction notice.

On the night they squabbled over unpaid bills, Lionel did not enter their bedroom until after the sunlight of a new dawn had seeped in. Caren fell asleep assuming that her husband would go out drinking. But when he finally lay beside her, the scent of alcohol was neither heavy on his breath nor in his behavior. He had not left the apartment and consumed only one beer. Lionel wanted his mind clear to think, and that is what he did plenty of. Yet the only resolution he came up with was trying extra hard to fix things on his own. He would hit the pavement with a vengeance, perhaps find a new employer willing to give him an advance on his salary. His drinking was doing him no good, so he would cut down, maybe even quit altogether.

It was a fine plan. But each day passed as a clone of its predecessor. Lionel's earnestness did nothing to convince anyone to hire him, nor persuaded the hierarchy at the factory to give in to the employees' demands. His belief that these ordeals were best handled sober was short lived. He spoke very little of his daily lessons in humility, but his pain screamed out in the silence.

Caren headed to the sofa for a well deserved rest. She prayed her husband would return with good news for a change. This hope vanished the moment he walked into the apartment and slammed the door behind him.

"We've been replaced."

He spoke without passion, only resignation. Bad luck was as much a part of him as the flesh covering his bones.

"The beautiful part is, I went back to beg for that piece of shit job. Everybody saw me go in. They knew what I was about to do. They watched me stabbing them in the backs."

"Oh, Lionel."

He took off his coat and hung it up on the coat rack. When it immediately slipped off and fell to floor, he simply ignored it. He looked exhausted, about ready to collapse limply as if possessing no more spine than the coat. It wasn't a tiredness caused by lack of sleep, but rather, by lack of will to keep on fighting the good fight.

"But I went in anyway. I was going to join the scabs. What choice did I have? My family comes first, before solidarity, before pride. I didn't know their decision had already been made. And my boss didn't say a word. He waited until I was through degrading myself. Then he told me."

Lionel leaned his head against the wall. Caren draped her arms around him.

"It's going to be all right," she said.

"I tried to believe that, but I can't no more."

Caren held on tighter still to show her husband that he *could* still believe, that he must.

He returned her embrace. They let the encompassing warmth overcome them, swaying gently as if to the sultry intonations of Sarah Vaughan that they had fallen in love to long ago. If the moment could somehow be frozen, if everything but the feel of Caren's touch was banished from existence, then things would be okay after all. But of course this was not to be. A knocking at the door brought tenderness to an end and reintroduced reality. Slowly they let go of each other. Lionel opened the door and regretted it instantly.

"Hello, Mr. Weldon. How are you today?"

"To tell you the truth, not too well."

Shane Weldon walked, or to be more precise, waddled into the apartment. He had stopped growing upwards after barely clearing five feet. His body made up for this deficiency by spreading out from front to back and side to side.

"I'm sorry to hear that," Lionel said, his line of sight directed towards the super's chest.

"No need to be, Johnson, because you can remedy my situation. It seems some tenants have yet to pay this month's rent, not to mention last month's and over half of the month before. Guess who heads that list."

“Yes, I know. You see, I've been..."

"Save the speech, Johnson. I've heard it enough times. I didn't come here for lame excuses. I came to collect the rent. Do you have it?"

Mr. Weldon unselfconsciously probed one of his nostrils, then wiped the finger off on his pants. This was not an unfamiliar demonstration on his part. Yet as disgusting as the man's personal hygiene was, considerably more nauseating was his condescending demeanor. In his presence, Lionel was made to feel like a badly behaved child who had gotten caught in an improper act. Most white people in positions of authority diminished him in such a manner. With Weldon it was particularly humiliating, because the emasculation took place in his home, before his family. The very things Lionel tried hardest to hide were exposed; his forced subservience, his expendability, his failings as protector and provider.

"Not all of it," he answered.

"Do you recall signing a lease that says you owe rent, the full amount I might add, at the beginning of each month?"

"Yes I do. It's just that..."

"Save it, Johnson." Mr. Weldon put his hands in his pockets and looked around the room. "There are a lot of people who would love to have this apartment. People who would pay for it."

Lionel ached to tell the portly building manager who did double duty as superintendent what he could do with his lousy apartment, lousy building, lousy toupee that wouldn't have fooled a blind man, but he didn't say a word. He couldn't even bring himself to look him in the eyes.

"I'll tell you what I'm going to do," Weldon said. "I'm coming back at the end of the week. You either have every penny of the money you owe, or else have your things packed and ready to move out."

He surveyed his surroundings again, making a mental list of repairs to ready the place for its next tenants. The odds were long that he would perform any of them. He simply liked to make mental lists. After hiking up his ill-fitting pants, he left the unhappy couple in his wake.

Caren closed the door. She turned towards her husband, waiting for him to explode. The warning signs were there. His fists were clenched tightly and his dark eyes had grown as ominous as the portal to hell. But that was where it ended. There was no ranting and raving, no banging of fist against wall. Instead he remained curiously silent, and this made Caren more uneasy than his yelling ever had. She was wary of his yet to be expressed anger, understanding that the path being laid out for it was best to be avoided, whether or not she was its cause.

"Are you okay, honey?"

"Yeah, I'm fine."

"What are we going to do?" she asked, nervous about posing the question that might finally set him off, but knowing it had to be asked.

"I don't know. Maybe we start packing."

"Packing for where?"

No destination was provided, not even a shoulder shrug was offered.

"We have to do something."

If he agreed with his wife's summation, Lionel gave no indication of this. "I'm going to take a walk."

"Take a walk? Lionel, we have to decide what..."

"I'm going to take a walk," he repeated, soft in volume but firm in tone. "I need to clear my head. You do whatever it is *you need* to do."

"Promise me you won't go out drinking."

"What good is a promise from me?" Lionel bent to grab his coat from off the floor, but instead of straightening back up, remained hunched over. He held one hand to his stomach, the other firmly gripped the doorknob.

"Are you okay?"

His only reply was to sway unsteadily, hanging on to the door like a life preserver on a stormy sea. Caren saw that the pain was bad enough to bring tears to her husband's eyes. He released the doorknob and dropped to one knee.

"Lionel, what's the matter?"

He still didn't answer, but the pain seemed to be subsiding for his breathing was coming easier. Caren's head swiveled as she looked maniacally around the room, for what she wasn't quite sure. She often dealt with medical emergencies at the nursing home she worked at and had become expert at it. Despite her attempts not to become personally attached to people so close to death, many of them endeared themselves to her. When the grasp they each had on their long lives was at last being wrenched away, she reacted to these situations like a professional, but later mourned as a friend. Now she found herself completely unprepared, immobilized with concern for the man she loved.

"I'm going to call for an ambulance," she said, finally having determined a plan of action, yet momentarily clueless as to where the phone was.

"No need for that." Lionel rose unsteadily to his feet. He would have preferred to stay down a while longer, but wanted to reassure his wife that he was okay.

"Are you sure?"

"Yeah. It's not like they'll come rushing into this neighborhood. I'd be better off walking."

"Should I call a cab?"

"I'll be all right. Probably something I ate. I think I'll go lie down."

"Take some Pepto Bismol for your stomach first."

"I hate that stuff."

"You have to take something."

"Yeah, whatever."

The anticipated explosion had manifested itself as an implosion. Caren wondered why when things fell apart, they couldn't do so in an orderly fashion rather than all at once. Her philosophizing was kept brief because of the long list of items clamoring to be first in line for her to worry about. Since it now appeared that Lionel would be okay, her family's financial problems took top billing. Mr. Weldon could not be held off much longer. They needed to get their hands on rent money. She and Lionel were both aware of what needed to be done, but only she was willing to do it.

* * *

Tony looked up at the banner that had recently been hung on a wall within Lincoln High School. It read; "Get Better Soon, Teddy." Wishful thinking that according to the newspapers had little chance of coming true. Teddy Wilkins had not opened his eyes since the night he was repeatedly struck by a baseball bat for the folly of loving with his heart instead of his head.

Since the day of Janet's visit, Tony had been receiving the silent treatment from his father. But upon learning of the attack on Teddy, Lionel was unable to resist breaking it to say - "I guess times haven't changed as much as you thought."

"Before you cross all the way over, you better be sure of where you're going," had been C.J.'s comment on the matter.

Charlie was concise and unmindful that he was repeating himself. "Fucking white boys."

Even his mother and sister cautioned him. He knew they meant well, so refrained from responding that the only thing he had in common with Teddy Wilkins was French class.

"Sorry I'm late, sweetie."

He turned his attention from the banner to his girlfriend. "Did you get an extension?"

"Three more days." The exasperation in Janet's voice indicated that something was bothering her beyond the writing of a term paper.

"What's the matter?"

She was hesitant to reply. Tony guessed that she too had been assailed by warnings from well meaning and not so well meaning friends. He sensed that she wanted to admit to this, but wished for the words to somehow be spoken without having to take responsibility for them.

"Nothing really."

"Is there anything I can do to help?" Tony asked in attempt to gently coax her into speaking truthfully.

"No."

"Is that because *I'm* the problem?"

Janet sighed deeply. "It's nothing you've done."

"Okay. But is it something I am?"

"I don't understand what you mean."

It was Tony's turn to deeply exhale, but none of his frustration was expelled by the action. "I think you do."

They had been skirting the issue from early on in their relationship, putting it aside in hope that it would drift away. Instead it had grown too large to be met any other way but head on. The longer Janet remained silent, the more Tony worried that she did so for reasons he had better find out about.

"It's just that now that I'm not dating Roger anymore, I haven't been hanging out with my friends very much. They've been giving me a hard time about it."

"You forgot to mention that they can't stand me." He expected her to deny this, to hang on for as long as she could to a state of blissful ignorance. Instead she shrugged and offered the same half hearted explanation he had once taken for gospel, before losing his religion.

"You did get into a fight with him last year. I guess they feel like I've chosen you over them."

Seeing the banner for Teddy had triggered something. Tony suddenly found himself unwilling to leave sleeping dogs undisturbed. Let them awaken and bark and bite at will. Let matters be attended to and the consequences for them paid. One of them may have been starboard while the other was port, but he could no longer deny that he and Teddy Wilkins were in the same boat on the same stormy sea. Now it was Janet's turn to acknowledge reality.

"Is that all there is to this? Or are you leaving something out?"

She averted her eyes from his lie detector stare.

"Hey, Janet." The two of them turned towards Erin McRory, practically needing to shield their eyes from the glare off of her braces which preceded her path down the school hallway like headlights. She reminded Tony a little of the Raggedy Ann doll his sister used to play with. "Is it true?"

"Is what true?"

"I heard through the grapevine that you have a new boyfriend, someone here at Lincoln. How does he compare to Roger? Ever since junior high you've always ended up with the hottest guys."

"He's even hotter," Janet said, rolling her eyes with moderate subtlety. "And he's standing right in front of you. Erin, this is my boyfriend Tony."

"Oh. Really? Oh. Hi." Erin twirled one of her pigtails around a finger, then popped a strand of strawberry blonde hair into her mouth, no doubt to be ground to shreds by her metallic covered molars. Tony responded to her confused greeting and quickly worn welcome with a blank expression.

"I gotta get to band practice. Nice meeting you, Tommy. See you guys around, I guess."

Tony returned to the subject that had been at hand before they were interrupted by Janet's nitwit friend, who strangely enough, he now recalled was in two of his Honors classes. His father's words about book smarts versus common sense came to mind.

"Does me being black have anything to do with it?" he asked, wanting to believe he was mistaken, that Janet would laugh away his absurd reasoning. He demanded the truth while crossing his fingers for anything but.

Janet put a gentle hand to his cheek. No further response was necessary.

"Well, then fuck 'em"

"They're my friends. Some of them I've known since I was little."

"Then it's about time you got new friends."

"It's not that easy."

Tony could not understand her way of thinking. If the people she associated with were racists, she shouldn't want to be around them. It was that simple. Her choice was either him or them, and apparently he was not the automatic selection.

"No, I suppose the easy thing would be to listen to them. Break up with me and get back with Roger. Maybe that's for the best. After all, I don't want anyone using *me* for batting practice."

"You're blowing this way out of proportion. They aren't like that at all. It's just that ... It's just that some things take time to get used to."

"Like you dating a nigger?"

"Don't talk like that, Tony."

"Why not? Isn't that how they talk?"

"No, it isn't. And what does it matter how they talk? It only matters how *we* feel for each other. Doesn't it?"

His anger was softened by the logic and tenderness of her words. They helped him realize that he was playing right into the hands of those who were awaiting his first misstep. He was forgetting what was most important. He and Janet were meant to be together.

"I'm sorry. I know I'm trippin'. I love you so much. I don't want to lose you."

"You won't lose me."

"Promise."

"Scout's honor."

Tony marveled at the fragility of love as he pulled Janet into his arms and kissed her. She was his world. He could scarcely recall life before her, and regardless of how the idea nagged at him, refused to imagine one after.

CHAPTER SIXTEEN

C.J. prettied himself up before the bathroom mirror. He wore an intimidating scowl for most of the world, but had to look good for his girl. From the corner of his always alert eyes, he noticed that he was being observed through the open door. His mother's dour expression caused him to abandon the task at hand.

"What's up, Mom?"

"Nothing much, Carl. How are you doing?"

"It's all good."

"Is it really?" Caren asked somberly.

"Yeah."

His mother obviously had something she wanted to say, but seemed unsure of how to go about it. The gap between them went well beyond generational.

"It's been a long time since we had a good talk," she remarked, tentatively inching closer to the subject she wished to broach.

"I'm on my way out if that's what you have in mind. Did I do something?"

"No, I did. I let you raise yourself."

"What are you talking about, Mom?"

C.J. did in fact know what his mother meant, and began mentally preparing himself for the all too familiar lecture.

Caren took the bandanna from his hand. A parent's job was to make sure things like this didn't happen. But it did happen. She had failed her youngest child.

"I don't know a whole lot about what's going on with you nowadays. I'm not proud of that. But I do know that much of it isn't right."

"I'm just getting by. The same as everybody else."

"No, that isn't true. Everybody isn't getting by that way."

"It's basically a club, Mom. Just a bunch of guys hanging out, killing time, scoping girls. The usual stuff."

"If it's so easy for you to lie to your mother's face, I can't imagine what else you have no problem doing."

Tony and Lisa had accustomed C.J. to justifying himself, but his quick and ready answers were less effective against his mother's aura of disappointment. He wanted to take away her shame, but any such attempt was destined for failure. She would have to settle for only one perfect son, because he could never be what she hoped for.

Caren handed him back his colors. It was too late to change him. From as early on as when he first learned to walk, rather than heading towards the arms held out for him he would toddle off in whichever direction he saw fit. Whether or not he arrived safely at his chosen destination was a matter for the hands of God.

"I love you, Mom."

"You better, or else I'll kick your butt."

C.J. laughed along with her. She would always be his mom, no matter how often he let her down. Her unconditional love was a wondrous thing. He probably didn't deserve it, but he would take it. He gave her a kiss on the cheek as he headed out.

"Be good," she told him.

"I'll try."

"Promise?"

"I promise to try."

With that he was out the door, and though Caren didn't have much faith in his ability to resist the overwhelming temptations of the streets, she would have to make due with his word.

As he rode the elevator to ground level he pondered his mother's concerns. There had been no way to adequately explain to her that the Kaos Krew was like family to him. Stronger than family. The Krew did not judge him. They expected and demanded nothing but his loyalty. In return, they supplied him with an identity that may have been scorned by many, but could be regarded lightly by none. In a world where danger lurked indiscriminately around every corner, the Kaos Krew always had his back. They would kill or die for him without reflection or reservation.

When he joined, for the first time he felt like things were going his way. Maybe he wasn't a top student like his brother. He wasn't a big time jock or the most popular kid in school either. But when he was seen proudly bearing his colors, he was looked at with the respect that fear demands.

People urged him to leave the Krew because they believed this to be the only way to avoid tragedy. But as he saw it, all lives ended tragically. Might as well live fully, other people's opinions be damned, until the inevitable end came about.

Besides, if he did try to walk away from the Kaos Krew he would be deemed a traitor. No one quitted his set. Not unless his intention was also to quit breathing.

Neither his brain nor his heart felt inclined to follow the advice of loved ones. From their point of view, what they said made perfect sense. To his ears, it was gibberish. Not jail, nor the grave, nor a guilty conscience was enough to dissuade him. There were worse fates that awaited men. Life without living, without achieving, without mattering.

Everybody kept talking, and perhaps everybody was right. But there were all kinds of rights and all kinds of wrongs, and C.J. chose to live by those of his own choosing.

* * *

Tanya alternated between casually glancing through the notes she'd taken in class to prepare for tomorrow's French exam and studiously reviewing the latest issue of *Vibe* magazine for gossip about her favorite celebrities. After getting the scoop on which actors and musical artists were sleeping with each other, she put the magazine away and looked through her purse. From it she retrieved a stick of gum and a photograph. She popped the former into her mouth and gazed at the latter even more lovingly than she had at the photo shoot of L.L. Cool J in *Vibe*. It was a picture she had taken, and its subject was the man of her dreams and her waking hours. She had looked at the photo many times before, but never in this new light that shone upon it. Eric was no longer just some really cute guy, or merely the guy she was talking to, or simply her boyfriend. He was the man she had given herself completely to, the man with whom her tumultuous journey from girl to womanhood was shared. Eric was her lover, the only first she would ever have.

Someone knocked at the door. Tanya put the photograph back into her purse and got up to let in her visitor.

"Hey, Pookie."

"Hi Daddy. What's up?"

"Nothing much. I have some free time, so I thought I'd relax at home for a while. I have an interview in an hour. Making doughnuts of all things." Lionel sat down on his daughter's bed and Tanya took a seat beside him.

"Think you're going to get it?" she asked.

"No, not really."

"Come on, Daddy. You have to go in there expecting to get the job. When they see how confident you are, they'll have to hire you."

Lionel smiled. When his offspring were young children he doted on each of them, was captivated by watching the world being discovered through their new eyes. As they grew up and the wonders of the world became old hat, his paternal affection decreased proportionately. Only with Tanya did he continue to feel comfortable in the role of nurturer. He loved his sons no less, but found it more difficult to show. Perhaps his sons were seen as truer reflections of his own flawed self, whereas Tanya reminded him of gentler qualities, particularly those he had become enamored of in Caren. He did not give excessive thought to this for the same reason he didn't contemplate much why the sky was blue or the grass green.

"If you say so, I'll have to try it. How come you're not in school?"

"The juniors are at Great Adventure today. I didn't feel like going."

"You have something against class trips?"

"No."

"Something against amusement parks?"

Tanya shrugged her shoulders.

"Then level with me. Why would you choose to sit around at home instead of going out and having fun with your friends?"

"I just figured the money could be spent in better ways."

Tanya had not intended to throw salt in her father's wounds, but succeeded in doing so nonetheless.

"You should have asked me," he said. "I don't want you to stop having fun because you think we can't afford it. I want to pamper my princess."

Tanya smiled. It wasn't meant to be patronizing, but Lionel could not help perceiving it that way. They both knew he was in no position to pamper anyone.

He looked around the room, taking stock of the collection of men who graced his daughter's walls. It seemed that just yesterday ponies and kittens had been up there.

"I guess you're not so little anymore. All the boys must be chasing after you. You look just like your mom when she was your age. How are things going with that boyfriend you had so much trouble saying goodnight to?"

"Okay."

"He treating you right?"

"Yes, Daddy."

The truth was that Tanya had no idea what to make of the way Eric was treating her. She only knew that things weren't the same between them. It was barely seventy two hours after her virginity was surrendered when the first sign of trouble appeared.

On that day, Eric swore up and down that she was responsible for the hickey on his neck. She did not recall creating the incriminating mark of passion, but since it was not outside the realm of possibility, she decided to let the matter slide. A few days later, however, word reached her ears that he had been seen hanging out with his ex-girlfriend.

Once again she forced herself not to rush to judgment. Rumors floated constantly around their school. Many proved to be nothing but nonsense. She knew that other girls had their eyes on Eric and would resort to any tactic to free him up. Accusing him falsely would not be beneath them, all being warlike in love.

But there were also clues not as visible to the eye or audible to the ear, yet no less piercing to the heart. She had expected that making love with Eric would cement their relationship. Instead, he seemed to have begun distancing himself immediately after his final heave on top of her. As he lay gathering his breath, passion spent and body no longer taut, he may as well have committed murder rather than sex. Though the loss was not tangible, the musky air was permeated by the thought that something had just ended rather than begun. When he looked at her from that point on, it was not as he used to. When he spoke to her, the depth of tenderness in his voice was not as it had once been. Tanya did not speak to him of these things, for they were too vague to substantiate. She could discover no proof, yet could not shake the suspicion that her foothold in paradise was already lost.

"So, you up for a game of Gin?" Lionel asked.

"Sure."

He shuffled the deck found on top of her bureau and dealt them each a hand. The game commenced.

"How did you know you loved Mom?" Tanya asked as she surveyed her cards. "How did you know she was the one?"

Lionel smiled resignedly. His baby girl wanted to talk about love. The days of piggyback rides and lollipop bribes definitely belonged to the past. He was no longer the main man in her life, merely the one to whom all future suitors would be compared. This would have to do. He considered the question at hand, then answered it.

"I woke up one morning and thought about my future with her in it or out of it. I decided life would go on either way, but in only one version would I be happy."

"That sounds like a good reason."

"It must have been. She's still putting up with me. Now what makes you ask such a question? Are you in love with this Eric fellow?"

"I guess so."

"Guessing has nothing to do with it. Save hunches for multiple choice questions or the race track. Places where you can afford to be wrong."

Tanya's surrender to Eric's pleas was based on what she now feared had been a false assumption. She believed that once her love was expressed in the manner he required, he would return that love in the form she needed. But if his feelings were based on conditions, did this not prove them to be something other than love?

Matters of the heart were proving to be very confusing. She wondered if this must be so, or if people unnecessarily complicated things with their desires, vices, insecurities, and the rest of the junk they dragged into relationships. Was love ever easy for anyone? If less complicated, would this make it less appreciated? Perhaps love was difficult for good reason. Perhaps everything on God's green earth was the result of a flawless plan, even that which seemed most muddled.

"That was deep, Daddy."

"All fathers are deep. You just have to ask what you want to know. But I suppose I'm not always so understanding. You forgive me?"

"Yes, I forgive you for being a bonehead sometimes."

"Hey, that's not what I said."

"But that's what you meant."

"Yeah, I guess I did", Lionel conceded. "You know, if I get this job today..."

"When you get it."

"When I get it, with my first paycheck I'm going to take you shopping for something pretty. Whatever you want. Or maybe I'll take the family to Great Adventure."

"It's a date."

"I once thought I would give my family whatever money could buy. I didn't want you guys to miss out on anything."

"That's okay, Daddy. Everything will be all right. You're going to get that job and bring home more money and doughnuts than we can stand."

Lionel pantomimed pulling off Tanya's nose and placing it in his pocket. She made a mock frown, so he put it back in place.

"Daddy."

"Yes. You have another question about love?"

"No. I have something to say."

"What is it, honey?"

"Gin."

* * *

The restaurant was teeming with ravenous appetites. An equal number of hungry people stood salivating on line outside, staring through the window at diners they were anxious to replace. Waiters and waitresses rushed about to keep the assembly line eating experience running smoothly. They succeeded in creating a cheerfully raucous atmosphere, so long as bellies were filled and post meal wetnaps were provided.

"What do you think?" Charlie asked above the din, wiping barbecue sauce from his chin.

"You were right, she's pretty hot." Tony grabbed a handful of onion rings from the pyramid of them at the center of the table. "Damn I love these things. This place was a great choice."

"I told you it was the joint. Where else can you get dinner for two in Manhattan for under ten bucks? I take all my dates here."

"I give credit where it's due," Tony said. "You did good."

"No one knows cheaper ways to get laid than I do. I should write a book."

"Just make sure it has plenty of pictures if you want Taneshia to understand." Tony nearly choked from laughing at his own humor while wolfing down grease-laden ringlets.

"That's fucked up, man. Do I rag on your girl?"

"If Janet's IQ was lower than a bowl of soup, I'd expect you to dog her out. Hell, I'd require it. But you wouldn't catch me in public with a girl who thinks a condiment is a form of birth control."

"She was joking."

"Yeah, right. Face it, Charlie. She's fine and all, but she ain't too quick."

"Maybe she just can't cook."

They were still laughing when their dates returned to the table.

"What's so funny?" Janet asked.

"You had to be there," said Tony. "Let me ask you two a question. Why do girls always go to the bathroom together?"

"To talk about their dates, silly."

"I hope you weren't too hard on Charlie. This is his first time out since the operation."

"You didn't tell me you were sick," Taneshia said.

Tony and Janet forced themselves not to look at one another, or else the laughter they were constraining would erupt.

"I was kidding", he said. "He was born looking that way."

"Huh?"

Janet kicked Tony in the shin and buried her face in her napkin. Tony shoved more onion rings into his mouth.

Charlie's quest to seduce Taneshia had been going on for over two months. Upon first meeting her, he was floored by her beauty and convinced she would be an easy conquest. Her beauty was undeniable, but it turned out that she was as chaste as she was slow witted. Having his intellectual standards, although they were quite malleable, he was anxious to break up with her because she fell far short of them. But not until his mission was accomplished. He had spent many hours listening to her innumerable thoughts about fashion when all he wanted was to get her undressed. There had to be a well deserved reward at the end of his long journey of mind numbing conversation and ten dollar meals.

"I love your necklace, Taneshia," said Janet.

"Thanks. I bought it at a flea market uptown, right by my school. They have a lot of cute stuff."

"What school would that be?" asked Tony. Taneshia was slightly older than Charlie. Thinking of which institutions of higher learning were in uptown Manhattan, Columbia University sprung to mind. If that was her answer, he decided he would launch a thorough investigation into their admissions process.

"Ralston Academy. It's like Barbizon."

"So you're an aspiring model?"

"Uh huh", answered Taneshia, seeming uncertain of her answer. Tony guessed that the word aspiring had thrown her. He wondered if she thought it meant sweating on one's ass.

"I knew a girl who tried to become a hand model," he said. "She didn't get any work because she had no thumbs."

Charlie smacked his forehead. "What do you see in this guy?" he asked Janet.

"It makes you wonder, doesn't it?" she teased.

"Why did she want to be a hand model then?" asked Taneshia.

Tony studied her expression intently, praying she was matching his admittedly corny joke with one of her own. The only thing found in her eyes was earnest desire for an answer to her question.

"I don't know. I guess some people aren't too bright."

He and Janet spent the rest of the meal playing footsie, gazing affectionately at each other, and devouring their high cholesterol meal. They anxiously looked forward to being alone so they could devour each other. Taneshia went on about her modeling plans while Charlie feigned interest and urged her to finish her oversized pina coloda. He was hoping that alcohol and sugar would accomplish what his charm had been unable to.

"I need to drain the weasel," said Charlie towards the end of the meal. "Care to join me, Tony?" he asked, mimicking the previous joint trip by Janet and Taneshia.

"I think I can squeeze out a few drops. Don't miss me too much," he said to Janet.

"Don't ask for the impossible."

For Tony, this night had been the perfect antidote to the stress of the past several weeks. He felt as if he and Janet were under a microscope, their relationship watched for the first sign of collapse. The world seemed to be rooting against them on general principle. Good times with good friends put such thoughts out of mind, at least temporarily.

“Don't miss me too much either," Charlie said, but Taneshia was too busy wolfing down her corn bread to answer him.

"I better hit that tonight," he said on the way downstairs to the restrooms. "I've waited long enough."

"Good luck," Tony responded with total sincerity. He wanted things to work out for Charlie as well as they had for himself. Taneshia was clearly not the great love of his life, but at least she had proved useful in distracting him from his ex. He could do better than both Sheila and Taneshia, and eventually he would. Good fortune reached most everyone in due time, and it just so happened that in the arena manned by Cupid, Tony had beaten his friend out in landing a one-in-a-million kind of girl.

"Janet's all right."

"She's great, ain't she?"

"Any girl who appreciates the beauty of Scarface earns points in my book,” said Charlie in reference to an earlier topic of conversation. “I need to find me a girl like that."

"Taneshia doesn't like Scarface?"

"Taneshia needs a dictionary to watch a Disney flick."

Tony laughed. "She does have a great body though, which is pretty amazing considering how much she eats."

"No it's not. She pukes on purpose after almost every meal."

"You're shitting me."

"I shit you not."

"Well, she just wants to look good for her man. The things we do for love."

"The things we do for a blow job," said Charlie as he and Tony approached adjacent urinals. "Then again, same difference."

* * *

Caren nervously twirled a strand of her hair in one hand and held the telephone receiver in the other until the dial tone died and an automated voice advised her to hang up and try again. This was easier said than done. She had been trying again for the last ten minutes. She almost gave up on the task entirely, then remembered that surrender was not an option and marched right back to the phone. Dialing the required eleven digits was the most difficult, heart wrenching thing she'd ever had to do. It would stir up a hornet's nest, and she was the one guaranteed to be stung. Nevertheless she obeyed the instructions, hanging the phone up, bringing it back to her ear and mouth, and finally summoning the courage to place her call.

"Hello," answered the voice on the other end of the line.

"Manny, this is Caren."

"Caren! Great to hear from you. It's been too long."

"Yes it has. How are things with you guys?"

"Ah, couldn't be better. How are things in the Bronx?"

"Well, you know. Things are tough all over, why should we be left out?" It was difficult for Caren to be patient with small talk when there was such big conversation to get to.

"This is Tony's last year in high school, right? Is he thinking about college?"

"He wants to go. That's kind of a sore topic around here. He and Lionel don't see eye to eye."

"So I take it my brother hasn't changed much. Not that I expected different. They don't come any more stubborn than Lionel."

"I suppose not."

"Last time I saw him, I was really hoping we would be able to put the past behind us. But he likes it up front."

"Like you said, he's a stubborn man."

"I walked out of Angie's house swearing I was through with him. But I'll always hope the next time might be the charm."

Caren was half listening, half envisioning Lionel's reaction once he found out about this call. Maybe it wasn't worth it. She could end the conversation now and ... And be out on the streets.

"So what's up?"

Caren crossed herself as she had been doing her whole life in hope of things that usually didn't heed the pious gesture. Then she bluntly answered Manny's question.

"The reason I called is because Lionel is out of work. Unless we get some money fast, we're going to be evicted from our home."

"I see. Well we can't let that happen. I'm curious about something, though. It isn't my brother's style to have others do his dirty work for him. Does he know you're calling?"

"No, he doesn't," Caren admitted.

There was a pause from Manny's end that seemed to last a thousand years. Caren was about to ask if he was still there, genuinely afraid he was not, when his voice reappeared.

"It would be no problem to put a check in the mail or have someone deliver the money to you. But I'm not going to do that."

Caren couldn't believe her ears. She was being refused. Her last shot had been a blank.

"Lionel is going to face me, and we're going to settle things between us once and for all."

"What are you saying, Manny?"

"I'm saying your husband is about to be paid a visit from his brother, and this time I'm not going to let him push me away."

"Nothing would make me happier," Caren said, a sigh of relief silently exhaled. "But you know how he is," she then hastened to remind her brother-in-law.

"Yes, well I can be as hard headed as him if necessary. I've put this off long enough. Like it or not, we're family. It's time we started acting that way."

Caren had done it. She had saved the day, kept a roof over her family's head, betrayed her husband. There was nothing left to do but batten down the hatches in preparation for the storm.

CHAPTER SEVENTEEN

Tanya scanned the lunchroom, but Eric was nowhere to be found amongst the bustling student body. There appeared to be little cause for concern on the faces that passed by, but for Tanya such lightness of spirit belonged to a distant past. Recent days had been marked by a succession of broken promises on Eric's part. Try as she might to remain optimistic, it was getting close to impossible not to believe the worst.

"What's up, beautiful?"

She turned to regrettably face Darryl Monroe. He had been hitting on her since the first day of school in their freshman year. At the time he sported a wispy moustache, or rather, about a third of a moustache. Her current relationship status had not changed his behavior any, and the intervening years had neither enhanced the development of his facial hair nor discouraged his attempts to woo her. She usually tried to keep conversation with him to a minimum, but since he and Eric were in the same class before lunch, she asked if he knew where her boyfriend might be found.

"There is more to life than Eric, you know."

"Does that mean you haven't seen him?"

"I didn't say that."

"Then you have."

"Maybe," Darryl said coyly. "But maybe you don't really want to know where he is."

"Trust me, I do."

He remained in flirt mode, fingering the scant hairs over his upper lip, unaware or simply not caring that she had even less patience for him today than usual.

"What do you see in a guy like him? You need a man who will be good to you, a brotha who will treat you right."

"Where is he, Darryl?"

"Room 304", he finally answered with an unsettling grin.

Tanya headed off at a brisk pace to find out why Eric had stood her up. By the time she reached the third floor she was trotting nervously, not fully understanding her anxiety, but not questioning it either. She stopped and peeked through the little window in the door of the specified classroom. Nothing was seen but scribblings on the chalkboard and a row of empty seats. It seemed that Darryl was playing a juvenile practical joke. She opened the door and stepped into the room.

That was when she saw them. Up against the wall. The girl's blouse halfway unbuttoned. Eric's hands and his lips doing things to a stranger that were supposed to be reserved for her. Tanya burned to halt what was going on before her eyes, but was powerless to do anything but masochistically stare.

At last they stopped. Eric looked straight at her, yet didn't say a word. The silence was maddening.

"How could you?"

A hint of remorse may have been accepted as the deepest apology. A simple "I'm sorry, I'll never do it again", may have been enough for him to earn forgiveness. This would never be known, because the words never came.

"I don't know what to say," was all he could come up with.

The girl, who was not even the ex-girlfriend Tanya had heard too much about but someone else altogether, quickly left the room. She did not want to be the victim of a jilted lover's violent reaction. Tanya waited for a more in-depth explanation.

"Look, it wasn't meant to be." No signs of guilt or regret were displayed. "Don't get emotional on me."

"How could you?" Tanya repeated, her needle stuck on this one agonizing question.

"I didn't plan to do it like this, but I guess it's for the best." Eric reflexively started to turn his cap, but Tanya snatched it off his head and threw it to the floor.

"I never mattered to you, did I?"

"Look, I didn't buy you a fucking diamond ring. We had some good times, some real good times, but you're the one who wanted to get all serious."

The advice of Cheryl rang in Tanya's ears. Cheryl had seen little reason for holding out, but neither did she feel that love was the proper motivation for sex. As she saw it, sex was something which provided pleasure on occasion, but even more frequently was useful as a tool to obtain gratitude from boys eager to please and to spend. It was simply a game to her, and as with all games, it was most fun when not taken too seriously. Her body was the playing piece, but her heart stood far removed from the scene.

This was what Cheryl had learned about sex to date, but she was unable to persuade Tanya of the merits of her mindset. The role of teacher was reserved for Eric, who taught without compassion.

He bent down and picked up his cap, checking it for dirt. It was one of many he owned. To Tanya it was now obvious that they were more cherished and respected by him than she ever was.

"Okay, so I played along," he confessed. "I said what I had to in order to get me some."

"You asshole."

"That's good, get it out of your system."

She followed his directions and slapped him across the face. "I hate you." Eric put up a hand in defense of further strikes, but this was unnecessary. Tanya realized that any pain she could inflict would be meager in comparison to that which she was feeling.

"Your cherry was going to be popped eventually. And you know you wanted to hit it as much as I did, probably more. You came to my door, remember? So don't act like I stole something. We both got what we wanted."

"How can you say that? How can you be so cruel?" Tanya felt tears beginning to form, but held them in. She would not give him the satisfaction. He had been given enough.

"I can say it because it's true. I'm not ready to be with just one girl. You're fly and all, but so are a whole lot of honeys. No hard feelings, okay? Catch you later, babe."

With that he was gone. Tanya was left with nothing more to say or do, other than allow her tears to fall freely.

* * *

The second floor of an abandoned tenement building, ravaged one year earlier by a suspicious fire, was what the Kaos Krew called home. When vacant, the charred ruins were guarded by the gang's pitbull, Man-eater. Though bred to be vicious, unlike his masters he held no animosity towards others based solely on what they wore. He was the only one amongst them who was color blind. But like the rest, he was trained to attack on command. The members of the Kaos Krew were sitting on the floor in a semi-circle, except for Louis, who stood before his reverent flock.

"This is it, guys. Time we give the Dawgs what they've been asking for."

The rest of the Krew roared their approval of the plan, rousing Man-Eater from his sleep. As they quieted down, a knock was heard. Not just any knock, but their coded signal. Three taps, then two taps, then three again. Everyone who was supposed to be there was accounted for. Louis, knife in hand, opened the door cautiously. Standing on the other side with an ear to ear smile was Tyrone.

Louis lifted him from the ground with his hug. "Tyrone, what the hell are you doing here?" he asked happily.

"You know I wouldn't miss this for the world. It's judgment day."

The members of the Kaos Krew came up and greeted him one by one. C.J. was last in line.

"What's up, homey?"

"I'm just psyched about kicking some Dawg ass."

"How'd you get released so early? I thought you were supposed to be laid up for at least another week. And how did you get out of your house? I figured your parents would have you under lock and key."

"My parents don't know I'm out. The hospital probably doesn't even know yet."

"You broke out?"

"I had to. When you told me we were going to take out the Raw Dawgs today, I went crazy thinking I wouldn't be there. I had to get my payback."

"But aren't you still hurt?"

"Never felt better. It'll take a lot more than one measly hole in the chest to stop me."

"Are you sure you're up to this, man?"

"Of course he's sure," said Louis, coming over and putting his hand on Tyrone's shoulder. "I'm proud of you, Little T." Tyrone beamed from his leader's words of praise.

Today was the end of the small time. Once their primary rivals were taken care of, their rule would be uncontested. The Kaos Krew paid little heed to those who supposedly controlled their neighborhood. They felt nothing but disdain for landlords, store owners, politicians, and especially cops, who were considered to be nothing more than a better funded gang. The boys in blue thought they called the shots, but were deluding themselves. The streets belonged to those most intimate with them.

Even if the Krew was wrong about today, the day was sure to come soon. Louis intended for them to get serious. Serious meant guns, semi-automatic weapons that killed indiscriminately, as easy to obtain as chewing gum once the right connection was made. Their enemies would have to be taught, if not today easy then tomorrow hard, that fun and games were over. Ruthlessness was required to obtain and sustain a monopoly. They needed to stake their claim now. There were too many dollars at stake to fool around any longer.

The Kaos Krew charged forth, avoiding by second nature the stairs their feet would go straight through, and emerged from the building with savage intentions. First the sun's rays struck. Fast on its heels were the Raw Dawgs.

It took place with great speed and efficiency, leaving little room for reaction. The Dawgs had been waiting for them, a perfectly planned and executed sneak attach. This would be their day.

C.J. felt an intense wave of pain in the back of his head as it was struck. And then, nothing.

* * *

"Awesome dinner, Mom," said Tony, shoveling food into his mouth as quickly as his hand and digestive system would allow. "Does this mean Dad got a new job?"

"Not exactly, but things are looking up."

Tony did not bother to question why this was so. He was too excited about having something besides the stew his mother had been making and re-making every day. The only thing he could think about was clearing his plate for seconds.

Caren was pleased to see her son's enjoyment of the meal. It felt good to do some genuine home cooking for her family. There were far more vital matters on her mind than food though. She walked into the living room just as her husband was entering through the front door.

"He been here yet?"

For a moment Caren thought Lionel somehow knew about her call to Manny, but then she realized that he was talking about their superintendent.

"No, not yet. How did it go today?"

"Same as every other day. Nobody is hiring. Nobody's hiring me, anyway. You think we'll be able to talk him into giving us more time?"

Caren didn't answer. She just lowered her eyes sheepishly, waiting for the chaos she had conjured to materialize.

"No, I don't think so either." Lionel walked into the kitchen and took in the sight of his son gorging himself.

"Great to have a real meal again," said Tony between bites.

Lionel grabbed a can of beer from the fridge. He wondered why his wife had decided to splurge after being so frugal the past several weeks. She must have decided to make their last dinner in this apartment a good one. Still, they were going to need every penny they had. The YMCA wasn't free, and God willing, they would be able to avoid ending up in the places that were. He walked back into the living room. Before he could ask Caren about the food, a knock at the front door redirected his steps.

He cleared his throat for the verbal tap dance he was about to perform that would hopefully buy a little leniency. Then he opened the door and instead of Mr. Weldon, he found the one person whose presence was even less desired.

"What the hell are you doing here?"

"I was in the neighborhood and thought I'd stop by," Manny answered, a little less assuredly than he had planned to sound. He would never grow accustomed to the high powered blasts of anger that came from Lionel. Absence would almost make him forget how fervently his brother hated him. But Lionel was always quick to remind him whenever their paths crossed, or rather, collided.

"Well you've just been uninvited."

"I've come a long way. You can at least show me some hospitality."

Lionel looked back at Caren. "You couldn't respect my wishes, could you?"

"Don't blame your wife for my being here. I invited myself. Thought you might want to catch up."

Lionel turned towards his brother like an exasperated lion on its unsuspecting trainer. Manny did what a man is supposed to do when trapped by a beast of far greater strength. He stood perfectly still and hoped to be left in one piece.

"I don't want you in my home. You're not welcome here. Have I made myself clear?"

"You never had any trouble in that area." Manny straightened his tie, because he figured that a casual gesture would give the appearance that he was more comfortable than he actually was. Then it occurred to him, not entirely comically, that he may have inadvertently tipped his brother off to the easiest way to wring his neck.

"Then why are you still here?"

"Because we need to talk."

"I don't know or care what *you* need to do, but *I* don't need to do a damn thing. This is my home. That's my doorway you're standing in. If Caren gave you the impression that we wanted you to come here, then I'm afraid you've been misled. Nothing has changed. It's time for you to do what you do best. Turn around and leave."

Had he taken his brother's advice, Manny would have walked right into Shane Weldon. The super ignored Manny's presence and got directly to the business he had come to settle.

"Well Johnson, you have my money?"

Manny took an envelope from his breast pocket and placed it into the greasy hand that was held out. "Here you go."

Weldon scrutinized the well dressed man giving him money and recognized the strong resemblance to his deadbeat tenant.

"I take it you two are related."

"I'm Lionel's brother."

"Is that right? Pleasure doing business with you, Mr. Johnson. By the way, that's a mighty fine looking suit."

"Thank you," said Manny, turning to face Lionel again. Seeing that he had been dismissed, Weldon headed to the elevator, refraining from probing his nose until after the doors began to close.

"I suppose you expect me to be grateful, *Mister* Johnson." Lionel had neither missed nor appreciated how his brother commanded instant respect from Weldon. This was accomplished easily enough by a custom fitted suit and an expensive watch casting its gleam on manicured fingernails that held out hundreds of dollars as if it was pocket change. Lionel and Manny were both surnamed Johnson, but only Manny earned the right to be referred to as “mister”, to be seen as a man.

"I owe you much more than a few dollars."

Lionel glared curiously at Manny for this was the first time he had ever admitted to owing him anything.

"So, may I come in?"

"If you think paying my rent earns you an invite, think again. You should have held on to your money."

It was difficult to keep from being drawn into a war of words with Lionel. Manny wasn't accustomed to being assaulted without fighting back. It was his nature to dismantle an opponent's attack. He had come prepared to grovel, but pride was an instinct not easily overcome.

"You really get off on thinking of me as the enemy, don't you? As long as I'm the bad guy, you don't have to account for anything. I get to take the blame for everything."

Lionel took a step forward. Manny stalwartly held his ground.

"Let's get this straight. I don't blame you to feel better about myself. I don't blame you because I've got nothing better to do. I blame you because you deserve to be blamed."

Manny sped recited the Greek alphabet in his head, his version of counting to ten in order to keep from responding rashly. As usual, Lionel had gotten to him. But this time would be different. He would be patient and let his brother's emotions run their course while keeping his own in check. Then the two of them could finally move beyond the accusations and denials and counter attacks.

"I know I'm at fault," said Manny in the tone he usually reserved for distraught clients. "That's why I've come here. To ask for your forgiveness."

"For somebody with a law degree, you sure ain't too bright." Lionel continued to guard his doorway with the discipline of a Roman sentry. "I didn't ask for your help, and I don't want your lame attempt at an apology either."

"Then what do you want? Tell me what it is and I'll do it."

"You can stay the fuck out of my life. And you can burn in hell." Lionel shoved past his brother on the way out to wherever he suddenly felt compelled to be.

"Lionel!" Caren called out to her husband's tensed back. She received no reply but the slam of a door as he entered the building's stairwell.

Manny finally stepped into the apartment.

"Don't worry, Caren. He'll be back. And I'll be here waiting for him."

CHAPTER EIGHTEEN

The Johnson's kitchen was taken over by the drool inducing scents of goat meat drenched in curry sauce; tender slices of ham; baked macaroni and cheese; candy sweet coleslaw; and rice browned by beans and seasoning. This was a standard special occasion meal in their household, usually reserved for Thanksgiving, Christmas and Easter. The avoidance of eviction ranked high enough to warrant a holiday feast. Lionel had not yet returned, Caren was in the living room on a phone call, Tanya claimed not to be feeling well and had taken a plate of food into her room, and C.J. was still out roaming the streets. This left only Manny and Tony at the dinner table.

"I always did love your mother's cooking," said Manny in between generous mouthfuls. "Not that I've had many opportunities to sample it."

"I haven't had much chance myself lately," said Tony to the man he so much admired. His uncle had garnered achievements of heroic proportions. He started out with nothing but dared to yearn for all the world had to offer, and the daring paid off.

"Things have been tough around here, huh?"

"Yeah, you could say that." Tony did not bother to elaborate. "How's the practice going?"

"It's going well. Very well actually. I was recently made a full partner."

"That's awesome. Congratulations."

"Thanks," said Manny without recognizable enthusiasm. "I've been fortunate. A lot of wonderful things have come my way."

"You've earned them."

Manny lowered his head. The last thing he needed was praise. Being in Lionel's home was a potent reminder of how tainted his own achievements were, and of how meager his brother's had turned out to be. A new topic was needed.

"So, you have a girlfriend?"

Tony's smile answered the question in advance of the words he spoke.

"Yeah. Her name is Janet."

"Is it serious?"

"As Romeo and Juliet."

"I hope you come to a better end than they did."

"We will. Janet is amazing. She's beautiful, and smart, and creative, and sweet, and funny, and did I mention beautiful? She's everything I ever wanted."

Manny held his tongue rather than warn his nephew about the dangers of going after your fondest desires. It was his experience that life worked under the same guidelines as a capitalistic society. In order to get what you wanted, it was usually necessary to give up something in return. Sometimes gaining what you defined as everything meant losing what you most needed.

"What are your college plans?"

Tony brightened at the prospect of discussing yet another of his favorite subjects. It was a rare treat to be in the company of someone who was openly supportive of his goals.

"I'd like to major in business, probably finance. I have pretty good grades and kicked butt on the SAT's, so I'm hopeful for scholarships from some decent schools."

"I hear you and Lionel don't see eye to eye on your plans."

"You heard right."

"I know it's hard to make sense of. I'll put in a good word for you while I'm here."

"Thanks, Uncle Manny. I don't think it will do much good, though. I gave up on changing my dad's mind a long time ago. When the time comes, I'm just going to do what's best for myself. I don't need his blessing or his support. You can't miss what you never had."

Manny recognized an earlier version of himself. His children were still quite young, their personalities not yet fully formed, but it was clear enough that they both favored the traits of their mother over his own. Tony possessed much ambition and tenacity, which would bode well for him in life, but no doubt worked against him within the confines of home. Manny understood as he listened to his nephew and heard the discontent beneath the surface of his words that Tony must have been having a difficult time being his father's son. He and Lionel were two trains running in opposite directions on the same track, neither of them willing to give way. The outcome would be messy.

"Your father has had some tough breaks. When your dreams slip away it's hard not be angry about it."

"So he blames you."

"I'm probably number one on the list."

"But not the only one," Tony said, eager to censure his father now that he had found a pair of sympathetic ears to vent into. "He blames white people for holding him down. He blames me for pretty much anything he can think up. Mainly for not buying into his line of bullshit."

"Hey!" exclaimed Manny in a forceful tone much too reminiscent of Lionel's. "Show some respect. Your father has his faults the same as anyone, but he has always put other people's needs ahead of his own, especially family. That's a rare and laudable thing. He's who you came from and who has gotten you this far, and that's no bullshit. That's something you need to keep in mind."

Manny regretted the intensity of his reprimand immediately. Tony did not deserve to be attacked for his feelings. He was not responsible for the way things were, merely a victim of the aftereffects.

Ordinarily, whatever Manny said to his nephew was treated as solemnly as a biblical commandment. But in this matter, Tony was by no means a compassionate jury easily swayed by a passionate closing argument. His perspective was a decidedly hostile one, and not even the verbal gymnastics of his uncle could bring him around.

"I do keep that in mind. But the way I see it, good men don't get drunk off their ass every night. They don't smack their wives around. They don't belittle their sons for having their own opinions and their own plans."

The more he spoke, the more he realized he had to say. Not a single ill feeling would remain on his chest. He did not need to be reminded from whom he came. Every day he tried to forget.

"He wants you to feel bad about doing better for yourself than he did. Why should you? You're where you are because of who you are, and the same goes for my dad. You chose to work for what you wanted while he chooses to complain about what hasn't been handed to him. I know you don't need me to tell you this, but sometimes I need to remind myself. You hear something often enough, it gets hard not to believe it after awhile. But I won't. I won't believe his lies, and I won't feel guilty that I don't."

Rising emotions had stolen Tony's appetite, but nothing could confiscate his feeling of righteousness.

"He thinks he can change me, that he can break me with his put downs. But I wear them like a badge of honor. The less he thinks of me, the better a man I must be."

Manny was stunned mute. Far deeper wounds had been inflicted than he had been prepared to mend. Lionel's disappointment and disillusionment had acted as tetanus to his family's bloodstream.

His piece said, Tony got up and left the kitchen as his mother entered. Someone was at the front door. If his father was back then he would certainly be drunk and agitated, always a lethal combination. The door opened and C.J. walked into the apartment.

"Christ, what happened to you?"

His clothing was smeared with blood. He held a hand to the back of his head as he staggered towards the bathroom. Tony grabbed his brother's arm because it was clear that his injuries were not fatal or particularly serious, but the same could not be said about his stubbornly foolish mindset.

"You're one stupid fuck. You won't stop till you're dead, will you?"

No answer or resistance came. Tony grew worried. Maybe this was beyond C.J.'s routine bumps and bruises. He appeared to be in shock.

"Say something, man. What's the matter with you?"

"He's dead," was the barely audible reply.

"What? Who's dead?"

"They killed him. He was just a kid. Just a fucking kid."

Tony squeezed his brother's arms to help him focus. "What are you talking about? Who's dead?"

"We don't know what the fuck we're doing. We're playing ourselves. We're dying cause we've got nothing better to do."

C.J.'s crazed expression resembled that of junkies minutes after he supplied them with what they needed to have. But Tony could see it was grief that had invaded his brother's system. He was anything but high.

His surroundings had been little more than a blur when he awakened from the blow to his head. Slowly the objects about him began to take solid form, until at the very center of his vision he found the point in space where life as he knew it came to a screeching halt, replaced with uncertainty and unshakable fear.

He crawled towards the prone body, turned his fallen comrade over, and found just what was expected. There was no need to check for breathing or a pulse. He knew death when he saw it.

"It looked like he was asleep. I knew he wasn't, but I started shaking him. I kept hoping it was some fucked up nightmare. I was going to wake up, and then he was going to wake up, and we would be back in his room looking at comic books and playing video games."

C.J. removed his hand from the back of his head. The wound had re-opened. The look on his face as he watched crimson drops fall to the carpet suggested fascination more than pain or concern.

"The crazy part is, he was out of it. He was locked up in the hospital and when he got out his parents were going to take him away."

It had been over a few city blocks that they decided to claim as their own. They believed if they pretended hard enough, the harsh truth could be denied. They would never own anything substantial. They would never be anything of legitimate worth. When all was said and done, they were miniscule fish in a bottomless ocean. They killed and died in a ridiculous attempt to create a tidal wave, when in fact, the most they could cause was a splash. That splash had been the death of C.J.'s best friend.

"Damn," Tony said as he placed the final pieces of the puzzle. "It's Tyrone, isn't it?"

"He was my boy. Wasn't afraid of nothing or nobody. Maybe he should have been."

Tony could not help thinking that Tyrone had asked for what he received. It may have been a cruel thought, but this made it no less true. Just because you have no regard for life, doesn't mean it has no regard for you. He had never felt sorry for those who committed suicide, even if it was done by another's hands.

"He died for nothing," C.J. said. "The only thing different is that he's gone."

Tony wondered what he should say. Certainly not what he was thinking. Then he decided that his brother didn't need answers, only the opportunity to liberate his grief.

"You were right, Tony. But I didn't get it. Not until I saw him dead. Then I understood. I understood everything."

C.J. slumped into his brother's arms. He had finally run out of words and strength. When Tony looked up, he saw that they were no longer alone. Their mother and uncle had come out of the kitchen and Tanya had emerged from her bedroom. They were all staring with sadness and wonder as the brothers clung to one another in the blood stained night.

CHAPTER NINETEEN

Manny's slumber was interrupted by bright light penetrating his protesting eyelids. The lamp directly above his head had been turned on. For a moment he was uncertain of his whereabouts. Then he looked up into familiar angry eyes and remembered. According to his watch it was four o'clock in the morning. According to his brother's expression, the start of Armageddon.

"Didn't I tell you to leave my home? Do I have to call the cops and have you arrested for trespassing?"

Rest was out of the question, as was civility. Lionel had obviously fortified his nerves with his liquor of choice. He was now sufficiently prepared to play the role of bouncer.

"I can't leave until I say what I came here to say." Manny shook off the last of his sleep and hoped to the creator of all things that sincerity would be apparent in his words. "I was wrong for abandoning the family like I did. I was wrong for abandoning you."

He rose to his feet. It was bad enough dealing with so much guilt without being literally looked down upon.

"Mostly I was wrong for not telling you this a long time ago. Chalk it up to useless pride. I'm sorry."

Over two decades had passed between the offense and the apology. Less than two seconds went by between the apology and its refusal.

"Did that clear your conscience? Can you go back to your perfect life now that the one little thing bothering you has been taken care of?"

Lionel sat down in his worn but reliable easy chair. He could care less whether he was looked up or down at. Exhaustion of both the physical and emotional variety dictated his actions. He plucked a cigarette from the pack in his breast pocket. Ordinarily he didn't smoke at home out of respect for his wife's wishes, but today was no ordinary day.

"I never wanted it to turn out this way," said Manny.

"I believe I know a thing or two about how you wanted your life to turn out. Everything you ever wanted is in plain sight for everyone to see. Right there in the palm of your hand."

"In my mind I had two choices." Manny was unable to resist falling back into his habit of self-defense. "Leave and make something of myself, or stay and be nothing. That's the only way I could see it."

"Looks like you were right. We're living proof of that, ain't we?"

Lionel rose and met his brother face to face. Manny was mesmerized by the not quite steady gait, the smell of cigarette smoke and alcohol, the aura of pure rage, pure pain. For a brief but overpowering moment, it seemed to Manny that an appearance was being made by the apparition of their father.

"Your new found guilt doesn't mean a damn thing to me," Lionel said. "Maybe it would have once. When I was young enough to still think I could do something with my life. But I lost those delusions a long time ago. Like it or not, this is it. Nothing either of us can do about it now."

He walked to the door and held it open. "The only worthwhile thing you can do for me is to leave."

The invitation was tempting. Lionel's sense of self was largely formed by the fact that he had been wronged. He was hurt and angry and deservedly so. If he granted forgiveness, what would he do with the rest of his days? If not the enraged sibling, who exactly would Lionel Johnson be? But Manny would not be leaving. He would stay and see this through to the unavoidably bitter end.

"It doesn't have to be this way."

"Sure it does."

"No it doesn't." Manny had one last line of argument to employ. "It can't. Because this goes beyond just you and me. I'm willing to take as much as you can dish out. I know I deserve it. But how about when I'm not around to be the scapegoat for everything that has ever gone wrong in your life? That leaves Caren and your kids to bear the brunt of your anger."

Manny had come to make amends, not war. He had since concluded that war was sometimes necessary to clear the space needed for peace.

"I treat my family just fine," Lionel said, each word punctuated like spikes into a railroad track. "Maybe I don't have much to give them. But I do the best I can, and you of all people have no right to judge me."

Lionel had entered his home a drunken man, but had since grown frightfully sober. In a life filled with failure he had found one thing to be proud of. His family had been put above everything, including himself.

"Now are you going to leave my home, or do I have to show you the way out?"

"Leave him alone, Dad."

Neither of them had noticed Tony's presence in the doorway of his bedroom.

"Get back in your room," Lionel commanded.

"He has every right to be here," Manny said. "This is about him too."

"Let's get something straight. That's *my* son. He'll do whatever the hell I say. So you can wrap up his rights with your self serving apologies, and I think you know where you can shove them."

Lionel walked towards Tony, determined to wield the authority that had been wrenched from his grasp. His role as provider may have been diminished, but he could still pull off the part of ass kicker if need be.

"Didn't you hear me, boy?"

Tony stood his ground, casting a glance of solidarity towards Manny.

"What the hell are you looking at him for? *I'm* the one talking to you. *I'm* your father. Or have you forgotten that?"

Tony had not forgotten. He knew it only too well. He was tempted to say this aloud, but his father hadn't raised any fools.

"Well, are you going?" Lionel was posing a threat, not a question. Tony would not dare choose Manny over him. There had to be a limit to how much his brother could take.

Upon being awakened by the argument, Tony's instinctive reaction was to rise and protect. He naturally assumed that his mother was in harm's way. When he found that the threats were directed towards his uncle, the urge to protect was replaced by a wish to support. Having stood up to his father on behalf of Janet had emancipated him. He would not allow his principles to be steamrolled by his father's ever again. He looked towards Manny to assure him that together they could not be moved.

"That's it."

"Lionel, no!"

Tony watched the back of Lionel's hand come within an inch of his face, where it stopped and hung in mid air. Manny had managed to grab his brother's arm before it did any damage. He then tried to contain Lionel in a bear hug, but years of manual labor had made Lionel much the stronger of the two. He easily broke free of the hold and shoved Manny to the ground.

Lionel turned back towards his son. Tony recognized the beast from his dream and knew that whether asleep or awake, there was no escape.

It was then that the look on Lionel's face turned from outrage to anguish. He clutched his stomach and groaned pitifully. "Help me," he gasped, stretching out for assistance from Tony, who remained stone faced and still as his father fell to the floor.

* * *

The sun patiently climbed the sky, illuminating all in its path. The beginning of another day was heralded, and with it would come a new set of births and deaths, moments of exultation and of heartbreak. It was from the setting of many such events that the Jonhsons took their leave. They were walking through the parking lot of the hospital where Lionel had been admitted.

"He's been having stomach pains for months," said Caren, visibly shaken by the events of that morning. "I should have insisted that he have himself checked out."

"Try to relax, Caren." Manny knew there was little chance of his advice being heeded.

"I hate leaving him there. I should go back."

"Now what good would that do? You saw him when we left. He was as ready to get up and go as we were. We'll know the results of his tests soon enough. I'm sure it's nothing serious."

Manny had no idea how serious Lionel's condition was, but was doing his best to be of comfort, to himself as much as to Caren.

"I don't know what I would do without him."

"Don't go talking like that. He'll be home before you know it."

"I hope to God you're right."

Manny held his arm around Caren's shoulders, not wanting the quaking of her grief to figuratively and perhaps even literally shatter her to pieces. Beside them, C.J. lent a similar arm of support to his devastated sister. On their heels marched a solitary soldier.

In times such as these, petty differences were supposed to be laid aside. Old grudges and past offenses should simply disappear. So Tony tried to put the welfare of his father first and foremost in his thoughts. But he could not. It was as if novocaine had been administered to the section of his being that allowed him to care. He found himself envying the despondency of his family, for it showed that they had each been able to move past their own issues. The humanity within them enabled love and forgiveness to take place, tidying up Lionel's transgressions, sweeping that which had caused them pain under a shielding rug. It restricted the scope of their vision until the only thing seen was the blood that bound them.

Tony was shamed that this could not be said of him. As diligently as he scavenged within himself, nothing could be found but the memory of a hand headed to strike him. His heart was overstuffed with resentment. There was simply no room for compassion.

CHAPTER TWENTY

Tony scrutinized his appearance in the mirror above his bureau. Not bad, but best to get a second opinion. He must not underestimate the value of any decision, no matter how trivial it seemed. What better way was there to judge a person than by the choices he made?

"What do you think of this tie?"

"I think you're out of your mind," Charlie answered. "That's what I think."

"Will you make yourself useful for a change?"

"You never get dressed up when you come to my house."

"I just want to make a good first impression."

"Then you might want to wear matching socks."

"Shit."

Tony had tried to convince himself that there was nothing to be nervous about. He had met parents of girlfriends' before. But this time was different, expectations and apprehensions heightened. The SAT's was supposedly the big test to determine his future, yet he calmly breezed through that in two socks of the same color. He couldn't shake the feeling that everything important to him was on the line tonight, dependant on his being no less than perfect. The Mitchell's must be shown that their daughter had chosen wisely.

He put on his tie of choice and decided it would have to do. "Well, this is as good as I'm going to look."

"Tragic, but true," said Charlie. "When are you heading over to Janet's crib?"

"In a few minutes. My uncle is giving me a ride."

"Time for me to split anyway. I'm going out with Taneshia tonight."

"Still putting in overtime for that booty? Maybe you should cut your losses while you can."

"I ain't hardly sweatin' that girl no more. But I need to stay on her good side while I'm moving on to her model wannabe buddies. I think I've hit the mother load this time. Might not be as glamorous as hanging out with some girl's parents, but I think I'll manage to enjoy myself."

"You do that."

"Right back atcha."

For most of the 48 hours to have passed since the early morning face off with his father, Tony had been trying to think about anything else. He had done his best to block out concern over the mysterious pain that had brought such a strong man to his knees, opting to believe that his father would be fine, seeking shelter in the comfort zone of denial. As for their relationship, Tony gave it scarcely a thought. He was resigned to the fact that it was beyond repair.

The timing of the invitation to have dinner with Janet's family was somewhat of a blessing, because focussing on winning over her parents was a preferable form of stress to that caused by thinking about his father. But as he stepped out of the leather interior of his uncle's luxurious car and stood before their home, willing himself to walk towards it turned out to be a greater challenge than anticipated.

"Don't be nervous," said Manny. "Go on and knock them out with that Johnson charm."

"I sure hope it doesn't skip a generation."

Manny laughed. "Everything will be fine. They're just people."

This was true. They were merely the two people who would judge if Tony was worthy to remain in the paradise their daughter had ushered him into.

With great determination he traveled the final yards of his journey and rang the doorbell. He was able to tug on his tie one last time before the door was opened.

"Hi. Come on in."

Janet had never looked more beautiful.

"Are you nervous?" she whispered.

"Not really," he lied.

She took his hand as they entered. Tony was impressed. He was reminded of houses seen in the copy of *Better Homes and Gardens* gathering dust in his dentist's reception area. There was a subdued elegance to his surroundings demonstrating that the Mitchell family was a couple of income levels removed from his own family. The only other person he knew to have furnishings in such good condition was his godmother in Brooklyn, who kept just about everything covered in plastic.

Seated at the head of the dining room table was Janet's father, awaiting his daughter's suitor and his meal. Her mother was in the kitchen taking dishes from a cabinet.

Janet started the introductions. "Mom, Dad, this is..."

"This is the boy you're having over tonight?"

"Yes, Daddy. I would like you to meet my boyfriend Tony."

"I see."

Tony shook Mr. Mitchell's hand, reminding himself to grip firmly, and took the seat Janet offered him. Janet's mother placed a set of plates on the table. She seemed quite focussed on the task at hand. Tony waited to meet her gaze with a warm smile, but had to settle for grinning self-consciously in her general direction.

"So, you two are dating," said Mr. Mitchell.

"Yes, sir. We've been going out for a while now."

"My wife and I are coming up on twenty years together. That's a while. You two hardly know each other, really."

"Well, what I do know, I like."

Janet's father peered at him unblinkingly. Tony competitively held the eye contact, realizing that his every move and word was being evaluated. No benefit of the doubt would be granted. The trust and welcome of Janet's parents would have to be earned. He felt certain that he was up to the task.

The eyes of Mr. Mitchell and his daughter initially seemed to mirror each other, but close inspection revealed a crucial difference. While hers reminded one of the sky on a cloudless summer day, his were a steely blue that seemed to be searching for something hidden beneath the surface of whatever they were looking upon.

"One thing about my daughter," he said. "She's full of surprises."

No response to the remark seemed fitting, so Tony gave none. The next several minutes passed by quietly, save for the clattering of silverware against china. Finally, Mr. Mitchell resumed his line of questioning.

"Where do you live, Tommy?"

"That's Tony. The Westwood Houses, sir."

"I see." Either his wife's cooking was not to his liking tonight, or else Tony's home address was responsible for Mr. Mitchell's vague expression of distaste. Or perhaps he held a strong preference for the name Tommy.

"You planning on going to college?"

"Yes I am." Tony was grateful to at last give what was surely a suitable response to a question. "I'm trying to decide between Columbia, NYU, and St. Johns. My preference..."

"College isn't cheap, you know. It's in your best interest to think realistically."

Tony wondered what Mr. Mitchell considered realistic for him to ponder. Did he believe that the only career paths for black men from the projects to choose from were drug dealer or pimp? No one was more aware than Tony that attending a good college would be financially challenging, but that did not make the idea beyond the scope of realism.

"I'll get by."

Janet's father flashed a plastic smile. "Maybe the negro college fund thing will help you out."

His pronunciation of "negro" was an unsettling sound to Tony's ears.

"You give any thought about going to one of those black colleges?"

"Black" was technically acceptable, but did not strike a more melodious chord.

"Like I said, since I plan to stay local. It's between Columbia, St. Johns, and NYU."

"Right, right. So what's your game?"

"Excuse me."

"Basketball, football, track?"

Tony placed his fork down on the plate before him. His appetite had vanished nearly as swiftly as Mr. Mitchell's hospitality. He briefly considered that perhaps Janet's father meant no offense by his question, but he had run completely out of benefit of doubt.

"I've given it a lot of thought, sir. Despite my inability to dunk a basketball or outrun a horse, I still figure I'll give college a shot. Maybe even pick up a degree while I'm there."

"I'm sure he'll be offered tons of scholarships," Janet interjected. "He gets straight A's. Why do you think my grades have gone up this semester?"

Tony continued to cling to the hope of turning this evening around, even though the odds were clearly decreasing by the second. If he was unable to win over Janet's parents, it might only be a matter of time before she began to see him in the same disapproving manner that they obviously did. It was critical that he keep his temper in check and his eyes on the prize.

He picked up his fork and scooped some rice and chicken into his mouth. "This is a great meal, Mrs. Mitchell." The dinner was in fact nothing beyond adequate, but flattery seemed the wisest way to go.

"Thank you," she mumbled, not bothering to look up from the food she was scarcely touching.

Desperate for a kindred spirit in a world gone topsy turvy, Tony glanced across the table. At least he wasn't the only one thoroughly confused. Janet appeared to be wondering if she was in the right house.

"You remind me of a girl at work," her mother said quietly, continuing to be mesmerized by her plate as she spoke.

"What do you do for a living?"

"I work in a real estate office."

"Commercial or residential?"

"Maybe I can arrange for you to meet her."

"Meet who?" Tony asked, easily accepting that his question would not be answered because the more time passed, the less surprised he was by the peculiarities of Janet's parents and this bizarre evening.

"The girl at my job. Her name is Rachel. She's very sweet and quite lovely. Born in Jamaica. Charming accent."

It seemed unreal, yet actually was happening. Mrs. Mitchell was trying to set him up. Either that, or else she thought all black people should get to know one another. He exhibited a counterfeit smile of his own, but since Janet's mother was determined not to look directly at him, the gesture was wasted. As for Janet, she seemed to be in a paralytic state of shock. This was a shame because Tony was in dire need of assistance.

"What do your folks do?" Mr. Mitchell asked.

"My mom is a nurse's assistant at a home for the elderly. My dad worked at a meat packing plant. Unfortunately, he recently lost his job."

Up to this point his father's vocation had been regarded with neither shame nor pride. It was simply what he did, what he bitterly complained about while hypocritically discouraging any attempt to avoid a similar plight. Observing the brief but blatant look of derision which graced Mr. Mitchell's face, Tony experienced an unfamiliar desire. He wished to stick up for his father. But he could think of nothing to say.

"This isn't the best time to be out of work," said Mr. Mitchell as if having revealed a divine truth. "Not that there's a good time. But with so many jobs going the way of the computer nowadays, you practically need a Master's from Harvard to get a job flipping burgers."

Tony's father was out of work because he was uneducated and ignorant. Mr. Mitchell had not said as much, but might as well have. He was obviously at ease summing up the prospects of a perfect stranger. This was because black people were as one in his eyes, their stories all the same. With every word Mr. Mitchell spoke, Tony understood a little more clearly what type of man he was dealing with.

"He'll be fine."

"With your talk of college, I guess you're not planning on following in his footsteps."

"You guess correctly."

"He must be very proud."

"One would think so. But not everything works out like you think it will."

"He *must* be proud," Mr. Mitchell insisted.

"My dad isn't a huge supporter of higher education."

"Is that right?"

"My dad and I don't see eye to eye on a lot of things. I plan to choose my own education, my own career, and my own woman to love. If he happens to disapprove of what I want, that's *his* choice."

The switch from defense to prosecution of his father had been effortless.

"You're quite headstrong," said Mr. Mitchell, almost but not quite with admiration. "You seem to know exactly what you want, and that's rare for your age. But you're young. As time goes by you'll find yourself wanting things you never thought about before, and forgetting things you once valued a great deal."

"The things I want now, I don't see changing any time soon."

"You and Rachel really are alike," said Janet's mother. "I think you two would definitely hit it off."

“Mom”, exclaimed Janet as if finally emerging from the effects of a stun gun.

"I already have a girlfriend, Mrs. Mitchell. That won't be changing any time soon either."

This effectively ended the interrogation. Everyone began focusing on cleaning their plates without the backdrop of forced conversation so the evening could be brought to early termination. Tony wondered why Janet hadn't warned him about her parents. Probably for the same reason he had kept quiet about his dad. He didn't want to be in her house a moment longer, but could think of no convenient reason to excuse himself. Nor did he wish to hurt Janet's feelings by leaving too hastily. As uncomfortable as the situation was, she was worth the sacrifice.

Tony was nearly finished eating when the stormy silence was broken by the entrance of someone at the front door. Janet had mentioned having an older brother.

"Looks like the happy wanderer has finally arrived," said Mr. Mitchell.

Tony turned around, but his view was obstructed by dozens of ceramic animals holding court on the wall unit dividing the living and dining rooms.

"You promised you'd be home in time for dinner."

"I got here as soon as I could, Dad."

The voice was familiar. Tony had little time to dwell on this thought before Janet's brother entered the dining room.

"Howard!?"

"Tony! What are you doing here?"

"I was invited for dinner. This is your house?"

"You two know each other?" asked Mr. Mitchell.

"Yeah, we work together," Howard answered. "You're the guy Janet's bringing home tonight?"

"You're Janet's brother?"

"This is fucking unreal."

"Watch your language, Howard."

"There's more important stuff going on than my grammar, Dad."

"Howard, take a seat," said Mr. Mitchell, trying to restore a semblance of order at his dinner table.

"We've got to talk," Howard said to Tony as he sat down. There was an inexplicable shortness to his tone and sternness to his glare. The two of them had spent hour upon hour together without a single harsh word between them, yet considerable animosity was now detected.

Tony shook his head in exasperation. Not only had his attempt to make a favorable impression on Janet's parents been in vain, but he would not even be getting an endorsement from his supposed friend. He rose to his feet.

"I think I should leave."

"No, don't," Janet feebly protested.

"I get the feeling I've outstayed my welcome."

He briskly strode out of the Mitchell's home. Once outside, Howard called after him. Against his better judgment he stopped and waited.

"Coming for a goodnight kiss?"

"What the fuck is going on here?"

"Seems pretty obvious to me," answered Tony. "The girl I've been seeing is your sister. Only I didn't know that until tonight. I can see you have a problem with it. Mind telling me why?"

"Tony, you're an okay guy. But I love my sister."

"I love her too. You already know that, though. I've told you plenty of times."

"You didn't tell me you were talking about Janet."

"You have different last names. How was I supposed to figure it out? And what the hell does this change?"

"Everything."

"Why?"

"Cause it does."

This was as much of an answer as Howard was willing to give. Not that it really mattered. Tony wasn't asking anything that hadn't already figured out for himself.

"I thought we were friends."

"That's got nothing to do with this."

"Then what does?" Tony was determined to make Howard speak the awful truth, to own up to his racist views.

"How about we make a deal. I won't date your sister and you won't date mine."

"Janet and I love each other and we're staying together. If you can't accept it, that's your problem."

Tony did not wait for a response. He wanted nothing from Howard but distance between them, and that is what he created. Several blocks were traveled before emotions other than outrage began to demand his attention. The evening had gone terribly, just the opposite of what he'd been hoping for. It wasn't his fault though. It couldn't have been. Janet's parents loathed him on sight. Before he could say a word, their damning opinion was formed.

He came to a stop. The Mitchell's house was now beyond his sight, and he feared that happiness with Janet may have slipped beyond reach as well.

* * *

Back in that house Janet lay in bed searching through her memory bank for anything that might have served as warning sign. Her parents had no black friends that she knew of. She recalled a few ethnic jokes that her father laughed at when told to him, though she could not remember any he told. Occasional remarks directed at the television when a heinous crime was committed by a black person took on added significance in hindsight. These instances had been relatively few and far between. Individually, the offenses were too minor to warrant recognition. They were just things people said and did from time to time, not indicators of anything she needed to be concerned about. Such had been her way of thinking, until this night provided so much evidence to the contrary.

Janet did not want to think of her family as they had just shown themselves to be. Instead she reasoned that they had been taken by surprise. Time was needed for tempers to cool and rational explanations to be given. Sometimes it was necessary to get used to new ideas before they could be embraced. Things said and done by people who had been taken off guard could be excused. Eventually acceptance would come about and a night such as this one would fade from memory. In the meantime, Janet wanted to blot it from existence, to focus solely on her love for Tony. This, and only this would make the confusion and hurt go away. But what if it was he who stayed away?

Janet rose from her bed and watched the weeping willow in her backyard perform a forlorn ballet in the breeze.

A pebble bounced off the window, startling her. Looking out, she saw a figure standing below. His features were hidden in shadow, but his identity was no mystery. She hurried downstairs and outside to join him.

"I'm so glad you came back. I'm sorry ..."

Tony cut off the rest of the apology with a kiss. "You didn't think you could get rid of me that easy, did you?"

"It wasn't supposed to be like that."

"I know it wasn't. You and me against the world. Maybe that's just how it's meant to be."

"I thought I knew them," Janet said. "How can I stand to go back in there, knowing how they feel?"

"Take it from an expert on the subject. You get used to it."

Tony caressed Janet's tear dampened face. He had never loved her so much as he did right then, which made what he said next all the braver.

"If you want to call it quits, I'll understand."

"No way. You're stuck with me for good. You and me against the world, right?"

"Right."

Tony and Janet sealed their pact with a kiss. For the time that it lasted, heartache drifted away. There was nothing else, there was no one else. The kiss was all.

* * *

Originally Tony intended to call his uncle to pick him up from the Mitchell's, but this was not a night in which things went according to plan. So he headed home on foot, at a relaxed pace the second time around with reassurance that his relationship with Janet was secure. He daydreamed along the way about the two of them on a deserted island. The vision was so clear that he had to look down to make certain his feet were indeed stepping on pavement, not tropical sands.

The instant he opened the door to his home, fantasizing ceased. His mother was crying. Uncle Manny tried valiantly to stem her tears, but his own pain rendered the words of consolation largely incoherent. Sitting in their father's easy chair weeping in a quieter manner was Tanya. C.J. stood with his back against a wall, staring blankly across the room. He locked eyes with Tony and answered the unspoken question.

"Dad's got cancer."

The three words hit Tony like a sledgehammer to the gut, knocking the breath out of him. He felt dizzy and nauseous. A terrible pounding began inside of his head.

"Oh God, why him?" Caren cried out. "He's been through so much."

Tony wished he could answer the question his mother had addressed to the heavens, because he knew God wouldn't bother to. He turned back to his brother.

"How bad is it? Does he have a chance?"

C.J. shrugged his shoulders. "The only things I know for sure are that he's got cancer, and that cancer kills people."

Accustomed to feeling that it was necessary to correct the error of C.J.'s thinking, Tony instinctively refuted the statement.

"Nothing's strong enough to take Dad out. He's too damn stubborn. He's gonna live forever."

"No such thing as forever."

"There must be something we can do," Tony said, because he irrationally refused to accept that his world could be turned upside down with no warning. "We can't just let it happen."

"We're not letting anything happen. It just is. All we can do is watch."

Tony glared at his brother. He was infuriated not by what C.J. said, for it was undeniable fact, but by the way it was stated. As if they were talking about the weather or something of equally casual effect on their lives.

"How can you be so fucking calm and collected? He's our father."

"That ain't going to keep him alive, is it?"

"You cry for your damn hoodlum buddies. Can't you spare a tear for Dad?"

C.J. flipped Tony's tie over his shoulder in disgust. "Don't worry about what I can spare and how I feel. You're the one who hates him, remember?"

Not bothering to wait for a denial, C.J. turned away and went into their bedroom to deal with the sorrow in his own way. He had unwittingly become an expert in such matters.

Tony, however, was still a novice. For this reason he could think of nothing to do but stare at his weeping family and try to wish his brother's words away. But they weren't going anywhere.

CHAPTER TWENTY-ONE

Caren walked about on automatic pilot performing household chores. Then she stopped in the middle of cleaning something that didn't particularly need to be cleaned. Staying on her feet suddenly required a gargantuan effort. Over a week had passed since the doctor's pronouncement, since time stopped for her. There was nothing else to life but the fact that Lionel might soon be gone from it.

Someone knocked at the unlocked front door. When Caren failed to respond, the person on the other side simply let herself in.

"I'm so sorry."

Ellen's regrets were offered for more than her friend would ever know. She did not think that Lionel would have confessed about the night when drunkenness, frustration, lust and loneliness dictated her actions. So repercussions for her moment of weakness was not a concern. What Ellen did fear was not being able to look Caren in the eyes without her shame showing through.

"I didn't know I could hurt this bad."

"Everything's going to be okay," Ellen said, wrapping her arms around Caren as if they could shield her from the onslaught of heartache. Her shame no longer mattered. Caren was in pain, and it was Ellen's duty to do everything in her power to be of comfort.

"No, things will never be okay again."

"You must have faith. How many times have you said that to me?"

The advice had been sincere on every occasion it was given. Caren's unswerving belief in the wisdom of God's plan had helped her persevere in the face of much adversity. Unquestionable knowledge that behind the most devastating of tragedies lay a divine purpose bestowed serenity that was not easily shaken. Yet when she groped blindly for her convictions this time out, what she came across was debilitating fear and paralyzing uncertainty. Despair was proving itself a formidable foe.

Caren was finding it increasingly necessary to remind herself that God had not forsaken her. She knew goodness and devotion did not grant one immunity from hardship, that she was not excused from being handed a heavy cross to bear. But despair had coated her palms with sweat, making her grip on that cross slippery.

"All I ever wanted was for my family to be healthy. Was that too much to ask?"

"No, honey."

Ellen did not share her friend's religious beliefs. What she did have faith in was the idea that bad breaks were no more or less avoidable than good ones. She was also convinced that people were rarely given more hardship than they could stand. The hollowness Caren felt was no doubt unbearable. For this very reason, it would not go on indefinitely.

Like pain, happiness was not built to last either. Sometimes it left of its own accord. On other occasions it was thrown away for an endless variety of foolish reasons. Whether in times of feast or of famine, it could be counted on that times would change. God was as good a name to call the fickle nature of fate as any.

If Caren felt temporarily abandoned by her God, Ellen would do her best to be a substitute source of solace. Considering the sins she had to atone for, it was the very least she could do.

* * *

Manny had come to the doorstep of his brother's modest home expecting a mighty struggle. This was not because there had been a great many arguments between them since Manny's departure for college twenty five years earlier. Arguments required words, and Lionel had been mostly unwilling to spare them. His resentment was instead characterized by what was left unsaid, but not unexpressed through maintained distance. Manny decided to forcibly bridge the divide, leaving his brother no choice but to strike out in defense. Lionel's animosity could be dealt with, but the distance between them would no longer be tolerated.

Patience and steadiness of pulse would counter Lionel's fury. Backing down was not an option. If he remained resolute, Manny was convinced that sooner or later something would be said or done to make a crack in the wall Lionel had erected around his jagged heart. Eventually it would come crashing down.

But it hadn't. Good intentions were no match for the refusal to forgive that Lionel clung to like a miser to his money. Manny's apology was seen as just another selfish act, done for the sake of conscience cleansing.

This was a popular opinion of late, also held by his wife. That was why instead of trying to work their problems out, she had filed for divorce. Caroline claimed he had been neglecting her and their children in favor of his job. She also accused him of having had an affair. The former was a matter of debate that he had little chance of winning. The latter was irrefutable fact. His indiscretion had been nothing serious, just casual sex to help him deal with the pressure of work. That was how he chose to categorize it. That was what he tried to make fly. But Manny could no longer deny the obvious. He had once again failed at being there for his family.

Although her unhappiness had been evident for quite some time, Caroline's knowledge of his infidelity and her resolution to end their marriage was an unforseen bolt of lightning, its flash illuminating the sins Manny had made himself blind to. With his gift for rhetoric, he made skillful arguments in defense of his hurtful behavior. Never before had so little been so late.

This led Manny to conclude that the timing of the phone call from Caren was an omen. A temporary cease fire was desperately needed. So he left for the Bronx, full of lofty aspirations with secret side benefits. He would try to make amends with Lionel, who might be satisfied to see him finally off his high horse and down on bent knee. And perhaps the time apart would dampen his wife's determination to deny forgiveness.

"You must be Lionel's brother."

"That I am," said Manny. The man who had interrupted his thoughts possessed rusty hair and eyes that reminded one of a priest, full of kindness and inviting of confessions.

"I'm a good friend of his. The name's Phil."

"Nice to meet you. I wish it was under better circumstances. A hospital is no place to meet someone for the first time, other than our children."

The men shook hands to cement the bond of concern that they shared.

“Have you seen him yet?” asked Manny.

“Yeah. I just left his room.”

“How did he seem?”

"Okay, I think. He didn’t act too depressed. Actually, he changed the subject whenever I brought up the fact that he’s sick. I guess he’s not ready to deal with it yet. All he wanted to talk about was baseball and, and everything except for the fact that he's got cancer."

Manny shook his head in both bafflement and a degree of admiration. Not even the specter of death could make a dent in his brother's obstinate nature.

"I half expected him to jump from the bed and tell me it's just a practical joke," Phil said. "I'm not sure what this is, but it definitely ain't no joke."

Manny also had been hesitant to accept the severity of Lionel's condition. Better that it be a trick pulled to avoid confrontation. But not even Houdini could have created such an effective illusion.

"As long as we're on unpleasant topics," said Phil, "I'm going to speak my piece. I may not be family, but I have been listening to the story of what happened between you and your brother for a good many years now, so I feel that entitles me to an opinion. I know you've come to settle things with Lionel. I commend you for that. But considering what he's going through, I really think the best thing you could do for him is to go back home."

Manny was dumbfounded. Lionel had actually recruited a tag team partner to help push him away.

"You've only heard one side of the story."

"Seems to me there is only one side. He got screwed and you did the screwing."

Manny wondered if Phil was right, if perhaps making the easy exit might not be the right thing to do this time around. The longer it was contemplated the less confident he grew of the ground he was standing on.

"I'm not going to deny anything," he said quietly. I'm not blaming anyone but myself." His voice rose in defiance as he finished the declaration. "But I'm not running away either. Not again."

"He doesn't want you around. Don't you understand that?"

"I understand it all too well. But he's my brother. That has to count for something. If you'll excuse me."

Moments later, Manny entered his brother's room. Lionel glanced towards the doorway, then turned back to the

TV as if his ears had deceived him and his eyes had discovered only empty space.

There was a great deal to say. So much to make up for, so much love to express. Once they had been brothers in the truest sense of the word. Manny desperately wanted to return to that place, but had mislaid his map and forgotten the directions.

He was helpless in every respect to do anything of use. He couldn't stop the cancer raging through Lionel's body. He couldn't give him back his dreams. He couldn't take away his brother's physical torment, or that which ran even deeper. He could only speak his heart.

"I love you. Hate me if you want. Hate me if it makes you feel better. But that's just a step away from hating yourself."

Lionel waited to make certain Manny had said everything he came to say. Then came his rebuttal.

"Fuck you, Manny. Fuck your six figure income and your oversized house in Connecticut. Fuck your country club membership, your rounds of golf, your his and her luxury cars, the prep school enrollments for your spoiled rotten kids. Fuck your stock portfolio, your cleaning service, your tax shelters and your tailored suits. Fuck it all. Not because I envy what you have, but because I pity you for what you're lacking.

Manny involuntarily took a step backwards from the force of his brother's hateful words. "Maybe you have a point," Lionel continued, wanting to keep Manny's momentum going until he was gone for good from his sight. "Maybe I do hate myself. But don't you for one second think it's because we're one and the same. I suppose you were hoping I would get soft hearted because I'm sick. Sorry to disappoint, but no can do. You've made a tidy profit from selling your integrity. Be happy with that and leave me be."

Lionel turned up the volume of the television as far as it would go, making certain that any response his brother may have would be drowned out by nonsensical noise. He need not have bothered. Manny realized that there was nothing else for him to do but leave, and that is what he did.

Alone again, Lionel lay still and waited for the rate of his breathing and thumping of his heart to slow down to normal. Then he raised up and hurled the remote against the wall for no purpose other than to watch it smash into pieces.

* * *

Room 6C of the Bussing Motel stood in for the deserted island of Tony's imaginings. He left his worries at the door, hid out there for a blissful hour or two with Janet. But turmoil had managed to discover their hiding place.

"Did you go today?"

"I got as far as the parking lot. I just couldn't do it."

Tony sat up and stared at a constellation of stains throughout the expanse of carpet, some of them probably blood, others most likely vomit, the majority indeterminate. If the carpet could talk, it would no doubt have many interesting stories to tell.

"Why not?" asked Janet.

“I don’t know.”

“Do you hate him?"

"If you'd asked me that before, I think I might have said yes." Tony paused a beat to consider what he had just said, what it meant. "Yeah, I probably would have. So why should anything change now?"

"Because it has. He's your father. The only one you've got. So when he's gone, he's gone."

"I know." Tony peeled a piece of plaster from the wall. He noticed a syringe lying in a corner, missed by a lackadaisical cleaning person, courtesy of the room's previous guests. "I also know how I feel, and I can't just wish it away."

A passing siren sounded, the urban version of a coyote on the plains. Somewhere not too far away another tragedy had unfolded, and the usual vultures were flocking to the scene.

"Can you get your parents to stop hating me?"

"I don't want to talk about this again, Tony."

She said this as if they had spoken considerably more on the subject than the few words Tony had been able to pry from her. Janet had come to view her family as an open wound that would close given time, but not if constantly prodded. Maybe there was sense to this way of thinking, but Tony could not help but be frightened by her silence. He wanted her to rail against them, demanded proof that she truly was different. He was ashamed of this desire, but shame is often no match for desire.

"Why not?" he asked. "Don't tell me you've accepted how they feel."

"I didn't say that." Janet sat up as well. She had a pretty good idea what Tony was seeking. He couldn't look at her without seeing her mother, and father, and brother. He needed to know for certain that she would never share their point of view, one which saw nothing beyond the color of his skin.

Janet wanted to abolish his doubts but could not, for the simple reason that she did see Tony's color. The genesis of their love was physical attraction, and his complexion had lured her the same as hers undoubtedly pulled him. It was not his blackness that she fell in love with, but it was a part of him, and therefore, a part of what she loved.

She wanted him to realize that there were no legitimate reasons for his fears. The hang ups of her parents and brother had nothing to do with her. Tony was her first true love, so therefore, all she knew of it. He feared that she might not love him enough, when in fact, it was not possible for her to love him any stronger, or deeper, or higher, or wider. Tony had created the extent to which her love could reach. If he couldn't see what should have been as recognizable as his own reflection, she could think of no way to make her feelings more plain.

"They hate me because I'm black," he said. "Because I put my black hands on their daughter."

"Stop it."

Tony did not want to stop. He wanted to continue badgering until Janet began to see things as he did, as they should be seen. But he realized that this would only push her away, giving those who tried to deny their happiness precisely what they longed for. And so he put his anger aside, full knowing that the cease fire was finite, that there was a limit to how long he would be able to suppress honest emotion.

"You really want to talk about something else?"

"That would be nice."

"Okay then, how about this? I love you, Janet."

"I love you too."

"Then what else matters?"

If she knew, she wasn't telling. Tony snuggled up against her and let the silence being paid for by the hour envelop them, rather than considering possible answers to his question.

CHAPTER TWENTY TWO

Tony and Howard unloaded boxes with the smooth efficiency bred by familiarity. Sounds of labor were the only ones being manufactured. The co-workers had not spoken a word to each other, except out of necessity, since the night of Tony's aborted meal with Howard's family.

When the truck was emptied, they sat down for a hard earned break. Howard picked up his thermos and took a swig. Tony perused the newspaper he had bought on his way to work.

"All right, they caught the bastards," he exclaimed.

Howard looked to see what he was gloating about. The perpetrators of the attack on Lincoln high school student, Teddy Wilkins, had been apprehended.

"They probably won't even serve any time," said Tony to himself, but Howard could no longer endure being ignored when it was far more common for him to be the center of attention. If giving a say in the matter, he would take being hated over being neglected.

"Why wouldn't they?"

Tony answered as if speaking to a child who had disturbed his relaxation with one too many silly questions.

"Because they're white, and Teddy was black, and this is America."

"If they're guilty, they'll pay for it."

"There ain't no if about it. They're definitely guilty, and chances are they'll get away with it."

"I remember you saying ..."

"Never mind what you remember. My eyes have opened quite a bit since then."

"Here we go again," said Howard. "The black man's theme song. White people make you poor, white people make you steal, white people keep you dumb. Total bullshit."

Tony found this conviction so pathetically ridiculous that it almost, but not quite, brought a smirk to his face. An occasion came to mind when Howard had described him as being “not really black". He was no stranger to such remarks since C.J. and his father often stated more or less the same thing, and for pretty much the same reasons. Somehow they had gotten it into their heads that the more melanin one had, the more frequently they were supposed to be found hanging out on street corners at four in the morning, doing nothing more constructive than grabbing hold of their crotches, bopping their heads to hip hop music, and downing malt liquor. To live otherwise could disqualify a brown skinned person from their God given race. Non-slang usage of the English language and mainstream ambitions were traitorous acts, audacious breaks of the Black Man’s first commandment, which was to always keep it real, whatever *it* happened to be, no matter how ridiculous the definition given to *real* was.

When his father and brother questioned his blackness, they were being harshly critical of him for not displaying more pride in his heritage. But Howard’s intent was not only to be facetious, but also in a fashion, complimentary. As a result, he had not snapped back in righteous indignation.

Tony wished now that he had reacted strongly, that he had said something on every occasion a racist remark was directed towards him, or within his earshot. There was a time when he used to qualify such statements based on the degree of malice behind them. Now he realized that there was never benign intent behind prejudice, no matter how light hearted the delivery, just plain ignorance that needed to be corrected.

"Yeah, you're right, Howard. We're all on the same playing field, equal opportunities for everybody."

"More than equal I'd say, with quotas and affirmative action programs everywhere. Half my friends who graduated last year still don't have jobs. Know why that is? Cause they were given away to less qualified blacks out of liberal guilt."

"That guilt sure didn't kick in at your house." Once at the Mitchell's dinner table, Tony had been "really black" beyond the shadow of a doubt.

"All I'm saying..."

"You're saying you don't think about black people one way or the other. As long as we stay in our place."

Howard's face contorted to shape the response he planned to make, but could not quite release.

"I have a question for you," Tony practically spat in disgust. "How come you never mentioned that your sister went to Lincoln? How come you never asked if I knew her, or suggested that I introduce myself to her?"

“I didn’t want it getting back to my dad where I was working.”

“You could have mentioned it after he found out.”

“Guess it slipped my mind by then.”

"I don’t think it slipped anything. You just figured I wouldn't run in the same circles as Janet did, and that was the way it should be. The last thing I could ever be was the guy she was dating."

Howard's expression might have been translated as sorrow, but not the kind where forgiveness is asked for or remorse felt. Perhaps he felt badly over the end of a friendship which had been genuine to him, but was unwilling to change his feelings or acknowledge he was wrong to have them. Losing Tony as a friend may have been a sacrifice of sorts, but one he was willing to make rather than accept the alternative. Maybe his bigotry was like the love he professed for his girlfriend - something he would stick by in the end, despite all contrary behavior.

Then again, perhaps the look meant nothing. As for Tony, he had no regrets. He hated Howard and wanted this to ring through loud and clear.

"How's it going fellas?"

Tony walked past Mr. Jordan with scarcely a glance as he answered his question.

"I quit."

"You do? "Why?"

"Ask him."

Mr. Jordan turned to Howard. Before he could inquire what was going on, Tony had left the store for good.

* * *

Tanya's closest friends Cheryl and Yolonda were seated in bright orange plastic chairs that had certainly not been molded to maximize coziness, but were quite easy to disinfect. As was often the case, they were of vastly different opinions on the matter of discussion. Physical discomfort, ideological disagreement, and shared nervousness quickly transformed their conversation into a quarrel. Yolonda was an avid reader of paperback novels in which long tressed heroines clung passionately in their corsets to bare chested, equally tressed studs. Living vicariously through these fictional women helped to compensate for her short hair, acne, braces, and lack of romance in her life. Yolonda possessed a beautiful voice that was the envy of mockingbirds. She did not merely verbalize a song, but inhabited it, furnished it with passion, heated it with revelry. Therefore she was routinely nudged by the head of her church choir to perform solos, but these efforts were in vain. The spotlight held nothing but dread for Yolonda. She preferred to be one of many voices in the midst of flowing robes.

If Cheryl had been gifted with an equally golden throat, she would have barged into the office of the nearest record executive and belted out unsolicited tunes until signed to a deal. She saw no advantage to introversion. Cheryl was someone who usually knew what she wanted, and was rarely shy about striving to obtain it.

She waved her hands frantically about to gesticulate her points, and the effect was remindful of a night sky on Independence Day. Each of her lengthy fingernails was a tiny canvas for a colorful display of designer cuticle art.

Yolonda secretly admired her friend's freedom of spirit, but disagreed with many of her manifestations of it, particularly Cheryl's casual attitude about sex. Or rather, her strict attitude that sex be kept casual. Sometimes Yolonda wondered if God had blessed her with the face and figure He had bestowed upon Cheryl, would she conduct herself in a similarly lusty manner. Yolonda claimed to deny herself pleasures based on her principles. But to what degree were these principles caused by her circumstances? To what degree were everybody's?

"I didn't put a gun to her head," said Cheryl in defense of the advice she had given Tanya. "She made the decision, not me. Suppose I said you should jump off the Empire State Building. Would you do it?"

"If I was in her state of mind I might." Yolonda would not be acknowledging the questions she asked of herself today. Regardless of circumstances, at some point a person had to take responsibility for their actions.

"But you would at least wear a parachute."

Their debate was taking place in the reception room of the free clinic a few blocks away from school. Tanya had fallen ill in her last period class. Being that the clinic's usual clientele consisted of strung out junkies and other lowlifes best kept at a maximum distance, her friends advised recovering at home, or even visiting their unsettling school nurse. Anything but the domain of the living dead. That was when Tanya told them what she suspected to be the cause of her symptoms.

"We both know who the one to blame is," Cheryl said. "Eric is a dog, plain and simple. She should have seen that from the beginning."

Yolonda was not buying this reasoning. Of course Eric was at fault. What he had done was deplorable. But this didn't change the fact that Tanya placed herself in position to be abused. Eric only did what he had been allowed to do. By giving up her body before she was ready, Tanya showed herself no respect. So why should she expect it from any man? Certainly not because he made pretty promises and had a nice smile.

Cheryl looked through her purse. A quick glance told Yolonda that her friend would never use unavailability of birth control as an excuse for getting pregnant.

"What's done is done. Let's just hope it's a false alarm." Cheryl found her cigarettes and was bringing one to her mouth when Yolonda knocked it to the floor.

"You can't smoke in a hospital."

"This ain't a hospital, it's a cesspool."

"You still can't smoke here."

"Look, I'm nervous, okay."

"If you're so nervous, you shouldn't have told her to do it in the first place."

"I didn't tell her not to use nothing," said Cheryl. "No dick gets near me without a jimmy hat."

"You shouldn't..." Yolonda cut herself short when she saw Tanya coming towards them. Neither she nor Cheryl bothered to ask what the diagnosis had been. Tanya's tears served notice.

Yolonda stood up and hugged her. "Everything's going to be okay."

"Have you decided what you're going to do?" asked Cheryl.

Tanya wiped her eyes. "I have to get out of here. I need to be by myself for awhile."

"Are you sure you want to be alone?" Yolonda asked.

Evidently she was, for Tanya ran out of the clinic and continued to sprint blindly for a couple of blocks. Then it dawned on her that no speed would be fast enough or distance far enough. So she came to a stop, taking a seat on the dented and rusted hood of a car that had seen better days, much like herself.

She rubbed her stomach as if it were a genie's bottle. A life was held beneath. Her child. The one possession she could truly call her own. Would its life have to be sacrificed? If not, wouldn't that mean sacrificing her own?

Tanya continued to sit and cry and wait for answers. They continued not to come.

* * *

Louis was in rare form. He spoke the gospel of the streets with conviction that rivaled any bible belt preacher. It was easy to imagine that had life placed him on a different road, he could have been convincing people to place their trust in God, or to vote for him come election time. But he was born a black male in the Bronx, and his instruction to the young urban warriors before him was to shed blood.

His words did not fall on deaf ears. The members of the Kaos Krew proclaimed their willingness and readiness to exact revenge. They would retrieve what they believed had been lost - honor, dignity, self respect. Perhaps they would never learn that these things could never be taken by another, only given away.

C.J. alone remained silent, unmoved by that which usually set a fire burning in his heart. He paid little attention to what Louis had to say, just catching bits and pieces. Something about waiting to recuperate; their plan of attack; an arsenal of guns that would soon be in their possession;

having pride in being a part of the Krew; etcetera. It didn't matter. C.J. no longer belonged here.

When the meeting concluded, he told Louis that he needed to speak to him. He didn't know where he would find the courage to deliver his message, but hoped to stumble upon it.

"Haven't seen much of you lately," Louis said after the room cleared out. "I was wondering if you would even show up today."

"I've had a lot on my mind."

"Don't sweat it, man. I know how tight you and Tyrone were. It's real fucked up, him going out like that."

"Yeah, it is. It's fucked up that any of us have to go out like that. I was headed in the same direction. But not anymore."

Louis' eyebrows arched. This was as expansive a reaction as he was prone to make.

"What are you saying?"

"I'm saying I'm out. This ain't worth dying for."

There it was. Nothing left to do but await the sentence. C.J. did not expect to be kept in suspense very long. Whether dispensing punishment or clemency, Louis' leadership was characterized by swift and decisive resolutions.

Louis tugged on one of his matted locks of hair as he pondered what to make of this turn of events. "If I was you I'd think this over a little more. Make sure you know what you're doing."

"I'm trying to make my life worth something."

"No. What you're doing is making it real short." Despite the threat of his words, Louis' tone was no different than if he was informing someone of the time. He was a killer. C.J. could only hope that he would be a reasonable one.

"Why it got to be like that? I have no beef with you. I just can't hang no more."

"The Dawgs have really got you scared, don't they?"

"I'm scared all right," admitted C.J. "But not of them. Just of wasting my life instead of trying to figure out what to do with it. You understand what I'm saying?"

"I understand fine. Now it's my turn to school you."

Louis grabbed C.J. by the throat and shoved him against the wall. With his other hand he withdrew a knife and pressed the blade against C.J.'s temple.

"You're trippin' nigga. Your little homey went out, so you scared you might be next. Figure if you break out now, maybe you won't get smoked. Wrong, mother fucker. Cruise now, you get smoked for sure."

The blade nicked C.J.'s flesh, just hard enough to break the skin and send a bead of blood trickling down his face. Louis returned the knife to his pocket, then delivered a solid punch to the kidneys which dropped C.J. to his knees.

"Don't fuck with me, or you'll be wishing it was you who went nice and quiet like Tyrone."

Louis walked out, feeling his point had been sufficiently made to the heap he was leaving on the floor. As if to congratulate C.J. for taking a stand on behalf of newly discovered convictions, Man-Eater came over and licked his face. C.J. petted the love starved beast.

"I hope you get out one day too, boy."

CHAPTER TWENTY THREE

Once again Tony was unable to will his feet towards their intended destination, although he went further on this occasion than any of the others. Each time out he surpassed what had been accomplished the time before, but he always came up short. Today he managed to enter the hospital and ask for his father's room number. Upon being told, he mulled the information over for a minute, then walked out. What did one say to his dying father? "Dad, I love you. I'll miss you terribly. You're the best father a boy could ever have." This wouldn't be believed even if he could somehow manage to say it.

After much reflection on the matter, he concluded that if there was some accomplishment his father could take pride in, all self-worth would not have been pinned on the color of his skin. Their lives would have been a whole lot easier if instead of force feeding his prejudices, he had allowed his children to become who they naturally gravitated towards being. Of course, maintaining bitterness for such a length of time was quite the accomplishment in itself. Unhappiness was no easier to master than contentment, but for his father, it seemed to be a breeze.

In light of recent events, Tony could no longer be certain that his father's mindset was without justification. The instant negative opinion formed by Janet's parents; the attitude of her friends; and most strikingly, the personality change undergone by Howard; were each blatant examples that skin color mattered to many people. Very much so.

Yet he still left the hospital in his wake. It had ceased to matter whether his father was right or wrong. When they last stood face to face, there was no word other than hate to name that which had flowed like scalding water from his father's eyes. Like father like son, Tony could give it as good as he got.

"What up, Johnson?"

Larry Faulk had been a classmate of his since seventh grade, but for most of that time their acquaintance was casual at best. Before and after gym class during their junior year, Larry would find himself at the mercy of some football players he had unintentionally rubbed the wrong way with his sardonic humor. The usual initiator of the harassment was Lincoln's varsity quarterback, Roger Lane. One day Roger was getting particularly rough, and without quite knowing why, Tony stepped into the fray. The result of his intervention was a small scuffle and the budding of a friendship.

"Not much, Larry. How's it going with you?"

"I was just kickin' it with your boy. Trying to get that nigga to hook me up with some of them modeling honies he's always bragging about. Charlie ain't that good looking and got no bank, so he must throw some dope lines."

Tony smiled at his friend's employment of hip hop vernacular. He wondered if Larry caught as much flack at home for "acting black" as *he* did for supposedly "acting white".

"Actually, he's just real persistent and knows how to bullshit," Tony explained.

"That the key to mad success with the females?"

"That's the key to success in a lot of things."

"Well you would know," Larry said. "How's your shorty? She drop your ass yet like an out of service area call or what?"

"I'm still hanging in there. Off to meet her now, as a matter of fact."

"Give her my regards. And tell your sister I said hi too."

"My girlfriend, my sister. Damn, Larry! Who's next, my mom?"

"Hey, it's not my fault God surrounded you with so many dimes. The least you can do is share the wealth."

"Keep dreaming, Larry. I have to get going."

"Yeah, me too. Be good, man."

"I always am."

After walking another three blocks, Tony entered a grocery store that was imaginatively named *Grocery Store*. He pulled from his pocket the brief shopping list his mother had provided and began to search. A box of sugar, a bag of rice, and toothpaste were the items he needed to acquire. It was while determining which brand of toothpaste was the best bargain this week that he noticed his every move was being scrutinized. The store employee had a dull gleam in his eyes that made him appear vaguely retarded, as if the mere idea of forming a thought more complex than 'I'm hungry/thirsty/sleepy' would tax him to the point of total exhaustion. Tony nodded to the Korean man, went with Crest, and moved on. A minute later he realized that his new found shadow was yet to be shaken.

"I don't need any help, thank you." Tony grabbed a generic box of sugar and went into the next aisle. There was no price tag on the five pound bag of rice. Depending on how much it cost, he might have enough money left over to buy Janet a discounted bouquet of flowers with a few hours of fresh appearance left in them.

He set out to look for the assistance. As it turned out, he needed to take no more than a single step, for the grocer was peering around the shelves at him. The inept spy quickly pretended to be examining cans of dog food, but his true purpose was obvious. This was not the first time Tony had been tailed in a store, but he decided it would be the last time he kept his annoyance to himself.

"What are you following me for? I have money. I don't appreciate being treated like a criminal. Do you understand me?"

"You buy or go."

"Fuck you."

Tony threw down his would be purchases and left the store, noting with no small degree of satisfaction that the box of sugar had burst open upon hitting the floor. This man, this foreigner who could barely speak the English language, had the nerve to come into *his* neighborhood and judge him. And not even to judge fairly. Only a single look was required for his verdict to be rendered. Did the grocer decide he had an A student before him? Did he conclude that his customer was someone with a bright future who should be treated with courtesy and respect? No. The brown skinned people who came in and out of his store were one and the same to him. All he saw was a kid who most likely intended to steal. All he saw was black.

He considered returning for the purpose of adding to the two words he had hastily spewed, but decided it wasn't worth the effort. The man wouldn't understand him, and even if he did, he wouldn't change. People never changed when it came to stuff like that.

Ten minutes later he arrived in front of Lincoln high school. Janet would be getting out of cheerleading practice soon. Since he no longer had a job to go to, Tony figured he would meet up with her. He was in dire need of the solace found in her arms.

The girls began filing out. Janet did not appear amongst them. He decided to wait a little longer. Five minutes went by uneventfully, leaving him to wonder if she had skipped practice today for some reason that she had neglected to tell him. Another five minutes passed without any sign of her. He was about to leave when the door of the school opened. It was Janet. Their eyes met, but before he could say a word someone appeared behind her.

"I have to go," Janet said to her companion.

"Just think about what I said. That's all I ask."

Roger headed off, but not before displaying a taunting smile. Before it could be reacted to, Tony felt a pair of lips against his own.

"Hi, honey. Shouldn't you be at..."

"Let's not change the subject, Janet."

"What subject?"

"That asshole is the subject. What the hell were you doing with him?"

"I wasn't with him," Janet said, taken aback by a degree of anger she had never before witnessed in Tony, though she did understand how what he had just seen must have appeared to him. "I mean, not like you're implying. He was waiting for me after practice. We just talked."

"About what? What are you supposed to think about?"

"Nothing I plan to."

"Then you won't mind telling me."

Janet did not answer right away for she obviously did mind. But she could see no way out of being truthful.

"He wants us to get back together."

It did not seem possible that this could be happening, except that it was. Tony's ears had confirmed that his eyes were not playing tricks on him. What he cherished most was slipping away.

"And what did you say?"

"What do you think? I told him I already have a boyfriend."

Everything she said was plausible. Her attitude seemed not to be one of guilt, merely bafflement that there should be any need to defend herself. But the vision of her with Roger had taken Tony's imagination hostage.

"I wish I believed you."

"Don't you trust me?"

"Trust doesn't change what I just saw."

Janet stared at him for a hard eight seconds to see if a retraction would be made. In the ninth second she conceded that none would be forthcoming.

"Fine, if that's how you feel."

She turned and walked away. Tony stared helplessly at the departure of his happiness, unable to comprehend what he had done. Then he realized it was far more important to immediately figure out what should be done next.

The answer reached his legs before his mind. When once again before Janet, he froze. How could this damage possibly be undone? No words seemed up to the task.

"I'm sorry."

Janet didn't say anything back. She accepted Tony's apology with a forgiving kiss that cast his fears into oblivion.

* * *

It was a perfect plan. The two of them would get married. He would find a job and they would get their own place. Then she would have the baby and they would be together forever. Just like in the movies.

Tanya had not spoken to Eric since the awful day he betrayed her, callously tossed aside the love she had deluged him with. She had sworn not to forget nor forgive his actions. Time would pass, the wounds would heal, he would become nothing but a distant memory.

That's what she told herself. That is what she tried to make happen. But the truth hung in the air before her like a persistent storm cloud. She would always love him. He would always be with her.

Tanya looked down at her stomach. Now he was literally a part of her. At first she had been terrified. She had been banished to hell for the sin of loving with too much vigor and not enough discretion.

Then came a revelation, causing her tragedy to be seen with new eyes. The baby would bring Eric back to her.

With the exception of Cheryl and Yolonda, no one knew she was pregnant. She wouldn't be able to keep it hidden much longer. Eventually her secret would tell itself. But if she was to get married to Eric, everything would be okay. Her life would be everything she ever wanted of it, just ahead of schedule.

So her mind was made up. Today she would tell him that he was going to be a father. She had asked him to meet her in the park at 3:30. It was now 3:42. She turned the band of her watch around so the face would be out of view, refusing to let time mock her with its habit of moving either too swiftly or too slow when closely observed.

"Hi."

It took all of her willpower not to rush into his arms.

"So what's this important thing you have to tell me?"

"I've missed you."

For two or three plodding seconds, he showed no reaction. Then he smiled, and it was like the re-emergence of the sun after an annihilating hurricane.

"I've missed you too. I picked up the phone to call you every day. But I knew how mad you were. I figured you'd never forgive me."

Tanya was stunned silent, so just listened as Eric said everything she had hoped to hear.

"I want you to know that girl means nothing to me. She's just a run of the mill skeezer. I don't know what I was thinking. I guess I got scared about how serious we were getting." Eric sat down and draped an arm around Tanya. "I love you, baby. I know this is asking a lot, but ..."

"I love you too."

Suddenly Tanya was back in the embrace of the man she loved, resuscitated by his kisses, resurrected by his touch. She had been petrified that her hopes for reclaiming him were childish fantasies. But those hopes paled in comparison to the reality which came to be. Love had not let her down. She had her Eric back.

"Let's go," he said once their lips parted.

"Go where?"

"My parents won't be home for a couple of hours. We have plenty of time to make up."

Reality set back in. What she had just been anxious to reveal, Tanya was now terrified to confess. She did not want to risk losing Eric immediately after reuniting. But what choice did she have?

"There's something I have to tell you first." She took the deepest breath of her life. "I'm pregnant."

Eric's arm withdrew. He spun his baseball cap around as if it were an antenna picking up what he hoped to have misheard.

"What are you telling me this for? You trying to say I have something to do with this?"

"Of course it's your baby," Tanya said. "You're the only one I've ever..."

"Bullshit! My pops warned me about girls like you. You go sleeping around and then try to convince some sucker that he's responsible for the trouble you've gotten your whoring ass into."

"Stop it, Eric, stop it. You know you were the only one."

"I don't have any money. So if you're trying to get me to foot the bill for an abortion, you picked the wrong brotha."

"I'm not trying to..."

Tanya swallowed the remainder of the sentence as her fairy tale crumbled around her. Happiness with Eric, much like his professed love for her, was merely an illusion. He was the person she had allowed herself to be most intimate with, but Tanya now clearly saw that before her was a stranger. What he had seemed to be was in fact the fanciful creation of her mind. Eric didn't give a damn about her. When he spoke of love, it was in the manner of someone who can recite a phrase in a foreign language but has no idea what it means. He only knows that it sounds pretty.

"I don't want you to do anything. Just leave."

Eric didn't need to be asked twice. He stood up and was quickly gone from sight.

Tanya had nothing to show for her ordeal with him but an unwelcome dose of reality and an unwanted child in her womb. The very fate prognosticated by her father. At the time she had hated his saying such a terrible thing, but this failed to stop her from living it out.

She knew three girls who had gotten pregnant while in high school. The situation had turned out fairly well for Rene. She ended up marrying the father about a month before giving birth. He quit school along with her and found a decent job as a mechanic. The last time Tanya saw them they were still together, still happy, with two more kids added to the mix. Their story had been her inspiration for a brief period, but Eric obviously had no intention of playing his part in such a scenario.

Jackie had been a mess long before getting pregnant. She was heavily into drugs and did whatever it took to whoever would obtain them. One of these guys insisted on not wearing a condom, and seven months later she was in labor. Motherhood did nothing to change Jackie's ways. Her son was born prematurely and an addict. Once he was out of her womb and in a harsh world, Jackie went immediately back to her old lifestyle until she overdosed. Her grandmother took custody of the child, exchanging a full grown crackhead for a miniature one.

Finally there was Maxine, who seemed stable before getting pregnant but was completely overwhelmed by the responsibilities of caring for an infant. She was sent to prison shortly after her baby was found dead in a dumpster.

Tanya rubbed her stomach. Just minutes before she had held lofty designs for her unborn child. But she now knew without doubt what must be done. She would get an abortion. Her uncle could provide the money. If he was willing to keep the secret to himself, her parents would never have to find out.

She loved the unformed being inside of her too much to ruin her baby's life because she did not yet have control of her own. Now that she was resolved, a sense of calm came over her. Like removing a bandage, she must act quickly. Pain was inevitable, but procrastination and indecision would only increase its intensity. The sooner this was done, the sooner she could start getting over it.

* * *

Lionel stared blankly at the flittering images on the television set. He recalled once finding amusement in the antics being played out before him, but that had been in a lifetime now beyond recognition.

His list of treasures was brief, but appreciated all the more because of this. Cold beer; a Mets game; Monday night football; the food and music of soul; making love to his wife; observing the poetry of a bird in flight. Maybe he couldn't afford the pleasures of a rich man, but his own served him just fine. Now he was being told that even these would soon be taken from him.

Lionel couldn't and wouldn't buy into that. He would leave this earth when he was good and ready, not a moment sooner. The cancer would have to find another life to pilfer, because he refused to let it take his. Enough had been taken from him already.

He didn't care what the so called medical experts had to say. They didn't know him. They had no idea what he had endured, how much glory he had aspired to, only to watch it slip away. No man would be cruel enough to pronounce his death sentence if he knew these things.

"Lionel, are you awake?"

He turned and saw his wife standing in the doorway. She came forward to take his outstretched hand. Lionel didn't have much, but he did have her, and often that was enough.

"How are you feeling?" Caren asked, already having broken the promise she had made to herself. Every time she came to visit, she swore she would not cry. Then she would see her husband lying helplessly and her resolve would fall to pieces.

"I'm feeling like dimming these lights, taking out a bottle of Ernie and Julio, putting on a Nat King Cole record. I think you know the rest."

Caren smiled and lay down beside him. Lionel ran his hand up and down her leg like he had done thousands of times before, but never with quite as much tenderness and poignancy.

"I've missed you," he said.

"What are you talking about? You see me every day."

"What I'm missing, you don't need eyes for. If I remember correctly, you keep yours closed."

"Not always. Sometimes I like to watch you."

Caren fingered the hairs in Lionel's mustache. For the past several weeks she had existed solely for the hours spent by his side. The rest of time was an iron maiden punishing her ceaselessly for reasons unknown. Each night she would dream of being in his arms, only to awaken to the merciless disappointment of a cold, vacant side of the bed.

"I'm going crazy in here," said Lionel. "I want to breathe real New York City air, not this sterilized shit. I want to feed the pigeons, have a beer, watch a ballgame in the comfort of my home. I want to be with my family. I want to make love to my wife."

"You'll have those things soon, honey. How much longer till you get the results of your tests?"

Lionel veered his gaze away from eye contact with Caren and answered quickly to keep himself from stopping mid-sentence. "Actually, my doctor was in here a little while ago."

Caren sat up. "What did he say?"

"What's it matter? It's what I know that counts."

"What did he say, Lionel?"

"What matters is that I'm not planning on going anywhere just yet. My family needs me. I promised I'd take care of you, and I meant it."

Caren did not press further. She waited for the truth to grow too unwieldy for her husband's grasp.

"What do these doctors know anyway? They're about as reliable as the weatherman, who as you may recall, said it was supposed to rain today. I see nothing but sunny sky through my window."

Lionel had told Dr. Weisman he wanted to deliver the news personally to Caren. Nearly twenty four hours had passed since his fate was etched in stone by medical science. But twenty four years would not have been long enough to find a way to sugarcoat his answer.

"He said the cancer has spread too far." Repeating the words to his wife was even more painful than hearing them the first time around. "Must've gotten bored laying about in my pancreas and decided to visit some other organs. They're not real hopeful."

"Oh God, no."

"Don't worry, baby," he said, desperate to convince her that the battle was not yet lost, for if she would believe perhaps her hope might be passed back to him. "Miracles take place everyday. One happens every time you smile."

He tilted Caren's face upwards towards his own.

"I know I've broken a lot of promises. I know I've let you down over and over again. But I won't this time. I can beat this."

He ran his fingers through her hair. Lionel loved her hair. And the nape of her neck. The tip of her nose. The bell of her ear. The slight swell of her belly. The gentle curve of her hips. The knuckles of her fingers and the nails on her toes. The suppleness of her lips. The serenity in her eyes. He loved everything about her. If a time machine existed, he would go back just to tell her that more often.

"I used to want a lot of things. Now I know I need nothing more than a lifetime with you. Do you believe in me, baby? Do you still believe in me?"

Caren nodded. It was easier to gesture a lie than speak it.

"You just wait and see," Lionel said, for he still needed to verbalize his thoughts no matter how little faith he had in them. "We're going to grow old together."

* * *

"Bartender, I'll have another."

Manny was drinking in the first bar he had come across, which happened to be the same one his brother frequented. Ordinarily he was not much of a drinker. Heavy burdens pressed down on him and he hoped alcohol might temporarily lighten the load. It succeeded merely in numbing his senses. The sounds about him; iced scooped into glass; liquid shaken and poured; reverent conversation about sports, missed opportunities, and lost loves; combined to create a gentle, almost melodic hum. Weighted eyelids and foggy retinas made it appear that all movement was slower and less steady than usual.

The day was not going well. His phone conversation with Caroline an hour earlier had confirmed that she was not softening in the least. She said she would not be in their house upon his return. He managed to talk her out of this by saying that if either of them was to leave, it should be him. She agreed to pack up his belongings so he'd be able, no matter how unwilling, to make his return home a short one. As the cherry on top she wanted full custody of their children, reasoning that he was scarcely ever around to take much notice of them anyway.

Manny said little in opposition, and not solely because he was given scarce opportunity and was also stunned beyond comprehension. His wife's responses to what he did manage to mutter were curt, spoken in a controlled monotone that was devoid of passion. With each calculated word, the futility of any attempt to sway her became increasingly obvious. Once her anger subsided to a somewhat rational level, he knew she would not continue in her insistence that his children be kept from him. She was just trying to make the earliest proceedings of their divorce as painful to him as possible, trying to match up with the hurt she was experiencing. In time her feelings about the destruction of their marriage would grow closer to a dull throb than the searing ache of freshly drawn blood. Cruelty was foreign to her nature, but for the moment she was trying her best to excel at it. Manny did not hold this against her. He was the only bad guy in this story and could not pretend otherwise.

His effort to patch the severed ties with his brother was going equally poorly. Lionel was likely to be soon buried with accusations of stolen dreams on his lips. And so, Manny was all out of self-coerced optimism. Monstrous reality was left in its place. Lionel had every right to feel as he did, and would not be relinquishing that right. Caroline would remarry and his children would grow up largely without his presence. Since Manny had spent a lifetime acting primarily on his own behalf, he would end up suitably alone. The punishment neatly fit his crimes.

He took a bitter swallow of his drink, hoping this would be the one to finally chase his problems away. It just added another trumpet to the brass band playing woefully off-key within his skull.

"How goes it?"

Manny turned and found his brother's friend. Perfect, another person who hated him.

"I've been better." He poured more of the potent elixir down his throat. "I don't think I'm up to another sermon on how much of a jerk I am. You can't bring me down any lower than I've managed to get on my own."

"Actually, I'd like to apologize," said Phil. "I was way out of line before."

"No you weren't. Everything you said was true."

Having been somewhat of a con man in his teen age years, Phil was usually able to recognize when a game was being run on him. Manny's current state aided in the cause since drunkenness tended to make men more themselves. One of its dangers was that it made them too much themselves. They became incapable of denying their pain. To the contrary, they feasted on it.

"You're being too hard on yourself," Phil said as he nodded at the bartender to indicate placement of his regular order, a fresh pour from the domestic beer tap.

"Nothing's ever been hard for me. I've gotten everything I ever wanted. I'm living the American dream. I don't give a damn about Lionel. I don't give a damn about anyone but me." Another gulp of bourbon served as exclamation point.

"If that were true I don't think you'd be here. Drinking yourself into oblivion isn't part of the American dream. Not in this dive anyway."

"You were right, Phil. I'm only adding more troubles to what he already has to deal with. Tomorrow I'm going back ..."

He had planned to say “home”, but since the house he had shared with Caroline and raised their children in would be no more than a pit stop on his journey, the word no longer seemed valid.

"I'm leaving. Lionel is better off with me as far away as possible."

"I think you're making a big mistake."

"Why?"

"Because he's your brother and he needs you,” Phil answered. “And as much as I hate to say this, it might be now or never. If I was in your shoes, no way could I just walk away."

"Haven't you heard? That's what I do."

"You also come back." Phil took a sip of his beer. "You said I didn't know your side. I've got some time to kill. Why don't you tell it to me."

"I don't have anything to say that you haven't already heard from Lionel." Manny prepared to finish his drink, but stopped. He stared at the glass as if surprised to find it in his hand. In fact, he was surprised to learn that he was in the mood to talk after all.

"This," he said. "This is the story. When my dad drank enough, he got mean. Very mean."

Phil nodded in understanding.

"Dreams are the story too. Big ones. He failed to make them come true, but just couldn't dream smaller no matter how drunk he got."

Manny held his hands before his face. His cuticles were expertly shaped, not a single callous marred his long fingers. This however, is not what he was seeing.

"Color. The bottom line is that being black prevented him from becoming the man he wanted to be. His anger and the liquor didn't mix, so he turned it on us, especially when he saw that Lionel and I had dreams of our own. Maybe he was trying to spare us, figuring he had done enough suffering for everybody. Or maybe he envied that we were taking our dreams further than he'd been able to."

Manny closed his eyes, transporting himself back to when he hit the crossroads of his life. It was a trip taken many times before, but never had the ride been so turbulent. Bourbon was not the smoothest of fuels.

The choice he made that long ago summer had defined his character. From then on, what he wanted would always prevail over what was right.

"After I passed the bar I had an ego the size of Texas. The world seemed to be lining up to kiss my ass. Then I'd see Lionel getting paid minimum wage, living in a dump, hardly surviving. I tried to help him out, but that just made it worse between us. I felt awful about how lopsided things had turned out, about the raw deal he'd gotten. But underneath my sympathy was always gratitude that his life hadn't happened to me."

"You would've had regrets either way," said Phil. "You went with the ones you minded least."

"Which makes me everything my brother's ever accused me of being, and worse."

"Which makes you human."

It was much too confusing, and the fact that the room was spinning didn't help. Maybe Phil was right, maybe not. Manny had only learned one thing for certain. He would never be a heavy drinker like his father and brother. He didn't have the constitution for it.

"Why don't we get out of here," Phil suggested.

"Sounds like a good idea." Manny hopped off the stool and was startled by how far away the floor had gone. Only the quick reaction of Phil prevented him from falling on his face. No sooner were they outside then did Manny bend over to throw up what he had spent the last couple of hours drinking down.

"Why do people drink?" he rhetorically asked after regaining a semblance of composure. "Give it enough of a chance and it can kill you."

"Maybe that's why."

Phil helped Manny to his feet and the two of them headed towards the nearest cup of coffee they could find.

CHAPTER TWENTY FOUR

Tony walked the empty hallways of Lincoln High School, being there after school hours because his intramural volleyball team had advanced to the final round. This event would receive little press in the recorded annals of mankind and no free trip to Disney Land was at stake. Nevertheless, it was a refreshing change to feel good about something. For the time that the game lasted, his concentration had been on nothing but the ball and the net. Thoughts of his dad or of Janet's disapproving family or of any other matters failed to penetrate his consciousness. And when the game's outcome was decided by no less than a spike by his own hand, it was as if all the joy he was capable of was suddenly released. Sometimes a win in volleyball is just what it takes.

His revelry ended when he turned the corner and came across the banner dedicated to Teddy Wilkins lying on the floor, spray painted letters blasphemously scrawled on the wall in its place. He looked to see if the authors were still lurking about. Finding no one, he focused his gaze back on the message that had been scripted in blood red. It consisted of merely one word, but spoke volumes.

Laughter trickled down the hall, followed by four members of Lincoln's varsity football team. Linebacker Jeff Fulgram, who allegedly popped steroids as if they were no more potent than Flintstones chewable vitamins; Vinny Ferrante, the prematurely balding offensive lineman; Tim Rhodes, the starting tight end whose matinee idol looks were offset by chronic bad breath; and at the head of the quartet of jocks was the team's star quarterback, Roger Lane.

Upon spotting Tony their conversation ceased. They looked at the defaced wall as if never having seen it before, but needn't have bothered with the playacting. He had no doubts that they were the ones responsible.

"I'm surprised you spelled it right."

Roger ignored the accusation.

"You're out of your league, Johnson. I really pissed Janet off, and you know how chicks are into revenge. But I didn't think she'd take it this far. I gotta give credit where it's due. She's made her point and then some. It won't last much longer though. I've let her know I give in. She can clean up and come home now."

Tony considered that if he brought this confrontation to blows, it would be four against one. Taking on Jeff alone would be the equivalent of rushing at an armored tank with a butter knife.

"I know you can see what's going on," Roger continued. "All you gotta do is open your eyes to see the writing on the wall." To accentuate his point he again scanned the offensive graffiti.

Tony was prepared to damn the odds and attack. Fear and discretion had taken a back seat to outrage. But he remained immobile. Even as the four of them walked away. Even when he noticed the confirming splotch of red paint on the back of Tim's sneaker. He was frozen not from fear of bodily harm, but in contemplation of what Roger had suggested.

The wall again exerted its magnetic pull. It was just a word. It took nothing from him. It made him feel only as low as he allowed himself to feel. His own brother used it in conversation habitually. But not in the same way - filled with malice, overflowing with insult. He couldn't tear his eyes away, shook with lust for retribution. Six little letters making one huge statement. NIGGER.

He pounded his fists against a locker, then another one, then another. Helpless to stop anything, to create anything but noise. The last few months had given him a lesson in human nature he would not soon forget. He had seen the soul of man at its darkest. All for the love of a girl.

Was it some of them or were none exempt? Did even Janet have trace amounts of bigotry lurking in her subconscious, waiting to strike when the time was right? Would she one day realize that she agreed with those who opposed them, that she was incapable of truly loving him?

Remembering his destination, Tony resumed walking towards the gym where he was supposed to meet her. The pain his tantrum had inflicted on his hands was beginning to set in.

There she was, twenty yards away, immersed in conversation with her friends from the cheerleading squad. Tony stopped. He had seen Janet with this crowd plenty of times, but something had changed.

He looked them over one by one. They were the same somewhat ditzy, head turning girls as always. Most of them stuck up, overly preoccupied with their looks. Susan Wilkes and Barbara Fischer were in the group. They were the respective girlfriends of Vinny and Jeff. That must be why he saw them differently. But no, that wasn't it.

Then it hit him. They had never seemed so glaringly white before. It was as if a spotlight was aimed at the girls, highlighting the features that defined them as Caucasian. The straight hair; deflated lips; narrow hips; thin noses; polkadot freckles; and the wall to wall, pale, bleached, ashen, wan, pasty, sickly, bloodless, lifeless, characterless, colorless flesh.

His sights again settled on Janet. The woman he loved. The most beautiful girl in the world, made of the very components which now seemed alien to him, repulsive even. A single thought overwhelmed everything else. He didn't belong here.

Tony could love in spite of rejection by Janet's family, the malice of her friends, the ignorance of his father. But not without regard for his own feelings, and he was no longer certain what they were.

Before she noticed him, he turned and headed outside. He couldn't be with her right now. His brain had spent the past few weeks on spin cycle. He needed to condense his contradictory beliefs into a single notion that his whiplashed mind could grasp.

* * *

The frigid gusts of a New York winter afforded Tanya the privacy she desired. She had the park bench upon which she sat to herself. Before learning that she was pregnant, most of her hours were spent as part of a group or half of a couple. Now she cherished isolation. As she placed her hand on her belly though, she recognized that even by herself, she was not alone.

At least things had become less complicated. She had gone to Eric because only he knew the words to the spell that could turn her confusion to clarity. And he cast it. Not as she had hoped. But by illustrating that the happily-ever-after life she envisioned would remain relegated to story books, so it was time to restore her old familiar one.

Now the matter had turned, as they often do, to money. She needed a few hundred dollars to pay for an abortion. Her uncle could spare the money, but would probably not do so without questions. If her condition was never revealed, she might eventually be able to forget. Once it was out, it would always be with her. She would never be able to leave behind the baby she had abandoned.

Applying pressure on Eric to live up to his responsibilities was an option. It wasn't fair that she had to deal with this mess on her own. But she wanted nothing to do with him anymore. If possible, she wanted to pretend away his existence and the damage wrought by his two faced love.

A lone teardrop made the epic journey down her sullen face. It was the first one shed in quite some time. She had thought herself no longer capable of them, her supply exhausted. About halfway down her cheek, the tear was captured on a fingertip. Tanya looked up towards the person who had intruded on her solitude.

"You dropped this," he said, sitting beside her.

"Larry I don't mean to be rude, but if you don't mind..."

“Actually, I do mind. And I do care. That’s why I followed you here.”

“Followed me?”

She slid a little further away from her brother’s friend. Tanya had always considered him to be a nice guy with a good sense of humor who was kind of cute for a white boy, and sometimes she vaguely suspected that he had a little crush on her even though he was older. But his talk of following her caused Tanya to worry that she might have a stalker to deal with, now of all times.

“What for?”

“I wanted to talk to you about something,” Larry answered.

“This really isn’t the best ...”

"I know, Tanya."

"You know what?"

"I know you're pregnant."

"What?” Tanya could not believe what she was hearing. Somehow Larry had become knowledgeable of her most sacred secret. Apparently her situation had become front page news. Just when she thought her life could not spiral any further out of control, yet more insanity had been tossed into the mix.

“How the hell?” she stammered. “Who told you?"

"That's not important."

"Who told you?" Tanya was stupefied that after treating her like dirt on the bottom of his Nikes, Eric had apparently gone around school bragging about his virility. It seemed there was no end to his cruelty.

"I promised that I..."

"Who told you?"

Larry understood from the tone of her voice that his promise would have to be broken.

"Yolonda did," he confessed. "But don't be mad at her. It's not her fault. She was doing a friend a favor."

"How is blabbing to everyone that I got knocked up doing me a favor?" Tanya couldn't believe she was having this conversation, that there was no one she could trust.

"She didn't tell everyone, just me. And *I'm* the one she did the favor for."

Larry spoke clearly and succinctly, but what he said was registered like writing reflected in a mirror. Even though she was familiar with the language, it was nearly impossible to make sense of his words.

"I don't understand."

"She told me because she's the only one who knows how I feel about you. Until now."

"How you feel about me?"

"Don't worry, my timing isn't this bad," said Larry with a reassuring grin. "I didn't come here to make a play for you. It's just that Yolonda figured I'd be willing to help."

"To help?"

"To lend you money for an abortion," he clarified. "I even know a place you can go. My cousin works there. It's a little out of the way, but I have a car now, so I figured I'd give you a ride. If you want it."

Larry saw that she was having great difficulty assimilating so much new information. As for his part, the words he spoke had not rolled effortlessly off his tongue. He had always viewed his feelings for Tanya as something that would remain secretive. If anything was meant to ever happen between them, he figured he would be given a sign.

Being told that she had been impregnated and abandoned in short order was a bit more sign than anticipated. Nevertheless here he was, acknowledging fate's calling card.

"I don't know what to say."

Tanya could not have been more honest. She had never thought about Larry in a romantic way, and at present, romance was the very last thing on her mind.

"No strings attached," he said. "Like I said, this isn't a play. We can handle it strictly as a loan. You can pay me back in installments. Whatever you can afford whenever you have it. No hurry."

"You like me?"

"We can talk about that if you want. But later. First things first."

As tempting as it was to ride this gift horse directly to the bank, Tanya needed a reality check. Solutions to problems of such magnitude typically didn't just pop up like a jack-in-the-box. Not without a catch.

"I don't want to lead you on, Larry. You're going to expect me to pay back more than just money. You're going to want your feelings returned. And I don't know if I can feel that way about you, or about anybody. Not for a long while anyway."

Larry took hold of Tanya's hands. Her instinctive reaction was to pull away. The last thing she wanted or needed was a man's touch. But the look in his eyes, sincerity it seemed, and an indescribable something more, kept her hands still.

"I'm doing a favor for a good friend's sister. I owe him one, and this should cover it. You can do with your feelings whatever you like. I'm not asking for promises. I'm not asking for anything."

Tanya could only stare at him in amazement, thinking that sometimes you find a way, and sometimes the way finds you.

CHAPTER TWENTY FIVE

A member of the Kaos Krew passed by C.J. and Lisa as they walked hand in hand through McKinley High School. The scowl on his face indicated bad intentions. C.J. kept his own expression blank, refusing to show concern much less fear. The only evidence of his discomfort came moments later as he attempted to open his locker and turned the wrong combination on his lock.

In the past few days verbal and written messages had appeared steadily. Most of them were threatening. A few were earnest pleas for C.J. to rejoin before it was too late.

Louis had declared a deadline for him to change his mind by. Today was it. Whatever was to be done would take place soon.

C.J. was gambling considerably more than he was willing to lose. But when he thought about the death of Tyrone; about how much his leaving the Krew had pleased Lisa; about the sense of pride he had sprouted these past few weeks; it seemed the bet had paid off.

Every day since declaring independence, he had found out something new about himself. Individually they were minor finds, but collectively these discoveries reformed him. He delighted in the unearthing of each piece. By becoming one of the Kaos Krew he had virtually sold his soul to the devil. Snatching it back was a dangerous act, for the devil was not disposed to giving refunds.

Getting the right combination the second time around, C.J. opened his locker. Its contents were mutilated. The pages had been torn from his textbooks, and far more painfully, from his comic books. A crude drawing of a skull and crossbones with KK written beneath it left no doubt as to who the perpetrators were. He closed the door quickly, but not fast enough to achieve his purpose.

"C.J., what's going on?"

He had managed to keep the threats a secret from Lisa up till now. His motivation was that he did not want to upset her, but even more, silence was the best way to remain in a state of denial.

"Nothing to worry about."

"Don't give me that. I want to know the truth. Did they really say it was okay for you to leave?"

C.J. shook his head.

"Why didn't you tell me?"

"I didn't want you getting worked up over nothing. I know Louis. He's trying to scare me by talking tough, but talk is all it is."

"This is my fault. You told me this would happen, but I wouldn't listen. What are we going to do?"

"Don't sweat it, Boo. It's just a bluff. They make their point, make me a little nervous, and then time passes and the whole thing is history. They've got nothing to gain by coming after me. If there's nothing in it for the Krew, they don't waste their time or energy."

"But suppose it isn't a bluff. Suppose ..." The remainder of the supposition was too terrible to verbalize.

C.J. gripped Lisa by the shoulders. He didn't want to see her frightened. It did nothing to strengthen his already shaky resolve.

"Do you want me running with them again?" he asked.

"No."

"Then trust me. Everything is going to be fine. Now let's get to work on what I really have to worry about, passing that damn algebra test."

* * *

Tony stared at the picture he kept in his wallet. He and Janet with cheeks pressed together, expressions of bliss on both of their faces, a moment of tenderness captured for eternity. It had been taken in a photo booth at the movie theater they went to most weekends. That had been a great day. They had seen something he couldn't remember, except that it was funny and romantic, gorged on White Castle hamburgers and rock solid milkshakes, then made love in Room 6C of the Bussing Motel.

The photograph was a little more than one month old, but its subject matter belonged to a past which had drifted almost beyond the point of recognition. He and Janet could not be together lately for more than five minutes without an argument breaking out. He found himself taking offense at one issue after another, translating the most neutral of statements as insults and criticism.

At night he stared at the cracks in the plaster of his bedroom ceiling, trying to figure out what had gone wrong and how to make it right again. He knew Janet was still the same girl who first captivated him. But *he* was no longer the same. It made little difference whether an alteration was made to a viewer's perspective or to that which was viewed. Either way, the original sight was lost.

Sometimes Tony would almost be able to convince himself that his old feelings were not gone for good, just temporarily misplaced. But then the anger would return. At what, he didn't even try to determine. It was just deaf, dumb and blind rage coursing through his veins, turning his blood to ice water, his heart becoming hard as iron. Love didn't stand a chance.

The previous night he had lain beside Janet, half listening to her words of consolation. “It happens to everyone,” she said. How would she know? It wasn't a concern she ever had to worry about. And he doubted her one and only former lover ever failed to perform his duties. How could Roger, or any red blooded heterosexual male for that matter, not be aroused by her? As for himself, Tony placed the blame on random thoughts. Thinking was the chief adversary of action.

He felt more irritated than ashamed or embarrassed. His heart wasn't into it, so why should he expect blood to be pumped as required to other organs? He might have worried, except that Janet's voice annoyed him too much to allow the indulgence.

"We can just talk," she said next. Tony was damned if he was going to spend his hard earned money on something he could do anywhere for free. The meter on their love nest was running. He closed his eyes and concentrated until her voice faded away. He stepped out of himself and into new skin. He was a slave fresh off a ship from Africa, alone with his master's wife. She couldn't pry her eyes off his naked, gleaming, black, forbidden flesh. The white man had taken his freedom and dignity. He would take something in return.

Janet didn't notice that their problem had been resolved until she was shoved back roughly and entered rougher still. Tony sought no pleasure, nor strove to give any. He was primal and relentless, and afterwards, silent.

Despite his ambivalence, breaking up with Janet was not a consideration. If he did, Roger and his friends would think they had won. They would believe they had intimidated him into running away. Knowing that they would be wrong offered no consolation. He would stay with her if for no other reason than spite, and at the moment, that was the best reason he could think of.

Tony approached Lincoln as the cheerleaders were leaving. Seeing no sign of his girlfriend, he entered the building. The first thing he saw was Janet and a football player discussing something in a manner far too cozy for his liking.

As he came within hearing distance, the conversation conveniently ended. The departing athlete was a blur of red due to his complexion and flame-like hair.

Janet kissed Tony in greeting. No sooner were her lips removed than her betrayal began.

"Did you have anything definite planned for us this weekend?"

"Not really. Why?"

"I was just invited to a party out on Long island. I'd kind of like to go. Some friends I haven't seen in ages will be there."

"Knock yourself out," Tony said stoically. "I don't want to get in the way of a good time. I'm *only* your boyfriend."

"Stop being silly. I want you to come with me, of course."

"I don't think so. Something tells me it won't be my kind of scene."

"It's a party, same as any other," said Janet. "It will be fun."

"For you no doubt. Judging from who the invitation came from, I'm guessing I'd be best off staying away. But you should go. You have no problem with that crowd. Hell, you *are* that crowd. And I'm not going to fight you over it anymore."

Janet's face screwed up into an expression of bewilderment intertwined with irritation. What she thought was to be a harmless discussion had escalated into yet another quarrel.

"What are you saying?" she asked.

"I see no good reason for you to be so chummy with the football team, considering what they think of me. Of us."

Janet sighed in exasperation.

"Do you want me to hide in a cave because you and my last boyfriend don't get along? I doubt he'll even be there. There's another party being thrown this weekend that he'll probably go to."

"Isn't it convenient that you happen to know his itinerary? For someone you're no longer seeing, you've certainly kept up to date on what he's doing and where he's doing it."

"Tony, you've got to get over this already. You're so hung up on these people. Nobody is conspiring against you. You're the one I love. You're the one I want to be with. There is nothing to be paranoid about except what you've invented in your head."

Janet's attempt to placate was a failed one. Tony saw right through her rationalizations and didn't like what was found.

"You want it back, don't you?" he asked. "The whole ball of wax. Best girl of the quarterback, center of this school's little universe."

"If anyone's missing anything, it's you," Janet countered. "You're the one doing all the complaining. You probably have friends you don't bring me around, places you avoid when you're with me. If you do, I would understand. I certainly wouldn't try to make you feel bad about not including me in every little thing. We're a couple, but we're also two separate people. It's okay that we have lives outside of each other. It's healthy."

The most ridiculous theory could be made to seem reasonable if twisted into a deceiving shape. Tony was not to be fooled. He understood the difference between a healthy relationship and one that was rotting at the core.

"You obviously don't know shit about my friends, or about me. Don't try to throw this back in my face, because I'm not the one who's been caught."

"Caught doing what?" Janet asked, her voice rising along with emotions no longer being held at bay. "Wanting to go to a party? When did that become a crime?"

"I don't want to feel like I'm keeping you from something, like I'm this burden you have to lug around. Just be honest with me."

Janet knew that Tony had been hurt by her family's reception of him. She understood that conflicting feelings about his father were beating him up. Questions had been raised in his mind that he was having difficulty grappling with. Confusion more often than not leads to anger. Janet had been willing to accept this anger. She loved Tony, had felt confident that if she remained patient and supportive, eventually his old self would return.

But her plan had failed. The Tony she knew wasn't coming back. He had become someone else, someone who was short tempered and self centered. Janet would tolerate it no longer. At least not silently.

"You want honesty, how's this? I'm sick of fighting with you and not knowing what the hell we're fighting about. I'm tired of being accused of, of nothing, but accused just the same. I'm tired of defending myself when I've done nothing wrong. If you don't love me anymore, at least have the decency to admit it, and to tell me why."

Tony did love her, and wanted more than anything to explain why this had become unbearable. But when he opened his mouth to speak he discovered that far more than clarity, what he wanted to bestow upon Janet was a share of his pain.

"It's a black thing. You wouldn't understand."

"Fuck you, Tony."

"What did you say?"

"I said fuck you. Fuck you, fuck you, fuck..."

Janet's stream of curses was cut short abruptly as Tony's open hand struck her cheek, snapped back her head, and pushed their relationship beyond redemption. The lovers became deathly silent and sent daggers with their eyes.

Janet's had transformed into the icy blue of her father's. Tony didn't care whom he resembled.

"Congratulations," Janet said. "You're finally getting what you wanted." She walked away, her gait as steady as her voice had remarkably been.

"You couldn't wait to go back, could you?" Tony shouted, determined to get the last word in. "To your old boyfriend, your old friends, your old life. Sorry I kept you so long."

Janet turned to respond, but changed her mind. She went back to her original course, going through the doors leading outside, leaving Tony on his own.

CHAPTER TWENTY SIX

One of the urban street poets that C.J. idolized shouted a rhythmic message from the radio by his bedside. Beside him was a pad full of the rhymes he had concocted. Perhaps this would be his way out. He felt his stuff was better than that of a lot of guys who received record deals and radio play. They had made it, changed their lives into something really worth living, made themselves the envy of all pretenders to their throne, so why not him? It was simply a matter of making the right connections. He hoped to one day rival the skills and success of his two mentors, Tupac Shakur and the Notorious B.I.G., who unfortunately had both been gunned down in their prime for the sin of living their lyrics.

The door to his room opened and Tanya entered. She had knocked first, but C.J. was oblivious to any sounds beyond the stereo speakers.

"What's up, sis?" When she didn't answer, C.J. got the hint and turned down the music.

"I need some money," Tanya said, seeing no reason to stall before getting to the point. "I thought you might have it."

She had decided not to take Larry up on his offer. Regardless of what he said, she saw strings attached to his money. He claimed his intentions were good, but she had learned to bestow trust with extreme caution. She had also determined that her uncle would not be the safest best, for he was likely to be inquisitive about what the money would be spent on, and his loyalty would probably to be her parents. So she turned to her closest friends, borrowing what she could from Yolonda and Cheryl. When this came up considerably short of what she needed, she next went to Tony, but he was broke. So she would now try to obtain the bulk of what she needed from her little brother, who was likely to have sufficient funds in his possession but not necessarily a willingness to part with it. C.J.'s money was tainted by how it had been earned, but Tanya rationalized that it would be applied to a worthy cause. Well, not exactly worthy. An awful one actually, but she was in no position to be choosy or righteous.

"How much we talking?"

"Two hundred dollars."

"Two hundred. Shit, I was thinking it would be more like twenty. Do I get it back?"

"Yes. It will probably take me awhile though."

“What do you need it for?”

“I’d rather not say.”

C.J. fidgeted with his chains as he contemplated parting with such a sizable amount of cash.

"I get the feeling this ain't for new gear, or hair extensions, or any of the usual bullshit you girls waste money on. You all right?"

Tony had asked the same question and received an identical reply.

"Depends on your answer."

An hour later Tanya sat in the waiting room of the clinic nervously waiting for her name to be called. All the arrangements had been made. Being a single, sixteen year old mother was no life for her. So this was the way it would have to be.

If only things had turned out differently, maybe her decision would have as well. If Eric had chosen to marry her, or at least accepted responsibility for their baby. If it didn't look as if her father might soon die. If. What a word. Things were as they were, like it or not. Ifs created the illusion of rising hopes that were in fact anchored firmly and permanently to the ground.

Tanya hadn't given up on happy endings. She still believed life could be like a fairy tale. But what good would it be to finally meet up with Prince Charming if she was holding a kid in her arms? He would just climb back on his horse and ride away.

Her choice was based on the soundest of logic. She would no doubt have regrets, but everyone accumulated their allotted share of those. Just about all the black girls in the Bronx that she knew adhered to the rules of their world. Not even Oprah was much help in motivating them to be the exception to those rules. The stereotypes would always greatly outnumber the odds breakers. Daydreaming that there was a much better fate in store for her than that awaiting her peers came to an abrupt end the minute she learned she was a pregnant, a statistic with nothing special or unique about her but CSI DNA type stuff and her social security number.

The daydreams had been put aside for the time being, but not permanently discarded. Eventually she would have kids who she would raise with her handsome, loving husband in their big house in the country. Perhaps they would go horseback riding or boating on weekends. She refused to relinquish this idyllic vision of the future at such a young age no matter how unrealistic she knew it to be.

But look at what she was disposing of instead.

"Tanya Johnson," the nurse's voice shrieked. Tanya caressed her stomach, which showed practically no sign of a person being formed beneath it. She had not experienced cravings, or swollen feet, or the majority of pregnancy traits she was familiar with. Movement was yet to be felt in her womb. It was almost as if nothing was there. But almost didn't count and wouldn't last for long.

"Tanya Johnson," the shrill voice repeated.

Fate had wrenched freedom of choice from her grasp. Like it or not, there was but one thing for her to do. As unfair as this may have been, nothing could change it.

Tanya stood up and walked towards the nurse. She continued right on past the woman, whose face unfortunately matched her voice, and kept walking until she was outside. Tanya drew a deep breath as if having emerged from underwater seconds before drowning. She could not avoid making a choice, but she could postpone it a little longer.

* * *

After loaning money to Tanya, C.J. drifted back into his music. The decibel level was as he liked it, slightly below deafening. He recited the rapid fire lyrics with eyes closed, picturing himself performing on stage. About half an hour had passed when a shadow fell across his face, informing him that he was no longer alone. He waited for the inevitable lowering of the volume by his brother. When the music continued to blare, C.J. opened his eyes. Tony had sat on his bed and was staring down at the carpet, apparently unable to think of anything more interesting to do. C.J. turned the music off.

"What's up?"

When his question went ignored, C.J. took an educated guess at the answer. He recognized the expression on Tony's face. It was the one that typically accompanied losing something precious.

"Trouble with Barbie?"

Tony remained silent as he reflected on what he had thrown away. Viruses of insecurity and doubt had polluted the bloodstream of his relationship with Janet. Resentment built upon itself like a snowball rolling down a hill. A love that once made him feel he was the luckiest man alive had come to bring more bad with it than good. So he cut his misery and losses short. Solitude was chosen over the corrosiveness of resentment.

The lack of response told C.J. that his guess was accurate. His brother had obviously been blindsided by whatever went down, even though to C.J., such an end result to Tony's relationship with that white girl was a predictable conclusion. When he first found Tony staring at her picture, he had looked like a child in a candy store. His eyes were wide open while the part of his brain that housed common sense was boarded shut. Tony devoured the sweets before him without considering if it might be bad for him.

His desire for Janet was considered by C.J. to be weakness, a sickness even. And in the end, pointless. No matter how many white lovers and half white babies a black man went through, he would always be running a losing race away from who he was.

C.J. rose to leave the room, pausing on the way out to pat his brother's shoulder.

"Things will get better. Probably won't get worse, anyway."

C.J. was now officially the winner of their arguments, but it made no real difference which of them could claim victory. The matter had ceased to be about blackness and whiteness. Tony had just lost his girl. That was the alpha and the omega of what he was going through. Any tears he may shed would be colorless.

* * *

Manny's footsteps faltered at the doorway of his brother's hospital room, but with grim determination he continued forward until reaching the bed. The sight before him brought about an involuntary shudder, but he forced himself not to look away. If Lionel felt half as bad as he looked, the pain must have been unimaginably malicious. Shifting position, Lionel discovered the unwelcome intruder.

His eyes flared in recognition. Strength may have abandoned his body, but passion remained in his dark eyes.

"Still slumming in my neighborhood? Don't you have a fancy job to go to?"

"I'm on vacation."

"You must have a lousy travel agent. This definitely ain't Disney Land."

Manny grinned. As boys they were as close as could be, and wherever they were to be found, the joyous sound of their laughter could be heard. As men, laughs between the two of them were few and far between. Even a small smirk was a rare treasure.

He had returned to his brother's bedside with slim hope of Lionel finally recognizing that he was not a villain, merely a selfish man who had made mistakes, done his penance, and should be granted clemency even if he didn't quite deserve it. Manny thought he finally detected a glimmer of this hope being realized. Or perhaps Lionel was simply too weak to fight anymore.

"How are you feeling?"

"They tell me I'm going to be worm food soon. The chemo hasn't done much. The doctor says the most I got is four to six months."

The words were a punch to the stomach. Manny's flaws of character had not brought this terrible situation about, but he felt guilty nonetheless. After years of denying responsibility for the results of his actions he was now willing to accept blame for all of the world's ills.

"What does he know?" Lionel continued. "I'm sure I still have a few years left on my warranty. They diagnose whatever costs the most to treat. If anything's killing me it's the designer drugs they're pumping me full of."

"I remember when you thought a doctor was the noblest thing a man could be."

Manny was bringing up the past, which was akin to tossing gasoline on an open fire. But it would be coming up sooner or later. It always did. So why wait?

"I was a kid, what did I know? To me a doctor was someone who helped people, saved lives. But they only care about ripping off the insurance companies, avoiding lawsuits, and making their tee off times."

Lionel began to cough, his torso heaving violently with each expulsion of air. When able to resume normal breathing, he finished his thought.

"It's the lowest level a man can sink to. Make that second lowest. I almost forgot about lawyers they hire to defend them against the lawsuits."

Another joke. Manny was glad to see that Lionel hadn't lost his edgy sense of humor. Then again, he may very well have been serious.

"I'd like to think had I made it, I would have been different. I never got the chance to find out, did I?"

"No, you didn't. I wish you would believe how sorry I am about that."

"I believe you," said Lionel

Manny wasn't sure how to respond to this. He could not help but wonder if a trap was being laid for him. Might his brother not get a perverted kick out of pretending to grant forgiveness, only to then pull the rug out from underfoot? This seemed rather absurd, yet it made equally little sense that their battle could end so abruptly, on such a muted note. Lionel had given no indication of anything but scorn for him up until now. Why should this change? Was it due to realization that the end was close at hand?

"I believe you're sorry I didn't become a doctor," Lionel continued. "You're sorry I have cancer. You're sorry I can't support my family."

The picture was beginning to come into focus. Accepting the sincerity of one's sympathy was not the same as forgiveness. Manny was as empty handed in that department as ever.

"If you could snap your fingers and make everything better, I'm sure you would. Unfortunately you can't, and that's all there is to this."

"No, that isn't true" said Manny with undisguised desperation. "There's a lot more to this. You have every right to be angry, Lionel. But people refuse their rights every day."

"I'm not wasting any more time being angry. I have one thing to concentrate on, and that's getting out of here."

Manny could offer nothing but another apology doomed to rejection. "I can't say enough times how sorry I am about everything."

"Yeah, I know. You're sorry, the doctors are sorry, my friends are sorry. Everyone might as well save their breath. I don't need anyone's pity because I'm going to beat this thing. I'm going to walk out of here, find a decent job, pay off my debts, including the one to you, and get my house back in order. I have a family depending on me."

Lionel paused, perhaps daring Manny to refute his claims, but the silence was left untouched. When no argument was offered, he proceeded to dispute himself.

"Then again, maybe they'll be better off without me. I haven't exactly given them a life of luxury."

"You mean much more to your family than the size of your paycheck," Manny said.

"That's a hell of a lot easier for you to say than me."

"No it isn't. It's harder". Manny decided to offer proof. "Caroline wants a divorce."

It felt as if the words were spoken by someone else. His unwillingness to accept the erosion of his marriage had been quite successful. On each occasion he was forced to acknowledge reality, it was like finding out for the first time.

"Seeing how much Caren loves you has made me realize ... Well, it's helped me to see what a fool I've been. To be honest, it's made me envious of you."

Manny did not lack for acquaintances. He spent a considerable amount of social time with associates at cocktail parties, power lunches, golf courses, and tennis courts. But he was not close with these people. He did not confide his most personal feelings to them. Outside of Caroline, there was no one to share such thoughts and emotions with. He needed a brother now more than ever. The irony did not escape him. Lionel was confined to a hospital bed, his remaining breaths finitely numbered, yet he was still the stronger of the two.

Manny reproached himself for not trying in earnest to make amends sooner. He sent a curse towards God, or nature, or whatever it was that had caused his brother's cells to rebel against him. Looking into Lionel's eyes, one saw a great deal reflected back. Fervent pride, indomitable will, unquenchable determination to be master of his destiny. But one look at his withered form made it plain that this plague would not be overcome.

"I had an affair," Manny reluctantly admitted, for each person who learned of his wretched behavior increased his degree of shame over it. "It meant nothing to me, which is something I take no pride in claiming, but that didn't make it any less real to Caroline. I never meant to hurt her. Guess that's not much of an excuse. What we mean doesn't count for a whole lot, I guess. Only what we do."

He hated to think of the day when Caroline confronted him, but did so all the time. His life was like a record that had been scratched precisely at the point where his marriage ended, causing the needle to stop and echo the moment indefinitely. Manny had tried his best to lie, then once this failed, to explain. But usually dependable words failed him. The tremor in his wife's voice was more than he could take.

Lionel gave no response to the confession, deepening Manny's frustration. When Lionel was telling him off, there was little room for misinterpretation. Silence could mean anything, or nothing at all.

"I'm trying to change. It's taken a hell of a lot to open my eyes. A lot of casualties. But I am trying."

Lionel continued to give no indication of caring one way or another about what he was being told. He seemed to be laying in wait for something. Manny felt he had no choice but to keep talking.

"I want you to know that you don't have to worry how Caren and the kids will get by financially. I'll make sure they are well provided for. I'll watch out for them the best I can."

Lionel finally chose to speak. "Lose one family, adopt another. You've found the one thing I have that you don't, so now you want to take that too. You want to make sure I'm left with nothing."

"Come on, Lionel. You know better than to think craziness like that."

"No, I think I've hit it right on the nose. But it doesn't matter. You're out of luck this time, Manny. I've got a little secret to tell you about sick people. Sometimes they get better. And that's just what I intend to do. So I suggest you go back to your own wife, try begging her a little harder for forgiveness, because mine ain't available."

Lionel wished he could drag Manny out of the room, out of the hospital, out of the Bronx, and out of his life for good. But he couldn't even rise to his feet.

"Get the hell out of here," he commanded in an impotent whisper.

"And then what? You think everything will get better once I'm gone? Do you believe your cancer will go away, your bills will go away, your problems will vanish simply because you told them to?"

"You have no idea how much I hate you."

The result of this statement was unexpectedly emancipating to Manny. Since his goal of reconciliation was obviously beyond reach, guilt and sympathy were put aside. He was free at last to speak his mind, to express how pissed off Lionel was making him. Like a pack of junk yard dogs that had brought the gate which imprisoned them crashing down, long muffled anger was set loose, anxious to devour.

"I have every fucking idea. That's why I've done all I could to make peace with you. But enough is enough. I can handle as much bile as you can dish out, but I can't knock the chip off your shoulder because I'm not the one who put it there. You managed that for yourself."

"I knew you hadn't changed. When have you ever decided that something *was* your fault? When's the last time you thought about anyone other than yourself?"

"This isn't about me, Lionel. This isn't about choices made when we were kids. Remember how badly we wanted to stop Dad from drinking? We couldn't take that bottle from his hand, could we? It was his choice alone to make.

"I thought you should have gone to college with me. I hoped with all my might that you would. But it wasn't up to me. The only actions I had control over were my own."

Manny clenched his fists to maintain stillness and calm, for his composure was on the verge of slipping away. Once tempers were lost, so was any opportunity at reconciliation. If debate gave way to yelling and cursing, all hope was eliminated. The fine line between passion and fury could not be crossed if there was to be any chance of reaching common, stable ground. Reason needed to dominate emotion no matter how daunting a challenge this was. Lionel could goad with the best of them. Manny's objective was to refrain from taking his bait.

"I know all about the actions you had control over," Lionel said. "You could have stuck around to help look out for Mom and Angie. You could have given back a tiny fraction of what was given to you."

"Yes, you're right," Manny admitted. "I could have. But I didn't. I made my choices. I lived my life the way I wanted to live it, right or wrong. I was a selfish bastard. I deny nothing. Not anymore. How about you, Lionel? When are you going to start taking accountability? When are you going to figure out that pushing around the people who are trying to love you can come to no good, unless your goal is to end up despised and alone? When are you going to realize that blaming other people doesn't fix anything? It doesn't even make you feel better, does it?"

"You arrogant son of a bitch. How dare you judge me?"

"I dare because I'm made of black flesh and red blood, same as you. I had the same opportunities to step up or get stepped on. I chose to put my fate in my own hands because I didn't like the look of the future if I just sat back and waited for it to happen. I won't pretend I'm not grateful that my kids don't have to want for anything. But that doesn't mean I don't feel terrible about the position I left you in. You're the last person I ever wanted to hurt. I wanted the world for both of us. But I wasn't as strong as you, Lionel. If I didn't leave when I did, I knew I would die there. I knew Dad would hold me back as strongly as he held on to a last call drink if I didn't take off fast and keep myself from looking back."

"You think feeling badly is enough?" Lionel asked. "Do you believe that's all you owe?"

He grimaced after posing these questions, a not so subtle reminder that the cancer was still hard at work. Manny wished the pain could be transferred to him, and that he had left poor enough alone. If this was how Lionel wanted things to be, perhaps this desire should have been respected. The rift between the two of them had been ignored for twenty five years. What good could result from attempting to vault it now?

Lionel's discomfort slowly subsided. He waited a moment after the pain had departed to catch his breath and round up his thoughts. Then he expressed them without censor.

"I want you to listen up good, Manny, because I don't intend to repeat myself and I don't plan to discuss this any further. The reason I'll never forgive you is because you looked into the eyes of your family and said: 'To hell with you. You can die for all I care. The only thing that matters is that I get what I want.' Maybe you didn't literally say those words, but that's what you meant, and that's what we heard. Life may be cruel and Satan may be a real son of a bitch. But when it came to being the asshole of all assholes, you took the cake, ate it up, and loved every mother fucking bite."

Lionel wanted to add an ounce of pain to his brother's guilt stacked conscience for each hour of back breaking labor he had endured, every dollar which had not turned up in his pocket when needed, every time he had cursed his fortune. Judging by the hurt in Manny's eyes, it had been accomplished. The score was as even as it was ever likely to be. If only this was enough.

"I'm working on becoming a better person," said Manny with quiet defiance. "Some days I feel I've made real progress. Some days I'm not so sure. But no matter how much I change, I can't undo a single thing. What's done is done."

Time had taught him that whether his sins were pardoned or left unforgiven, they would remain committed. Tomorrow he would hopefully choose wiser, with a stronger measure of compassion.

"I can't make you forgive me," he continued. "That too is out of my hands. The most I can do is try to make up for what I've done. As for you, you have two choices. You can spend your time feeling cheated. Or you can accept what's happened and what's going to happen, maybe find peace of mind while you're at it. I personally would trade every cent I've earned for some of that."

There was no dishonor in failure if everything to be given had been offered. Manny had nothing left. His heart had been emptied. He started to walk out, but Lionel's voice brought him to a halt.

"I'm tired of accepting what I don't want. Why can't I say no just once? No, I don't want to have cancer. No, I don't want to die."

Lionel wiped his face hard, obliterating any evidence of weakness to have temporarily appeared. Then he did something even more mystifying than the shedding of tears. He reached out. Manny tentatively stepped forward and took hold of his brother's outstretched hand.

"Do what you promised," Lionel said. "Take care of them for me."

The welfare of his family was his responsibility till death and beyond. The resentment he felt towards Manny must not be allowed to jeopardize their well being. His remaining hours were far too scarce for him to make any more bad decisions.

"Guess I better prepare for the inevitable. A man's got to do what a man's got to do. Dad's one piece of wisdom. Remember?"

"Yeah, I remember," Manny answered.

It was impossible to forget. Manny had clung to those words for solace as he spent sleepless nights in his dorm room. It had not been easy living with the knowledge that he had held his brother down in order to raise himself up, but desperate acts are born of necessity.

"I didn't want to end up like him," Lionel said. "A drunk who wasted his life dreaming about things that would never be. I fought it the best I could. I guess he did too."

Manny often recalled the day he had played hooky from school and came across the sight of his father emerging from a bar with a strange woman on his arm. The drunken beatings he may have forgiven, but this betrayal of his mother destroyed the last trace of a son's respect. In hope that she would gather her children up and take them someplace far away, Manny told her what he had seen. She in turn told him that she knew all about her husband's philandering, and that in spite of it, they would not be going anywhere. Manny could not understand why his mother chose to stand for such behavior. Years later when his own wife proved to be far less accommodating, he failed to comprehend how he had managed to become what he abhorred. Like Lionel, he had fought but ultimately lost the battle to escape their father's legacy.

"Despite everything I still loved him," Lionel said, drawing Manny from a tortured past to the merciless present. "I guess that's why you left while I couldn't. You refused to love anyone who wouldn't give it back. In the end Dad didn't give a damn about anything but the bottle."

They were to decide between attempting to save a drowning man who would probably drag them under with him, or turning away to save themselves. Condemning Manny for abandonment allowed Lionel to ignore the regret he felt over staying put. He had long claimed loyalty to family as his chief motivation, but there was much more to it.

Winning a college scholarship meant everything to Lionel, not only because of the opportunities made available but also for the statement of vindication proclaimed. It was proof that his intellect and humanity warranted recognition, despite claims to the contrary that formed the fabric of his existence. White people could call him any name they wanted. His father could rant till doomsday about how black folks were foolish to hope for better days to come, ignoring that he himself was the greatest perpetrator of this crime.

Lionel was deaf to such teachings. He knew he was inferior to no one, regardless of where he was made to sit, or eat, or learn. No matter how often he was warned that an uppity nigger was not too far off from being a dead one.

Then his brother took off and insecurity took hold. They had traveled from day one on a two seated bicycle, and it was always Manny up front steering, Lionel who occasionally stopped peddling and coasted. Manny's departure raised issues that little thought had been given to before. Most prominent amongst them was whether it was worth leaving Caren behind to chase what may never be caught. Despite her declarations of never ending devotion, there was no guarantee that she would be waiting upon his return from college. Once the familiar was discarded, change was inevitable, and not necessarily for the better. Lionel's conviction in the dreams once shared with his brother was not as strong when held alone. If he tried but failed to achieve them, he might be left with nothing. As long as he remained by Caren's side, there was no fear of coming up short. Her love was the safer bet.

"You know what I should have learned from Dad. No matter how much you love people, you'll never bother to show them if you're busy feeling sorry for yourself."

He leaned back and closed his eyes. Manny recognized the magnanimity of the gesture. Lionel had let down his guard. He was allowing a truce to be called.

"That's the funny thing about life. We get about an equal share of shit and roses. Nobody gets just one or the other. But we often see it that way."

"This is true," said Manny.

Lionel was done thinking of his father, through with dwelling on a past that refused to release its clutches. From here on out he would focus on the reality of here and now, for this was the only way to salvage a dwindling future. That future was not without promise, despite the fact that he was not long for this world. There were many tomorrows to be lived through his children. He could only hope that they would face them more courageously than he had, that his mistakes would serve as warning signs rather than crutches to lean on.

"I've fought Tony tooth and nail about everything he wants to accomplish, just like Dad fought us. It was my intention to teach him about owning up to his responsibilities. I wanted to prepare him for what it takes to be a man, especially a black man. I thought I could spare him from disappointment by smashing his illusions early on. But I guess I was really just trying to live his life for him. I was trying to get back at you, and at Dad, and at the entire world by training my sons to be as angry at it as I've been."

Lionel shook his head in disbelief of the years he had wasted and love he had squandered. "The only thing I accomplished was getting Tony to resent me. To hate me."

"You might think that's what you did," Manny said. "But some things are trickier to understand than others."

He pulled a rose from one of his brother's get well bouquets and breathed in its sweet scent. The smell of shit would always overpower that of a rose, unless the flower was held directly under one's nose.

"I believed I hated Dad for the longest time," Manny continued. "Then one day I saw him staring at me from the mirror and I knew different. He's a part of me. I owe him for my flaws, and for a thing a two that's halfway decent about me too. Plus I have a son who inherited that crooked grin of his. I have no choice but to love the old man even if I never liked him very much."

Lionel considered what his brother had said. After a few seconds he decided that it made about as much sense as anything else.

"I suppose no matter what happens and how you feel about it, your father will always be your father. Kind of like how your brother will always be your brother. And you know what, Manny? I've missed mine."

"Me too."

Manny smiled and Lionel followed suit, and the wall between them began to crumble.

CHAPTER TWENTY SEVEN

It was over. That was what it came down to, no more or less. Charlie pressed for an explanation. He wanted to know the progression of events which had led to such a conclusion. Tony tried to explain, more for his own sake than to satisfy his friend's curiosity. But anything he could think of to say fell far short of the truth.

Of two twin facts he was certain. He had loved Janet. She loved him in return. Yet he still wasn't clear on whether they ever really knew each other. Perhaps they only knew what the other was. She, a status symbol to be proudly displayed. He, an act of defiance against the conventions of society. This was by no means a recipe for happily ever after, assuming that such a lofty concept actually existed outside of fairy tales and Hollywood.

Love is not easy to grasp the first time around. It invariably becomes confused with other things. We define ourselves by what we choose and what we shun. In our search for an identity and a niche in the world, we use others to help us along the way. When their purpose has been served, we cast them aside. Tony suspected that he and Janet had exhausted each other's usefulness. Or was he just trying to convince himself of this because wounded hearts tended to medicate themselves with the bitter pill of cynicism? Was he striving to forget the flawless beauty of his time with Janet by reaching the ugliest imaginable conclusions?

Tony had no answers to Charlie's questions. He only knew that the reason he and Janet came to an end mattered no more than the reason they began. All flowers died, though some at least got to bloom prior to their demise. He would always remember the bloom of their relationship.

"Fortunately there's no pussy shortage," Charlie said, trying to lighten the mood. "It's waiting right where you left it. Everywhere. You've been ignoring a whole lot of fine sistas, but now that you're back and you're black, ain't nothing cures a broken heart better than some fresh coochie. Like I keep telling you, it's crazy to tie yourself down. Life will tie you to something soon enough."

Tony heard scarcely a word. He wasn't concerned with what awaited him. Hindsight was presenting a harsh vision. For everything he once believed, the opposite had turned out to be true.

"It's not like I didn't have plenty of warning about what would go down, especially from my dad. I haven't even visited him in the hospital, he pissed me off so much. But he's only been telling the truth."

Charlie had long felt that Tony's attitude towards his father was overly critical. Maybe Mr. Johnson fell short of Bill Cosby parenting standards, but the man had done what he could. He was a protector and provider for the woman he had married and the children she bore him. Charlie would have forgiven his own father for any atrocity, had he only bothered to stick around. He therefore believed Tony should have stood vigil in that hospital twenty four seven because Lionel had been a father to him, warts and all, not just a hit-and-run sperm donor.

These thoughts remained concealed. Tony was hurting too much to have someone dumping on him. Part of the art of friendship was knowing when to keep your mouth shut.

"I've been thinking about nothing but going to college and being with Janet," Tony continued. "I haven't given a damn about anything else. But there's more I have to look out for than myself. My dad has always tried to get that through to me, but I wouldn't listen."

"What are you saying, man?"

"I'm saying I can't go to college. Not for a while anyway."

"Why not? Didn't your uncle promise to help out?"

"Yeah. But I don't think we should take him up on it. Some money to pay the rent and our bills until I find a full time job is one thing. We don't have much of a choice. But expecting him to support us indefinitely *and* to put me through college is too much to ask."

"You're not asking," Charlie said. "He's offering. The man makes big bucks. He wouldn't have made the offer if he couldn't afford to. You're his family. Family is supposed to help each other out when the help is needed. So why turn it down?"

"Because accepting his handout would be an insult to my father. I'm not going to disappoint him. Not anymore."

Tony pushed the broccoli on his plate as far off to the side as possible. The force feedings of youth had failed to develop in him a taste for the stuff.

"Hey, what up guys?"

Larry joined them at the table they inhabited in Sanstone Diner. The restaurant's food was greasy and overpriced; the decor generic; the music piped in from hidden speakers, blander than that of any elevator. Nevertheless, Sanstone's was always packed. From morning till afternoon senior citizens filled the booths, reminiscing about days long gone by. When school let out for the day a new generation took over, one preoccupied with the pop culture of the moment. To the diner's staff there was little difference between the two physically disparate groups. They were equally messy and equally poor tippers.

"How's it going?" asked Charlie in greeting.

"Not bad for me. But there's an ugly rumor going around that Tony and Janet broke up. Say it ain't so, man."

"Yeah, it's so," Tony grumbled.

"What happened?"

The question had been asked of him once too often.

"What do you care? It's what you wanted, ain't it? She's available now, so go for it."

Larry jerked back as if struck by a punch that was not seen coming. "What? Come on, man. You know me better than that. We're homies, ain't we?"

"Right now, I don't think I could be friends with any of you people."

"You people? What's up with that noise? Breaking up with Janet must have really fucked you up."

"I think you should get out my face, Larry."

"Oh, it's like that?"

"Yeah, that's what it's like."

Larry shook his head, then obeyed Tony's wishes and walked away.

"That was definitely not cool," Charlie reproached. "What's the matter with you? Larry's down, you know that."

"I don't know a damn thing anymore. I got to get out of here. I need some air." Tony rose to leave, but stood still as a monument when a couple entered the diner.

Janet did not seem to notice him. It was as if he had become transparent to her oceanic eyes. Roger however, was thoughtful enough to send a wink and a smile his way. The regrets that had been clinging to him, whispering in his ear that he had thrown away the best thing ever to happen to him, finally dropped off. His suspicions were not unfounded. Janet *had* used him. And now she was flaunting what she had obviously wanted from the very beginning.

He watched them get seated in a booth. He thought Janet seemed to be averting her eyes so as not to be found paying attention to him. He hesitated a moment longer, giving her a last chance to acknowledge his existence. But she remained enrapt by Roger, gazing upon him as adoringly as a puppy before its master.

Tony left the diner. He walked towards someplace, any place else. Each step taking him further from the source of his torment, but no closer to relief from it.

CHAPTER TWENTY EIGHT

Tony sat watching the sun descend behind the projects. Young children played gaily around him. A few yards away slightly older children, but children none the less, exchanged drugs for money. It was a familiar scene. So familiar it was easy not to notice, to simply accept and grow into. But Tony had always noticed. The scope of his vision extended well beyond the asphalt jungle he had been born into. Real life lay ahead, somewhere behind these tenement buildings. Real life was in the land the sun went to every night.

He once believed that the fare to the sunset world was one he could afford. But it seemed he would have to spend his very soul, and he was not willing to pay that steep a price.

A couple of young men drinking from 40 ounce bottles of malt liquor, both wearing Negro League baseball jerseys, swaggered by. The taller of the two, sporting cornrows in his hair and at least three gold teeth, stared him down. Tony wisely ignored him, not least because of the suspicious bulge in the shorter guy's back pocket. He saw no purpose in getting shot because someone was in a bad mood, or perhaps just plain bored. They got into a jeep parked at the corner and music came screaming from mega sized speakers in the back as the vehicle departed.

Tony's view of the future may have been altered, but his perception of the present had not. This was not where he wanted to be. This was not how he wanted to live. He did not wish to become these people.

But these were *his* people. Did this not mean that he was ashamed of who he was? What else could account for him seeking shelter in Janet's arms? Why had it taken white people's direct showing of hatred to finally make him question his value system? How far would he have gone from himself to get away from what he feared becoming?

A tennis ball bounced towards him, followed by a beautiful little girl with the biggest pair of hazel eyes he'd ever seen. She stopped and held out her hand. Innocence personified. He resisted the temptation to pinch her cheeks and returned the ball.

"Don't ever grow up," he said. She answered with a precocious smile, then ran back to her friends. No, Tony decided, it definitely wasn't being black that he hated. It was the poverty, ignorance, and desperation this girl would find herself mired in. It would take away her innocence and become part of her. The journey from playing with dolls and jumping rope to turning tricks for a quick high was a brutally short one. She had not chosen these circumstances. They were her birthright. The color of her skin had not made them so. They just were. They emanated from the credo of the ghetto - Get yours anyhow, any way, just as long as you get it fast, because you might not be around tomorrow, and that might not be such a bad thing.

Tony knew what he wanted from life and the surest way to get it. The one thing he hadn't figured out was people. He thought too well of them, refused to believe what his father preached and Charlie cautioned about. Surely theirs were clouded judgements; prejudiced by bad experiences; blind, deaf and dumb to good ones. Only an open mind could recognize the truth.

The truth which came to be was that he had been scorned and rejected, not for who he was, but what he was. A black man who had infiltrated territory forbidden to him, inhabited and guarded by those whose gravest fear was contamination by his kind. He'd had the audacity to fall in love with a native of this foreign land. But in the end she proved to be no better, no different than the rest.

So he decided to suffer from selective amnesia. Forgotten would be the sound of Janet's laughter; the feel of her lips against his skin; the way her hair spread out over his chest as they lay in repose; the look on her face as they made love; the sound of her voice when she said he was her sun and moon and stars. Only by deleting heaven from his memory did he have a chance to survive on earth.

But he could not free himself from the grip of nostalgia. Every time he saw her with Roger, a piece of him died. How many could he possibly spare? He sympathized with the three bears a million fold. Someone else was sleeping contentedly on his side of the bed. He craved Janet's touch, knew that his will was no match for the addiction. One tender look from her would be enough to shatter his china doll resolve. But she always held her gaze steady and beyond him.

Just about anything served as a bittersweet forget-me-not. Lyrics of songs addressed him personally, book and movie plots turned out to be pale duplicates of his life story, TV commercials for anything from deodorant to pre-owned cars found ways to strum his heartstrings. Besides these blatant instances there were also occasions when memories crept up on him with the stealth of a secret agent in masterful disguise. The ghost of their love affair proved able to haunt him through the laughter of a child, a scent wafting through the open door of a bakery, the way a particular cloud hung in the sky.

Had he been wrong to surrender what he treasured? By accusing Janet of wanting to be back with Roger, had he enforced a terrible prophecy? The most ridiculous of fabrications will be perceived as fact if repeated often enough. Tony's mounting insecurities had metamorphosed him from the man Janet loved into someone she could no longer tolerate. Roger must have seemed like a pretty good alternative considering.

On the other hand, science class taught that certain chemicals could not combine under any circumstances. If forced together, the result would be explosive. Towards the end of their relationship Tony's body had become a cauldron of obsession and resent. Loving Janet did not mix with these ingredients. He had pushed her away in order to prevent a catastrophe, and there had been no gentle way of doing so. Did this mean he had done the right thing?

He now realized that right and wrong were intertwined notions. His arms could not differentiate between just and unjust causes. They only knew that they were empty.

Three times he had almost given in, nearly confessing that he couldn't take things being this way. Not as long as he remembered how they had been, and that would likely be forever. He hung up after one ring the first time, after two the second. On the third occasion she picked up right away.

He had accused Janet of whatever his harried mind could concoct, employing any leap of logic that would connect the dots that formed a picture of her betrayal. As payback she made good on these accusations. They had both made pathetic attempts to deny what was painfully obvious, that they were meant to be together.

"Hello. Hello. Is anybody there? Who is this?" Then she hung up.

The sound of Janet's voice was not enough to dissolve Tony's shame. He could still feel the sting in his hand from when it struck her. Could she still love him even if she wanted to? How dare he expect her to accept romantic declarations after he had shown his darkest side, proven that his version of love wasn't always accompanied by innocent kisses, but if provoked, by a mindless, violent rage?

Striving to win back her love would likely gain him nothing but confirmation that she now hated him. Better not to know for certain. Better to learn how to keep the past in place. How not to be so trusting. Not to assume that people's motives were pure. To give up on the fallacy that in its blindness, love still managed to conquer every foe.

He would learn his lessons well.

There was one other matter to be taken care of. He must see his father, apologize for not listening, let him know that his message had finally gotten through.

Tony had to figure out the impossible. How could he stop loving Janet? How could he start to love his father again?

* * *

Caren, C.J. and Tanya stared at the television in silence. Not too long ago at this time of day, the Johnson household would be filled by their father's booming laughter. But much had transpired since then. Watching The Love Connection just wasn't the same.

The phone rang and C.J. went to get it. "What's up, man?" asked the voice on the other end of the line that was just beginning to deepen from puberty. It belonged to Duane Langston, a member of the Kaos Krew.

"What do you want?"

"You already know what we want, but you wouldn't be down with that. Guess what though. Louis says he's willing to give you another chance. Just drop by and apologize, and it's all good."

"That shit is over for me. Why can't you niggas accept it and leave me be?"

"You been around long enough to know it don't work like that," Duane said. "Now, I'm going to ask you one more time. You coming or not?"

"I ain't going nowhere."

"That's what I thought you'd say. Tell me something. How's that fly girlfriend of yours? You seen her the last couple of hours?"

C.J. didn't answer, but his body shook at the implication of the question.

"She's one fine piece of ass. You better look out for her. I know a lot of guys who wouldn't mind getting themselves some of that."

C.J. could do nothing but wait for his most terrible nightmare to be revealed.

"I'm disappointed in you, man. All this time I thought you were some kind of stud, boning a sweet thing like her. I can't tell you how surprised I was to find out she was a cherry. Of course, she wasn't a cherry no more by the time my turn came. Not even close."

This was no bluff. Duane was not merely trying to lure him. Something in his voice rang horrendously true.

"We loosened her up a bit for you. Consider it a goodbye present. Why don't you come by and pick her up. I think she's ready to go home now."

It took the sound of the phone landing on the kitchen floor to awaken C.J. from his trance. Then he was off and running.

He went to his bedroom and tore through the lowest drawer in the dresser he shared with Tony. At the bottom he found what he was looking for. It had been kept as sort of a souvenir, but was never again to be used for its deadly purpose. Now he would have to break the promise he had made to himself. He was to do battle one more time.

Minutes later C.J. was pedaling his bike feverishly, a modern day knight on a desperate quest. Every second spent knowing what Lisa must be enduring was torture. His legs grew weary as he rode uphill. It was neither gravity nor physical exhaustion that he fought against, but knowledge of the part he had played. The life he had led; the choices made; the temptations succumbed to; had worked in unison to guide fate towards this day. He should have known what the consequences of his actions would be.

Tomorrow and every day thereafter he would embrace these facts like a whore, with equal measures of shame and passion. He would not forget the lessons learned, regardless of how much anguish their recollection stirred. Forgetting sins was often followed by repeating them. Lisa must never suffer again.

He was conscious of the knife in his back pocket with every stride. Not long ago, with the Krew's colors atop his head for the world to see and his heart filled with malevolence, he set out to kill and discovered he could not. He had been a hard core gang banger on the outside, a frightened child beneath the guise. Since then he had changed his ways, put aside the trappings of hood life in favor of old fashioned happiness. The new C.J., purified and innocent as a baby in baptismal water, knew he would have no qualms about killing tonight.

The threat of physical harm or perhaps death flashed into his head, only to exit twice as quickly. No space was reserved in his subconscious for fear. Lisa needed him.

C.J. jumped off his bike and ran up the rotting staircase that led to what he most abhorred, to what could never be left entirely behind him, and to all that truly mattered. He pushed at the door his former brethren and their captive were behind. As usual, it was barred shut.

"No one gets in here unless they do the knock," said a familiar voice. "You ought to know that."

The code was pounded and the door opened. Directly across the room lay Lisa. C.J. felt his knees buckle and barely managed to contain the bile rising up his throat.

Most of Lisa's clothing had been torn from her. She did not react to the sight of C.J. but remained still, quietly sobbing, covered with blood. Standing above her was Louis, tossing a knife from hand to hand in a carefree manner.

"Don't be upset. She really seemed to enjoy it. The first time is always special."

Snickers came in surround sound. He and Louis were center stage in a barbarous play.

"I can't believe she was a cherry. Could that mean you are too? Damn shame to die a virgin."

Louis`casually stepped over Lisa's body as if it were a toy that he was done playing with. C.J., standing taut as a piano wire, forced his eyes away from her and withdrew his weapon.

Louis could have easily arranged to take him out by surprise. At any point in any place an anonymous gun barrel might have been placed to the back of his head, quick and painless restitution. Instead he would be made to suffer. He was also being given a chance, although it was a slim one, for they were to engage in a game at which Louis was by far superior. C.J. was adept at handling his knife but Louis handled one like it was a natural extension of his arm, reflecting on how best to manipulate it no more than a bird considered the physics of flight or a spider pondered the negotiation of a web. A monumental task stood before C.J. To get what he wanted, he would have to earn it. This was the Krew's way.

"You had such promise," Louis said. "Why'd you go soft? Was it for that piece of pussy I just had? It wasn't all that great. Certainly not worth dying for."

C.J.'s initiation into the Kaos Krew consisted of crossing this very room while he was beaten on mercilessly. Arriving consciously at the other end had been the requirement to get in. Leaving the room alive was now what it would take to get out.

He lunged forward but the anticipated move was easily avoided by Louis, who took the opportunity to slice his knife across C.J.'s upper arm. C.J. ignored the sting and sight of his blood. He feigned another lunge, then swung his knife backhand. Louis instinctively leaned back, avoiding death by inches.

Now it was Louis' turn to be the aggressor and he attacked with fervor, tearing the air to shreds. C.J.'s widened eyes paid attention to the most minute details of Louis' body language in order to remain beyond reach of the hungry blade. He tripped over Lisa's feet while backing up and Louis rushed towards him to take immediate advantage. C.J. lashed out as he tried to regain balance and his knife fortuitously found a piece of Louis' forearm, stalling the gang leader's momentum.

Louis briefly regarded his newest scar to be, then beckoned for C.J. to follow him to the center of the room.

"There's some people you don't want to fuck with. If I've taught you nothing else, remember that."

The lesson was ignored. No sooner were the words spoken than was C.J. within kill or be killed range, flailing wildly. In Louis' years of street wars no one had ever come at him so ferociously. He was unaccustomed to being in retreat. Unable to fend C.J. off any longer, he yelled out as the knife pierced his shoulder. Emboldened that weakness had been exposed in his mentor, C.J. stalked with singleness of purpose.

He thrust his knife at Louis' stomach but the target was never reached. Louis side stepped and kicked the weapon from C.J.'s grasp, clear across the room. C.J. stumbled to his knees, defenseless. Louis pounced to bring the murderous matter to an end, but C.J. tumbled to avoid the strike, then scrambled towards his knife. He could feel Louis' breath hot on the back of his neck in pursuit, preparing to plunge sharpened steel into his spine. He dove to the ground in calculated desperation.

As soon as the handle was felt beneath his fingertips, C.J. swung his arm behind him. The tip of the blade was pointed where he hoped Louis would be. He felt it tearing deeply into flesh, muscle and tendon, and knew he had guessed correctly.

Louis staggered backwards, hands plastered to the hole in his abdomen in a futile attempt to stem the flow of blood rapidly draining him of life. His knife lay harmlessly out of reach on the floor. With neither haste nor hesitation, C.J. walked towards him. He stared into Louis' eyes, fascinated by the fear in them, and by the fading of the light. Now he at last knew what it felt like to kill a man. No big deal.

"Look at you shaking like a bitch. I always thought you were better than the rest of us, that death couldn't catch you. Guess I was wrong. You're a punk mother fucker who bleeds like a pig when he gets stuck, same as everybody else."

C.J. wanted to hurt Louis beyond physically, to make his death as torturous an ordeal as possible. He hoped that in so doing he might earn a measure of satisfaction, taste a small sip of pleasure in the midst of his agony. But this was not to be. He saw the terror and helplessness engulfing Louis and felt nothing but coldness inside. And so he advanced, prepared to dispose of another human being in the same manner that a garbage man tossed trash into the back of his truck. It was simply a job he had to do.

Then the look on Louis' face changed. What C.J. initially mistook as a grimace turned out to be a smile. Louis withdrew his right hand from his stomach and reached towards the small of his back. C.J. understood immediately that he had been conned, that he had fallen for a bluff from a master.

The occurrences to follow were seen as little more than a blur to onlookers. C.J. springing forward with feline quickness. Louis' bloody hand resurfacing with a gun. The gang leader's eyes widening as he saw the charge of his assailant and the reddened blade headed towards his throat. The blade reaching its target, sinking in with awful finality.

The simultaneous explosion and searing pain that filled C.J. as Louis completed his final act - pulling a trigger.

Their bodies collapsed to the floor. The battle was over. As usual there was no real winner because sooner or later, if not today then perhaps tomorrow, they were all going down. One by one, two by two. Whatever.

The rest of the Kaos Krew, knowing that the sound of gunfire might bring police at any moment, began rushing from the building. There was no use showing loyalty to their fallen leader. Loyalty is wasted on corpses.

C.J. was unaware of the room being emptied. He was too busy dragging his body and the bullet imbedded in it across the floor. Lisa had been in a state of shock, only semi-aware of what was going on around her. The gun shot brought her back to her senses. She crawled towards C.J., meeting him half way.

"I love you, Lisa. Don't ever forget that."

They clung to each other with as much strength as they could muster. C.J. felt darkness closing in on him and fought it off the best he could. Yet despite this struggle, he had never been more at peace. The girl he loved was in his arms, and he in hers. What could possibly matter beyond that?

* * *

Bored with sitting still, Tony set forth on a restless and aimless walk. If answers wouldn't come to him, he would go out in search of them. But it had been over an hour and he had only come across new questions. How would he support the family when his father died? Would it mean giving up his college dreams for good? Or had he already let them go for entirely different reasons?

He had always considered himself a responsible person, but in truth, up till now he didn't have much to be held accountable for. His carefree days were dwindling down to the last precious few. Then he would have to trade in his role of son for one he didn't quite know what to name.

A police siren shattered the silence of the evening. Flashing lights signaled mayhem ahead. More of the same old same old. It didn't matter how badly he wanted out of this place. It wasn't willing to let him go.

A mob of people loitered about the area where three patrol cars and an ambulance had stopped. They were gathered in front of an abandoned building. Curiosity getting the better of him, Tony stopped to join the onlookers. Minutes later, a docile pitbull came trotting out followed by two policemen escorting a hysterical young girl wrapped in a blanket. The cops looked strong but were still having difficulty keeping her under control. As they were guiding her towards the ambulance and awaiting paramedics, something about her struck Tony as familiar. He placed the face that was distorted by panic and grief a second before she shouted out.

"C.J.! Oh my God! Somebody help him!"

Tony shoved his way through the crowd, past the cops who were keeping people at bay. He ran up the stairs and into an open room, passing a body that was covered by a sheet, beyond hope or prayer.

An attempt to preserve the life of the second injured party was still underway. Tony dropped to one knee beside his brother. Though there was no choice in the matter, he begged C.J. not to die.

"No, C.J. No."

The response to his plea came in a muted whisper. "It meant something. You understand?"

Tony took hold of his brother's hand and nodded. "Yeah."

C.J. would never hear another word. His life had reached its conclusion. A tear leapt from Tony's cheek and was absorbed by the river of blood.

It may have been the creaking of the decrepit structure, or perhaps the play of rats beneath the floorboards, but the sound Tony made out above the din seemed to him the weeping of angels. His sole thought was of the stack of looseleaf papers contained in a shoebox that the lyrics of his brother's songs were composed on. They had been accompanied by beats that played only in C.J.'s head. Tony wondered if any of the songs could serve as funeral dirge, and if so, how might the music be released now.

Tony felt himself being pulled away. He saw the ambulance workers drape a sheet over his brother's face and take him out on a stretcher. An onslaught of questions was directed towards him. What they were didn't matter, nor did his replies.

C.J. was dead.

CHAPTER TWENTY NINE

It was as if nature had chosen to pay homage to the memory of C.J. The sky darkened to the color of granite as the sun lay low behind a phalanx of clouds. A breeze escorted vibrantly colored but lifeless leaves around the tombstones, whispering the announcement that a new resident had entered the room behind death's door.

A figure in black stood before a sorrowful congregation. He rambled in a nasally voice distractingly remindful of Porky Pig about a kid he hardly knew. Tony didn't pay him much attention. What could this holy man have to say about his brother? To him, Carl Langston Johnson was just another gang banger whose luck had run out and whose fate was now in greater hands.

Tony knew that like himself, C.J. had wanted to chart his own course rather than be at the mercy of life's currents. Knowledge was Tony's chosen helm, and he now knew that lessons taught in textbooks and spouted by scholars and supposed experts with their own agendas were suspect at best. C.J. opted for a bandanna and band of roving brethren. Tony came into the world feeling he had the inalienable right to stake claim on everything before him. C.J. reserved nothing but the luxury of digging his own grave, because if others could dictate how he lived, he damn sure wouldn't let them choose his death as well.

As Tony stared vacantly, the pine box was lowered and swallowed whole by the carnivorous earth. He had often berated his brother for being in a gang, endlessly recited reasons to get out. His words of wisdom were finally heeded. Here was C.J.'s reward.

Yet it was not quite so simple. A jaded police report, neighborhood gossip, or brief mention in the newspaper failed to reflect a full reality. These things, in attempting to be literal interpretations of unfortunate and soon to be forgotten events, missed the point. It was not the decision to leave his gang which had doomed C.J., or even the choice to join in the first place. His fate had been determined the moment he was born a black male into a white world. Since the color of his skin cost him the respect he deserved, he intended for the colors he wore to earn it back. When he realized how much was being offered to others but not to him, he decided to take what he wanted. He reasoned that being bad was better than being invisible.

He had now paid the price for his sins. The preacher wouldn't say that. He didn't want to offend the dearly departed's family by saying if one lived by the blade and bullet, chances are he would die that way as well. The boy whose spirit was being blessed had tread the well worn path of fools, so what did that make of him?

The preacher's saintly wisdom failed to inform him of just one thing, but it was a critical piece of information. In striving to have his worth acknowledged, C.J. learned at long last that it was love rather than power that could accomplish this.

Tony wished a peaceful rest upon his brother's spirit. He understood what C.J. had died for. It wasn't meaningless.

He looked towards Lisa and watched the tears roll down her battered face, each one a liquid capsule of hurt. Her life had been sadistic. She had endured the worst a person could. This would be enough to destroy most people. But here she was, summoning strength from God knew where to say goodbye to her beloved.

Then Tony looked at his mother, but had to quickly turn away. Seeing her pain directly was like staring at the sun.

It was easiest to fault Louis, for he had pulled the trigger. Others would accuse C.J. of bringing this end upon himself, because of the lifestyle he embraced. But Tony knew without question that the color of his brother's skin had brought about his demise. The blame lay on those who refused to see beyond it.

* * *

For about half an hour Caren handled herself commendably. She accepted condolences, made certain that everyone was taken care of, was a gracious hostess. But the attempt to keep herself distracted was ill fated. Something came to be said or done that forcefully reminded her of the purpose of the gathering, and she could no longer maintain her stoic facade.

She was taken to her bedroom where Ellen, Angie and Caroline tried to console her. Her best friend and sisters-in-law said all the appropriate things that women say to one another on such a sad occasion, but their compassion fell on deaf ears. Tears were Caren's last refuge and she would not be denied them.

Her grief did not subside, but eventually did begin to manifest itself in a quieter and seemingly controlled manner. She clutched a pillow as tenderly as if it was the baby boy she had given birth to fifteen years earlier, rocking back and forth no longer to soothe an upset child, but to generate a body rhythm that would hopefully lull her into a meditative state. Caroline took the opportunity to get Caren a drink of water. Moments later she came upon her soon to be ex-husband alone in the kitchen.

"How is she?" he asked.

"As well as can be expected."

Caroline filled a cup with tap water. Manny held a glass of wine out to her.

"You look like you could use it."

"I can."

He handed the wine glass to his wife, avoiding direct contact with those eyes of hers which were so lightly colored, he sometimes felt it might be possible to look straight through them and read her mind. The impression was misleading, for Caroline possessed a remarkable poker face that could conceal the strongest of emotions. Manny had no idea how to act around this woman who had shared his bed for at least as long as forever. There was no way to tell if she was on the verge of wavering, if all hope was lost, or if their marriage was stuck someplace in the middle.

"I'm glad you came. I thought you might refuse to be in the same room as me no matter what the circumstances."

"Don't mean to deflate your ego, Manny, but my being here has nothing to do with you."

His concentrated effort not to say the wrong thing had succeeded for all of ten seconds. There were no right things he could say to his wife, and no one to blame for this but himself.

"Of course not."

Caroline softened in deference to the occasion.

"It's great that you've been here for them. This is too much for Caren to handle on her own."

"I'm a poor substitute for the man she really needs. God only knows how much I owe my brother and his family."

"They're not the only ones," said Caroline. "I'm sorry, I shouldn't have said that. Not now anyway."

"That's okay. I deserve it."

"Yes, you do. I should be getting back." She started to walk out but Manny reached over to prevent her from leaving just yet.

"For the last couple of months we've talked about nothing but divorce proceedings. Now it's ..., all of this. When do we talk about us?"

"I don't recall you having much to say. Let me think. Oh yeah, I think you said you were sorry a few times."

"I *am* sorry, Caroline. I love you."

"Yes, you tossed in a couple of those as well."

"For God's sake. You don't make it very easy to ask for a second chance."

"Why should I?"

The majority of responses that came to mind would be seen by Caroline as flimsy at best. Yes, they had two decades of shared lives. They were raising wonderful children together. They had vowed before God and man to remain true to one another. But since Manny had broken his part of the deal, all bets were now off.

"Because you love me too."

Manny thought he detected a change in his wife's eyes, a refraction of light that indicated she had been moved in some way. But he needed confirmation.

"I know I don't deserve forgiveness, but I'm begging for it anyway. Please allow me to spend the rest of my life making this up to you."

She was such a beautiful woman. Manny tried but failed to remember the last time he had told her so.

"I never meant to hurt you," he said instead. "I have no excuse for what I did except incredible stupidity. Baby if you would only give me another shot, I promise to earn it."

Caroline allowed her husband's plea time to settle in. The second hand of the clock hanging on the kitchen wall moved a few ticks, and then she spoke and Manny understood perfectly where he stood in her graces.

"You're a changed man now, is that it? Is that what you expect me to believe?"

"You're supposed to believe that saving our marriage is at least worth thinking about."

"I do think about it, Manny. I think about it day and night."

Caroline brushed back her hair as she always did when about to read someone the riot act. The gesture had first been seen by Manny on the day they first met, introduced by a mutual friend in college whose name escaped recollection. She had pushed back her bangs and attacked him for his stance on the Vietnam War. Three quarters of the way through her argument, his assessment of the situation was changed. By halfway through he had fallen in love.

"But when I do, what comes to mind are the times our kids asked for you and I told them you were working hard and would be home soon. Does screwing your secretary fall under the category of working hard? Please don't answer that."

"She meant nothing to me," Manny said feebly, knowing it was of little consequence what definition he gave to the significance of his former secretary. "If I could undo it, I would."

"If you could undo it, it still wouldn't matter. This is about more than your inability to keep your pants zipped. That was just the icing on the cake."

In the years they had been together, his wife had not budged on anything her mind and heart were set on. Her strength of conviction was amongst the things Manny admired most about her. She had gone along with his wishes on numerous occasions for the sake of harmony, but her opinions and desires remained undisturbed.

"You want me to believe you've changed," Caroline said. "Well I'm the one who has changed. I'm no longer the naive girl you could overwhelm with promises. I want to believe in you but I can't, no matter how hard I try."

Caroline stood before Manny in the flesh, but may as well have been an old photograph. All the yearning in the world could not retouch the image of her leaving, nor reclaim what had once been. The tug of war for their love had been lost, not because Manny did not pull hard enough, but because his wife opted to let her end go. It did not matter how much she meant to him because he had destroyed everything he meant to her. She was as resolved to abandon their marriage as Manny had been years earlier to leave home for college. The pleas of loved ones went unheard. The choice had been made, and it was a keeper.

Caroline rushed out of the kitchen. The only physical trace of her to remain was the lipstick stain on her wine glass.

* * *

Tony had spent the afternoon in a corner, staring absently at people milling about his living room. Periodically someone tried to engage him in conversation. They would tell him how sorry they were, how terrible they felt. But Tony wasn't much in the mood for talking. He didn't give a damn about their sorrow. It wasn't going to bring his brother back.

As the hours dragged, his patience diminished. He wanted to do something besides feeling miserable, longed for the hurt to fade, but instead it grew until it had taken on a life of its own and he was merely the vessel of containment.

He brushed past the person currently saying something uselessly trite and went into his bedroom. The urge to break something, to bring about destruction, was overwhelming. He turned about in circles in search of just the right object. Then he stopped, for a new idea had come to mind. He pulled open a drawer that was reserved for C.J.'s clothing and discarded all garments until coming across what he was looking for.

Tony examined the piece of cloth closely, remembering his first sight of it. C.J. had walked into the room with a back eye, a bloodied lip, a badly bruised cheekbone, and the bandanna on his head. Pride radiated from his toothy grin. He was only thirteen years old, but had passed the test.

Of course Tony told him he was crazy. He said their father was going to make the ass kicking just willingly undergone look like a wrist slap. But C.J. only cared that he had earned his colors. He was a real live gang banger now.

After tying the bandanna on, Tony peered curiously at his reflection in the mirror. Then he went to the closet and pulled out a baseball bat. Accessories in place he left his room, parted the sea of mourners, and walked out of the apartment.

Six climbed flights of stairs later he arrived at the top floor of the building. A thin chain which was routinely busted and replaced and busted again was the only impediment between him and the roof. Beyond the half hearted security system lay a site for illicit sex, drug use of various kinds, and numerous other activities he was better off not knowing about. Tony swung the bat over his shoulder and brought it down with as much force as he could generate. Seconds later he stood atop his neighborhood.

It was one of those evenings he had thought magical as a child. The sun and moon simultaneously stood in the sky, one either early or the other late. Tony stared at the ultimate source of illumination and its majestic reflector, and finally tears began to stream down his face.

He walked to the roof's edge and looked down at passing traffic and people going about their business. Then he looked out towards the surrounding tenement buildings, checkers of light being the only indication that behind each window was a set of triumphs and failures, trials and tribulations, hopes and prayers. This was the world his brother had wanted to rule, and he to flee. The only world they had ever known. It had devoured C.J. for his desires. What did it hold in store for him?

Tony understood how it had shaped him to date. Unnatural conditions had been imposed on both his love and his hate. Gone were the days of innocent intentions, fearless ambitions, and heedless passions. Suspicion, mistrust and resentment were the poor substitutes.

A procession of images passed before his mind's eye as if neatly presented in a slide show. He saw the still and silent form of his brother encased for eternity. His mother lying on the floor she had been mercilessly thrown to. A bed soaked with the tears, fear and shame elicited by his domineering father. The hospital room he could not will himself to dutifully enter.

Upon a rooftop that featured a view of virtually every path traveled in his relatively small number of days, Tony contemplated which one might be taken next. He was terrified of venturing forward as he stood perched not only on the ledge of a roof, but also at the dawn of a new century, a brand new life. Yet neither staying put nor heading back to the cocoon of childhood were options available to him.

He would have to go downstairs soon. There were weighty responsibilities awaiting him. Looking for an easy way out was tempting. The crack pipes littered about indicated that many others had come to this roof for that very reason. But Tony's purpose was to take a solitary moment to say goodbye to his brother, make his mind as clear as the sky above him, and spend his final minutes as a boy before returning home a man.

And so he wiped away his tears, took a deep breath, then unleashed a primal scream towards the dual celestial orbs that were the only witnesses to his rite of passage.

* * *

Staring out of his window, Lionel observed the mating ritual of two pigeons that had perched on a ledge a few stories above him. Their heads bobbed rhythmically with each step they took. The male puffed himself up, almost doubling his size. The female briefly resisted, then let her man go about his business. A few flaps of wings later it was over. The pigeons seemed to briefly regard their audience, then without warning took flight. Lionel followed their path, watching them grow smaller and smaller until they were no more than patches of grey against the pale blue sky.

Lionel thought of his two sons, the younger one now departed from this world, the elder alienated beyond the point of return. In Tony he saw the long lost ambition of his youth mirrored back, his pride before it was annihilated. C.J. on the other hand, reflected Lionel's dark and stormy acceptance of life's inequalities. Tony was the young dreamer from Georgia who envisioned a better way to live. C.J. was the bitter realist in the carnivorous slums of New York City, getting by the best he could.

Tony may have turned out as he had because pipe dreaming and unquenchable ambition were in their genes, but C.J. learned by the example of a father who had already surrendered and could do little more than lash out at a world that was impervious to his feeble blows. Much friction was created because Tony embodied what he new rejected. Conversely, his younger son's acts of rebellion were not questioned, challenged or discouraged. Though Caren often pleaded with him to get more involved, for the most part he let C.J. do as he pleased, reasoning that boys will be boys.

He had failed both of his sons because he was too consumed with self-pity to be the father he should have been. The results could not have been more conclusive. Tony abhorred him. C.J. had just been lowered into the ground.

Lionel knew he had fallen far short of the man he promised Caren he would one day be. It was therefore a reasonable conclusion that his family would be better off without him. Manny would make good on his promise to provide for them. Tanya wouldn't have to miss out on things because money was too tight to spoil her with. Tony would make a success of himself. Caren would find someone to treat her the way she deserved. As for C.J., it's not a crime unless there is a victim.

Death would soon claim Lionel as well, but he was no longer in fear of this prospect. Upon reviewing his list of things to live for, he found that the arguments ceased to compel him. Life was hard and cruel, only rewarding the lucky or wise. He had been neither, and didn't have enough time allotted to change the pattern of his existence.

In two weeks he would get to go home, something he had stopped looking forward to. Being temporarily out of work had made him feel useless. How was he to feel now, being practically an invalid, nothing but a burden to be pitied? He could not support his family in any way. The only thing he would be able to give them was a close up view of a dying man.

And so he wept. His tears were cold and lonely and as silent as death. When a sound made him turn towards the doorway, he found his wife standing there.

Tears rushed down her face also, accompanied by sobs of anguish. Her body quivered like a lone leaf futilely resisting the force of an Autumn wind, refusing to give way so that new life could replace it the next Spring.

"He was a good boy," she said. "He wasn't perfect. God knows none of us are. But he was never as hard as he pretended to be. I just can't get myself to believe he's gone."

As his wife lay beside him, Lionel realized there was something he should do, something he should say. As it was, he found it exhausting simply to keep his arms around her. Physically and emotionally, his strength had deserted him. It hardly mattered that C.J. was dead. Caren's teardrops did not move him. He could feel no pain, no grief, no anger, no pity. He was capable of merely one emotion, a desire for release. He wanted the cancer in his body to finish its job.

"Are you okay, honey?"

The question seeped through the consolation-proof window that Lionel cowered behind. He was unaware of how long Caren had been speaking, or what she might have said prior to her question. He only knew that she would have to get through this on her own.

"Yeah, I'm fine."

Caren recognized the truth that contradicted this claim. Beside her was merely a shell of the man she had loved these many years.

She held tight to him and began leafing through memories. Not those to be cherished, but the ones usually kept in cold storage. She recalled the times that her husband's frustration was directed her way with such swiftness that there was little opportunity to raise her guard or duck. With equal aplomb, she withstood baseless accusations and the callused knuckles to follow in the bleakest of hours.

These occasions came to mind without judgment or resentment. Caren understood that love is never granted free of charge. Once one's heart was surrendered, it became subject to the whims of its captor. She complained little of its mistreatment, because it had been her choice to give it away.

A fine line existed between acceptance and submissiveness, and she had stopped trying to decipher it a long time ago. She chose not to ask questions of herself which led to answers best left unexamined. Ellen called this living with her head stuck in the sand. To Caren, it was simply getting by as she knew how.

The good and the bad of life with Lionel were as inseparable as the flip sides of a coin. Again and again her fate had been tossed into the air. In each instance, whatever came up, came up. When the bad showed its face, Lionel was always sorry afterwards. Small consolation perhaps, pitiful even. Others in Caren's shoes might have used them to walk. She had opted to stay put, to take the blows that preceded the kisses of regret, and to love with everything she had in her.

Caren drew Lionel's head to her bosom and rocked him as if he were an infant. She had come to find solace in his arms, but it was clear that she would have to do the comforting this time around.

"Everything's going to be all right," she said, for it was her turn to lie.

CHAPTER THIRTY

Yesterday C.J. had been buried. Today mountains still stood tall; trees swayed in the breeze; rivers flowed to seas; the world kept spinning round. The events of tomorrow were anybody's guess.

Lionel heard someone enter his room but did not turn to see who it was. He had been paid one too many visits from doctors, nurses, and unwanted visitors who desired a last look and the opportunity to say goodbye. Now that he had been liberated from fear of dying, feelings of tenderness towards most of those who once possessed his friendship and kindest regards had been turned off. He was tired of people looking at him uneasily, feeling sorry for him. Resignation to the inevitability of his fate had made him impatient to move it along. But he could do without the constant reminders that he would be missed, especially since he did not particularly believe them.

"Hey, Dad."

Emotions upon hearing the prodigal voice competed against one another - grateful relief versus resentment of his son's procrastination. In the end it was shame that won out over both. He had given Tony good reason to stay away.

"Hello, son."

Tony walked over to the window, needing to gather himself before looking back at the fragile body that housed his father. This should not be. Some things were never supposed to change. His mother would always be loving. His father would always be strong. If these were only temporary conditions, what could possibly last? Would the oceans eventually run dry? Would birds one day forget the secrets of flight and song?

"I'm sorry I didn't come sooner, Dad. Everything's been so crazy."

"That's not why you haven't come."

"No, I guess it isn't," Tony admitted, not bothering to elaborate. He took a seat next to the bed. This conversation would not be easy. There was much to say, no clear start off point delineated.

A shadow on the wall startled him. He could have sworn for half a second that the outline belonged to the grim reaper, but it was only his father's IV.

Tony looked out the window and watched an ambulance pulling in, transporting mortality as if it was furniture, one set to be dropped off so another could be picked up. He had believed his thoughts to be gathered before leaving home, but the looming presence of death in the hospital room had scattered them again.

It didn't seem fair that he must apologize and accept total responsibility. He felt his father should own up to the hurt he had caused and express some measure of regret. But this was selfish thinking that was immediately cast aside. Tony would shoulder all the blame for this was the least his father deserved, the least that any dying man should be granted.

He shook his head to push back a budding tear, a tradition amongst the Johnson men.

"I wouldn't listen to you, Dad, but I learned anyway. You were right all along. And I was wrong. Wrong about what I believed, and wrong for not trusting your word. I know now that when white people look at me, they don't really see me. They just see the color of my skin. They just see another nigger. And no matter how hard I try to live like they do, to consider myself no different than them, they'll always see me the same way."

Tony waited for a response. Would his father be pleased by this surrender? Would he be a gracious winner, or grin and say "I told you so"? Would he want to know what had finally brought him around? None of the above. Lionel's eyes remained empty, his tongue still.

An extended hacking cough broke the silence. It was an inhuman sound, as if contained within lungs made of tin. He offered his father the glass of water by the bedside, but Lionel gestured that he did not want it. Tony needed to make amends, if by only a small symbolic act, but his father refused any gesture of kindness. Deathbed apologies apparently had no effect on him. Or maybe he simply wasn't thirsty.

"C.J. understood," said Tony once Lionel's breathing had returned to normal. "They couldn't fool him. But it still didn't do him any good."

He had steadfastly refused to heed his father's warnings. The messenger was blamed because the message was so awful. Now Tony wanted to offer at least his respect and duty back, if not his love. But his father had reached a stage where nothing other than ease from his physical discomfort was of much use to him. Anything not serving this purpose would be thoughtlessly refused.

"I'm sorry I've always given you such a hard time, Dad. I'm sorry I wouldn't listen to you, that I've been such a fool and such a disappointment. I should have understood you were only trying to look out for me."

He thought he saw his father's lips twitch and waited anxiously for him to say something, it no longer mattered what. False alarm. Lionel remained maddeningly mute.

"I'll leave you to get some rest. I'll be back to visit again real soon." Tony started to walk out, mission accomplished with the bare minimum of satisfaction.

"Your Jets surprised me. They've actually managed to win some games this year."

Tony turned and looked at his father in bewilderment, then said what came naturally.

"I told you so."

"I should have listened when you said things were looking up for them. But they've been bums for so long. Who would have figured they had it in them to change?"

"I guess some things never change," Tony said. "Until they do."

"Yeah, I guess."

It wasn't much, minutiae in comparison to what had been hoped for, but it would have to do. Lionel closed his eyes for some much needed rest. Tony walked to the doorway where he remained for half a minute in case his father would have anything else to say, then concluded his visit with the lone tear failing to obey his command.

* * *

Lionel had wanted to speak to his son about matters of much greater weight than football. He knew how difficult it must have been for Tony to accept what he had long refused to see. Tony's eyes were now open. In the end this was probably a good thing. But Lionel still vividly recalled the day he learned what it meant to be called nigger. The lesson may have been a necessary one, but this made that particular pill no easier to swallow.

For every word his son had spoken, hundreds more undoubtedly remained buried. Tony had expected a return apology, but what would be the point of making amends now? It would be easier on him to lose a father that he hated.

"I'm sorry," said Lionel to the empty room. Forgiveness wasn't granted, but the damned know to keep their expectations to a minimum.

In his sleepless slumber Lionel saw himself young again, full of ambition, determined to take on the world. He recalled how it felt to fall in love the very first and last time. His wedding day. Holding his first healthy born child moments after he entered the world. The first steps each of his children took. Boarding a train to leave his childhood home behind for good, taking his bride to a place where the limitations of future good fortune would be theirs to set.

He thought of these monumental events and also of numerous small happenings permanently lodged into his memory. He tried to wish a few of the less significant recollections away to make room for matters of greater consequence that remained frustratingly out of reach, but it didn't work. No matter how hard he tried, he could not remember the face of the woman he had bequeathed his virginity to, nor the supple lines of the hooker's body. As unforgettable as the experience had seemed, in the end it formed nothing more substantial than a shadow of his past. Yet with little effort he was able to picture every exterior and interior detail of the one car his father ever owned. Its time of service to them was less than one year, and Lionel got to drive the mobile junk pile fewer than a dozen times. Among those occasions was a trip to the whorehouse for Negroes on the outskirts of town. The place he and Manny scraped up enough money and courage to visit one apparently not so memorable night after all.

Things did not turn out as wonderful as imagined while watching America roll by the window on that long ago train ride towards the promise of the north. A hearty share of failure and disappointment had been dished out in the years to follow. Yet Lionel loved life anyway. He loved it for the few pleasures it occasionally doled out, and for the infinite possibility of more that it held. So he mourned the passing of that which had been, and that which never came to be.

Last but not least, never least, he recalled the day his first child was stillborn. Caren was destroyed when unable to deliver him safely. She looked at Lionel with eyes that pleaded with him to ease her suffering, but he could not return the gaze. In fact, he could not fully share her pain. His son had been taken out of the room, but was all he could see, no matter how hard he tried to wish the vision away. It was not the tiny lifeless body in his mind's eye, but the child's light complexion that taunted him. It suggested he should be grateful that his namesake would never take a breath.

Nine months earlier he had arrived at Loehman's Antique Store to pick Caren up for their weekly Friday night date. He saw immediately that something was very wrong. She was putting up the bravest front she could, for it was her intention to keep what her boss had done a secret. Yet it did not take much time or effort for Lionel to pry the truth free.

"I tried to keep him off of me. I scratched and hit and did everything I could to get away. He was drunk, and I prayed that would make him too weak to hold me down, or unable to do what he planned on doing. I fought him as hard as I could. I fought until I couldn't fight anymore."

Caren had only just recently gifted Lionel with her virginity in a moment of tender passion. Now she had been branded by the curse of sex when fueled by lust and inhumanity and ill conceived feelings of entitlement. She would never be the same. *They* would never be the same.

Lionel's hands trembled as he imagined the neck of the man responsible for this between them. Caren wrapped her arms tightly around him. She was afraid he would not be able to look at her as he used to, that the defilement of her body by the devil in a white man's skin would mutate his love. There was no need for this fear. It was not of love that Lionel thought. Nor did he continue to think of vengeance. Reality had already begun to settle into his thoughts. He would not be killing anyone. He would not go to the police. He would not even confront Caren's boss for forcing himself upon her.

There were laws on the books of their sleepy southern town that were for display purposes only, and unwritten rules which had better be followed. These ignored laws and invisible rules existed for the purpose of enforcing the white man's place in their society, and to remind the black man of his own lowly position. There had always been white men who raped black women for leisure. They routinely escape punishment and maliciously persecuted black fathers, brothers, husbands and lovers who chose manhood over caution.

A good life with a good woman lay in wait for Lionel. He did not want to throw this away. So he muffled his fury. He pushed his pride so far down that it reached the bowels of the earth. He suffered in silence and helped Caren do the same. They would forget that the horror had ever taken place.

This plan worked for awhile. Caren's final day at her job was never mentioned. The rape was pretended into nonexistence. A few weeks later, however, their make-believe became impossible to maintain when she discovered that she was pregnant.

"I'm certain it's your baby. I know it is, even if I don't know how I know. I just feel it. This child was conceived in love. A woman knows about such things. That man's poison had nothing to do with it."

Lionel did not protest. Instead he married Caren and began searching for a way to leave their hometown far behind. The child in her womb would be given a chance. No matter if the baby was not his, which was a possibility he could not discredit as easily as Caren had done. If she gave birth to a child who was obviously half white, there would be no escape from the shame of how this came to be. So they would go someplace where they could be strangers, where anonymity could be worn like a cloak. They would start over.

Several years and substantial miles away later, Caren's second pregnancy resulted in a successful birth. There was no need for Lionel to doubt this time around that the boy was indeed his own. He was free to be grateful that this child had been delivered without an umbilical cord murderously wound around his throat. Nothing should have prevented Lionel from unadulterated celebration in becoming a father.

Yet he could not help wondering about the lightness of his son's color. He madly theorized that the seed of Caren's rapist had lingered in her body and tainted another birth. Although this was ridiculous, the final remnants of his paranoia did not vanish until a few weeks passed and Tony's skin darkened sufficiently in that time. In a way though, it never went away. Lionel remained eternally on guard for the white man's evil. There was no telling where it would come from, or how it might gain entry into the unsuspecting souls of his children. Nearly twenty years transpired before the re-appearance, when it walked into his home in the guise of a pretty girl on the arm of his son.

Lionel opened his eyes and pulled out the handful of sleeping pills he had been hoarding for the past several weeks. He didn't have enough yet. Not in a hospital filled with doctors eager to come to everyone's rescue, regardless of whether their patients wanted to be saved or not. About another week's supply was needed to make certain it was done right. This could not be screwed up.

As far back as Lionel could remember, outside forces had determined how he would live. Poverty, bigotry, loyalty, betrayal and resentment. Now it was cancer. He was supposed to lay down defenselessly while it chewed him up and spit him out. The script had been completed and there would be no re-write.

Lionel could not bring back the years lost with his brother. He could not abolish his shameful treatment of the woman who loved him without limits. He couldn't take back the hurt which was Tony's only inheritance from him. He couldn't pamper his daughter. It was not possible to open the door to his sons' room and look upon C.J. again. But Lionel could have one thing, and that was peace.

He had been born with the deck stacked against him. For a long time he believed he might find the card hidden in his sleeve that would allow him to beat the house. But there was no card, or else it was hidden too well. His body went on for years after this realization, but the energy supply of his spirit dropped below empty. The remainder of his days would be a brutal formality, a slugfest against God in which he was defenseless against a myriad of thunderous blows, remaining upright solely on instinct. He was growing more tired with each passing day. So very tired.

Now the end was being made official. The most terrifying aspect of death was that it could take you whenever it saw fit, in any of a countless number of ways. But if a man assumed command of the options, he captured death's power, and thus had no reason to be afraid.

The way Lionel saw it, he could shrivel up and die while his loved ones watched and waited, or he could whip out the Ace that finally turned up after he stopped looking for it. From here on out he was calling the shots, defining the terms, writing rather than playing or being played by the rules.

Sweet release was foreseeable and unavoidable. While waiting for it he would indulge in pleasant diversions. The remote control by his bedside was able to access scores of cable networks, but the one televising game shows all day was the only channel he cared to watch. *The Newlywed Game* would be coming on in ten minutes. He liked to guess which of the couples in their dated outfits and hairstyles would stick it out, and which marriages would fail to endure. They all believed back then that love lasted forever. By now they surely knew as did he that forever was a treacherous myth, though probably a necessary one.

CHAPTER THIRTY ONE

The television was on more out of habit than for entertainment purposes. On screen, a rap artist who'd had two or three hit songs was giving a tour of his house, or rather his mansion, to MTV viewers. The obscenity of wealth on display did not seem fair to Tony. As for the showboating gold toothed rapper, he seemed unconcerned with fairness, or with the irony that his lyrics glorifying the dangers of surviving on mean streets enabled him to reside on Easy Street. Tanya leafed through a copy of Seventeen magazine, flipping by a montage of pretty, carefree, mostly Caucasian girls. She had once examined these pages for fashion tips and advice on how to navigate her angst filled teenage years. Her priorities had changed substantially since then. There were no articles on getting knocked up in the current issue, so like the television it was merely a diversion. Not really killing time, just slightly injuring it.

Tony watched a cockroach ascend the wall. It seemed to have no particular destination or duty as it risked the perils outside whichever crack it resided in. Perhaps the quick execution brought about by a single strike of TV Guide was preferable to dying of boredom. Death was favored over risk free existence. C.J. would have admired the little guy.

"Do you think God is letting him blast his music in heaven?" Tanya asked.

With C.J. gone and their father terminal, the remnants of the Johnson family had been spending a great deal more time in each other's company. In the past they had rushed past one another on individual agendas. They loved each other, but in an abstract way, taking for granted that everyone would always be around. As the size of their family diminished, the remaining survivors clung tighter together.

"I think God is letting him do whatever the hell he wants."

It was not often that they spoke aloud about their brother's death. Tanya in particular rarely mentioned his name, any reminder that he was gone being too painful. When they did speak of him it was like their reaffirmed love for each other, communicated not in words, but looks and innuendoes. Telepathically they spoke volumes about how the world they once knew had fallen apart.

"There's too many things to be sad about, Tony. Whenever my mind gives me a break from C.J., I start thinking about Daddy. If I'm able to push that away for a few minutes, I think about..."

Tanya stopped herself short. She had momentarily forgotten that her pregnancy was still a secret. Not long ago, her entire days were spent contemplating her condition and its possible resolutions. Personal concerns had been pushed to the back burner in the wake of more immediate crises. But they couldn't stay there much longer.

"About Eric and stuff."

Tony nodded. In addition to mourning the loss of a brother and dreading the worst for his father, Janet frequently jumped to the forefront of his thoughts.

"I'm scared to fall asleep at night," Tanya said. "I feel like I need to keep my eyes on everybody, listen for their breathing."

Tony put an arm around his sister's shoulders. Gone were the days when wounds of the skin could be repaired by a kiss and a Band-Aid, wounds of the heart by a hug of consolation. Ready or not, the demise of childhood had come to pass. Being lovesick over Janet and crossing his fingers about college seemed as distant as sucking his thumb and wetting his bed.

"They say whatever doesn't kill you makes you stronger," he said, the moment seeming as appropriate a one for a cliché as any.

"Then we should be able to take on Samson, Hercules, and King Kong."

Tony and Tanya looked towards the voice. Their mother's entrance had gone unnoticed.

"We're not catching a whole lot of breaks," Caren said. "But God has not forsaken us. He'll make a way for us to get by."

Tony wondered if she really believed what she said, or was just mindlessly parroting what years of church going had drilled into her head. Recent events should have dictated that her beliefs be revised. When it came to looking out for the welfare of the Johnson family, God apparently was on vacation, or at the very least, an extended coffee break.

Caren read her son's thoughts. He had forgotten about the ability to speak and listen without tongue or ear that they had each acquired.

"Having faith isn't easy, and I don't just mean in God. Carl didn't have enough faith in himself, or else he never would have needed that gang"

She sat down between her children. It was time to verbalize what they were going through. It was time to start healing. As strong as her belief in God's benevolence was, she knew He had to be met halfway. God preferred not to give free handouts. His love was not welfare.

"As for your father, he was once a remarkable man. He had more self-confidence than anyone I've ever known. You might find that difficult to believe, but it's true. He just got broken along the way."

When as a young woman Caren thought it impossible to make it through another day in a loveless home, Lionel supplied the support she needed. When she found herself pregnant and ejected, he did not let her down. Self reliance became unnecessary because he was always there.

As alcohol and disappointment began to take more of a toll than Lionel could bear, depending on him grew increasingly hazardous. But old habits like old drunks, tend to die hard. Caren continued to believe that her husband would come through when needed, that he would relocate the optimism and fervent conviction of his self-worth that had initially attracted her to him. Sadly he would discover only excuses, causes to be angered, and drinks within arm's reach.

Caren stared at a photograph hung on the wall, smiling in remembrance of the day it was taken in a mall eight years earlier. Her family posed before a pretend scenic view, a framed time capsule of happier, simpler times. She would always have fond memories of yesterday, but it was necessary to deal with today and figure out how to get to tomorrow in one piece.

"Don't get me wrong. Your father's faults have never lessened my love for him. I wouldn't trade our life together for anything. But in more ways then we'll ever know, we lost out when he stopped believing in himself."

Like the cancer eroding his organs, resentment had diligently eaten away at Lionel's soul. This corrosion resulted in bouts of cruelty. It changed him day by day into someone Caren could scarcely recognize. The glimmer of his true self that shined beneath years of wear and tear steadily grew dimmer. Caren had been unable to resist contemplating on occasion how much longer her heart could remain faithful. Now she knew for certain that she would be able to love her husband until her dying day, just as she had sworn to do.

"There is much joy ahead," she told her children. "Those we love are never really gone if we don't let go of what was best in them. We must remember the good. The bad will be forgiven on its own."

Tony and Tanya had grown accustomed to seeing their mother pushed around. Listening to her now, they viewed her as if for the first time. She was indeed a wise woman. She was a teacher. Her lessons would be in how to survive, for she possessed a PHD in the subject.

"It isn't looking good for your father. It's not going to get any easier for a while. But we still have each other."

"Aren't you scared?" Tanya asked.

"I'm petrified, sweetie. Hope and fear go hand in hand. Love causes both of them."

Tony and Tanya had never met the magnificent version of their father who had been spoken about, but at long last they were being introduced to their remarkably strong mother.

CHAPTER THIRTY TWO

It seemed the calendar had progressed at an accelerated rate since Manny left behind that which was familiar for the wilds of the Bronx. Several weeks which bore the weight of hair graying years later, it was time to return. But to what? At home his belongings would be packed and waiting for him to remove them. He had tried to rehearse what he might tell his children to make certain they realized he was not abandoning them, that he loved them more than anything. All he'd come up with was to say he was sorry, the very words that had failed so miserably when stated to his brother and to his wife. He could only hope that because his kids were less jaded than adults tended to be, they would grant more clemency.

"So you're splitting," Phil said.

"Yeah. Everyone's got a pretty heavy case load. They need me back as soon as possible."

The two men were lounging in Phil's small, well tended backyard. Phil walked over to a basketball lying on the ground, dribbled it between his legs, then released it in a smooth arc towards a net that hung from the porch.

"Nice shot," Manny said.

"My son keeps me in practice. He's only twelve years old and it takes all I've got to beat him. In a year he'll be wiping up the court with me." He took another shot that dropped smoothly in.

"I used to be pretty good at this game," Phil continued. "Had a skyhook that would have made Kareem ask for pointers. I practically lived on the playground courts. Seems like it was yesterday, but I guess it wasn't. Where did the years go?"

"I'm not sure where they went, but I do know that they aren't coming back."

"For the NBA championship." Phil's next shot rolled teasingly around the rim before falling to the ground.

"You'll get 'em next year, champ."

"There's always next year," said Phil. "At least there used to be. Now I'm not so sure."

The ball bounced over to Manny, who scooped it up and took a jumpshot that fell woefully short. "I'm a little out of practice," he understated.

Phil's wife, a diminutive Guyanese woman whose adorably round face featured a slight overbite that added to rather than detracted from her appeal, brought out a couple glasses of soda and then left the men to their games. For several seconds after she was gone, Manny stared towards the space she had occupied. Then he asked Phil a question that he had already sensed the correct answer to.

"How would you say your marriage is?"

"Not in any danger as far as I know."

"Yeah, but are you happy?" Manny pressed. "Does it still have that kick like in the beginning?"

Phil stopped dribbling the basketball and considered how to respond.

"You can't stay high forever. Everything has to come down eventually. But I'm happy. As far as I can tell, Dana is too."

Manny watched as Phil spun the ball on his finger. He would have to learn how to do that. His son was too young to care much about the legal cases his dad won, but surely he would be impressed by a basketball defying gravity on his fingertip. Would he soon only be able to spend time with Jason and his daughter Stacey when visitation rights allowed? The absurdity of such a notion made it practically comical, but absurd events were no less real than the commonplace, and the lump that had developed in his throat over the thought made laughter impossible.

"We're not floating around with our heads up in the clouds like a couple of sex crazed teenagers," Phil resumed. "But we enjoy each other's company. We've built a life together. Not a perfect one, but a damn good one."

Manny thought back to the days before dissatisfaction supplanted comfort in his marriage, back when he and Caroline were able to appreciate each other's presence, when being together was its own reward. He was amazed by how deeply he had to go into his memory bank to make this withdrawal. It was nearly impossible to notice that each day they grew an inch further apart, but over the years those inches had added up to miles between them, the stretch of an ocean which seemed even larger than it was because he lacked a compass. Manny could not reclaim what had been lost and had no idea how to start over and make Caroline fall in love with him all over again.

"Camelot is for the young," said Phil. "I realized I was no longer a kid when the fruit of my loins started to dominate the boards. But I think I have something considerably more substantial than Camelot."

Manny had once believed the very same thing. Now he was left to wonder if he would ever get to feel that way again.

"If Caroline would only give me another chance," he said mostly to himself. "But she won't. She's walking away and as much as I want to, I can't stop her."

"Maybe she just needs more time."

"She's filed for divorce, Phil. She's not asking for a little time, she wants an eternity. An eternity away from me. I've tried everything to change her mind. I don't know what more I can do."

"I guess you hope for a miracle."

"That's your advice," Manny said incredulously and somewhat irritably. "To sit around and wait for the impossible."

"If you've tried everything, what else can you do?"

"I suppose thinking like that might work fine for some people. Unfortunately I stopped believing in miracles a long time ago. Working in the law business teaches you to be a realist."

"It should have also taught you something else.

"What's that?"

Phil turned to face away from the basket, took a peak over his shoulder to gauge its location, then shot the ball blindly over his head.

"Shit happens." Swish!

* * *

Tanya sat on the edge of her bed, lovingly caressing her belly that had just begun to grow. Only slightly, not really noticeable yet. But Tanya noticed. Inside of her, life was beginning.

Acceptance of this had come slowly. How could it be that she would soon be a mother? Her sweet sixteen party was still a fresh memory. The prom was less than two years away. This was supposed to be her time to shed girlhood for womanhood, not youth for reluctant acceptance of irreparable fate.

The structure of her day to day existence was collapsing. Sometimes she could think of nothing to cling to as the whims of God and man tossed her about but the idea of her baby. Simultaneously realized was the fact that thinking this way was ridiculous. She could not have been less equipped to handle the responsibilities that would need to be taken on.

Yet was it any more sensible for her father to be wasting away in a hospital bed? What was the logic behind her brother being here one day, gone the next? Becoming a mother seemed no less natural than these things. What did feel increasingly unnatural was the thought of bringing about the end of her child's life, especially while in the midst of losing loved ones against her will.

"You're beautiful when deep in thought."

Tanya's lips curved into the slightest of smiles, just enough for the outline of her dimples to form. This wasn't the first time she had temporarily forgotten his presence, but he never seemed to mind. He knew Tanya had a lot to think about, and he was a patient man.

"I should make a decision soon," she said.

"I suppose."

"I have to do it. No doubt about it. This weekend."

"Okay. But that's what you said last weekend. And the weekend before."

"I know, I know," Tanya agreed. "You're right. I've just got to do it already."

"Exactly."

"Or not do it."

"Exactly again."

"Larry, how would you feel if I didn't?"

"I'll be here for you either way.

"But I would have a baby, and it wouldn't be yours. Are you telling me you could hang with that?"

"I'm a great hanger."

"You wouldn't resent it, not even a little?"

"Why trip over what happened before I was around?" Larry said. "The way I figure, it's my own damn fault. If I had made my move sooner, Eric never would have made it into the picture. So why resent you or some innocent kid for my own mistake? Not that I'm making a move now."

"You're just hanging."

"Exactly."

"Is there anything I can do that would drive you away?" Tanya asked.

The question had not been anticipated. The concerned expression to come over Larry's face said as much. But if he was thrown off balance by the suggestion that the girl he was so crazy about might not want him around, his recovery was a swift one.

"Sure. Just tell me to go. Is that what you're saying?"

"No."

Larry failed to suppress a smile at the answer he had hoped to hear. "Then I'll continue to stick around."

"And I'll keep waiting for you to make your play."

Larry squeezed the teddy bear he had brought over as a gift. He stared at the pictures on the wall of Tanya's fantasy men, none of whom he came close to resembling. He asked himself if there was much chance of a predicament such as this one working out in his favor.

Then he ignored the logical answer, for right here and now he could think of no place else he would rather be. Love had coaxed him to this room and demanded that he be still.

"You've got some decisions to make first," he said. "I can't get in the way of that. But trust me, it will be worth the wait."

"That sounds like a line to me."

Larry took Tanya's hands in his own. "I'm not saying any lines, I'm not making any moves. I'm just..."

"Hanging."

"Exactly."

Tanya could not help but see that by her side was someone who cared deeply for her. Larry wasn't out to get something, except a chance to be loved in return. Would she give him this opportunity? Had she already done so? She had once received everything she thought to want out of a relationship with disastrous results. Now that she asked for absolutely nothing, Larry had arrived and presented his amazing ability to make her feel that no matter how things worked out, she would be okay. Perhaps the lesson to be taken from this was that love wasn't something that could be custom ordered. It came whenever it chose in whatever form it desired, whether the heart was ready or not. Or maybe, as she had come to learn about many of life's ups and downs, there was no lesson to be learned at all.

Someone knocked at the door and after Tanya said to come in, her brother entered the room.

"Tanya, guess what ... Larry?"

"What's up, bro?" said the last person Tony had expected to find in his sister's room, on her bed, mere inches away from her. The nature of the relationship that had blossomed was immediately obvious.

"Not much," Tony answered.

"Hey, no hard feelings about our little beef. Bad timing on my part."

"Bad judgement on mine."

"So everything's cool?" asked Larry.

"Cool? That's one word for it. I'll see you guys later."

Tony stepped back out and closed the door behind him, staring into vacant space for a moment until the apartment's buzzer snapped him out of his stupor. That would be Charlie. Then again, seeing how this day was going it would probably be best not to take anything for granted or to put much stock in assumptions. He looked again at his sister's door, searching for a termite who might have a clue to the ways of the world. Not finding one, he went to let in his friend.

* * *

Charlie plopped himself down on C.J.'s bed. This was the first time anyone had been on the bed since his death. It was as if a sacred place was being left for him to return to, just in case he decided to show up one day. But C.J. would not be coming back no matter how much he was missed, no matter how long a space for him was kept open. Some spaces could only be filled by time.

“It gets so quiet in here at night,” said Tony. “No one to bullshit with, no one to argue with. He used to snore like a fucking chainsaw. Kept me up for hours sometimes. I'd give anything to hear that snore again."

"How's the family coping?"

"The best we can. We have to go on. What choice do we have? So we're being sad and we're going on."

C.J.'s half of the room was just as he left it. Posters of Allen Iverson, Malcolm X, and an outrageously curvaceous swimsuit model were taped to the wall behind his bed along with a 5 x 7 photograph of Lisa. His clothing remained hanging in the closet or folded in drawers, more than a dozen pairs of his sneakers were lined up neatly on the floor. It wasn't this way for any cleaning his mother had done. C.J. may have led a chaotic life, but was very orderly when it came to the arrangement of his possessions.

Eventually this stuff would be thrown out or given away. Tony would then claim the entirety of the room as his own. But he was in no particular rush for this day to arrive. He would rather possess the echoes of C.J. evoked by that which had been left behind.

"Any word about your dad?"

Tony walked to the window he once believed tomorrow could be seen from, although the only view actually afforded from this vantage point was the brick wall of an adjoining building. None of his current misery had been foretold by the arrangement of cemented bricks.

"He's coming home soon. There's no stopping the cancer."

Charlie thought briefly of his own father, a man who left him with no choice but to carry on in his absence. This meant he was everywhere and no place. He may have been performing heroic deeds, or perhaps merely mundane acts, or maybe he was rotting in an obscure grave. The alternatives were as innumerable as grains of sand. His father might have been the devil incarnate, or he may have redeemed himself and gone on to lead the life of a saint who had forgotten his former address. Charlie would never know, and most of the time managed to convince himself that he didn't really care. Most of the time.

"I finally went to see him," Tony said. "It didn't exactly go as planned. I had this stupid fantasy where I would tell him I'm sorry, he would forgive me, we'd hug and cry and say we loved each other. But I didn't say much and he said even less."

"Your dad doesn't strike me as the hugging and crying type. He's more of a "go to hell" kind of guy. I think "go to hell" is a fucked up translation of "I love you". Sometimes you gotta read between the lines."

"I'll tell you this much, Charlie. When I have kids they're going to know I love them. They won't have to read between anything."

"When I have kids they're gonna know I'm their father because I'm going to be there. Might not sound like much, but it's a step up from what I had?"

Tony nodded his head in sympathetic agreement.

"Did you hear about Teddy Wilkins?" asked Charlie.

"No, I didn't. Is he dead?" After not knowing anyone personally to have died during the first eighteen years of his life, in the past few months death had become nearly as regular as the mail. Learning that a classmate of his had been killed once would have been stunning, devastating news. Now it was just one in a crowd of sad stories of unfulfilled potential.

"Just the opposite. He came out of the coma. His doctors are expecting a full recovery now. They're saying it's practically a miracle."

"No kidding. So God's still in the miracle business. Who would've thunk it?"

"Beats me. What's that you're holding?"

Not until he looked down did Tony remember the letter in his hand. He had intended to tell Tanya about it, but seeing Larry in her room distracted him. Then talking about C.J., and his father, and Teddy had kept his announcement under wraps. Meanwhile the most important document he had ever received lay in his grasp.

"It's from NYU. I was accepted with a full scholarship."

"No shit!" Charlie reached over to give his friend a congratulatory slap on the shoulder. "You did it, just like you said you would. I'm proud of you, man."

"Yeah," said Tony with no recognizable enthusiasm.

"I know it's tough to get excited right now. But this is amazing. All that studying paid off."

"College is way down on my priority list. I'm not even sure if I'm going to..."

"Trust me on this one," Charlie interrupted. "You're gonna accept the scholarship, get nothing but A's, and go on to do great things. It's your calling. You don't ignore a calling or else God punishes you with male pattern balding or a wife who forgets what sex is the minute the honeymoon is over."

Tony smiled despite himself. He had just about resigned himself into accepting that he would be passing on college, at least for the time being. Then the letter arrived. The future he had envisioned for so long was no longer a fantasy. It had become real, ironically when it was now amongst the least of his concerns.

He didn't know what he wanted or what to believe in anymore. On each occasion that he thought he had a fix on his mindset, something would happen to alter his perspective. His opinions on vital matters were once set in stone. Now they were like a branch carried along by a river's rapids, its course haphazardly altered by the position of rocks, fallen tree trunks, and various other impediments.

The sound of a couple's laughter was heard through the thin wall.

"Did you know that my sister is going out with our favorite homeboy wannabe?"

"I've seen them together a few times."

"Is that right?" Apparently he was the last to know. "How did I not know about this? You'd think it's the sort of thing she might bother to mention."

"Maybe it's a secret. Chicks are devious by nature."

"Why didn't *you* say anything?"

"Didn't seem to be any of my business. "You got a problem with it?"

"I guess not," answered Tony after a moment's consideration. "It's just weird. I never would have imagined them as a couple."

"I wonder if anyone ever said that about you and Janet."

Tony smirked, then tried to pose his next question nonchalantly.

"You seen her lately?"

"Who wants to know?" Charlie asked in return.

"I'm just curious about how she's doing."

"You never should have dumped her, my man."

"Since when did you start approving of Janet?"

"I never had anything against her," Charlie responded. "I just thought you were getting too serious, too fast, without really looking at what you were getting yourself into. You never even considered that there might be some hassles to deal with, which is the surest way to make sure they'll come up in spades.

"That's part of why I gave you such a hard time. The other part is probably because I was jealous. You had a real good thing going while my good thing was gone. Plus it seemed I hardly ever got to see you anymore. I guess I was being petty, just like everyone else who was trippin' about you guys being together. She's fine, she's cool to hang with, her ass ain't half bad for a white chick, and she was giving up the good stuff. What more can you ask for?"

Tony pondered the question. What beyond perfection *did* he seek? Janet's only flaw was skin complexion that didn't match his own in a world that made an inexplicably big deal of color coordination.

Charlie reached into his back pocket and withdrew a pick, which he applied to his rapidly sprouting afro. This had become an even more addictive habit than rubbing his smooth scalp.

"I ran into her earlier today," he said. "Told her I was planning to join the Marines, and she said she was going to NYU of all places. Then Roger walked by and she ignored him. I asked what the deal was and she told me she had broken up with him."

Tony tried to keep a reaction from showing. What was there to react to anyway? So Janet had dumped Roger. She was free now. What difference did that make? None whatsoever.

"He must have thrown one too many interceptions in the championship game."

"Actually," said Charlie, "I think she's in love with someone else. Someone she just may run into on her college campus."

Tony walked over to his bureau and extracted last year's Lincoln High School yearbook from the top drawer. He flipped it open to the page containing a close up of Janet. She hardly knew he existed back then as she posed in her cheerleading outfit, flashing her man-killer smile. She had not known that he was aching to be with her. Certainly she had no idea that one day his dreams would come true, he *would* get to hold her, only to let go. Then he would ache all over again, stare at her picture once again, wonder if dreams ever came true twice.

Despite his best efforts to defy sentiment, to reject forgiveness, his true feelings had been fossilized, preserved within a secret chamber of his heart, invulnerable to the destructiveness of wounded pride. Loving Janet came as automatically as breathing, and like this act, he could force himself to stop doing it only for brief periods of time.

Was loving her a form of betrayal? Could he give himself to her without relinquishing something essential in himself? Did he need to stick to his own kind in order to maintain his identity, even if he wasn't quite sure what that was?

The disapproval of others had done a fair share of damage to their relationship. Yet pressure from outside was negligible compared to that which came from within. Tony had suffered from uneasy suspicion that Janet was just biding her time, having a sordid little adventure with him until somebody more appropriate came along. He had lived and loved in fear of the moment when her lips would open to form the word "goodbye". In the end he practically forced her to say it so he could be put out of his misery.

When every pro is confronted by a con and the whims of the heart are met at every turn by a harsh comprehension of the mind, how is such a stalemate to be resolved? Tony needed to know.

"Let me ask you something. Did I seem different to you when I was with Janet?

Little insight was expected to be gained from the vague query, but Charlie's gift of clear sightedness made another one of its surprise appearances.

"Ever make yourself a full glass of Kool Aid when there was only enough mix left for half a glass?"

"Yeah, I guess.

"Then you know that what you end up with is red, tasteless water."

"Meaning?"

"It seemed to me that you were looking for a middle ground. You tried to be everything you thought Janet wanted, but at the same time, you didn't want to change from who you were. You didn't want the fact that you're black to be important, but you didn't want it to be forgotten either, least of all by yourself.

"I'm not saying you handled the situation wrong, because who knows how you're supposed to act when everyone is giving you such a hard time about something as natural as falling in love. Hell, I wasn't even in the relationship yet I went back and forth on how to feel about it, on whether to have your back or to turn mine. All I know is that sometimes there is no middle ground. There's just two opposite ends. You can stay the same or else you can change, but you can't do both. Satisfy your taste or else satisfy your thirst, but whichever one you pick means you have to give up the other."

Tony envisioned a future with he and Janet still together, married and with a child. He considered the plight of their pretend son or daughter - half black, half white. Would the two halves equal a whole, or would the result be a splintered soul in an endless search for affirmation? Neither sense of self nor of place ever satisfied.

"I'll be right back. You want a soda?"

"Sure. Unless you got Kool Aid."

Tony headed to the kitchen, but instead of opening the refrigerator he paused before the telephone on the wall. He knew it could change his life if he chose to use it for that purpose.

Hearing that Janet and Roger were no longer together was partially responsible for holding him in place. So was learning she would be attending the same college as him, assuming that he decided to go. He was also kept still by the recent response of his uncle when asked what the chances were of a reconciliation with Aunt Caroline.

"I'm not sure I'll ever get her to forgive me. I just know that I'll never stop trying, no matter what. Some things are worth any price. You just have to figure out what those things are, then start paying."

Tony was at a loss to figure out what he should do, what he was willing to sacrifice. There was a crucial question he had been unable to answer. Why had he fallen for Janet to begin with? Had he sought personification of the stereotypical beauty of the western word, and she happened to neatly fit this bill with her fair skin, cloudless sky eyes, and golden tresses? If this was so, it seemed almost reasonable to cast her aside for an equally frivolous reason.

Then again, perhaps both the question and its answer were inconsequential. Maybe there were an infinite number of reasons for one's soul to be pulled towards that of another, none of them more worthy than any of the others. He had fallen for Janet, he loved her still, and he had no choice in this matter. If he was now strong enough and if she was willing, it was possible that they could start anew. Otherwise, Tony knew that he would hurt for awhile longer. But the pain would fade over time, and he would wake up one morning to find that his heart continued to beat, cracks notwithstanding.

The first go around it was as if he was on trial for the originator of sins - longing for forbidden fruit. The situation was unchanged. The world was as it had always been. Yet he found himself contemplating whether to sin again, regardless of the severity of the punishment. Perhaps he would base his decision not on the color of his skin, but that of his blood, and the direction in which it pulled his heart.

Tony placed his hand on the telephone. He had tried to accept that for whatever reason, the time had simply been wrong for he and Janet. But his attempt failed. Or perhaps times were changing.

A ringing startled him. He picked up the phone receiver right away, not bothering to check Caller ID and planning to end the upcoming conversation quickly, for he had a call of his own to place.

"Hello. Hello. Is anybody there?"

Of course someone was there. He recognized the sound of her breathing - as sweet as honey, soft as satin. The inhale seemed to form the first syllable of his name while the exhale sighed the second.

"Is this you, Janet? If it is, please don't hang up. I was just about to call. Is it you?"

"I'm so sorry about C.J. I would have called earlier, but I didn't..." Janet left the remainder of her explanation to linger silently on the wires that connected them.

"Thanks for calling." The Bible, Koran and Torah combined contained less than what Tony left unsaid.

"How are you doing?"

"I've been better."

Proclamations of devotion demanded release, but Tony ignored this impulse. Was it out of respect for the more prominent issue of his brother's passing? Was he afraid to leave himself open to rejection? Would the stream of questions ever stop?

"I've missed you," Janet said.

She was letting him know that the runway was clear. She was making it easy for him.

"I should have understood how tough a time you were having. I should have been more patient. Things would have gotten easier to deal with after awhile. But I was selfish. All I cared about was having my old Tony back."

It was more than he could have dared to hope for. Nothing had been done to redeem himself, yet here Janet was forgiving him, welcoming him back. He needed only to accept the invitation he so much desired.

"I love you, Tony. I was wrong for not understanding, for going back to Roger, for not being there when you needed me most. I'm sorry."

"I love you too."

The days without Janet far outnumbered the magical ones spent by her side. But in that brief period she had become everything to him. The hours to have passed since their parting seemed a pale mockery of living. The air had become suffocating, his steps labored, food distasteful, music cacophonous.

Now suddenly what he once possessed and had been missing beyond measure was his again for the asking. Yet his response was delayed because he suffered from more than just loneliness. His equally potent doubts refused to lessen. If he took measures to end his suffering, the stoppage might be temporary. Should he deny himself the fix he craved in hope of an eventual cure?

Tony closed his eyes to picture Janet with phone pressed to ear, taking in what she was about to hear. What one has chosen to do at a given moment and what is ultimately done when anticipation gives way to action are often not one and the same.

"I wish that was enough," he said. "I wish my color didn't matter. I wish yours didn't. I wish upon every star in the sky that we could backtrack. That way C.J. would still be alive, my father would be healthy, I would be holding you in my arms."

It was of course impossible, but Tony could have sworn he heard a tear slide down Janet's cheek.

"I wish that wishing made a thing so. But I have no magic genie. I just have the way I feel, and what I feel is that no matter how much we love each other, it can't erase the hate."

"What happened to us against the world?" Janet asked. "Why should other people's hang ups be our problem? Are you going to base your choices on what other people think?"

"I'm not talking about other people. I'm talking about myself. I'm talking about the fact that no matter how hard I look, I just can't get myself to see you the same. Things changed between us, and even if it wasn't your fault or mine, I still don't know how to change them back."

Several seconds of silence followed, then a gentle click, and finally a harsh dial tone. But not as harsh as the truth now recognized by Tony. He loved Janet but hated the malice of mankind that being with her forced him to acknowledge. He could not forget how he had been treated. He could not forgive the way he had been seen. Janet was not amongst those to blame in either thought or deed. Only in a manner that was superficial and should have been insignificant, yet sadly, could not be ignored. Not by him. Not anymore. If they tried to go back to the way things were, the shape their relationship would take was unavoidable. Circumstances would generate anger, which would transform into cruelty. Tony would become a carbon copy of his father, funneling rage to whomever loved him most. This could not be risked. So he was forced to let Janet go.

A blind man given sight only to have the sense awakened to the bloody carnage of a battlefield might very well regret the gift. Tony learned how it felt to hold Janet in his embrace, and this led to discovering how much it would ache when he proved too weak to hang on.

He replaced the phone in its cradle but kept his hand on the receiver. Without pride or regret he thought of how he had accounted for himself up until the moment at hand - the boy he had been, the man he was struggling to become. He reflected on the knowledge he had gained, and at what cost.

In the time it takes a boy to become a man, an infinitude of events occur to transform him. As Adam grew from the soil and Eve from his rib, the final creation is far more complex than the base model. We are formed by every triumph, every failure, every laugh, every tear. The ingredients which comprise us are each ball caught, mile pedaled, knee bruised, kiss taken, heart broken, mended, re-broken, mended again. We become more sophisticated and savvy, but not necessarily more wise. Perhaps true wisdom is not gained over the time we travel from cradle to grave, but rather, lost.

A night came to mind when he and Janet had double dated with another couple. The four of them went to a local nightclub, and though the others were allowed in with a jovial smile, Tony was asked to provide ID which he did not have. They ended up going someplace else, but the indignity of the rejection clung to him like perspiration on a construction worker's brow.

If a similar event had occurred in the past, he probably would have chalked the experience up to bad luck. Perhaps the bouncer randomly selected people to proof based on criteria no more particular than eenie meenie minie moe. Maybe the age of every tenth or twentieth person was verified. His face may have displayed apprehension about being carded that the bouncer picked up on.

Tony immediately eliminated these possibilities. He was convinced that the decision to single him out was motivated by nothing but racism, for his eyes had come to view matters through a jaundiced perspective. Like a dog taught to sniff out narcotics, he had been trained to spot injustice headed his way. This sixth sense had become a part of who he was, like it or not.

Reality defuses the aura of paradise, rendering it as commonplace as a magic trick after the secret behind the illusion has been deciphered. The truth can be ignored, but cannot be unlearned. Even after the three monkeys made sure that evil was neither seen, heard, nor spoken of, they still knew it was there.

The ringing of the phone did not startle him the second time around, and a quick glance verified who it once again was. He may have felt a tremor in his fingertips before the sound was registered by his ears. Or perhaps he had been expecting the follow-up call, expecting that love would be more persistent than hurt, more resilient than pride.

The repetitive mechanical plea captivated him. He waited to see if his hand would obey the summons and bring Janet's voice to his ear. He waited for the divine intervention that his mother had such faith in to guide him. He waited to find out beyond the realm of doubt exactly what it was that he believed in, what sort of man he would choose to be. If he waited quietly and patiently enough, he felt certain that the answers would come.

Yet they did not. Instead he realized that much like our days in the womb, we are metaphysically in the dark. Just as all men before us did, and those after us will do, we spend our lives groping for that which cannot be described, but shall surely be recognized when found. On occasion we stumble upon what seems to be a truth. Compared to the surrounding blackness, it sparkles and dazzles our eyes. But are these actually truths? Are our eyes really feasting upon light? Or just patches of grey?

Tony and Janet had taken on the world and they had lost. The bravest of souls often lose heart and succumb to its indifference. If convictions make the man, when they are broken, who is there to be found in the mirror? People were fated by design to become strangers to themselves whenever they were unable to stand up for their principles. In failing to maintain his most instinctual beliefs, Tony had become someone incapable of being happy with Janet. But maybe all hope was not lost. Perhaps yet another version of himself would eventually come to be created. And it was possible that in the skin of this new incarnation he might cross paths with her again. There was even a chance that his rebirth was already underway.

When the answering machine kicked on, the call was abruptly cut off. Tony had not moved a muscle when thirty seconds later the phone in his hand began to ring again. This pattern would not continue indefinitely. Surrender by one of them was inevitable. Tony would either choose to pick up, or else he would decide, at least for now, to move on.